More Rivals of

SHERLOCK HOLMES

Stories from

The GOLDEN AGE of GASLIGHT CRIME

edited and introduced by

NICK RENNISON

NO EXIT PRESS

First published in 2019 by No Exit Press,
an imprint of Oldcastle Books Ltd,
Harpenden, UK
noexit.co.uk

Editorial comment © Nick Rennison 2019

A CIP catalogue record for this book is available from the British Library.

ISBN
978-0-85730-260-1 (print)
978-0-85730-261-8 (epub)

2 4 6 8 10 9 7 5 3 1

Typeset in 11.25pt Bembo
by Avocet Typeset, Somerton, Somerset, TA11 6RT
Printed and bound in Great Britain by Clays Ltd, Elcograf S.p.A.

To Eve with love and thanks

Contents

CONTENTS

8

INTRODUCTION

'After Holmes, the deluge!' the author and Sherlockian critic
Vincent Starrett once wrote. He was referring, of course, to
the vast number of private detectives and other crime-solvers
who peopled the pages of the English and American popular
magazines in the wake of the astonishing success of Sir Arthur
Conan Doyle's character.

The magazine press of the day had very nearly as voracious
an appetite for content and stories as TV does today. The most
significant of these magazines was *The Strand*. Founded by the
publisher George Newnes, it first appeared in January 1891. Its
editor was Herbert Greenhough Smith who was to continue in
that role for the next thirty-nine years. It was Smith who had the
perspicacity to spot immediately the potential in Conan Doyle's
Sherlock Holmes short stories. Forty years later, perhaps with a
little benefit of hindsight, he recalled the moment in 1891 when
he received the manuscripts of two of the stories. 'I at once realised
that here was the greatest short story writer since Edgar Allan
Poe... there was no mistaking the ingenuity of the plot, the limpid
clearness of the style, the perfect art of telling a story.' The first of the
Holmes short stories, 'A Scandal in Bohemia', was published in the
July 1891 edition of *The Strand Magazine*. A literary phenomenon
was born. The connection between Holmes and *The Strand* was to
last until 1927 and the publication of 'The Adventure of Shoscombe
Old Place', the final tale of the great consulting detective. Apart
from the first two novels, every Holmes story made its first British
appearance in the pages of *The Strand*.

However, *The Strand* did not just provide a home for Holmes and Dr Watson. Stories of other fictional detectives of the period, several of them represented in this collection, were published in its pages. These included Dick Donovan, created by Greenhough Smith's father-in-law JE Preston Muddock, EW Hornung's gentleman thief AJ Raffles, Lois Cayley, a feisty 'New Woman' who appeared in stories by Grant Allen, and Richard Marsh's Judith Lee. Arthur Morrison's Martin Hewitt made his debut in *The Strand* in 1894, at least in part to fill the gap left by Conan Doyle's decision to kill off Holmes in 'The Final Problem' which had been published the previous December.

Nor, of course, was *The Strand* the only such periodical on the newsstands. There were dozens and dozens of similar magazines in the 1890s and 1900s and nearly all of them featured crime stories. Arthur Morrison's Horace Dorrington stories made their first appearance in *The Windsor Magazine* as did Guy Boothby's tales of the occultist and criminal mastermind Dr Nikola and Arnold Bennett's Cecil Thorold stories. *The Idler*, edited for several years by Jerome K Jerome, author of *Three Men in a Boat*, published some of William Hope Hodgson's 'Carnacki' stories, about an investigator of the supernatural. (In 1892, *The Idler* also published the very first parody of Sherlock Holmes – 'The Adventures of Sherlaw Kombs' by Jerome's co-editor Robert Barr.) GK Chesterton's Father Brown stories featured in *The Pall Mall Magazine*. (There seemed to be a fondness at the time for naming periodicals after famous London streets.) Other, smaller magazines also had their detectives. Loveday Brooke, one of a number of female detectives in the fiction of the period, appeared in *The Ludgate Monthly*; Headon Hill's Sebastian Zambra was to be found in *The Million* and Victor Whitechurch's railway detective Thorpe Hazell, appropriately enough, graced the pages of *The Railway Magazine* as well as *The Royal Magazine* and *Pearson's Magazine*.

It is from this vast pool of periodical fiction that I have drawn the majority of the stories in this book. As with the first volume in this series (*The Rivals of Sherlock Holmes*) what I wanted to do more than anything was to demonstrate the sheer variety of crime stories published between 1890 and 1914. People often assume that there is little worth reading from that era other than the Holmes stories and that the fictional detectives of the time are all Sherlock clones. Neither of these assumptions is true. Conan Doyle was inarguably the best writer in the genre in the decades immediately before the First World War but that does not mean he was the only one with great talents. Arthur Morrison, R Austin Freeman and Baroness Orczy – to name just three – were all highly skilled writers of popular fiction who can be read with great pleasure today. And while there were undoubtedly characters who were cheap copies of Doyle's detective (I have included David Christie Murray's John Pym as an example of one of these) they were vastly outnumbered by those who were very different. It was almost a matter of pride among self-respecting authors to come up with a character that did not echo Sherlock Holmes. From the blind detective Max Carrados to Arthur Morrison's utterly ruthless, almost monstrous creation, Horace Dorrington, from Baroness Orczy's pioneering Scotland Yard detective Lady Molly to John Dollar, EW Hornung's 'Crime Doctor', there are plenty of characters who are memorable in their own right.

In this new volume of stories, I have avoided including any of the 'Rivals of Sherlock Holmes' who appeared in my first collection. It would have been easy enough to pick another Father Brown story by GK Chesterton or another tale about Jacques Futrelle's 'Thinking Machine', Professor Augustus SFX Van Dusen. There are plenty of very readable stories featuring those two characters from which to choose. However, in pursuit of my wish to demonstrate the variety and range of late Victorian and Edwardian crime fiction, I have picked fifteen entirely different 'Rivals' for this volume. And only one writer from the first book – Headon Hill - also makes an appearance in this one.

When fans of crime fiction refer to its 'Golden Age' they usually mean the era of Agatha Christie, Dorothy L Sayers and

Margery Allingham but there was an earlier period in the history of the genre that was just as rich and fascinating. The years between 1890 and the outbreak of the First World War saw the emergence and establishment of Sherlock Holmes as the greatest of all fictional detectives. No one disputes his pre-eminence but he had plenty of rivals. As Vincent Starrett pointed out, there was a 'deluge' of them. As I hope this second volume of stories proves, many of them deserve to be remembered and read today.

MR BOOTH

Created by Herbert Keen (fl. 1896)

Mr Booth (we never learn his Christian name) appears in a series of stories collectively entitled 'Chronicles of Elvira House' which were published in The Idler *magazine in 1896. They are narrated by Mr Perkins, an unworldly, middle-aged clerk in an insurance office who lodges at the boarding house of the title and persuades his friend Booth to take rooms there as well. Booth is a former detective and a much shrewder individual than his friend. In most of the stories Perkins or somebody he knows blunders into a tricky, possibly criminal situation and Mr Booth, through his knowledge of human nature, comes to the rescue. The 'Chronicles of Elvira House' are slight stories in themselves but they have a great deal of charm and are richly redolent of the era in which they were written. I have been unable to find any information whatsoever about the author Herbert Keen. Possibly it was a pseudonym; possibly he wrote nothing other than the stories of Mr Booth and Mr Perkins.*

THE MISSING HEIR

My friendship for Mr Booth was cemented by his rendering me a great personal service, for which I shall ever be grateful to him. I regret to say that he obstinately refused to admit that he had done anything to make me his debtor, when I in vain endeavoured to persuade him to accept some substantial recognition of my obligation. I did, indeed, succeed in forcing upon him a cat's-eye scarf-pin of his own selection, which I thought, not only hideous in itself, but ridiculously inadequate, even as a mere memento. If he survives me, however, the contents of my will may convince him that he cannot baulk my fixed determination; meanwhile, I can, at least, enjoy the satisfaction of relating the episode.

I have already said that I was a clerk in the Monarchy Assurance Office, and until a certain eventful evening, about a year after Mr Booth came to reside at Elvira House, I never imagined, in my wildest dreams, that any improvement in my position or prospects was likely to occur. I was already on the wrong side of fifty, and had reached the limit of salary allotted to the subordinate staff. Younger men had been promoted over my head to more responsible posts; and I had long since realised, without bitterness, that my services were not regarded as entitling me to especial consideration. I had no friends among the Directorate, no influential connections, and no outside expectations from any source whatever. Fortunately, I had always contrived to make my modest salary suffice for my requirements, and had even saved a little money: so that, being totally devoid of ambition, I was leading a perfectly contented existence, undismayed by the certainty of being forced to retire into private life at the end of another ten years or so on a pension of infinitesimal proportions.

I never had a spirit to contract a debt which I could not pay, and therefore I was quite calm when, on being summoned from the drawing-room one evening, I was informed by the faithful footman George, in an awe-stricken whisper on the landing outside, that a mysterious 'party', who refused his name and business, was waiting to see me. George, though young in years, was not without experience in the class of callers who are objects of distrust and perturbation to impecunious boarders. The Major, for instance, was never at home to anyone on any consideration whatever; and George understood that he was entitled to claim a shilling from his master for every obnoxious visitor whom he succeeded in turning away from the premises. Constant practice in this respect had sharpened the lad's wits, and his warning glance plainly told me that, in his opinion, the person below was a dun.

I descended, however, without the least apprehension on this score, and was confronted in the entrance-hall by a young man, who obsequiously addressed me by name. He handed to me a cheap card, on which was inscribed with many flourishes the distinguished appellation, 'Mr Farquhar Barrington'. He was a tall, slim, respectable-looking youth, neatly, though somewhat shabbily dressed, with rather prominent features, sandy hair, and a clean-shaven face. Before I could say a word he whispered hastily behind his hand.

'I have some valuable information of immense importance to you, sir, and must beg for a private interview.'

The man's manner, rather than his words, vaguely impressed me, and I invited him into the dining-room, which was then unoccupied. All traces of our recent meal had been cleared away, and the long table, denuded of its cloth, was ignominiously displayed in the guise of a series of wide boards, supported by trestles, and sparsely covered with green baize. While I turned up the one dim gas-jet which remained alight, my visitor carefully closed the door behind him, and threaded his way among the scattered chairs to the seat which I indicated by the fireplace.

'Mr Perkins,' he said solemnly, 'permit me to congratulate you.'

'Why?' I enquired, staring at him.

'Because you have only to say a single word to find yourself in possession of a handsome sum of money.'

'Indeed, how?' I enquired curiously, but not particularly moved.

'Never mind how, Mr Perkins. You shall know in one minute. At present nobody in the world knows or suspects but myself.'

This sounded rather startling, and I gazed at him with renewed interest while he sat facing me. He had a thin, curved, hawk-like nose, high cheek-bones, small light blue eyes, deep-set and close together, very thin lips, and a strong lower jaw. His complexion was yellow and freckled, and I now judged him to be considerably older than I had at first supposed. His dress consisted of a long frock-coat, much frayed and worn at the wrists and elbows, a tall hat bronzed with age, trousers with a threadbare pattern, and enormous boots, all bulged and cracked. His linen, what there was of it, was decidedly dingy; round his neck he wore a greasy old silk tie, and his large bony hands were gloveless. Yet, in spite of his unprepossessing exterior, his resolute manner, and the absolute calmness with which he submitted to my scrutiny, impelled a vague respect.

'You think I'm a beggar or a lunatic, of course,' he said quietly.

'I do not recognise your name,' I said, glancing in perplexity at his card.

'No, and what is more, you do not even know it,' he replied; and then, in answer to my look of surprise, he added, 'That is an assumed name. My real name will be forthcoming if we do business; otherwise I prefer to remain, so far as you are concerned, Mr Farquhar Barrington.'

'You might just as well have called yourself plain John Smith,' I said, inclined to laugh at the fellow's cool impudence.

'First impressions go for something. My appearance, I know, is not in my favour. I assumed a name that might attract,' he replied, in a matter-of-fact way.

'How can you expect me to do business, as you call it, if you don't tell me who and what you are?' I exclaimed, irritably.

'What does it matter to you, Mr Perkins, who and what I am?' he answered, imperturbably. 'It is much more to the point that I know who and what you are. I don't want anything from you; on the contrary, I come as a benefactor. If you will sign this, you will never regret it.'

He produced a folded paper as he spoke, and handed it to me. It was a short document, very neatly and formally written in legal phraseology, on a sheet of blue foolscap, with a red seal at the end. I opened it carelessly at first, and then read it through with attention. It was in the form of a bond, by which I undertook, in consideration of certain information, to pay to someone – a blank space was left for the name – one half of any money I might recover by means of such information.

'Your name is not filled in,' I remarked, when I had mastered this remarkable production.

'It shall be filled in when you sign,' he said, with a laugh.

I read the document again, but with the aid of all the intelligence I could muster, I failed to see anything in it that was not fair and straightforward. It pledged me to nothing except to pay this man half of any money I might receive through his information. It did not bind me to employ him about the business, and it left me entirely free to make use or not of his information, as I pleased.

'One half seems a considerable proportion,' I said.

'It is better than nothing,' replied Barrington, for so I suppose I had better call him. 'Take time, if you please, for reflection. Do you know of any money due to you from anyone?'

'No,' I answered, truthfully.

'Any expectations? Any rich relatives? Think, Mr Perkins!'

He spoke half mockingly, yet with sufficient earnestness to put me on my guard. I deliberately reflected, but without result, while he sat watching me with admirable self-control.

'I think you ought to tell me a little more,' I said at length, rather feebly.

'Not a word, unless you choose to sign,' he replied, with quiet determination.

'Very well,' I said abruptly, after a further pause, 'I'll sign.'

I now know that my decision was very hasty and unwise, but at the time I believed either that Barrington's boasted information would turn out delusive, or else that it referred to some small unclaimed dividend in a long-forgotten bankruptcy due to a remote ancestor of mine. I had heard of such cases, and of consequent disappointment, but so far as I was concerned, as I expected nothing, I was not uneasy.

'There seems to be no ink here, and we shall want a witness,' he remarked coolly, as he spread the document on the table, and screwed together a portable pen which he took from his pocket.

'What sort of witness?' I enquired, ringing the bell.

'Anyone who is intelligent enough to write his name and to prove, if necessary, that you signed the document of your own free will, Mr Perkins,' said Barrington, testing the nib of the pen on his thumb-nail.

I thought of the lad, George, but, alas it was before the days of School Boards, and I doubted whether he could write; therefore, when he appeared in answer to the bell, I requested him to bring the ink, and to ask Mr Booth, who was in the smoking-room, if he would be good enough to step this way.

'What is Mr Booth?' enquired Mr Barrington, as George departed on his errand.

'What is he?' I repeated, not seeing the drift of the question.

'He isn't a lawyer, I suppose. I won't have anything to do with lawyers,' said Barrington, for the first time showing a slight symptom of uneasiness.

'No, he isn't a lawyer. He is a private gentleman; a boarder here,' I answered.

I suppose there was a little hesitation in my tone, though I was not conscious of any intention to deceive, for it did not enter my mind that my friend's occupation was the least material. Barrington, however, looked at me sharply and seemed a trifle disturbed, until Mr Booth made his appearance, following on the heels of the lad who brought the ink. I noticed that my visitor seemed relieved at the aspect of the mild, benevolent-looking gentleman who entered, with his half-consumed cigar in his hand, bowing politely as he beheld the stranger. The latter, when the footman had left, dipped his pen into the ink with a reassured air, and was evidently proceeding to fill his real name into the blank space when I said, with assumed carelessness, which doubtless did not conceal my suppressed excitement:

'I want you to witness my signature to a document, Mr Booth.'

'I should like to see it first,' said he, glancing at Barrington over his spectacles.

Barrington immediately withdrew his pen, and looked annoyed, while I handed the paper silently across the table to my friend, who read it through between the whiffs of his cigar. Then he said quietly but decidedly:

'I shouldn't sign this, if I were you, Perkins; it wants considering.'

'Mr Perkins has considered,' said Barrington, quickly.

'What is it all about?' enquired Booth, strolling round the table, and dropping carelessly into a chair by my side.

I explained, and it is unnecessary to repeat the conversation that ensued, because it was practically a repetition of my previous questions put in more ingenious forms by Mr Booth, and of Barrington's guarded answers. But I soon perceived that the latter realised he had a very different person to deal with in my friend, and if he did not actually suspect Mr Booth's late occupation, he at least manifested considerable distrust of him. But he maintained his resolute bearing and would not budge an inch from his terms, though my friend tried to tempt him with alternative proposals, such as various percentages on the amount recovered, and finally, to my dismay, he commenced making deliberate offers to purchase the information for money down. He started with £100, and got as far as £200, then £300. Finally, he said:

'Come, Mr Barrington. £350! It is the last time!'

'No,' said Barrington, resolutely, to my secret relief. 'It is sign or nothing.'

'Well, well, there's no hurry, I suppose?' said Mr Booth, who seemed amused. 'The property won't run away.'

'It is in the hands of somebody who won't keep it long. What's more,' added Barrington, with an angry gleam in his eyes, 'if Mr Perkins won't decide tonight I'll sell my information to the other side.'

At this I nudged my friend warningly under the table, for I had worked myself into a foolish state of nervous excitement. It had become quite evident to me, from Barrington's refusal to be tempted by the large sums offered to him, that the money at stake was considerable, and I was fairly carried away by his resolute attitude.

But Mr Booth took not the slightest notice of my hint, and merely said:

'We will turn the matter over in our minds. Perhaps tomorrow I may be disposed to advise Mr Perkins to sign the document.'

He was proceeding to take it up, when Barrington pounced upon it, tore it across with an emphatic gesture, and threw the pieces on the fire. They were caught in a lingering blaze and instantly consumed, while Barrington stood by buttoning up his coat.

'Will you leave your address in case we wish to communicate with you?' asked Mr Booth, innocently.

At this Barrington laughed scoffingly, and made no answer.

'Perhaps you would prefer a message in the first column of the Times,' suggested Mr Booth, quite unmoved.

'As you please,' said Barrington indifferently.

'Will you write a form of advertisement?' said Mr Booth.

'You can write, I'll dictate,' replied Barrington, with a glance of contempt.

'Have you a slip of paper?' enquired Mr Booth, a little sharply, as he felt in his own pocket.

I hastened to feel in mine, but my friend kicked me under the table. Barrington, meanwhile, had instinctively commenced to unbutton his coat, but, desisting suddenly, he said with a sneer:

'I have none.'

Considering that the bulging of his coat plainly showed that his inner breast-pocket was full of letters, &c., it was obvious that his reply was untrue. However, Mr Booth only smiled, and said good-humouredly:

'I'll fetch some.'

He walked quickly from the room, and when he had gone, Barrington immediately turned upon me.

'Your friend isn't so clever as he thinks. He is causing you to make a fool of yourself, Mr Perkins.'

'I am satisfied to leave myself in his hands,' I replied angrily.

'Very well. Fortunately, you'll never know what it has cost you,' said Barrington, with a shrug.

I did not respond, for I was not best pleased at the turn of events, and was afraid of showing it. During Mr Booth's brief absence Barrington sat on the end of the table, frowning at the fire; he rose when my friend returned, and, strolling to the hearthrug, said sarcastically:

'Shall I dictate the advertisement?'

'Yes,' said Mr Booth, placing a sheet of notepaper before him on the table and taking up a pen.

'If you will put this in the first column of the *Times* any morning this week, I will call here at 9 o'clock on the evening of the same day, understanding that Mr Perkins will sign the document.'

'Well?' said Mr Booth, pen in hand.

'*Mr B admits that he is beaten*,' dictated Barrington, sneeringly.

My friend grinned as he wrote this down, and then carefully blotted it.

'The initial might mean either of us,' he observed slyly.

'You forget that Barrington isn't my name,' said the stranger, moving round the table to the door.

'No, I shan't forget,' laughed Mr Booth.

Our visitor, I could see, did not feel at all at his ease with my friend in spite of his pretended assurance, and without another word, except a muttered 'Goodnight', he strode from the room, and presently we heard the hall-door bang behind him.

Mr Booth and I sat looking at one another for a few moments across the table, and, no doubt, my expression conveyed my sentiments of mingled disappointment and anxiety, for Mr Booth suddenly burst out laughing,

'My dear fellow, don't look so glum,' he cried. 'I wonder you can resist laughing. That is one of the cleverest young fellows I've ever met. I've been at him for half an hour, and yet I don't know his name, his address, his handwriting, his occupation, his nationality – I haven't succeeded in eliciting a solitary shred of a clue. I'm a much older hand than he is, too.'

'I must confess I don't think it is a laughing matter,' I said ruefully. 'What about the money?'

'I'm firmly convinced, Perkins, that you are entitled to a fortune,' he replied, evidently quite in earnest.

'Good heavens! But where is it?' I exclaimed, my natural feeling of elation struggling with misgivings.

'I think it perfectly possible that, at present, he alone knows,' replied Mr Booth, lighting another cigar.

'And he has disappeared?' I murmured.

'Yes,' he nodded.

'I expect we shall have to insert the advertisement, after all,' I said tentatively.

'What, this?' he exclaimed, crushing up the slip of paper in his hand rather viciously, and jerking it into the fireplace. 'I would almost sooner you lost your fortune, Perkins, than give that fellow such a triumph. No, no! It was only a little dodge of mine to get a scrap of his handwriting, if possible. I hoped, too, he might have given me an old envelope with an address upon it, to write upon.'

'But he didn't,' I said shortly.

'No, he was pretty cute – yet he is not so clever as he thinks,' replied Mr Booth, unconsciously repeating Barrington's words about him. 'I set George to follow him.'

'When you went out of the room?'

'Yes; George is an intelligent lad. He may bring us some information; and now, old fellow, let us seriously consider your side of the question. Come up to my room and talk it over.'

Mr Booth occupied one of the largest of the private apartments in the house, which, by the way, consisted, strictly speaking, of two houses communicating with one another. He had partly furnished it himself, and, by an ingenious contrivance of curtains, had practically divided it into a sitting-room and bedroom. The fireplace was in the former, and seated on a couple of comfortable armchairs in front of it, with a genial blaze leaping up the chimney, and the table spread with glasses and decanters from his private store, my friend and I settled down to a private confabulation.

This consisted, mainly, of researches into my family history. I ransacked my memory to recall to mind all the relatives I had ever known or heard of, while Mr Booth laboriously constructed my pedigree on a slip of paper. Unfortunately, our occupation was not very encouraging in its results, for I was almost the only survivor of my own generation, and of my ancestors I could give but little information. I thought Mr Booth looked rather blue at the conclusion of our labours, though he said cheerfully:

'One never can tell. Of course, that fellow may be on a false scent, but somehow I fancy he has found out something which we can't at present. Come in!'

The last words were uttered in response to a knock at the door, and the next moment the lad George presented himself, looking flushed and excited.

'Well?' queried Mr Booth.

'Please, sir, I did as you told me. I slipped out and hired a hansom, and waited a few doors off till the party left this house,' said George breathlessly. 'He jumped on a passing 'bus and rode up to the end of Orchard Street.'

'Did he notice you following in the hansom?'

'No, sir... not then. He walked up Oxford Street to the Marble Arch. I got out of the cab, as you suggested, and hung on the step by the driver, who walked his horse as if he were plying for a fare.'

'Good lad! Yes?'

'The party took another 'bus at the Marble Arch, to the end of Hamilton Place.'

'Yes?'

'Then he strolled eastward along Piccadilly. I am afraid he twigged me then.'

'Ah!'

'Yes, sir, for he made a start into the roadway and jumped on a 'bus as quick as lightning, while I, as the traffic was blocked, followed on foot. It was lucky I did, for he suddenly slipped off the 'bus he was on and jumped upon the one in front.'

'Lucky you saw him.'

'Yes, sir, and being rather blown I got inside the same 'bus while he was mounting on the roof.'

'Five shillings for that, George!'

'Thank you, sir. Well, I kept a sharp look-out, and all of a sudden, just after we had passed the Egyptian 'All, I see'd him jump off.'

'On which side of the road?'

'Side he was agoing, sir; the left-hand side. I don't think he knew I was in the 'bus, but he was precious quick. He turned up a turning and disappeared before you could say "knife"!'

'You followed?'

'Yes, sir, but only just in time. The turning wasn't a street. There was a house at the end, with a flight of steps leading to it. I think they call it the Albany, sir?'

'Quite right,' said Mr Booth, with increased interest.

'Well, sir, he said a word to the porter, and passed into the building along a sort of corridor. I followed, but the porter stopped me and asked my business. Well, of course I hadn't got no business, nothing that I could tell. The porter wouldn't let me go in; couldn't persuade him anyhow, sir. I waited about for more than an hour, sir, but he never came out, so I returned.'

'There is an entrance at the other end,' observed Mr Booth, thoughtfully.

'So I remembered afterwards, sir, and I didn't think it worthwhile waiting any longer,' said George, apologetically.

'You did very well, George, and here is half-a-sovereign,' said Mr Booth, producing the money.

'Much obliged, sir, I'm sure, sir,' said George, pocketing the coin with intense gratification at my friend's commendation.

'Sharp lad that,' said Mr Booth, approvingly, when he had disappeared.

'But nothing has come of it all,' I exclaimed.

'H'm. I'm not so sure it isn't a clue. How did Barrington

manage to get past the porter? He must have mentioned the name of someone in the building. It doesn't follow, of course, that he called on anyone. Still, there is no knowing. Well, goodnight, Perkins,' he added, suddenly rousing himself, after some minutes' reflection, 'I'm more hopeful than I was five minutes ago.'

I took the hint and returned to my own room, somewhat cheered by my friend's last words, but feeling, upon the whole, rather depressed than otherwise. My head was a little turned by the vague expectations which had been aroused by the mysterious Barrington; and I was possessed by a sort of feverish impatience which made me inclined to blame Mr Booth for his interference. I passed an almost sleepless night in building castles in the air on the very unsubstantial foundation of Barrington's visit. But by slow degrees I became calmer; my common sense reasserted itself; the extreme improbability of an unexpected inheritance appealed to my sober judgment; and though I did not close my eyes till dawn, I awoke at the usual hour without a trace of my recent excitement. Nay, more, I can honestly assert that those short hours of mental disturbance had completely discounted the effect of any future development, however startling, and from that time forward I watched the progress of events with philosophical calmness, almost amounting to indifference.

'Well, Perkins, what do you think about it all this morning?' was my friend's greeting when we met at breakfast.

'I think it is all nonsense,' I replied quietly. 'And you?'

'I agree. Nevertheless, as a mere matter of curiosity, I propose to make an enquiry of the porter at the Albany. Will you come?'

So far from feeling disappointed at Mr Booth's reply, I was disposed to regard the suggestion as a waste of time and energy. However, I did not wish to appear ungracious, and curiosity, if nothing stronger, caused me to acquiesce in his proposal. I was rather surprised to find that my friend seemed to regard the affair more seriously than he pretended, but even this discovery failed to render me the least enthusiastic.

The porter at the Albany, a pompous individual in a red

waistcoat, displayed a very defective memory at first, but the magical effect of five shillings was that he recalled the circumstance of the incident which George had recounted, and recognised Barrington by our description.

'Why did you let him pass?' enquired Mr Booth, when relations between us had been established on this friendly footing.

'He said he had a message for Mr Halstead from his lawyers.'

'Mr Halstead resides here then?'

'Yes, last house but one.'

'Did you notice whether he called there?' enquired Mr Booth.

'No, sir, I didn't. The fact is that other impudent chap comes up at the moment and gives me a lot of his cheek. It was all I could do to turn him away.'

'Is Mr Halstead at home now?'

'I suppose so. He ain't often out so early as this,' said the porter, glancing at his watch.

'I think my friend and I will call upon him,' observed Mr Booth.

The porter politely made way for us, and we strolled up the corridor while Mr Booth said:

'I expect it was only a blind. Still, we will call, and enquire if Mr Halstead knows him. It is worthwhile.'

On arriving at the house indicated, however, we learnt from Mr Halstead's servant that his master was out of town; and further enquiry elicited the fact that no one answering to the description of Barrington had called the preceding evening. The valet, who seemed to be well informed about Mr Halstead's affairs, and was evidently in his confidence, had never seen or heard of such a person.

'Is he a wrong 'un, this Mr – what is his name – Barrington?' enquired the valet.

'That is just what I want to find out,' replied Mr Booth cautiously. 'He knows your master's name, at all events. By the way, who are Mr Halstead's lawyers?'

'Messrs Talbot & Black, of Lincoln's Inn Fields,' said the man promptly.

'Thanks,' said Mr Booth, as we turned away. 'Possibly he may be one of their clerks.'

The valet, who, no doubt, imagined that we were a couple of detectives on the track of a malefactor, manifested his discretion by refraining from asking any further questions, and we walked away to the Vigo Street entrance of the Arcade.

'It is quite clear he isn't known there,' said Mr Booth, thoughtfully. 'I should like to find out how he got hold of Mr Halstead's name, though I expect he only used it as a means of escaping through the Albany corridor. No doubt he was sharper than George imagined, and saw that he was being shadowed.'

'Why did you ask the name of Mr Halstead's solicitors?' I enquired.

'Because, although I don't think that anything will come of it, we may as well call upon them,' replied Mr Booth, hailing a passing hansom.

A short drive, during which my companion sat silent and thoughtful, brought us to our destination, and, as neither of the principals had arrived, we had an interview with the managing clerk of the firm. I envied and admired the easy self-possession which my friend displayed in obtaining the information he required. Instead of appearing to ask a favour, he contrived, by his tact and pleasant manners, to convey an impression of conferring an obligation, and caused the cautious old head clerk to produce his snuff-box with a deferential air, and to become quite friendly and confidential.

'No, sir, we have never heard of Mr Farquhar Barrington, as he calls himself,' said the old gentleman. 'We have never had a clerk of that name or answering his description during the fifty-two years I have been here.'

'That is quite conclusive,' said Mr Booth, smiling.

'And you say that this individual is passing himself off as a member of our staff? Really, sir, I am indebted to you – my principals will be indebted to you – for your friendly warning. We will be on our guard, sir, we will be on our guard.'

Mr Booth accepted these expressions of thanks with becoming modesty, and by degrees drifted into an amicable conversation on general subjects until, to my surprise, the name of Mr Halstead was introduced. How it came about I really cannot exactly remember; I think my friend made a casual reference to somebody he knew, who had once lived in the Albany; and so, insensibly as it were, the old clerk was led to speak of the firm's client.

Without manifesting any curiosity, and in the most natural way in the world, my friend became possessed of all the information he required about Mr Halstead. We learnt that he was an old bachelor, who had formerly been a clerk in one of the government offices; that he was eminently respectable, and fairly well off; that his family came from Leicestershire, and that there was no kind of mystery about him or his affairs.

'Well, Perkins,' said my friend quietly, as we parted on the pavement in front of Messrs Talbot & Black's office, at the conclusion of our visit, 'I think we need not pursue the matter any further; it is a false scent.'

'Then what is to be done?' I asked.

'We must consider. Barrington must be unearthed. Anyhow, we've got a week,' said Mr Booth, hopefully, in allusion to the period of grace so contemptuously accorded.

But during this interval, which quickly slipped by, I began to observe in my friend signs of gloomy irritation. He said very little to me about what he was doing, and, as I felt convinced that he was making unremitting efforts on my behalf, I forbore to question him. Curiously enough, as time went on, I felt much more concerned on his account than on my own. It would be affectation to pretend that I did not experience some disappointment as I instinctively realised the failure of his attempts to discover my mysterious visitor, but it grieved me to see how he took the matter to heart, and I dreaded to think of his bitter humiliation at having to confess himself baffled.

However, the apparently inevitable moment arrived, and one

morning he came up to me after breakfast, and silently handed me a slip of paper.

'What is this?' I enquired nervously, knowing full well.

'Tomorrow is the last day. That young fellow is too clever for me,' he replied quietly.

'You advise me to insert the advertisement and to sign the bond?' I said.

'I dare not advise the contrary. Mind you, I think, in course of time, I might find everything out. But it is a hard nut to crack. At present I have been able to do nothing.'

He turned aside as he spoke, with such an air of dejection and annoyance that I made, on the spot, a reckless resolve. Of course, I was influenced in some measure by his suggestion that he only needed time; but at the moment I felt in a mood to hazard everything rather than cause my friend pain.

My first impulse was simply not to insert the advertisement; but, on second thoughts, a better plan occurred to me. I took up a pen, and on a fresh slip of paper I wrote the words:

'*Mr Barrington is informed that he is beaten.*'

It was a mere piece of harmless bravado, designed to gratify my friend rather than to cause annoyance to his adversary. Still, I could not help chuckling at Mr Barrington's mystification when he beheld it, and I experienced quite a thrill of gleeful satisfaction when I handed the message across the desk at the *Times* office.

I kept my secret from Mr Booth, and next morning I watched with considerable amusement to see the effect upon him of my little manoeuvre. He was very late down – I think purposely – and when he arrived he distinctly avoided opening his private copy of the *Times*, which lay by the side of his plate. But at length, catching my eye, he unfolded the sheet with a studied air of indifference. I saw him glance at the 'agony' column, and then give a start of surprise, while his bald forehead grew rosy over the top of the page. The next moment he jumped up from his seat with a beaming countenance, and came round to the back of my chair.

'You old ass,' he murmured in my ear, giving me at the same time a friendly dig in the ribs.

After which little ebullition of feeling, he resumed his place at the table, and went on with his breakfast as though nothing had happened. For my part, between satisfaction at the evident gratification which I had caused him and an Englishman's nervous dread of being thanked, I made haste to despatch my meal, and hurried off to the office without giving him an opportunity of speaking to me.

I was in unaccountably good spirits all that day and felt rather relieved that my duties kept me mostly out of doors. I sometimes had a good deal of running about to do, and it happened that it was my turn to go the round of the various branches, so that I had little leisure to reflect upon the possible consequences of the step I had taken. I did not get back to my desk till after the doors of the establishment had been closed to the general public; and I then learnt that a lad had called during the afternoon with a note for me, but that, just before closing time, he had returned and asked to have the note handed back to him on the ground that, owing to my continued absence, it was now useless. I was annoyed to find that this request had been complied with, so that I had absolutely no idea who my correspondent was.

I naturally associated this rather mysterious incident with my advertisement in the day's *Times*, and hastened back to Elvira House as soon as I could to tell my friend about it.

George opened the door to me in a state of suppressed excitement, and after briefly saying, in answer to my enquiry, that Mr Booth had not yet returned, he blurted out:

'That there party is here, sir! I showed him in the smoking-room, as he said he would wait for you.'

'Did he ask for me?' I enquired, considerably startled.

'No, sir, he asked for Mr Booth first, and it's my belief he wouldn't have come in if I hadn't told him Mr Booth wasn't coming back tonight,' said George with a wink.

I felt exceedingly uncomfortable, for without my friend at my elbow I did not know what on earth I should say to my visitor. From Mr Booth's opinion of the fellow, I knew that I was no match for him in cunning, and, with regard to the bond, I should have considered it an act of disloyalty to have signed it behind my friend's back.

However, there was nothing to be done but to face the man, so, bidding George to warn Mr Booth if he returned before my visitor left, I hung up my greatcoat and hat in the hall, and walked into the smoking-room.

Barrington was standing on the hearth-rug with his back to the fire, looking much more prosperous than at our first interview. He was neatly dressed in a stout suit of blue serge, and on the table lay a brand new cloth-cap of the same material. He looked as though he were on the eve of a journey, and carried a railway rug across his arm.

'Ah! Mr Perkins,' he exclaimed, impatiently, as I entered. 'I sent a note to your office, but you were out.'

'You saw the advertisement, I suppose,' I said, taking the bull by the horns.

'Yes. I'm glad to find that you can do without me,' he replied, looking at me keenly.

'Thanks to my friend, Mr Booth,' I observed, as calmly as I could.

'He has found out everything, has he?' enquired Barrington, rather nervously.

'May I enquire,' I said, stiffly, feeling unpleasantly conscious that the tell-tale blush was mounting to my cheeks, 'the object of your visit?'

'I am going abroad, and my train starts for Southampton in an hour,' he said, still looking hard at me. 'I am afraid I must admit that I called simply out of curiosity.'

'You don't want me to sign that precious document then?' I said, hastily, to conceal my dismay at the news of his departure from England.

'Oh, no! It is too late. I made you a fair offer, Mr Perkins. I have sold my secret to somebody else,' he replied, gravely.

'You scoundrel!' I exclaimed, exasperated by his coolness.

'Strong language, Mr Perkins, won't disguise the fact that, as I expected, your advertisement was bounce,' he replied, in a tone of such evident satisfaction that I felt doubly annoyed with myself.

'How about Mr Halstead?' I exclaimed in desperation.

'Mr Halstead!' he repeated, pausing with an air of bewilderment in the act of taking up his hat from the table. 'Oh! You mean the old gentleman who lives in the Albany,' he added, after a few moments of puzzled reflection.

'Yes,' I said sullenly, perceiving that my chance shot had missed its mark.

'Ha! ha! ha!' he laughed boisterously. 'So that is the extent of Mr Booth's wonderful discoveries! Will you present my compliments to your friend and say that I knew that I was being followed that night. If I could spare the time I should like to see him to congratulate him upon his triumph.'

He took a step towards the door as he spoke, but before he could reach it I rushed forward and, with a desperate movement, turned the key. My action was so totally unexpected that Barrington at first looked simply amazed, while for my part, I was so carried away by excitement and anger at the thought of his quitting the country with his undisclosed secret that I had yielded to a desperate and unreasoning impulse.

'Mr Perkins! What does this mean?' exclaimed Barrington, quickly and sternly, when he realised the situation.

'You must wait to see Mr Booth,' I gasped, as I slipped the key into my pocket.

'I understood Mr Booth was out of town,' he said, in a startled tone.

'He will be back in time for dinner,' I answered.

'Open that door immediately,' cried Barrington, in a peremptory tone.

'Not until –'

'Mr Perkins, open that door, or –'

He did not conclude his sentence, but, with a determined air, produced suddenly a formidable revolver and levelled it straight at my head. I wish I could record that I displayed courage and firmness in this startling emergency. I am afraid I must admit that, on the contrary, I behaved with absolute pusillanimity. I endeavoured to convince myself that my assailant would not dare to carry out his threat, but it is not easy to reason calmly with the gleaming barrel of a revolver dazzling one's eyes and understanding, and Barrington's aspect was that of a desperate man. After a brief moment of hesitation, I sulkily threw the key on the table, and stepped out of range, while my visitor picked it up and, transferring the offensive weapon to his left hand, proceeded to unlock the door, keeping his eyes fixed, half sternly and half jeeringly, upon me.

We were both of us too much preoccupied, I suppose, in watching one another, to notice the sound of an approaching footstep in the hall outside; at all events it would be difficult to say which was the more startled – though with widely different emotions – when, the instant Barrington had turned the key, the door was quietly opened from the outside and Mr Booth, still wearing his hat and overcoat, quietly entered the room.

He appeared to take in the situation at a glance, and, before Barrington could recover from his surprise, closed the door behind him and stood with his back against it.

'You had better put that thing away,' he said, addressing my companion, referring contemptuously to the revolver.

'I'm in a hurry,' said Barrington, taking a step forward.

'You were thinking of starting on a journey?' enquired Mr Booth, blandly.

'Abroad,' I interposed, significantly.

'Will you be good enough to ring the bell, Perkins?' said Mr Booth.

'Stop!' exclaimed Barrington, as I was proceeding mechanically to obey. 'What for?' he added, turning fiercely upon my friend.

'I propose to give you in charge for threatening Mr Perkins –

and also myself – with a revolver,' said Mr Booth, smiling at the fellow's manifest discomfiture. 'What the ultimate result may be I can't say, but you will pass this night, at all events, in a police cell.'

'What is the object of this tomfoolery?' cried Barrington, angrily.

'That's my affair, but I can guarantee this much – that in twelve hours from now, you being safe under lock and key, I shall, with the assistance of the police, have discovered everything I wish to know – your name, your recent address, your present destination, the persons you have been in communication with, the nature of your business with them – in a word, everything.'

'You know nothing at present, at all events,' said Barrington, with an attempted sneer, though he could not disguise his consternation at my friend's words.

'You are going to tell me a good deal,' said Mr Booth, grinning with satisfaction, 'unless the prospect of having to put off your journey will not inconvenience you.'

'I was a d----d fool to come here,' exclaimed Barrington, half involuntarily.

'Oh, no. You needn't blame yourself too much,' said Mr Booth, condescendingly, 'you naturally wished to find out what the advertisement meant. You feared the money which is to be paid to you by certain parties might have been withheld at the last moment if everything had been discovered.'

'That is right enough,' replied Barrington, who seemed somewhat relieved by my friend's altered manner.

'Now the question is,' said Mr Booth, strolling from the door to the fireplace, a circumstance of which our visitor showed no disposition to take advantage in his evident perplexity, 'will it suit you better to be detained in a police cell for a night, and run the risk of getting nothing after all, or to be allowed to proceed on your journey with – say – twenty-four hours' grace?'

'Confound you! You've won after all!' exclaimed Mr Barrington, after an agitated silence, smiling in spite of his vexation.

'You see, you are in a cleft stick!' laughed Mr Booth, gleefully.

'Well, I suppose I must accept your terms,' said Barrington, hastily producing a well-filled pocket-book and extracting an advertisement cut from a newspaper, 'you must have discovered this for yourself, you know. I've told you nothing.'

'Not a word,' said Mr Booth gravely. 'Is this right, Perkins?' he enquired, passing on the newspaper cutting to me, after glancing at it.

'Yes!' I exclaimed excitedly, a moment later. 'Henry Eustace Barker was my father's first cousin. He went to Australia many years ago, and – well, to tell the truth, I had forgotten all about him.'

'Then we need not detain Mr Barrington,' said Mr Booth, bowing ironically.

* * * * * *

I have terminated the story at this point because I have no desire to weary my readers by detailing the legal formalities which resulted in my successfully establishing my claim as heir-at-law of my father's cousin. Mr Booth acted throughout as a zealous and shrewd adviser, and it was chiefly owing to his assistance that I recovered the greater part of the property. It turned out that Barrington – whose real name I charitably refrain from mentioning – had been a clerk in the office of the firm of solicitors who had some years previously inserted the advertisement which had escaped my notice at the time. How he discovered me was never clearly ascertained, for I am pleased to say that my existence was never suspected either by the solicitors referred to or by the distant relative who wrongfully inherited the fortune. It was this circumstance which caused me to overlook my relative's weakness in having yielded to temptation by purchasing Barrington's silence for a very large sum after the latter had revealed to him that I – the real heir – was still living. It is an episode in my family history which I prefer not to dwell upon. Suffice it to say, that I recouped him this outlay, and agreed to a compromise which did not leave him penniless; while, on the other hand, I became possessed of a handsome competence, which enabled me to retire from the office, and to present the capital sum I became entitled to in lieu of a pension, to the Monarchy Clerks' Benevolent Fund.

MAX CARRADOS

Created by Ernest Bramah (1868-1942)

Ernest Brammah Smith, whose writings all appeared under the name Ernest Bramah, began his working life as a farmer. Indeed, his first published book was about farming but he soon realised that a life on the land was not for him. He took a job as secretary to the humourist Jerome K Jerome and worked as an editor on several magazines before his own writing career took off. Bramah wrote in a variety of styles and genres. During his lifetime, his best-known creation was probably Kai Lung, an itinerant storyteller in Ancient China whose tales, sometimes fantastical in nature, were collected in volumes published over a forty-year period. (The Kai Lung stories are rarely read today and they are undoubtedly dated, although they have had some unlikely admirers, including Jorge Luis Borges.) Bramah's one science fiction novel, What Might Have Been, *a work of alternate history, was published in 1907. A later edition was reviewed by George Orwell and some critics have claimed it as an influence on* Nineteen Eighty-Four. *Bramah's blind detective Max Carrados first appeared in a volume of short stories published in 1914. Carrados is not the only blind detective from that era – the American writer Clinton Stagg created Thornley Colton at about the same date – but he is much the most interesting. Some of Carrados's abilities (he can read fine print by touch alone and shoot accurately at targets he cannot see) verge on the supernatural but, in other ways, he is a sympathetic and down-to-earth character. Like his creator, he was a numismatist and coins have a part to play in several of his adventures. All of them are well written and remain worth reading.*

THE TRAGEDY AT BROOKBEND COTTAGE

'Max,' said Mr Carlyle, when Parkinson had closed the door behind him, 'this is Lieutenant Hollyer, whom you consented to see.'

'To hear,' corrected Carrados, smiling straight into the healthy and rather embarrassed face of the stranger before him. 'Mr Hollyer knows of my disability?'

'Mr Carlyle told me,' said the young man, 'but, as a matter of fact, I had heard of you before, Mr Carrados, from one of our men. It was in connection with the foundering of the *Ivan Saratov.*'

Carrados wagged his head in good-humoured resignation.

'And the owners were sworn to inviolable secrecy!' he exclaimed. 'Well, it is inevitable, I suppose. Not another scuttling case, Mr Hollyer?'

'No, mine is quite a private matter,' replied the lieutenant. 'My sister, Mrs Creake – but Mr Carlyle would tell you better than I can. He knows all about it.'

'No, no; Carlyle is a professional. Let me have it in the rough, Mr Hollyer. My ears are my eyes, you know.'

'Very well, sir. I can tell you what there is to tell, right enough, but I feel that when all's said and done it must sound very little to another, although it seems important enough to me.'

'We have occasionally found trifles of significance ourselves,' said Carrados encouragingly. 'Don't let that deter you.'

This was the essence of Lieutenant Hollyer's narrative:

'I have a sister, Millicent, who is married to a man called Creake. She is about twenty-eight now and he is at least fifteen years older. Neither my mother (who has since died), nor I, cared very much about Creake. We had nothing particular against him, except, perhaps, the moderate disparity of age, but none of us appeared to have anything in common. He was a dark, taciturn man, and his moody silence froze up conversation. As a result, of course, we didn't see much of each other.'

38

'This, you must understand, was four or five years ago, Max,' interposed Mr Carlyle officiously.

Carrados maintained an uncompromising silence. Mr Carlyle blew his nose and contrived to impart a hurt significance into the operation. Then Lieutenant Hollyer continued:

'Millicent married Creake after a very short engagement. It was a frightfully subdued wedding – more like a funeral to me. The man professed to have no relations and apparently he had scarcely any friends or business acquaintances. He was an agent for something or other and had an office off Holborn. I suppose he made a living out of it then, although we knew practically nothing of his private affairs, but I gather that it has been going down since, and I suspect that for the past few years they have been getting along almost entirely on Millicent's little income. You would like the particulars of that?'

'Please,' assented Carrados.

'When our father died about seven years ago, he left three thousand pounds. It was invested in Canadian stock and brought in a little over a hundred a year. By his will my mother was to have the income of that for life and on her death it was to pass to Millicent, subject to the payment of a lump sum of five hundred pounds to me. But my father privately suggested to me that if I should have no particular use for the money at the time, he would propose my letting Millicent have the income of it until I did want it, as she would not be particularly well off. You see, Mr Carrados, a great deal more had been spent on my education and advancement than on her; I had my pay, and, of course, I could look out for myself better than a girl could.'

'Quite so,' agreed Carrados.

'Therefore I did nothing about that,' continued the lieutenant. 'Three years ago I was over again but I did not see much of them. They were living in lodgings. That was the only time since the marriage that I have seen them until last week. In the meanwhile our mother had died and Millicent had been receiving her income. She wrote me several letters at the time. Otherwise we did not correspond much, but about a year ago she sent me their new address – Brookbend Cottage, Mulling Common – a house that they had taken. When I got two months' leave I invited myself there as a matter of course, fully expecting to stay most of my time with them, but I made an excuse to get away after a week. The place was dismal and unendurable, the whole life and atmosphere indescribably depressing.' He looked round with an instinct of caution, leaned forward earnestly, and dropped his voice. 'Mr Carrados, it is my absolute conviction that Creake is only waiting for a favourable opportunity to murder Millicent.'

'Go on,' said Carrados quietly. 'A week of the depressing surroundings of Brookbend Cottage would not alone convince you of that, Mr Hollyer.'

'I am not so sure,' declared Hollyer doubtfully. 'There was a feeling of suspicion and – before me – polite hatred that would have gone a good way towards it. All the same there *was* something more definite. Millicent told me this the day after I went there. There is no doubt that a few months ago Creake deliberately planned to poison her with some weedkiller. She told me the circumstances in a rather distressed moment, but afterwards she refused to speak of it again – even weakly denied it– and, as a matter of fact, it was with the greatest difficulty that I could get her at any time to talk about her husband or his affairs. The gist of it was that she had the strongest suspicion that Creake doctored a bottle of stout which he expected she would drink for her supper when she was alone. The weedkiller, properly labelled, but also in a beer bottle, was kept with other miscellaneous liquids in the same cupboard as the beer but on a high shelf. When he found that it had miscarried he poured away the mixture, washed out the bottle and put in the dregs from another. There is no doubt in my mind that if he had come back and found Millicent dead or dying he would have contrived it to appear that she had made a mistake in the dark and drunk some of the poison before she found out.'

'Yes,' assented Carrados. 'The open way; the safe way.'

'You must understand that they live in a very small style, Mr Carrados, and Millicent is almost entirely in the man's power. The only servant they have is a woman who comes in for a few hours every day. The house is lonely and secluded. Creake is sometimes away for days and nights at a time, and Millicent, either through pride or indifference, seems to have dropped off all her old friends and to have made no others. He might poison her, bury the body in the garden, and be a thousand miles away before anyone began even to inquire about her. What am I to do, Mr Carrados?'

'He is less likely to try poison than some other means now,' pondered Carrados. 'That having failed, his wife will always be on her guard. He may know, or at least suspect, that others know. No... The common-sense precaution would be for your sister to leave the man, Mr Hollyer. She will not?'

'No,' admitted Hollyer, 'she will not. I at once urged that.' The young man struggled with some hesitation for a moment and then blurted out: 'The fact is, Mr Carrados, I don't understand Millicent. She is not the girl she was. She hates Creake and treats him with a silent contempt that eats into their lives like acid, and yet she is so jealous of him that she will let nothing short of death part them. It is a horrible life they lead. I stood it for a week and I must say, much as I dislike my brother-in-law, that he has something to put up with. If only he got into a passion like a man and killed her it wouldn't be altogether incomprehensible.'

'That does not concern us,' said Carrados. 'In a game of this kind one has to take sides and we have taken ours. It remains for us to see that our side wins. You mentioned jealousy, Mr Hollyer. Have you any idea whether Mrs Creake has real ground for it?'

'I should have told you that,' replied Lieutenant Hollyer. 'I happened to strike up with a newspaper man whose office is in the same block as Creake's. When I mentioned the name, he grinned. "Creake," he said, "oh, he's the man with the romantic typist, isn't he?" "Well, he's my brother-in-law," I replied. "What about the typist?" Then the chap shut up like a knife. "No, no," he said, "I didn't know he was married. I don't want to get mixed up in anything of that sort. I only said that he had a typist. Well, what of that? So have we; so has everyone." There was nothing more to be got out of him, but the remark and the grin meant – well, about as usual, Mr Carrados.'

Carrados turned to his friend.

'I suppose you know all about the typist by now, Louis?'

'We have had her under efficient observation, Max,' replied Mr Carlyle, with severe dignity.

'Is she unmarried?'

'Yes; so far as ordinary repute goes, she is.'

'That is all that is essential for the moment. Mr Hollyer opens up three excellent reasons why this man might wish to dispose of his wife. If we accept the suggestion of poisoning – though we have only a jealous woman's suspicion for it – we add to the wish the determination. Well, we will go forward on that. Have you got a photograph of Mr Creake?'

The lieutenant took out his pocket-book.

'Mr Carlyle asked me for one. Here is the best I could get.'

Carrados rang the bell.

'This, Parkinson,' he said, when the man appeared, 'is a photograph of a Mr — what first name, by the way?'

'Austin,' put in Hollyer, who was following everything with a boyish mixture of excitement and subdued importance.

'... of a Mr Austin Creake. I may require you to recognise him.'

Parkinson glanced at the print and returned it to his master's hand.

'May I inquire if it is a recent photograph of the gentleman, sir?' he asked.

'About six years ago,' said the lieutenant, taking in this new actor in the drama with frank curiosity. 'But he is very little changed.'

'Thank you, sir. I will endeavour to remember Mr Creake, sir.'

Lieutenant Hollyer stood up as Parkinson left the room. The interview seemed to be at an end.

'Oh, there's one other matter,' he remarked. 'I am afraid that I did rather an unfortunate thing while I was at Brookbend. It seemed to me that as all Millicent's money would probably pass into Creake's hands sooner or later I might as well have my five hundred pounds, if only to help her with afterwards. So I broached the subject and said that I should like to have it now as I had an opportunity for investing.'

'And you think?'

'It may possibly influence Creake to act sooner than he otherwise might have done. He may have got possession of the principal even and find it very awkward to replace it.'

'So much the better. If your sister is going to be murdered it may as well be done next week as next year so far as I am concerned. Excuse my brutality, Mr Hollyer, but this is simply a case to me and I regard it strategically. Now Mr Carlyle's organisation can look after Mrs Creake for a few weeks but it cannot look after her for ever. By increasing the immediate risk, we diminish the permanent risk.'

'I see,' agreed Hollyer. 'I'm awfully uneasy but I'm entirely in your hands.'

'Then we will give Mr Creake every inducement and every opportunity to get to work. Where are you staying now?'

'Just now with some friends at St Albans.'

'That is too far.' The inscrutable eyes retained their tranquil depth but a new quality of quickening interest in the voice made Mr Carlyle forget the weight and burden of his ruffled dignity. 'Give me a few minutes, please. The cigarettes are behind you, Mr Hollyer.' The blind man walked to the window and seemed to look out over the cypress-shaded lawn. The lieutenant lit a cigarette and Mr Carlyle picked up *Punch*. Then Carrados turned round again.

'You are prepared to put your own arrangements aside?' he demanded of his visitor.

'Certainly.'

43

'Very well. I want you to go down now – straight from here – to Brookbend Cottage. Tell your sister that your leave is unexpectedly cut short and that you sail tomorrow.'

'The *Martian*?'

'No, no; the *Martian* doesn't sail. Look up the movements on your way there and pick out a boat that does. Say you are transferred. Add that you expect to be away only two or three months and that you really want the five hundred pounds by the time of your return. Don't stay in the house long, please.'

'I understand, sir.'

'St Albans is too far. Make your excuse and get away from there today. Put up somewhere in town where you will be in reach of the telephone. Let Mr Carlyle and myself know where you are. Keep out of Creake's way. I don't want actually to tie you down to the house, but we may require your services. We will let you know at the first sign of anything doing and if there is nothing to be done we must release you.'

'I don't mind that. Is there nothing more that I can do now?'

'Nothing. In going to Mr Carlyle you have done the best thing possible; you have put your sister into the care of the shrewdest man in London.' Whereat the object of this quite unexpected eulogy found himself becoming covered with modest confusion.

'Well, Max?' remarked Mr Carlyle tentatively when they were alone.

'Well, Louis?'

'Of course, it wasn't worth while rubbing it in before young Hollyer, but, as a matter of fact, every single man carries the life of any other man – only one, mind you – in his hands, do what you will.'

'Provided he doesn't bungle,' acquiesced Carrados.

'Quite so.'

'And also that he is absolutely reckless of the consequences.'

'Of course.'

'Two rather large provisos. Creake is obviously susceptible to both. Have you seen him?'

'No. As I told you, I put a man on to report his habits in town. Then, two days ago, as the case seemed to promise some interest – for he certainly is deeply involved with the typist, Max, and the thing might take a sensational turn any time – I went down to Mulling Common myself. Although the house is lonely it is on the electric tram route. You know the sort of market garden rurality that about a dozen miles out of London offers – alternate bricks and cabbages. It was easy enough to get to know about Creake locally. He mixes with no one there, goes into town at irregular times but generally every day, and is reputed to be devilish hard to get money out of. Finally I made the acquaintance of an old fellow who used to do a day's gardening at Brookbend occasionally. He has a cottage and a garden of his own with a greenhouse, and the business cost me the price of a pound of tomatoes.'

'Was it – a profitable investment?'

'As tomatoes, yes; as information, no. The old fellow had the fatal disadvantage from our point of view of labouring under a grievance. A few weeks ago Creake told him that he would not require him again as he was going to do his own gardening in future.'

'That is something, Louis.'

'If only Creake was going to poison his wife with hyoscyamine and bury her, instead of blowing her up with a dynamite cartridge and claiming that it came in among the coal.'

'True, true. Still...'

'However, the chatty old soul had a simple explanation for everything that Creake did. Creake was mad. He had even seen him flying a kite in his garden where it was bound to get wrecked among the trees. "A lad of ten would have known better," he declared. And certainly the kite did get wrecked, for I saw it hanging over the road myself. But that a sane man should spend his time "playing with a toy" was beyond him.'

'A good many men have been flying kites of various kinds lately,' said Carrados. 'Is he interested in aviation?'

'I dare say. He appears to have some knowledge of scientific subjects. Now what do you want me to do, Max?'

'Will you do it?'

'Implicitly – subject to the usual reservations.'

'Keep your man on Creake in town and let me have his reports after you have seen them. Lunch with me here now. Phone up to your office that you are detained on unpleasant business and then give the deserving Parkinson an afternoon off by looking after me while we take a motor run round Mulling Common. If we have time we might go on to Brighton, feed at the "Ship", and come back in the cool.'

'Amiable and thrice lucky mortal,' sighed Mr Carlyle, his glance wandering round the room.

But, as it happened, Brighton did not figure in that day's itinerary. It had been Carrados's intention merely to pass Brookbend Cottage on this occasion, relying on his highly developed faculties, aided by Mr Carlyle's description, to inform him of the surroundings. A hundred yards before they reached the house he had given an order to his chauffeur to drop into the lowest speed and they were leisurely drawing past when a discovery by Mr Carlyle modified their plans.

'By Jupiter!' that gentleman suddenly exclaimed, 'there's a board up, Max. The place is to be let.'

Carrados picked up the tube again. A couple of sentences passed and the car stopped by the roadside, a score of paces past the limit of the garden. Mr Carlyle took out his notebook and wrote down the address of a firm of house agents.

'You might raise the bonnet and have a look at the engines, Harris,' said Carrados. 'We want to be occupied here for a few minutes.'

'This is sudden; Hollyer knew nothing of their leaving,' remarked Mr Carlyle.

'Probably not for three months yet. All the same, Louis, we will go on to the agents and get a card to view, whether we use it today or not.'

A thick hedge in its summer dress, effectively screening the house beyond from public view, lay between the garden and the road. Above the hedge showed an occasional shrub; at the corner nearest to the car a chestnut flourished. The wooden gate, once white, which they had passed, was grimed and rickety. The road itself was still the unpretentious country lane that the advent of the electric car had found it. When Carrados had taken in these details there seemed little else to notice. He was on the point of giving Harris the order to go on when his ear caught a trivial sound.

'Someone is coming out of the house, Louis,' he warned his friend. 'It may be Hollyer, but he ought to have gone by this time.'

'I don't hear anyone,' replied the other, but as he spoke a door banged noisily and Mr Carlyle slipped into another seat and ensconced himself behind a copy of *The Globe*.

'Creake himself,' he whispered across the car, as a man appeared at the gate. 'Hollyer was right; he is hardly changed. Waiting for a car, I suppose.'

But a car very soon swung past them from the direction in which Mr Creake was looking and it did not interest him. For a minute or two longer he continued to look expectantly along the road. Then he walked slowly up the drive back to the house.

'We will give him five or ten minutes,' decided Carrados. 'Harris is behaving very naturally.'

Before even the shorter period had run out they were repaid. A telegraph-boy cycled leisurely along the road, and, leaving his machine at the gate, went up to the cottage. Evidently there was no reply, for in less than a minute he was trundling past them back again. Round the bend an approaching tram clanged its bell noisily, and, quickened by the warning sound, Mr Creake again appeared, this time with a small portmanteau in his hand. With a backward glance he hurried on towards the next stopping-place, and, boarding the car as it slackened down, he was carried out of their knowledge.

'Very convenient of Mr Creake,' remarked Carrados, with quiet satisfaction. 'We will now get the order and go over the house in his absence. It might be useful to have a look at the wire as well.'

'It might, Max,' acquiesced Mr Carlyle a little dryly. 'But if it is, as it probably is, in Creake's pocket, how do you propose to get it?'

'By going to the post office, Louis.'

'Quite so. Have you ever tried to see a copy of a telegram addressed to someone else?'

'I don't think I have ever had occasion yet,' admitted Carrados. 'Have you?'

'In one or two cases I have perhaps been an accessory to the act. It is generally a matter either of extreme delicacy or considerable expenditure.'

'Then for Hollyer's sake we will hope for the former here.' And Mr Carlyle smiled darkly and hinted that he was content to wait for a friendly revenge.

A little later, having left the car at the beginning of the straggling High Street, the two men called at the village post office. They had already visited the house agent and obtained an order to view Brookbend Cottage, declining, with some difficulty, the clerk's persistent offer to accompany them. The reason was soon forthcoming. 'As a matter of fact,' explained the young man, 'the present tenant is under *our* notice to leave.'

'Unsatisfactory, eh?' said Carrados encouragingly.

'He's a corker,' admitted the clerk, responding to the friendly tone. 'Fifteen months and not a doit of rent have we had. That's why I should have liked –'

'We will make every allowance,' replied Carrados.

The post office occupied one side of a stationer's shop. It was not without some inward trepidation that Mr Carlyle found himself committed to the adventure. Carrados, on the other hand, was the personification of bland unconcern.

'You have just sent a telegram to Brookbend Cottage,' he said to the young lady behind the brasswork lattice. 'We think it may have come inaccurately and should like a repeat.' He took out his purse. 'What is the fee?'

The request was evidently not a common one. 'Oh,' said the girl uncertainly, 'wait a minute, please.' She turned to a pile of telegram duplicates behind the desk and ran a doubtful finger along the upper sheets. 'I think this is all right. You want it repeated?'

'Please.' Just a tinge of questioning surprise gave point to the courteous tone.

'It will be fourpence. If there is an error the amount will be refunded.'

Carrados put down a coin and received his change.

'Will it take long?' he inquired carelessly, as he pulled on his glove.

'You will most likely get it within a quarter of an hour,' she replied.

'Now you've done it,' commented Mr Carlyle, as they walked back to their car. 'How do you propose to get that telegram, Max?'

'Ask for it,' was the laconic explanation.

And, stripping the artifice of any elaboration, he simply asked for it and got it. The car, posted at a convenient bend in the road, gave him a warning note as the telegraph-boy approached. Then Carrados took up a convincing attitude with his hand on the gate while Mr Carlyle lent himself to the semblance of a departing friend. That was the inevitable impression when the boy rode up.

'Creake, Brookbend Cottage?' inquired Carrados, holding out his hand, and without a second thought the boy gave him the envelope and rode away on the assurance that there would be no reply.

'Some day, my friend,' remarked Mr Carlyle, looking nervously towards the unseen house, 'your ingenuity will get you into a tight corner.'

'Then my ingenuity must get me out again,' was the retort.

'Let us have our "view" now. The telegram can wait.'

An untidy workwoman took their order and left them standing at the door. Presently a lady whom they both knew to be Mrs Creake appeared.

'You wish to see over the house?' she said, in a voice that was utterly devoid of any interest. Then, without waiting for a reply, she turned to the nearest door and threw it open.

'This is the drawing-room,' she said, standing aside.

They walked into a sparsely furnished, damp-smelling room and made a pretence of looking round, while Mrs Creake remained silent and aloof.

'The dining-room,' she continued, crossing the narrow hall and opening another door.

Mr Carlyle ventured a genial commonplace in the hope of inducing conversation. The result was not encouraging. Doubtless they would have gone through the house under the same frigid guidance had not Carrados been at fault in a way that Mr Carlyle had never known him fail before. In crossing the hall, he stumbled over a mat and almost fell.

'Pardon my clumsiness,' he said to the lady. 'I am, unfortunately, quite blind. But,' he added, with a smile, to turn off the mishap, 'even a blind man must have a house.'

The man who had eyes was surprised to see a flood of colour rush into Mrs Creake's face.

'Blind!' she exclaimed, 'oh, I beg your pardon. Why did you not tell me? You might have fallen.'

'I generally manage fairly well,' he replied. 'But, of course, in a strange house –'

She put her hand on his arm very lightly. 'You must let me guide you, just a little,' she said.

The house, without being large, was full of passages and inconvenient turnings. Carrados asked an occasional question and found Mrs Creake quite amiable without effusion. Mr Carlyle followed them from room to room in the hope, though scarcely the expectation, of learning something that might be useful.

'This is the last one. It is the largest bedroom,' said their guide. Only two of the upper rooms were fully furnished and Mr Carlyle at once saw, as Carrados knew without seeing, that this was the one which the Creakes occupied.

'A very pleasant outlook,' declared Mr Carlyle.

'Oh, I suppose so,' admitted the lady vaguely. The room, in fact, looked over the leafy garden and the road beyond. It had a French window opening on to a small balcony, and to this, under the strange influence that always attracted him to light, Carrados walked.

'I expect that there is a certain amount of repair needed?' he said, after standing there a moment.

'I am afraid there would be,' she confessed.

'I ask because there is a sheet of metal on the floor here,' he continued. 'Now that, in an old house, spells dry rot to the wary observer.'

'My husband said that the rain, which comes in a little under the window, was rotting the boards there,' she replied. 'He put that down recently. I had not noticed anything myself.'

It was the first time she had mentioned her husband; Mr Carlyle pricked up his ears.

'Ah, that is a less serious matter,' said Carrados. 'May I step out on to the balcony?'

'Oh yes, if you like to.' Then, as he appeared to be fumbling at the catch, 'Let me open it for you.'

But the window was already open, and Carrados, facing the various points of the compass, took in the bearings.

'A sunny, sheltered corner,' he remarked. 'An ideal spot for a deck-chair and a book.'

She shrugged her shoulders half contemptuously.

'I dare say,' she replied, 'but I never use it.'

'Sometimes, surely,' he persisted mildly. 'It would be my favourite retreat. But then –'

'I was going to say that I had never even been out on it, but that would not be quite true. It has two uses for me, both equally

51

romantic; I occasionally shake a duster from it, and when my husband returns late without his latchkey he wakes me up and I come out here and drop him mine.'

Further revelation of Mr Creake's nocturnal habits was cut off, greatly to Mr Carlyle's annoyance, by a cough of unmistakable significance from the foot of the stairs. They had heard a trade cart drive up to the gate, a knock at the door, and the heavy-footed woman tramp along the hall.

'Excuse me a minute, please,' said Mrs Creake.

'Louis,' said Carrados, in a sharp whisper, the moment they were alone, 'stand against the door.'

With extreme plausibility Mr Carlyle began to admire a picture so situated that while he was there it was impossible to open the door more than a few inches. From that position he observed his confederate go through the curious procedure of kneeling down on the bedroom floor and for a full minute pressing his ear to the sheet of metal that had already engaged his attention. Then he rose to his feet, nodded, dusted his trousers, and Mr Carlyle moved to a less equivocal position.

'What a beautiful rose-tree grows up your balcony,' remarked Carrados, stepping into the room as Mrs Creake returned. 'I suppose you are very fond of gardening?'

'I detest it,' she replied.

'But this *Glorie*, so carefully trained –?'

'Is it?' she replied. 'I think my husband was nailing it up recently.' By some strange fatality Carrados's most aimless remarks seemed to involve the absent Mr Creake. 'Do you care to see the garden?'

The garden proved to be extensive and neglected. Behind the house was chiefly orchard. In front, some semblance of order had been kept up; here it was lawn and shrubbery, and the drive they had walked along. Two things interested Carrados: the soil at the foot of the balcony, which he declared on examination to be particularly suitable for roses, and the fine chestnut-tree in the corner by the road.

As they walked back to the car Mr Carlyle lamented that they had learned so little of Creake's movements.

'Perhaps the telegram will tell us something,' suggested Carrados. 'Read it, Louis.'

Mr Carlyle cut open the envelope, glanced at the enclosure, and in spite of his disappointment could not restrain a chuckle.

'My poor Max,' he explained, 'you have put yourself to an amount of ingenious trouble for nothing. Creake is evidently taking a few days' holiday and prudently availed himself of the Meteorological Office forecast before going. Listen: "Immediate prospect for London warm and settled. Further outlook cooler but fine." Well, well; I did get a pound of tomatoes for *my* fourpence.'

'You certainly scored there, Louis,' admitted Carrados, with humorous appreciation. 'I wonder,' he added speculatively, 'whether it is Creake's peculiar taste usually to spend his weekend holiday in London.'

'Eh?' exclaimed Mr Carlyle, looking at the words again, 'by gad, that's rum, Max. They go to Weston-Super-Mare. Why on earth should he want to know about London?'

'I can make a guess, but before we are satisfied I must come here again. Take another look at that kite, Louis. Are there a few yards of string hanging loose from it?'

'Yes, there are.'

'Rather thick string – unusually thick for the purpose?'

'Yes; but how do you know?'

As they drove home again Carrados explained, and Mr Carlyle sat aghast, saying incredulously: 'Good God, Max, is it possible?'

An hour later he was satisfied that it was possible. In reply to his inquiry someone in his office telephoned him the information that 'they' had left Paddington by the four-thirty for Weston.

It was more than a week after his introduction to Carrados that Lieutenant Hollyer had a summons to present himself at The Turrets again. He found Mr Carlyle already there and the two friends awaiting his arrival.

'I stayed in all day after hearing from you this morning, Mr

Carrados,' he said, shaking hands. 'When I got your second message I was all ready to walk straight out of the house. That's how I did it in the time. I hope everything is all right?'

'Excellent,' replied Carrados. 'You'd better have something before we start. We probably have a long and perhaps an exciting night before us.'

'And certainly a wet one,' assented the lieutenant. 'It was thundering over Mulling way as I came along.'

'That is why you are here,' said his host. 'We are waiting for a certain message before we start, and in the meantime you may as well understand what we expect to happen. As you saw, there is a thunderstorm coming on. The Meteorological Office morning forecast predicted it for the whole of London if the conditions remained. That was why I kept you in readiness. Within an hour it is now inevitable that we shall experience a deluge. Here and there damage will be done to trees and buildings; here and there a person will probably be struck and killed.'

'Yes.'

'It is Mr Creake's intention that his wife should be among the victims.'

'I don't exactly follow,' said Hollyer, looking from one man to the other. 'I quite admit that Creake would be immensely relieved if such a thing did happen, but the chance is surely an absurdly remote one.'

'Yet unless we intervene it is precisely what a coroner's jury will decide has happened. Do you know whether your brother-in-law has any practical knowledge of electricity, Mr Hollyer?'

'I cannot say. He was so reserved, and we really knew so little of him –'

'Yet in 1896 an Austin Creake contributed an article on "Alternating Currents" to the American *Scientific World*. That would argue a fairly intimate acquaintanceship.'

'But do you mean that he is going to direct a flash of lightning?'

'Only into the minds of the doctor who conducts the post-mortem, and the coroner. This storm, the opportunity for which he has been waiting for weeks, is merely the cloak to his act. The weapon which he has planned to use – scarcely less powerful than lightning but much more tractable – is the high voltage current of electricity that flows along the tram wire at his gate.'

'Oh!' exclaimed Lieutenant Hollyer, as the sudden revelation struck him.

'Some time between eleven o'clock tonight – about the hour when your sister goes to bed – and one thirty in the morning – the time up to which he can rely on the current – Creake will throw a stone up at the balcony window. Most of his preparation has long been made; it only remains for him to connect up a short length to the window handle and a longer one at the other end to tap the live wire. That done, he will wake his wife in the way I have said. The moment she moves the catch of the window – and he has carefully filed its parts to ensure perfect contact – she will be electrocuted as effectually as if she sat in the executioner's chair in Sing Sing prison.'

'But what are we doing here!' exclaimed Hollyer, starting to his feet, pale and horrified. 'It is past ten now and anything may happen.'

'Quite natural, Mr Hollyer,' said Carrados reassuringly, 'but you need have no anxiety. Creake is being watched, the house is being watched, and your sister is as safe as if she slept tonight in Windsor Castle. Be assured that whatever happens he will not be allowed to complete his scheme; but it is desirable to let him implicate himself to the fullest limit. Your brother-in-law, Mr Hollyer, is a man with a peculiar capacity for taking pains.'

'He is a damned cold-blooded scoundrel!' exclaimed the young officer fiercely. 'When I think of Millicent five years ago –'

'Well, for that matter, an enlightened nation has decided that electrocution is the most humane way of removing its superfluous citizens,' suggested Carrados mildly. 'He is certainly an ingenious-minded gentleman. It is his misfortune that in Mr Carlyle he was fated to be opposed by an even subtler brain –'

'No, no! Really, Max!' protested the embarrassed gentleman.

'Mr Hollyer will be able to judge for himself when I tell him that it was Mr Carlyle who first drew attention to the significance of the abandoned kite,' insisted Carrados firmly. 'Then, of course, its object became plain to me – as indeed to anyone. For ten minutes, perhaps, a wire must be carried from the overhead line to the chestnut-tree. Creake has everything in his favour, but it is just within possibility that the driver of an inopportune tram might notice the appendage. What of that? Why, for more than a week he has seen a derelict kite with its yards of trailing string hanging in the tree. A very calculating mind, Mr Hollyer. It would be interesting to know what line of action Mr Creake has mapped out for himself afterwards. I expect he has half-a-dozen artistic little touches up his sleeve. Possibly he would merely singe his wife's hair, burn her feet with a red-hot poker, shiver the glass of the French window, and be content with that to let well alone. You see, lightning is so varied in its effects that whatever he did or did not do would be right. He is in the impregnable position of the body showing all the symptoms of death by lightning shock and nothing else but lightning to account for it – a dilated eye, heart contracted in systole, bloodless lungs shrunk to a third the normal weight, and all the rest of it. When he has removed a few outward traces of his work Creake might quite safely "discover" his dead wife and rush off for the nearest doctor. Or he may have decided to arrange a convincing alibi, and creep away, leaving the discovery to another. We shall never know; he will make no confession.'

'I wish it was well over,' admitted Hollyer. 'I'm not particularly jumpy, but this gives me a touch of the creeps.'

'Three more hours at the worst, Lieutenant,' said Carrados cheerfully. 'Ah-ha, something is coming through now.'

He went to the telephone and received a message from one quarter; then made another connection and talked for a few minutes with someone else. 'Everything working smoothly,' he remarked between times over his shoulder. 'Your sister has gone to bed, Mr Hollyer.'

Then he turned to the house telephone and distributed his orders.

'So we,' he concluded, 'must get up.'

By the time they were ready a large closed motor car was waiting. The lieutenant thought he recognised Parkinson in the well-swathed form beside the driver, but there was no temptation to linger for a second on the steps. Already the stinging rain had lashed the drive into the semblance of a frothy estuary; all round the lightning jagged its course through the incessant tremulous glow of more distant lightning, while the thunder only ceased its muttering to turn at close quarters and crackle viciously.

'One of the few things I regret missing,' remarked Carrados tranquilly; 'but I hear a good deal of colour in it.'

The car slushed its way down to the gate, lurched a little heavily across the dip into the road, and, steadying as it came upon the straight, began to hum contentedly along the deserted highway.

'We are not going direct?' suddenly inquired Hollyer, after they had travelled perhaps half-a-dozen miles. The night was bewildering enough but he had the sailor's gift for location.

'No; through Hunscott Green and then by a field-path to the orchard at the back,' replied Carrados. 'Keep a sharp look out for the man with the lantern about here, Harris,' he called through the tube.

'Something flashing just ahead, sir,' came the reply, and the car slowed down and stopped.

Carrados dropped the near window as a man in glistening waterproof stepped from the shelter of a lich-gate and approached.

'Inspector Beedel, sir,' said the stranger, looking into the car.

'Quite right, Inspector,' said Carrados. 'Get in.'

'I have a man with me, sir.'

'We can find room for him as well.'

'We are very wet.'

'So shall we all be soon.'

The lieutenant changed his seat and the two burly forms took places side by side. In less than five minutes the car stopped again, this time in a grassy country lane.

'Now we have to face it,' announced Carrados. 'The inspector will show us the way.'

The car slid round and disappeared into the night, while Beedel led the party to a stile in the hedge. A couple of fields brought them to the Brookbend boundary. There a figure stood out of the black foliage, exchanged a few words with their guide and piloted them along the shadows of the orchard to the back door of the house.

'You will find a broken pane near the catch of the scullery window,' said the blind man.

'Right, sir,' replied the inspector. 'I have it. Now who goes through?'

'Mr Hollyer will open the door for us. I'm afraid you must take off your boots and all wet things, Lieutenant. We cannot risk a single spot inside.'

They waited until the back door opened, then each one divested himself in a similar manner and passed into the kitchen, where the remains of a fire still burned. The man from the orchard gathered together the discarded garments and disappeared again.

Carrados turned to the lieutenant.

'A rather delicate job for you now, Mr Hollyer. I want you to go up to your sister, wake her, and get her into another room with as little fuss as possible. Tell her as much as you think fit and let her understand that her very life depends on absolute stillness when she is alone. Don't be unduly hurried, but not a glimmer of a light, please.'

Ten minutes passed by the measure of the battered old alarum on the dresser shelf before the young man returned.

'I've had rather a time of it,' he reported, with a nervous laugh, 'but I think it will be all right now. She is in the spare room.'

'Then we will take our places. You and Parkinson come with me to the bedroom. Inspector, you have your own arrangements. Mr Carlyle will be with you.'

They dispersed silently about the house. Hollyer glanced apprehensively at the door of the spare room as they passed it but within was as quiet as the grave. Their room lay at the other end of the passage.

'You may as well take your place in the bed now, Hollyer,' directed Carrados when they were inside and the door closed. 'Keep well down among the clothes. Creake has to get up on the balcony, you know, and he will probably peep through the window, but he dare come no farther. Then when he begins to throw up stones slip on this dressing-gown of your sister's. I'll tell you what to do after.'

The next sixty minutes drew out into the longest hour that the lieutenant had ever known. Occasionally he heard a whisper pass between the two men who stood behind the window curtains, but he could see nothing. Then Carrados threw a guarded remark in his direction.

'He is in the garden now.'

Something scraped slightly against the outer wall. But the night was full of wilder sounds, and in the house the furniture and the boards creaked and sprung between the yawling of the wind among the chimneys, the rattle of the thunder and the pelting of the rain. It was a time to quicken the steadiest pulse, and when the crucial moment came, when a pebble suddenly rang against the pane with a sound that the tense waiting magnified into a shivering crash, Hollyer leapt from the bed on the instant.

'Easy, easy,' warned Carrados feelingly. 'We will wait for another knock.' He passed something across. 'Here is a rubber glove. I have cut the wire but you had better put it on. Stand just for a moment at the window, move the catch so that it can blow open a little, and drop immediately. Now.'

Another stone had rattled against the glass. For Hollyer to go through his part was the work merely of seconds and with a few touches Carrados spread the dressing-gown to more effective disguise about the extended form. But an unforeseen and in the circumstances rather horrible interval followed, for Creake, in accordance with some detail of his never-revealed plan, continued to shower missile after missile against the panes until even the unimpressionable Parkinson shivered.

'The last act,' whispered Carrados, a moment after the throwing had ceased. 'He has gone round to the back. Keep as you are. We take cover now.' He pressed behind the arras of an extemporised wardrobe, and the spirit of emptiness and desolation seemed once more to reign over the lonely house.

From half-a-dozen places of concealment ears were straining to catch the first guiding sound. He moved very stealthily, burdened, perhaps, by some strange scruple in the presence of the tragedy that he had not feared to contrive, paused for a moment at the bedroom door, then opened it very quietly, and in the fickle light read the consummation of his hopes.

'At last!' they heard the sharp whisper drawn from his relief. 'At last!'

He took another step and two shadows seemed to fall upon him from behind, one on either side. With primitive instinct a cry of terror and surprise escaped him as he made a desperate movement to wrench himself free, and for a short second he almost succeeded in dragging one hand into a pocket. Then his wrists slowly came together and the handcuffs closed.

'I am Inspector Beedel,' said the man on his right side. 'You are charged with the attempted murder of your wife, Millicent Creake.'

'You are mad,' retorted the miserable creature, falling into a desperate calmness. 'She has been struck by lightning.'

'No, you blackguard, she hasn't,' wrathfully exclaimed his brother-in-law, jumping up. 'Would you like to see her?'

'I also have to warn you,' continued the inspector impassively, 'that anything you say may be used as evidence against you.'

A startled cry from the farther end of the passage arrested their attention.

'Mr Carrados,' called Hollyer, 'oh, come at once.' At the open door of the other bedroom stood the lieutenant, his eyes still turned towards something in the room beyond, a little empty bottle in his hand.

'Dead!' he exclaimed tragically, with a sob, 'with this beside her. Dead just when she would have been free of the brute.'

The blind man passed into the room, sniffed the air, and laid a gentle hand on the pulseless heart.

'Yes,' he replied. 'That, Hollyer, does not always appeal to the woman, strange to say.'

MISS FLORENCE CUSACK

Created by LT Meade (1854-1914)
& Robert Eustace (1854-1943)

LT Meade was the pseudonym of Elizabeth Thomasina Meade Smith, an almost impossibly productive writer of the late Victorian and Edwardian eras who made her first appearance in print in the 1870s and went on to publish close to 300 books. At one stage in her career she was writing ten novels a year. In her lifetime she was best-known as the author of stories for girls, often with a school setting, but she also wrote many crime stories, sometimes in collaboration with other writers. One of her most regular collaborators was Robert Eustace (real name Eustace Robert Barton), a doctor and part-time writer. With Eustace she created a number of series characters including a remarkable femme fatale and supervillain called Madame Sara, John Bell, a professional ghost-hunter, and Diana Marburg, a palmist and occasional solver of crimes. Eustace outlived Meade by several decades and continued to write fiction in the crime and mystery genre. He also continued to collaborate with other writers, including Dorothy L Sayers with whom he wrote The Documents in the Case, *first published in 1930. Meade and Eustace's female detective Florence Cusack appeared in a series of short stories first published in* Harmsworth Magazine *between 1899 and 1901. The stories are narrated by one Dr Lonsdale. Indeed, he also does much of the legwork in them but it is the glamorous Miss Cusack – 'this handsome girl with her slender figure, her eyes of the darkest blue, her raven black hair and clear complexion' – who provides the final insights and solves the crimes.*

THE ARREST OF CAPTAIN VANDALEUR

One soft spring day in April I received a hurried message from Miss Cusack asking me to see her immediately.

It was a Sunday, I remember, and the trees were just putting on their first green. I arrived at the house in Kensington Park Gardens between four and five o'clock, and was admitted at once into the presence of my hostess. I found her in her library, a large room on the ground floor fitted with books from wainscot to ceiling, and quite unlike the ordinary boudoir of a fashionable lady.

'It is very good of you to come, Dr Lonsdale, and if it were not that my necessities are pressing, you may be sure I would not ask you to visit me on Sunday.'

'I am delighted to render you any assistance in my power,' I answered; 'and Sunday is not quite such a busy day with me as others.'

'I want you to see a patient for me.'

'A patient?' I cried.

'Yes; his name is Walter Farrell, and he and his young wife are my special friends; his wife has been my friend since her schooldays. I want you to see him and also Mrs Farrell. Mrs Farrell is very ill – another doctor might do for her what you can do, but my real reason for asking you to visit her is in the hope that you may save the husband. When you see him you may think it strange of me to call him a patient, for his disease is more moral than mental, and is certainly not physical. His wife is very ill, and he still loves her. Low as he has sunk, I believe that he would make an effort, a gigantic effort, for her sake.'

'But in what does the moral insanity consist?' I asked.

'Gambling,' she replied, leaning forward and speaking eagerly. 'It is fast ruining him body and soul. The case puzzles me,' she continued. 'Mr Farrell is a rich man, but if he goes on as he is now doing he will soon be bankrupt. The largest fortune could not stand the drain he puts upon it. He is deliberately ruining both himself and his wife.'

'What form does his gambling take?' I asked.

'Horse-racing.'

'And is he losing money?'

'He is now, but last year he unfortunately won large sums. This fact seems to have confirmed the habit, and now nothing, as far as we can tell, will check his downward career. He has become the partner of a bookmaker, Mr Rashleigh – they call themselves "Turf Commission Agents". They have taken a suite of rooms in Pall Mall, and do a large business. Disaster is, of course, inevitable, and for the sake of his wife I want to save him, and I want you to help me.'

'I will do what I can, of course, but I am puzzled to know in what way I can be of service. Men affected with moral diseases are quite out of an ordinary doctor's sphere.'

'All the same it is in your power to do something. But listen, I have not yet come to the end of my story. I have other reasons, and oddly enough they coincide. I know the history of the man whom Walter Farrell is in partnership with. I know it, although at present I am powerless to expose him. Mr Rashleigh is a notorious swindler. He has been in some mysterious way making enormous sums of money by means of horse-racing, and I have been asked to help the Criminal Investigation Department in the matter. The fact of poor Walter Farrell being in his power has given me an additional incentive to effect his exposure. Had it not been for this I should have refused to have anything to do with the matter.'

'What are Rashleigh's methods of working?' I asked.

'I will tell you. I presume you understand the principles of horse-racing?'

'A few of them,' I answered.

'Mr Rashleigh's method is this: He poses as a bookmaker in want of capital. He has had several victims, and Mr Farrell is his last. In past cases, when he secured his victim, he entered into partnership with him, took a place in the West End, and furnished it luxuriously. One of the Exchange Telegraph Company's tape machines which record the runners, winners, and the starting prices of the horses was introduced. As a matter of course betting men arrived, and for a time everything went well, and the firm made a good business. By degrees, however, they began to lose – time after time the clients backed winners for large sums, and Rashleigh and his partner finally failed. They were both apparently ruined, but after a time Rashleigh reappeared again, got a fresh victim, and the whole thing went on as before. His present victim is Walter Farrell, and the end is inevitable.'

'But what does it mean?' I said. 'Are the clients who back the horses really conspirators in league with Rashleigh? Do you mean to imply that they make large sums and then share the profits with Rashleigh afterwards?'

'I think it highly probable, although I know nothing. But here comes the gist of the problem. In all the cases against this man it has been clearly proved that one client in particular wins to an extraordinary extent. Now, how in the name of all that is marvellous does this client manage to get information as to what horse will win for certain? And if this were possible in one case, why should he not go and break the ring at once?'

'You are evidently well up in turf affairs,' I replied, laughing, 'but frauds on the turf are so abundant that there is probably some simple explanation to the mystery.'

'But there is not,' she replied, somewhat sharply. 'Let me explain more fully, and then you will see that the chances of fraud are well-nigh at the vanishing point. I was at the office myself one afternoon. Walter Farrell took me in, and I closely watched the whole thing.

'It was the day of the Grand National, and about a dozen men were present. The runners and jockeys were sent through, and were called out by Mr Farrell, who stood by the tape machine; then he drew the curtain across. I made some small bets to excuse my presence there. The others all handed in their slips to him with the names of the horses they wished to back. The machine began clicking again, the curtain was drawn round it, and I will swear no one could possibly have seen the name of the winner as it was being printed on the tape. Just at the last moment, one of the men, a Captain Vandaleur – I know of him well in connection with more than one shady affair – went to the table with a slip, and handed it in. His was the last bet.

'The curtain was drawn back, and on Captain Vandaleur's slip was the name of the winning horse backed for five hundred pounds. The price was six to one, which meant a clear loss to Walter Farrell and Mr Rashleigh of three thousand pounds. The whole transaction was apparently as fair and square as could be, but there is the fact; and as the flat-racing season is just beginning, if this goes on Walter Farrell will be ruined before Derby Day.'

'You say, Miss Cusack, that no communication from outside was possible?'

'Certainly; no one entered or left the room. Communication from without is absolutely out of the question.'

'Could the sound of the clicking convey any meaning?'

She laughed.

'Absolutely none. I had at first an idea that an old trick was being worked – that is, by collusion with the operator at the telegraph office, who waited for the winner before sending through the runners and then sent the winning horse and jockey last on the list. But it is not so – we have made inquiries and had the clerks watched. It is quite incomprehensible. I am, I confess, at my wits' end. Will you help me to save Walter Farrell?'

'I will try, but I am afraid my efforts will be useless; he would resent my interference, and very naturally.'

'His wife is ill; I have told her that you will call on her. She knows that I hope much by your influence over her husband.'

'I will certainly visit Mrs Farrell, but only as an ordinary doctor goes to see a patient.'

'I believe you will do the rest when the time comes,' she answered.

I made no reply. She took out her watch.

'The Farrells live not ten doors from here,' she said. 'Will you visit Mrs Farrell now? Walter will in all probability be at home as it is Sunday afternoon. Ask to see Mrs Farrell; I will write my name on your card, and you will be admitted immediately.'

'And am I to come back and tell you the result?' I asked.

'As you please. I shall be very glad to see you. Much depends on what you do.'

I saw by the expression on Miss Cusack's face how intensely in earnest she was. Her enthusiasm fired mine.

'I will go at once,' I said, 'and hope that luck may be with me.'

I left the house, and a few moments later was ringing the bell of No 15 in the same road. A butler in livery opened the door, and on inquiring for Mrs Farrell I was admitted immediately. I sent up my card, and a moment later a quiet-looking woman tripped downstairs, came to my side, and said in a gentle, suppressed sort of voice, 'My mistress is in bed, doctor, but she will be pleased to see you. Will you follow me? Come this way, please.'

I followed the maid upstairs; we passed the drawing-room floor, and went up to the next storey. Here I was ushered into a large and luxuriously furnished bedroom. In a bed drawn near one of the windows where she could see the setting sun and some of the trees in Kensington Gardens, lay the pretty girl whom I was asked to visit. She could not have been more than nineteen years of age. Her brown hair lay tossed about the pillow, and her small, smooth, unlined face made her look more child than woman. A hectic spot burned on each of her cheeks, and when I touched her hand I knew at once that she was in a feverish and almost dangerous condition.

'So Florence Cusack has sent you, Dr Lonsdale,' was her remark to me.

'I am Dr Lonsdale. What can I do for you, Mrs Farrell?'

'Give me back my strength.'

The maid withdrew to a distant part of the room. I made the ordinary examination of the patient. I asked her what her symptoms were. She described them in a few words.

'I have no pain,' she said, 'but this intolerable weakness

increases day by day. It has come on most gradually, and no medicines give me the least relief. A month ago I was well enough to go out, and even walk; then I found myself too tired even to drive in a carriage, then I was too weary to come downstairs, then too prostrate to sit up. Now I stay in bed, and it tires me even to speak. Oh! I am tired of everything,' she added, 'tired of life, tired of –' her eyes filled with tears – 'tired of misery, of misery.'

To my dismay she burst into weak, hysterical crying.

'This will never do,' I said, 'you must tell me all, Mrs Farrell. As far as I can see, you have no active disease of any sort. What is the matter with you? What is consuming your life?'

'Trouble,' she said, 'and it is hopeless.'

'You must try to tell me more.'

She looked at me, dashed away her tears, and said, with a sudden spurt of spirit which I had scarcely given her credit for, 'But has not Florence Cusack told you?'

'She has certainly said something.'

'Ah, then you do know all; she said she would speak to you. My husband is downstairs in the smoking-room: go and see him – do what you can for him. Oh! He will be ruined, ruined body and soul. Save him! Do save him if you can.'

'Do not excite yourself,' I said. I rose as I spoke, and laid my hand with a slight pressure on hers. 'You need not say any more. Between Miss Cusack and me your husband shall be saved. Now rest in that thought. I would not tell you a thing of this kind lightly.'

'Oh! God bless you,' murmured the poor girl.

I turned to the maid, who now came forward.

'I will write a prescription for your mistress,' I said, 'something to strengthen and calm her at the same time. You must sit up with her tonight, she is very weak.'

The maid promised. I left the room. The bright eyes of the almost dying girl followed me to the door. As I stood on the landing I no longer wondered at Miss Cusack's attitude in the matter. Surely such a case must stir the depths of the most callous heart.

I went downstairs, and unannounced entered the smoking-room. A man was lying back in a deep leather chair, near one of the windows. He was a dark, thin man, with features which in themselves were refined and handsome; but now, with the haggard lines round the mouth, in the deeply set, watchful, and somewhat narrow eyes, and in a sort of recklessness which was characterised by his untidy dress, by the very set of his tie, I guessed too surely that Miss Cusack had not exaggerated the mental condition of Mr Walter Farrell in the very least. With a few words I introduced myself.

'You must pardon this intrusion, Mr Farrell. I am Dr Lonsdale. Miss Cusack has asked me to call and see your wife. I have just seen her; I want to say a few words to you about her.'

He looked anxious just for a moment when I mentioned his wife's name, but then a sleepy indifference crept into his eyes. He was sufficiently a gentleman, however, to show me the ordinary politeness, and motioned me to a chair. I sat down and looked full at him.

'How old is Mrs Farrell?' I said, abruptly.

He stared as if he rather resented the question; then said, in a nonchalant tone, 'My wife is very young, she is not twenty yet.'

'Quite a child,' I said.

'Do you think so?'

'Yes, little more than a child – just on the verge of life. It seems very sad when the young must die.'

I would not have made use of this expression to an ordinary man, but I wanted to rouse and startle Farrell. I did so effectually. A veil seemed to drop from his eyes; they grew wideawake, restless, and agonised. He drew his chair close to mine, and bent forward.

'What do you mean? Surely there is not much the matter with Laura?'

'No active disease, and yet she is dying. I am sorry to tell you that, unless a complete change takes place immediately, she can scarcely live another week.'

Farrell sprang to his feet.

'You don't mean that!' he cried, 'my wife in danger! Dr Lonsdale, you are talking nonsense; she has no cough, she complains of nothing. She is just a bit lazy – that is what I tell her.'

'She has no strength, Mr Farrell, and without strength we cannot live. Something is eating into her life and draining it away. I will be perfectly frank with you, for in a case of life and death there is no time, nor is it right, to stand on ceremony. Your wife is dying because her heart is broken. It remains with you to save her; the case is in your hands.'

'Now what do you mean?'

'You know what I mean. She is unhappy about you. You must understand me.'

He turned very white.

'And yet I am doing all that man can for her,' he said. 'She expects me to smile always and live as a butterfly. Men have troubles and anxieties, and mine are –'

'Pretty considerable, I should say,' I continued.

'They are. Has Florence Cusack been talking to you about me?'

'I am not at liberty to answer your question.'

'You have answered it by not denying it. Florence and Laura are a pair of fools, the greatest fools that ever walked the earth.'

'You do not really think that.'

'I do think it. They want a man to do the impossible – they want a man to withdraw when – there, Dr Lonsdale, you are a man and I can talk to you. I cannot do what they want.'

'Then your wife will die.'

He began to pace up and down the room.

'I suppose you know all about my connection with Rashleigh?' he said, after a moment.

I nodded.

'Well, then you see how I am placed. Rashleigh is hard up just now; I cannot desert him in a moment like the present. We hope to recoup ourselves this very week, and as soon as such is the case I will withdraw from the business. Will that content you?'

'Why not withdraw at once?'

'I cannot; nothing will induce me to do so. It is useless our prolonging this discussion.'

I saw that I should do harm instead of good if I said anything further, and, asking for a sheet of paper, I wrote a prescription for his wife. I then left the house to return to Miss Cusack.

The moment I entered her library she came eagerly to meet me. 'Well?' she said.

'You are right,' I answered, speaking now with great impulse and earnestness. 'I am altogether with you in this matter. I have seen Mrs Farrell and I have had an interview with Farrell. The wife is dying. Nay, do not interrupt me. She is dying unless relief comes soon. I had a long talk with Farrell and put the case plainly to him. He promises to withdraw from Rashleigh's firm, but not until after this week. He sticks to this resolve, thinking that he is bound in honour to support Rashleigh, whose affairs he believes are in a critical condition. In all probability before the week is up Mrs Farrell will die. What is to be done?'

'There is only one thing to be done, Dr Lonsdale – we must open Walter Farrell's eyes. We must show him plainly that he is Mr Rashleigh's dupe.'

'How can we do that?'

'Ah! There comes the crux of the whole situation. The further I go, the more mysterious the whole thing appears. The ordinary methods which have served me before have failed. Look here.'

She pointed to a page in the book of newspaper cuttings which lay by her side.

'Through channels I need not detail, I have learned that this is a communication of one of the gang to another.'

I took the book from her hands, and read the following words: *'No mistake. Sea Foam. Jockey Club'.*

'Gibberish!' I said, laying the paper on the table.

'Apparently,' she answered, 'but Sea Foam is Captain Halliday's horse entered for the City and Suburban race to be run on the 21st – that is next Wednesday – at Epsom. For five continuous hours I have worked at those few words, applying to them what I already know of this matter. It has been of no good.'

'I am scarcely surprised to hear you say so. One would want second sight to put meaning into words like those.'

'Something must be done, and soon,' she said. 'We must expose this matter on Wednesday. I know that Walter Farrell has lost heavily this month. There is not an hour to be lost in trying to save Laura. We must keep up her courage until Wednesday. On Wednesday the whole fraud must be discovered, and her husband liberated. You will help me?'

'Certainly.'

'Then on Wednesday we will go together to Mr Rashleigh's office. You must bet a little to allay suspicion – a few sovereigns only. You will then see him for yourself, and – who knows? – you may be able to solve the mystery.'

I agreed to this, and soon afterwards took my leave.

I received a note from Miss Cusack on Tuesday evening, asking me to lunch with her on the following day. I went. The moment I entered her presence I was struck, and almost startled, by her manner. An extraordinary exaltation seemed to possess her. The pupils of her eyes were largely dilated and glowed as if some light were behind them. Her face was slightly flushed, and her conversation was marked by an unusual vivacity and sparkle.

'I have been very busy since I saw you last,' she said, 'and I have now every hope that I shall succeed. I fully believe that I shall save Walter Farrell today from the hands of one of the cleverest scoundrels in London,' she said, as we crossed the hall, 'and consign the latter to penal servitude.'

I could not help being much impressed by the matter-of-fact *sangfroid* with which Miss Cusack spoke the last words. How was she going to obtain such big results?

'Have you no fear of personal rudeness or violence?' I asked.

'None whatever – I have made all arrangements beforehand. You will soon see for yourself.'

We partook of lunch almost in silence. As I was returning to Miss Cusack's library afterwards I saw, seated in the hall, a short squarely built, but well-dressed man.

'I shall be ready in a few moments, Mr Marling,' she said to him. 'Is everything prepared?'

'Everything, miss,' he replied.

Very soon afterwards we took our seats in Miss Cusack's brougham, and she explained to me that our companion was Inspector Marling, of Scotland Yard, that he was coming with us in the *rôle* of a new client for Messrs Rashleigh and Farrell, and that he had made all necessary preparations.

We drove rapidly along Knightsbridge, and, going into Piccadilly, turned down St James's Street. We stopped at last opposite a house in Pall Mall, which was to all appearance a private one. On either side of the door were brass plates bearing names, with the floor of the occupant engraved beneath. On one of the plates were the words, 'Rashleigh and Farrell, Third Floor'. Miss Cusack pressed the bell corresponding to this plate, and in a few moments a quietly dressed man opened the door. He bowed to Miss Cusack as if he knew her, looked at Marling and me with a penetrating glance, and then admitted us. We went upstairs to the third landing, though before we reached it the deep voices of men in the commission agent's suite of rooms fell on our ears. Here we rang again, and after what seemed a long delay the door, which was hung with a heavy velvet curtain on the inner side, was slowly opened. Farrell stood before us.

'I thought it must be you,' he said, the colour mounting into his thin face. 'Come inside; we are rather a large party, as it is an important race day.'

As I entered I looked round curiously. The room was thronged with a smartly dressed crowd of men and women who were lounging about in easy-chairs and on couches. The carpet was a rich Turkey pile, and the decorations were extravagantly gorgeous. At one side of the room near the wall stood a table upon which was a small gas-lamp, several slips of paper, and a 'Ruff's Racing Guide'. At the further end of the room, set back in a recess, stood the tape machine, which intermittently clicked and whirred while a long strip of paper, recording news automatically, unrolled from the little wheel and fell in serpentine coils into a wastepaper basket beneath.

At one glance I saw that, when the curtain that hung from a semi-circular rod above it was drawn, no one in the room could possibly read what the wheel was printing on the tape.

'Let me introduce you to Captain Vandaleur, Dr Lonsdale,' said Miss Cusack's voice behind me.

I turned and bowed to a tall, clean-shaven man, who returned my salutation with a pleasant smile.

'You are, I presume, interested in racing?' he said.

'I am in this particular race,' I answered, 'the City and Suburban. I am anxious to make a small investment, and Miss Cusack has kindly introduced me to Mr Rashleigh for the purpose.'

'What particular horse do you fancy?' he asked.

'Lime-Light,' I replied, at a venture.

'Ha! An outsider; well, you'll get twenties,' and he turned away, for at that moment the runners for the first race began to come through. Farrell stood by the tape and called them out. Several of the men present now went to the table and wrote their fancies on the slips of paper and handed them to Farrell. Vandaleur did not bet.

I watched the whole proceeding carefully, and certainly fraud of any kind seemed out of the question.

Miss Cusack was evidently to all appearance evincing the keenest interest in the proceedings, and betted pretty heavily herself, although the horse she selected did not turn out the winner. Another race followed, and then at 3.30 the runners and jockeys for the great race came through. Heavy bets were made on all sides, and at 3.40 came the magic word 'Off', to signify that the race had started.

Farrell now instantly drew the curtain round the glass case of the instrument, while the bets continued to be made. Some were very heavy, running to hundreds of pounds. In a few moments the machine began clicking and whirring again, probably announcing the name of the winning horse.

'Have you all made your bets, gentlemen?' said Farrell.

'One moment,' cried Vandaleur, going to the table and writing out a slip. 'It's a poor chance, I know; but nothing venture, nothing win. Here goes for a monkey each way Sea Foam – and chance it.'

He crossed the room and handed Farrell the slip.

'All right, Vandaleur,' he replied, 'plunging heavily as usual. Now then, anyone else want to bet? I am going to draw back the curtain.'

No one answered. Farrell's face was pale, and an unmistakable air of nervousness pervaded him. Everyone pressed eagerly forward in order to be as close as possible to the instrument. Each man craned and peered over the other's shoulder. Farrell snatched back the curtain, and a shout of 'Sea Foam first!' rang through the room.

I looked at Miss Cusack. She was still standing by the table, and bending over the chimney of the gas-lamp. At this instant she turned and whispered a few words to Inspector Marling. He left the room quietly and unnoticed in the buzz of conversation that ensued.

Sea Foam's price was twenty to one, and Vandaleur had therefore scored £12,500.

I went up to Farrell, who was standing near the tape machine. I saw drops of perspiration on his forehead, and his face was like death.

'I am afraid this is a heavy blow to you,' I said.

He laughed with an assumption of nonchalance, then he looked me in the face and said slowly, 'It is. Vandaleur is invariably lucky.'

He had scarcely spoken the words before Inspector Marling reappeared. His face betrayed that something exciting was about to happen. What it was I could not guess. The next moment he had crossed the room and going straight up to Vandaleur laid his hand on his shoulder, and said in a loud voice that rang through the room, 'Captain Vandaleur, I arrest you for conspiracy, and for fraudulently obtaining money by means of a trick.'

If a thunderbolt had fallen it could hardly have caused greater consternation.

Vandaleur started back. 'Who are you? What do you mean?' he cried.

'I am Inspector Marling, of Scotland Yard. Your game is up; you had better come quietly.'

The room was now in the utmost confusion. Two other men had made a dash for the door, only to fall into the arms of two officers who were waiting for them outside. Farrell, with an ashen face, stood like one struck dumb.

'For God's sake explain it all,' he said at last.

'Certainly,' answered Miss Cusack, 'it is simply this: You have been a dupe in one of the most daring and subtle frauds ever conceived. Come this way, I will show you everything.'

As she spoke she led the way from the room and up the stairs which led to the fourth floor. We all followed her and entered a room which was over the one we had just left. It was barely furnished as an office, and to our utter surprise it contained another tape machine, which was working like the one below.

'Dr Lonsdale,' said Miss Cusack, 'you remember the advertisement? "No mistake. Sea Foam. Jockey Club".'

'Perfectly,' I answered.

'When Jockey Club is mentioned in connection with horse-racing, one would naturally suppose that *the* Jockey Club was meant,' she continued. 'That was what puzzled me so long. But there is another kind of Jockey Club. Look here.' She pointed to an open box containing several small bottles, and took one out. Removing the glass stopper, she handed it to me.

'Do you recognise that scent?' she asked, as I sniffed at it.

'Perfectly.' I replied. 'Jockey Club, isn't it? Still, I feel in utter bewilderment.'

'Now I will explain what it means, and you will all, gentlemen, see how abilities can be used for the purposes of crime.'

She went across to a little square deal table that stood in the corner, and moved it aside. Behind one of the legs which had effectually concealed it was what appeared to be an ordinary piece of gas-pipe that passed through the floor. The upper end of it was open and was fitted with a screw for a nut.

'Now see, all of you,' she cried, 'this pipe communicates with the lamp on the table in the room below. When the gas is turned off downstairs there is a free passage. The man who keeps this office, and who, I fear, has contrived to escape, is in league with Captain Vandaleur, and both are, or rather were, in league with Rashleigh. These three scoundrels had a code, and this was their code. As soon as the winner came through, and the machine up here communicated the fact to the man in this room, a certain scent corresponding to a certain horse was sent down through the gas-pipe.

'In this case Jockey Club corresponded to Sea Foam. By means of this spray pump the vapour of the scent was passed down through the pipe to the lamp in the room below. Captain Vandaleur had only to bend over the chimney to get the scent, and write out the name of the horse which it corresponded to.'

To express our unbounded astonishment and our admiration for Miss Cusack's clever solving of the mystery would require more space than I have at my disposal. As to poor Farrell, his eyes were completely opened; he looked at us all with a wild stare, and the next moment I heard him dashing downstairs.

'But how did you discover it? What made you think of it?' I said to Miss Cusack some hours later.

'Ah! That is my secret. That I cannot explain to you, at least not yet,' was her reply.

Rashleigh and Vandaleur have been arrested, and both

are now undergoing the punishment they so richly deserve. Farrell has learned his lesson: he has given up horse racing, and Mrs Farrell has recovered her strength, and also her youth and beauty.

JOHN DOLLAR,
THE CRIME DOCTOR

Created by EW Hornung (1866-1921)

Born near Middlesbrough, the son of a businessman originally from Hungary, Ernest William Hornung spent his late teenage years in Australia, where he worked as a tutor and began to write what became his first novel. He returned to England in 1886 and his first stories soon appeared in the magazines. The Bride in the Bush, *the novel he had begun down under, was published in 1890. Australia continued to provide the backdrop for later novels but he produced stories with all kinds of settings and rapidly became a familiar name in literary London. He married Arthur Conan Doyle's sister, Connie, in 1893. Hornung is best remembered for the creation of the elegant, cricket-playing gentleman-burglar Raffles who first appeared in 1898. Although never rivalling in popularity the works of his brother-in-law, Hornung's stories about Raffles, so redolent of the era in which they were written, have plenty of admirers. They have regularly been adapted for films and TV. Hornung also wrote a much less well-known sequence of stories about a character named John Dollar. These appeared originally in* Everybody's Magazine *in 1913 and were collected in book form the following year. Dollar is a trained physician and one of the first fictional detectives to approach crime from the perspective of a psychologist. Not only does he solve crimes, he also runs a sanatorium in which criminals are treated. He is an interesting character and deserves more attention from fans of late Victorian and Edwardian crime fiction than he has received.*

ONE POSSESSED

Lieutenant-General Neville Dysone, RE, VC, was the first really eminent person to consult the crime doctor by regular appointment in the proper hours. Quite apart from the feat of arms which had earned him the most coveted of all distinctions, the gigantic General, deep-chested and erect, virile in every silver-woven hair of his upright head, filled the tiny stage in Welbeck Street and dwarfed its antique properties, as no being had done before. And yet his voice was tender and even tremulous with the pathetic presage of a heartbreak under all.

'Doctor Dollar,' he began at once, 'I have come to see you about the most tragic secret that a man can have. I would shoot myself for saying what I have to say, did I not know that a patient's confidence is sacred to any member of your profession – perhaps especially to an alienist?'

'I hope we are all alike as to that,' returned Dollar, gently. He was used to these sad openings.

'I ought not to have said it; but it hardly is my secret, that's why I feel such a cur!' exclaimed the General, taking his handkerchief to a fine forehead and remarkably fresh complexion, as if to wipe away its noble flush. 'Your patient, I devoutly hope, will be my poor wife, who really seems to me to be almost losing her reason –' but with that the husband quite lost his voice.

'Perhaps we can find it for her,' said Dollar, despising the pert professional optimism that told almost like a shot. 'It is a thing more often mislaid than really lost.'

And the last of the other's weakness was finally overcome. A few weighty questions, lightly asked and simply answered, and he was master of a robust address, in which an occasional impediment only did further credit to his delicacy.

'No. I should say it was entirely a development of the last few months,' declared the General emphatically. 'There was nothing of the kind in our twenty-odd years of India, nor yet in the first year after I retired. All this – this trouble has come since I bought my house in the pine country. It's called Valsugana, as you see on my card; but it wasn't before we went there. We gave it the name because it struck us as extraordinarily like the Austrian Tyrol, where – well, of which we had happy memories, Doctor Dollar.'

His blue eyes winced as they flew through the open French window, up the next precipice of bricks and mortar, to the beetling sky-line of other roofs, all a little softened in the faint haze of approaching heat. It cost him a palpable effort to bring them back to the little dark consulting -room, with its cool slabs of aged oak and the summer fernery that hid the hearth.

'It's good of you to let me take my time, doctor, but yours is too valuable to waste. All I meant was to give you an idea of our surroundings, as I know they are held to count in such cases. We are embedded in pines and firs. Some people find trees depressing, but after India they were just what we wanted, and even now my wife won't let me cut down one of them. Yet depression is no name for her state of mind; it's nearer melancholy madness, and latterly she has become subject to – to delusions – which are influencing her whole character and actions in the most alarming way. We are finding it difficult, for the first time in our lives, to keep servants; even her own nephew, who has come to live with us, only stands it for my sake, poor boy! As for my nerves – well, thank God I used to think I hadn't got any when I was in the service; but it's a little hard to be – to be as we are – at our time of life!' His hot face flamed. 'What am I saying? It's a thousand times harder on *her*! She had been looking forward to these days for years.'

Dollar wanted to wring one of the great brown, restless hands. Might he ask the nature of the delusions?

The General cried: 'I'd give ten years of my life if I could tell you!'

'You can tell me what form they take?'

'I must, of course; it is what I came for, after all,' the General muttered. He raised his head and his voice together. 'Well, for one thing she's got herself a ferocious bulldog and a revolver.'

Dollar did not move a doctor's muscle. 'I suppose there must be a dog in the country, especially where there are no children. And if you must have a dog, you can't do better than a bulldog. Is there any reason for the revolver? Some people think it another necessity of the country.'

'It isn't with us – much less as she carries it.'

'Ladies in India get in the habit, don't they?'

'She never did. And now –'

'Yes, General? Has she it always by her?'

'Night and day, on a curb bracelet locked to her wrist!'

This time there were no professional pretences. 'I don't wonder you have trouble with your servants,' said Dollar, with as much sympathy as he liked to show.

'You mayn't see it when you come down, doctor, as I am going to entreat you to do. She has her sleeves cut on purpose, and it is the smallest you can buy. But I know it's always there – and always loaded.'

Dollar played a while with a queer plain steel ruler, out of keeping with his other possessions, though it too had its history. It stood on end before he let it alone and looked up.

'General Dysone, there must be some sort of reason or foundation for all this. Has anything alarming happened since you have been at – Valsugana?'

'Nothing that firearms could prevent.'

'Do you mind telling me what it is that has happened?'

'We had a tragedy in the winter – a suicide on the place.'

'Ah!'

'Her gardener hanged himself. Hers, I say, because the garden is my wife's affair. I only paid the poor fellow his wages.'

'Well, come, General, that was enough to depress anybody –'

'Yet she wouldn't have even that tree cut down – nor yet come away for a change – not for as much as a night in town!'

The interruption had come with another access of grim heat and further use of the General's handkerchief. Dollar took up his steel tube of a ruler and trained it like a spy-glass on the ink, with one eye as carefully closed as if the truth lay at the bottom of the blue-black well.

'Was there any rhyme or reason for the suicide?'

'One was suggested that I would rather not repeat.'

The closed eye opened to find the blue pair fallen. 'I think it might help, General. Mrs Dysone is evidently a woman of strong character, and anything –'

'She is, God knows!' cried the miserable man. 'Everybody knows it now – her servants especially – though nobody used to treat them better. Why, in India – but we'll let it go at that, if you don't mind. I have provided for the widow.'

Dollar bowed over his bit of steel tubing, but this time put it down so hastily that it rolled off the table. General Dysone was towering over him with shaking hand outstretched.

'I can't say any more,' he croaked. 'You must come down and see her for yourself; then you could do the talking – and I shouldn't feel such a damned cur! By God, sir, it's awful, talking about one's own wife like this, even for her own good! It's worse than I thought it would be. I know it's different to a doctor – but – but you're an old soldierman as well, aren't you? Didn't I hear you were in the war?'

'I was.'

'Well, then,' cried the General, and his blue eyes lit up with simple cunning, 'that's where we met! We've run up against each other again, and I've asked you down for this next weekend! Can you manage it? Are you free? I'll write you a cheque for your own fee this minute, if you like – there must be nothing of that kind down there. You don't mind being Captain Dollar again, if that was it, to my wife?'

His pathetic eagerness, his sensitive loyalty – even his sudden and solicitous zest in the pious fraud proposed – made between them an irresistible appeal. Dollar had to think; the rooms upstairs were not empty; but none enshrined a more interesting case than this sounded. On the other hand, he had to be on his guard against a weakness for mere human interest as apart from the esoteric principles of his practice. People might call him an empiric – empiric he was proud to be, but it was and must remain empiricism in one definite direction only. Psychical research was not for him – and the Dysone story had a psychic flavour.

In the end he said quite bluntly:

'I hope you don't suggest a ghost behind all this, General?'

'I? Lord, no! I don't believe in 'em,' cried the warrior, with a nervous laugh.

'Does any member of your household?'

'Not – now.'

'*Not* now?'

'No. I think I am right in saying that.' But something was worrying him. 'Perhaps it is also right,' he continued, with the engaging candour of an overthrown reserve, 'and only fair – since I take it you are coming – to tell you that there was a fellow with us who thought he saw things. But it was all the most utter moonshine. He saw brown devils in flowing robes, but what he'd taken before he saw them I can't tell you! He didn't stay with me long enough for us to get to know each other. But he wasn't just a servant, and it was before the poor gardener's affair. Like so many old soldiers on the shelf, Doctor Dollar, I am writing a book, and I run a secretary of sorts; now it's Jim Paley, a nephew of ours; and thank God he has more sense.'

'Yet even he gets depressed?'

'He has had cause. If our own kith and kin behaved like one possessed –' He stopped himself yet again; this time his hand found Dollar's with a vibrant grip. 'You will come, won't you? I can meet any train on Saturday, or any other day that suits you better. I – for her own sake, doctor – I sometimes feel it might be better if she went away for a time. But you will come and see her for yourself?'

Before he left it was a promise; a harder heart than John Dollar's would have ended by making it, and putting the new case before all others when the Saturday came. But it was not only his prospective patient whom the crime doctor was now really anxious to see; he felt fascinated in advance by the scene and every person of an indubitable drama, of which at least one tragic act was already over.

There was no question of meeting him at any station; the wealthy mother of a still recent patient had insisted on presenting Doctor Dollar with a fifteen-horse-power Talboys, which he had eventually accepted, and even chosen for himself (with certain expert assistance), as an incalculable contribution to the Cause. Already the car had vastly enlarged his theatre of work; and on every errand his heart was lightened and his faith fortified by the wonderful case of the young chauffeur who sat so upright at the wheel beside him. In the beginning he had slouched there like the worst of his kind; it was neither precept nor reprimand which had straightened his back and his look and all about him. He was what John Dollar had always wanted – the unconscious patient whose history none knew – who himself little dreamed that it was all known to the man who treated him almost like a brother.

The boy had been in prison for dishonesty; he was being sedulously trusted, and so taught to trust himself. He had come in March, a sulky and suspicious clod; and now in June he could talk cricket and sixpenny editions from the Hounslow tram-lines to the wide white gate opening into a drive through a Berkshire wood, with a house lurking behind it in a mask of ivy, out of the sun.

But in the drive General Dysone stepped back into the doctor's life, and, on being directed to the stables, he who had filled it for the last hour drove out of it for the next twenty-four.

'I wanted you to hear something at once from me,' his host whispered under the whispering trees, 'lest it should be mentioned and take you aback before the others. We've had another little tragedy – not a horror like the last – yet in one way almost worse. My wife shot her own dog dead last night!'

Dollar put a curb upon his parting lips.

'*In* the night?' he stood still to ask.

'Well, between eleven and twelve.'

'In her own room, or where?'

'Out-of-doors. Don't ask me how it happened; nobody seems to know, and don't *you* know anything if she speaks of it herself.'

His fine face was streaming with perspiration; yet he seemed to have been waiting quietly under the trees, he was not short of breath, and he a big elderly man. Dollar asked no questions at all; they dropped the subject there in the drive. Though the sun was up somewhere out of sight, it was already late in the long June afternoon, and the guest was taken straight to his room.

It was a corner room with one ivy-darkened casement overlooking a shadowy lawn, the other facing a forest of firs and chestnuts on which it was harder to look without an instinctive qualm. But the General seemed to have forgot his tragedies, and for the moment his blue eyes almost brightened the sombre scene on which they dwelt with involuntary pride.

'Now don't you see where Tyrol comes in?' said he. 'Put a mountain behind those trees – and there *was* one the very first time we saw the house! It was only a thunder-cloud, but for all the world it might have been the Dolomites. And it took us back... we had no other clouds then!'

Dollar found himself alone; found his things laid out and his shirt studded, and a cozy on the brass hot-water can, with as much satisfaction as though he had never stayed in a country house before. Could there be so very much amiss in a household where they knew just what to do for one, and just what to leave undone?

And it was the same with all the other creature comforts; they meant good servants, however short their service; and good servants do not often mean the mistress or the hostess whom Dollar had come prepared to meet. He dressed in pleasurable doubt and enhanced excitement – and those were his happiest moments at Valsugana.

Mrs Dysone was a middle-aged woman who looked almost

old, whereas the General was elderly with all the appearance of early middle age. The contrast was even more complete in more invidious particulars; but Dollar took little heed of the poor lady's face, as a lady's face. Her skin and eyes were enough for him; both were brown, with that almost ultra-Indian tinge of so many Anglo-Indians. He was sensible at once of an Oriental impenetrability.

With her conversation he could not quarrel; what there was of it was crisp, unstudied, understanding. And the little dinner did her the kind of credit for which he was now prepared; but she only once took charge of the talk, and that was rather sharply to change a subject into which she had been the first to enter.

How it had cropped up, Dollar could never think, especially as his former profession and rank duly obtained throughout his visit. He had even warned his chauffeur that he was not the doctor there; it could not have been he himself who started it, but somebody did, as somebody always does when there is one topic to avoid. It was probably the nice young nephew who made the first well-meaning remark upon the general want of originality, with reference to something or other under criticism at the moment; but it was neither he nor Dollar who laid it down that monkeys were the most arrant imitators in nature – except criminals; and it certainly was the General who said that nothing would surprise him less than if another fellow went and hanged himself in their wood. Then it was that Mrs Dysone put her foot down – and Dollar never forgot her look.

Almost for the first time it made him think of her revolver. It was out of sight; and full as her long sleeves were, it was difficult to believe that one of them could conceal the smallest firearm made; but a tiny gold padlock did dangle when she raised her glass of water; and at the end of dinner there was a second little scene, this time without words, which went far to dispel any doubt arising in his mind.

He was holding the door open for Mrs Dysone, and she stood a moment on the threshold, peering into the far corners of the room. He saw what it was she had forgot – saw it come back to her as she turned away, with another look worth remembering.

Either the General missed that, or the anxieties of the husband were now deliberately sunk in the duties of the host. He had got up some Jubilee port in the doctor's honour; they sat over it together till it was nearly time for bed. Dollar took little, but the other grew a shade more rubicund, and it was good to hear him chat without restraint or an apparent care. Yet it was strange as well; again he drifted into criminology, and his own after-dinner defect of sensibility only made his hearer the more uncomfortable.

Of course, he felt, it was partly out of compliment to himself as crime doctor; but the ugly subject had evidently an unhealthy fascination of its own for the fine full-blooded man. Not that it seemed an inveterate foible; the expert observer thought it rather the reflex attraction of the strongest possible horror and repulsion, and took it the more seriously on that account. Of two evils it seemed to him the less to allow himself to be pumped on professional generalities. It was distinctly better than encouraging the General to ransack his long experience for memories of decent people who had done dreadful deeds. Best of all to assure him that even those unfortunates might have outlived their infamy under the scientific treatment of a more enlightened day.

If they must talk crime, let it be the Cure of Crime! So the doctor had his heart-felt say; and the General listened even more terribly than he had talked; asking questions in whispers, and waiting breathless for the considered reply. It was the last of these that took most answering.

'And which, doctor, for God's sake, which would you have most hope of curing: a man or a woman?'

But Dollar would only say: 'I shouldn't despair of *anybody*, who had done *anything*, if there was still an intelligence to work upon; but the more of that the better.'

And the General said hardly another word, except 'God bless you!' outside the spare-room door. His wife had been seen no more.

But Dollar saw her in every corner of his delightful quarters; and the acute contrast that might have unsettled an innocent mind had the opposite effect on his. There were electric lamps in all the right places; there were books and biscuits, a glass of milk, even a miniature decanter and a bottle of Schweppes. He sighed as he wound his watch and placed it in the little stand on the table beside the bed; but he was only wondering exactly what he was going to discover before he wound it up again.

Outside one open window the merry crickets were playing castanets in those dreadful trees. It was the other blind that he drew up; and on the lawn the dying and reviving glow of a cigarette gave glimpses of a white shirt-front, a black satin tie, the drooping brim of a Panama hat. It was the nice young nephew, who had retreated before the Jubilee port. And Dollar was still wondering on what pretext he could go down and join him, when his knock came at the door.

'Only to see if you'd everything you want,' explained young Paley, ingenuously disingenuous; and shut the door behind him before the invitation to enter was out of the doctor's mouth. But he shut it very softly, trod like a burglar, and excused himself with bated breath: 'You are the first person who has stayed with us since I've been here, Captain Dollar!' And his wry young smile was as sad as anything in the sad house.

'You amaze me!' cried Dollar. Indeed, it was the flank attack of a new kind of amazement. 'I should have thought –' and his glance made a lightning tour of the luxurious room.

'I know,' said Paley, nodding. 'I think they must have laid themselves out for visitors at the start. But none come now. I wish they did! It's a house that wants them.'

'You are rather a small party, aren't you?'

'We are rather a grim party! And yet my old uncle is absolutely the finest man I ever struck.'

'I don't wonder that you admire him.'

'You don't know what he is, Captain Dollar. He got the VC when he was my age in Burmah, but he deserves one for almost every day of his ordinary home life.'

Dollar made no remark; the young fellow offered him a cigarette, and was encouraged to light another himself. He required no encouragement to talk.

'The funny thing is that he's not really my uncle. I'm *her* nephew; and she's a wonderful woman, too, in her way. She runs the whole place like a book; she's thrown away here. But – I can't help saying it – I should like her better if I didn't love him!'

'Talking of books,' said Dollar, 'the General told me he was writing one, and that you were helping him?'

'He didn't tell you what it was about?'

'No.'

'Then I mustn't. I wish I could. It's to be the last word on a certain subject, but he won't have it spoken about. That's one reason why it's getting on his nerves.'

'*Is* it his book?'

'It and everything. Doesn't he remind you of a man sitting on a powder-barrel? If he weren't what he is, there'd be an explosion every day. And there never is one – no matter what happens!'

Dollar watched the pale youth swallowing his smoke.

'Do they often talk about crime?'

'Always! They can't keep off it. And Aunt Essie always changes the subject as though she hadn't been every bit as bad as uncle. Of course, they've had a good lot to make them morbid. I suppose you heard about poor Dingle, the last gardener?'

'Only just.'

'He was the last man you would ever have suspected of such a thing. It was in those trees just outside.' The crickets made extra merry as he paused. 'They didn't find him for a day and a night!'

'Look here! I'm not going to let you talk about it,' said Dollar. But the good-humoured rebuff cost him an effort. He wanted to hear all about the suicide, but not from this worn lad with an old man's smile. He knew and liked the type too well.

'I'm sorry, Captain Dollar.' Jim Paley looked sorry. 'Yet, it's all very well! I don't suppose the General told you what happened last night?'

'Well, yes, he did, but without going into any particulars.'

And now the doctor made no secret of his curiosity; this was a matter on which he could not afford to forego enlightenment. Nor was it like raking up an old horror; it would do the boy more good than harm to speak of this last affair.

'I can't tell you much about it myself,' said he. 'I was wondering if I could, just now on the lawn. That's where it happened, you know.'

'I didn't know.'

'Well, it was, and the funny thing is that I was there at the time. I used to go out with the dog for a cigarette when they turned in; last night I was foolish enough to fall asleep in a chair on the lawn. I had been playing tennis all the afternoon, and had a long bike-ride both ways. Well, all I know is that I woke up thinking I'd been shot; and there was my aunt with a revolver she insists on carrying – and poor Muggins as dead as a doornail.'

'Did she say it was an accident?'

'She behaved as if it had been; she was all over the poor dead brute.'

'Rather a savage dog, wasn't it?'

'I never thought so. But the General had no use for him – and no wonder! Did he tell you he had bitten him in the shoulder?'

'No.'

'Well, he did, only the other day. But that's the old General all over. He never told me till the dog was dead. I shouldn't be surprised if –'

'Yes?'

'– if my aunt hadn't been in it somehow. Poor old Muggins was such a bone between them!'

'You don't suppose he'd ended by turning on her?'

'Hardly. He was like a kitten with her, poor brute!'

Another cigarette was lighted; more inhaling went on unchecked.

'Was Mrs Dysone by herself out there – but for you?'

'Well – yes.'

'Does that mean she wasn't?'

'Upon my word, I don't know!' said young Paley, frankly. 'It sounds most awful rot, but just for a moment I thought I saw somebody in a sort of surplice affair. But I can only swear to Aunt Essie, and she was in her dressing-gown, and it wasn't white.'

Dollar did not go to bed at all. He sat first at one window, watching the black trees turn blue, and eventually a variety of sunny greens; then at the other, staring down at the pretty scene of a deed ugly in itself, but uglier in the peculiar quality of its mystery.

A dog; only a dog, this time; but the woman's own dog! There were two new sods on the place where he supposed it had lain withering…

But who or what was it that these young men had seen – the one the General had told him about, and this obviously truthful lad whom he himself had questioned? 'Brown devils in flowing robes' was perhaps only the old soldier's picturesque phrase; they might have turned brown in his Indian mind; but what of Jim Paley's 'somebody in a sort of surplice affair'? Was that 'body' brown as well?

In the wood of worse omen the gay little birds tuned up to deaf ears at the open window. And a cynical soloist went so far as to start saying, 'Pretty, pretty, pretty, pretty!' in a liquid contralto. But a little sharp shot, fired two nights and a day before, was the only sound to get across the spare-room window-sill…

The bathroom was next door; in that physically admirable house there was boiling hot water at six o'clock in the morning; the servants made tea when they heard it running; and the garden before breakfast was almost a delight. It might have been an

Eden... it *was*... with the serpent still in the grass!

Blinds went up like eyelids under bushy brows of ivy. The grass remained grey with dew; there was not enough sun anywhere, though the whole sky beamed. Dollar wandered indoors the way the General had taken him the day before. It was the way through his library. Libraries are always interesting; a man's bookcase is sometimes more interesting than the man himself, sometimes the one existing portrait of his mind. Dollar spent the best part of an absorbing hour without taking a single volume from its place. But this was partly because those he would have dipped into were under glass and lock and key. And partly it was due to more accessible distractions crowning that very piece of ostensible antiquity which contained the books, and of which the top drawer drew out into the General's desk.

The distractions were a peculiarly repulsive gilded idol, squatting with its tongue out, as if at the amateur author, and a heathen sword on the wall behind it. Nothing more; but Dollar also had served in India in his day, and his natural interest was whetted by a certain smattering of lore. He was still standing on a newspaper and a chair when a voice hailed him in no hospitable tone.

'Really, Captain Dollar! I should have asked the servants for a ladder while I was about it!'

Of course, it was Mrs Dysone, and she was not even pretending to look pleased. He jumped down with an apology which softened not a line of her sallow face and bony figure.

'It was an outrage,' he owned. 'But I did stand on a paper to save the chair. I say, though, I never noticed it was this week's *Field*.'

Really horrified at his own behaviour, he did his best to smooth and wipe away his footmarks on the wrapper of the paper. But those subtle eyes, like blots of ink on old parchment, were no longer trained on the offender, who missed yet another look that might have helped him.

'My husband's study is rather holy ground,' was the lady's last word. 'I only came in myself because I thought he was here.'

Mercifully, days do not always go on as badly as they begin; more strangely, this one developed into the dullest and most conventional of country-house Sundays.

General Dysone was himself not only dull, but even a little stiff, as became a good Briton who had said too much to too great a stranger overnight. His natural courtesy had become conspicuous; he played punctilious host all day; and Dollar was allowed to feel that, if he had come down as a doctor, he was staying on as an ordinary guest, and in a house where guests were expected to observe the Sabbath. So they all marched off together to the village church, where the General trumpeted the tune in his own octave, read the lessons, and kept waking up during the sermon. There were the regulation amenities with other devout gentry of the neighbourhood; there was the national Sunday sirloin at the midday meal, and no more untoward topics to make the host's forehead glisten or the hostess gleam and lower. In the afternoon the whole party inspected every animal and vegetable on the premises; and after tea the visitor's car came round.

Originally there had been much talk of his staying till the Monday; the General went through the form of pressing him once more, but was not backed up by his wife, who had shadowed them suspiciously all day. Nor did he comment on this by so much as a sidelong glance at Dollar, or contrive to get another word with him alone. And the crime doctor, instead of making any excuse to remain and penetrate these new mysteries, showed a sensitive alacrity to leave.

Of the nephew, who looked terribly depressed at his departure, he had seen something more, and had even asked two private favours. One, that he would keep out of that haunted garden for the next few nights, and try going to bed earlier; the other an odd request for an almost middle-aged man about town, but rather flattering to the young fellow. It was for the loan of his Panama, so that Dollar's hatter might see if he could not get him as good a one. Paley's was the kind that might be carried up a sleeve, like the modern handkerchief; he explained that the old General had given it him.

Dollar tried it on almost as soon as the car was out of sight of Valsugana – while his young chauffeur was still wondering what he had done to make the governor sit behind. It was funny of him, just when a chap might have been telling him a thing or two that he had heard down there at the coachman's place. But it was all the more interesting when they got back to town at seven in the evening, and he was ordered to fill up with petrol and be back at nine, to make the same trip over again.

'I needn't ask you,' the doctor added, 'to hold your tongue about anything you may have heard at General Dysone's. I know you will, Albert.'

And almost by lighting-up time they were shoulder to shoulder on the road once more.

But at Valsugana it was another dark night and none too easy to find one's way about the place on the strength of a midsummer day's acquaintance. And for the first time Dollar was glad the dog of the house was dead, as he finished a circuitous approach by stealing through the farther wood, toward the jagged lumps of light in the ivy-strangled bedroom windows; already everything was dark downstairs.

Here were the pale new sods; they could just be seen, though his feet first felt their inequalities. His cigarette was the one pin-prick of light in all the garden, though each draw brought the buff brim of Jim Paley's Panama within an inch of his eyes, its fine texture like coarse matting at the range. And the chair in which Jim Paley had sat smoking this time last night, and dozing the night before when the shot disturbed him, was just where he expected his shins to find it; the wickers squeaked as John Dollar took his place.

Less need now not to make a sound; but he made no more than he could help, for the night was still and sultry, without any of the garden noises of a night ago. It was as though nature had stopped her orchestra in disgust at the plot and counterplot brewing on her darkened stage. The cigarette-end was thrown away; it might have been a stone that fell upon the grass, and Dollar could almost hear it sizzling in the dew. His aural nerves were tuned to the last pitch of sensitive acknowledgment; a fly on the drooping Panama-brim would not have failed to 'scratch the brain's coat of curd'. ... How much less the swift and furtive footfall that came kissing the wet lawn at last!

It was more than a footfall; there was a following swish of some long garment trailing through the wet. It all came near; it all stopped dead. Dollar had nodded heavily as if in sleep; had jerked his head up higher; seemed to be dropping off again in greater comfort.

The footfalls and the swish came on like thunder now. But now his eyelids were only drooping like the brim above them; in the broad light of their abnormal perceptivity, it was as if his own eyes threw a dreadful halo round the figure they beheld. It was a swaddled figure, creeping into monstrosity, crouching early for its spring. It had draped arms extended, with some cloth or band that looped and tightened at each stride: on the rounded shoulders bobbed the craning head and darkened face of General Dysone.

In his last stride he swerved, as if to get as much behind the chair as its position under the tree permitted. The cloth clapped as it came taut over Dollar's head, but was not actually round his neck when he ducked and turned, and hit out and up with all his might. He felt the rasp of a fifteen-hours' beard, heard the click of teeth; the lawn quaked, and white robes settled upon a senseless heap, as the plumage on a murdered pigeon.

Dollar knelt over him and felt his pulse, held an electric lamp to eyes that opened, and quickly something else to the dilated nostrils.

'O Jim!' shuddered a voice close at hand. It was shrill yet broken, a cry of horror, but like no voice he knew.

He jumped up to face the General's wife.

'It's not Jim, Mrs Dysone. It's I – Dollar. He'll soon be all right!'

'Captain – Dollar?'

'No – doctor, nowadays – he called me down as one himself. And now I've come back on my own responsibility, and – put him under chloroform; but I haven't given him much; for God's sake let us speak plainly while we can!'

She was on her knees, proving his words without uttering one. Still kneeling speechless, she leaned back while he continued: 'You know what he is as well as I do, Mrs Dysone; you may thank God a doctor has found him out before the police! Monomania is not their business – but neither are you the one to cope with it. You have shielded your husband as only a woman will shield a man; now you must let him come to me.'

His confidence was taking some effect; but she ignored the hands that would have helped her to her feet; and her own were locked in front of her, but not in supplication.

'And what can any of you do for him,' she cried fiercely – 'except take him away from me?'

'I will only answer for myself. I would control him as you can not, and I would teach him to control himself if man under God can do it. I am a criminal alienist, Mrs Dysone, as your husband knew before he came to consult me on elaborate pretences into which we needn't go. He trusted me enough to ask me down here; in my opinion, he was feeling his way to greater trust, in the teeth of his terrible obsession, but last night he said more than he meant to say, so today he wouldn't say a word. I only guessed his secret this morning – when you guessed I had! It would be safe with me against the world. But how can I take the responsibility of keeping it if he remains at large as he is now?'

'You can not,' said Mrs Dysone. 'I am the only one.'

Her tone was dreamy and yet hard and fatalistic; the arms in the wide dressing-gown sleeves were still tightly locked. Something brought Dollar down again beside the senseless man, bending over him in keen alarm.

'He'll be himself again directly – quite himself, I shouldn't wonder! He may have forgot what has happened; he mustn't find me here to remind him. Something he will have to know, and you are the one to break it to him, and then to persuade him to come to me. But you won't find that so easy, Mrs Dysone, if he sees how I tricked him. He had much better think it *was* your nephew. My motor's in the lane behind these trees; let him think I never went away at all, that we connived and I am holding myself there at your disposal. It would be true – wouldn't it – after this? I'll wait night and day until I know!'

'Doctor Dollar,' said Mrs Dysone, when she had risen without aid and set him to the trees, 'you may or may not know the worst about my poor husband, but you shall know it now about me. I wish you to take this – and keep it! You have had two escapes tonight.'

She bared the wrist from which the smallest of revolvers dangled; he felt it in the darkness – and left it dangling.

'I heard you had one. He told me. And I thought you carried it for your own protection!' cried Dollar, seeing into the woman at last.

'No. It was not for that'– and he knew that she was smiling through her tears. 'I did save his life – when my poor dog saved Jim's – but I carried this to save the secret I am going to trust to you!'

Dollar would only take her hand. 'You wouldn't have shot me, or any man,' he assured her.

'But,' he added to himself among the trees, 'what a fool I was to forget that *they* never killed women!'

It turned almost cold beside the motor in the lane; the doctor gave his boy a little brandy, and together they tramped up and down, talking sport and fiction by the small hour together. The stars slipped out of the sky, the birds began, and the same cynic shouted 'Pretty, pretty, pretty!' at the top of its strong contralto. At long last there came that other sound for which Dollar had never ceased listening. And he turned back into the haunted wood with Jim Paley.

The poor nephew – still stunned calm – was as painfully articulate as a young bereaved husband. He spoke of General Dysone as of a man already dead, in the gentlest of past tenses. He was dead enough to the boy. There had been an appalling confession – made as coolly, it appeared, as Paley repeated it.

'He thought *I* knocked him down, and I had to let him think so! Aunt Essie insisted; she *is* a wonder, after all! It made him tell me things I simply can't believe... Yet he showed me a rope just like it – meant for me!'

'Do you mean just like the one that – hanged the gardener?'

'Yes. *He* did it, so he swears... *afterward*. He'll tell you himself – he wants to tell you. He says he first... I can't put my tongue to it!' The lapse into the present tense had made him human.

'Like the Thugs?'

'Yes – like that sect of fiendish fanatics who went about strangling everybody they met! *They* were what his book was about. How did you know?'

'That's Bhowanee, their goddess, on top of his bureau, and he has Sleeman and all the other awful literature locked up underneath. As a study for a life of sudden idleness, in the depths of the country, it was enough to bring on temporary insanity. And the strong man gone wrong goes and does what the rest of us only get on our nerves!'

Dollar felt his biceps clutched and clawed, and the two stood still under more irony in a gay contralto.

'Temporary, did you say? Only *temporary*?' the boy was faltering.

'I hope so, honestly. You see, it was just on that one point... and even there... I believe he *did* want his wife out of the way, and for her own sake, too!' said Dollar, with a sympathetic tremor of his own.

'But do you know what he's saying? He means to tell the whole world now, and let them hang him, and serve him right – he says! And he's as sane as we are now – only he might have been through a Turkish bath!'

'More signs!' cried Dollar, looking up at the brightening sky. 'But we won't allow that. It would undo nothing and he has made all the reparation... Come, Paley! I want to take him back with me in the car. It's broad daylight.'

DICK DONOVAN

Created by JE Preston Muddock (1843-1934)

The impressively named James Edward Preston Muddock was born in Southampton, the son of a sea captain. After an adventurous early life, which involved travel in India and the South Seas, gold mining in Australia, and a lengthy sojourn in America, he took up writing in his late twenties. During a career that lasted more than sixty years, he published dozens and dozens of novels and hundreds of short stories. Muddock has the unusual distinction of having had a town named after one of his characters. His 1905 fantasy novel The Sunless City *follows the adventures of a prospector named Josiah Flintabbaty Flonatin who discovers a lost world at the bottom of a lake in the Rocky Mountains. The book became a favourite of Thomas Creighton, a real-life prospector who founded a township in Manitoba and called it Flin Flon after Muddock's creation. The town still exists under that name. However, Muddock's most famous character – so famous that the writer eventually used his name as a pseudonym under which to publish other books – was the detective Dick Donovan. Donovan first appeared in print at much the same time as Sherlock Holmes and initially the careers of the two detectives unfolded in parallel. Under the collective title of 'Romances from a Detective's Case-book' several stories featuring Donovan appeared in* The Strand Magazine *in 1892, the same year that many of the early Sherlock Holmes stories were first published there. In 1900, Muddock's daughter Dorothy married, as his second wife, Herbert Greenhough Smith,* The Strand Magazine*'s long-serving editor. All told, Muddock wrote more than 180 Donovan stories which were collected in a dozen or so different volumes in the late 1880s and 1890s.*

THE JEWELLED SKULL

Busily engaged one morning in my office in trying to solve some knotty problems that called for my earnest attention, I was suddenly disturbed by a knock at the door, and, in answer to my 'Come in!' one of my assistants entered, although I had given strict orders that I was not to be disturbed for two hours.

'Excuse me, sir,' said my man, 'but a gentleman wishes to see you, and will take no denial.'

'I thought I told you not to disturb me under any circumstances,' I replied, somewhat tartly.

'Yes, so you did. But the gentleman insists upon seeing you. He says his business is most urgent.'

'Who is he?'

'Here is his card, sir.'

I glanced at the card the assistant handed to me. It bore the name – Colonel Maurice Odell, *The Star and Garter Club*

Colonel Maurice Odell was an utter stranger to me. I had never heard his name before; but I knew that the Star and Garter Club was a club of the highest rank, and that its members were men of position and eminence. I therefore considered it probable that the Colonel's business was likely, as he said, to be urgent, and I told my assistant to show him in.

A few minutes later the door opened, and there entered a tall, thin, wiry-looking man, with an unmistakable military bearing. His face, clean-shaved save for a heavy grey moustache, was tanned with exposure to sun and rain. His hair, which was cropped close, was iron grey, as were his eyebrows, and as they were very bushy, and there were two deep vertical furrows between the eyes, he had the appearance of being a stern, determined, unyielding man. And as I glanced at his well-marked face, with its powerful jaw, I came to the conclusion that he was a martinet of the old-fashioned type, who, in the name of discipline, could perpetrate almost any cruelty; and yet, on the other hand, when not under military influence, was capable of the most generous acts and deeds. He was faultlessly dressed, from his patent leather boots to his canary-coloured kid gloves. But though, judging from his dress, he was somewhat of a coxcomb, a glance at the hard, stern features and the keen, deep-set grey eyes was sufficient to dispel any idea that he was a mere carpet soldier.

'Pardon me for intruding upon you, Mr Donovan,' he said, bowing stiffly and formally, 'but I wish to consult you about a very important matter, and, as I leave for Egypt tomorrow, I have very little time at my disposal.'

'I am at your service, Colonel,' I replied, as I pointed to a seat, and began to feel a deep interest in the man, for there was an individuality about him that stamped him at once as a somewhat remarkable person. His voice was in keeping with his looks. It was firm, decisive, and full of volume, and attracted one by its resonance. I felt at once that such a man was not likely to give himself much concern about trifles, and, therefore, the business he had come about must be of considerable importance. So, pushing the papers I had been engaged upon on one side, I turned my revolving chair so that I might face him and have my back to the light, and telling him that I was prepared to listen to anything he had to say, I half closed my eyes, and began to make a study of him.

'I will be as brief as possible,' he began, as he placed his highly polished hat and his umbrella on the table. 'I am a military man, and have spent much of my time in India, but two years ago I returned home, and took up my residence at the Manor, Esher. Twice since I went to live there the place has been robbed in a somewhat mysterious manner. The first occasion was a little over a year ago, when a number of antique silver cups were stolen. The Scotland Yard authorities endeavoured to trace the thieves, but failed.'

'I think I remember hearing something about that robbery,' I remarked, as I tried to recall the details. 'But in what way was it a mysterious one?'

'Because it was impossible to determine how the thieves gained access to the house. The place had not been broken into.'

'How about your servants?' I asked.

'Oh, I haven't a servant who isn't honesty itself.'

'Pray proceed. What about the second robbery?'

'That is what I have come to you about. It is a very serious business indeed, and has been carried out in the mysterious way that characterised the first one.'

'You mean it is serious as regards the value of the property stolen?'

'In one sense, yes; but it is something more than that. During my stay in India I rendered very considerable service indeed to the Rajah of Mooltan, a man of great wealth. Before I left India, he presented me with a souvenir of a very extraordinary character. It was nothing more nor less than the skull of one of his ancestors.'

As it seemed to me a somewhat frivolous matter for the Colonel to take up my time because he had lost the mouldy old skull of a dead and gone Rajah, I said, 'Excuse me, Colonel, but you can hardly expect me to devote my energies to tracing this somewhat gruesome souvenir of yours, which probably the thief will hasten to bury as speedily as possible, unless he happens to be of a very morbid turn of mind.'

'You are a little premature,' said the Colonel, with a suspicion of sternness. 'That skull has been valued at upwards of twelve thousand pounds.'

'Twelve thousand pounds!' I echoed, as my interest in my visitor deepened.

'Yes, sir; twelve thousand pounds. It is fashioned into a drinking goblet, bound with solid gold bands, and encrusted with precious stones. In the bottom of the goblet, inside, is a diamond of the purest water, and which alone is said to be worth two thousand pounds. Now, quite apart from the intrinsic value of this relic, it has associations for me which are beyond price, and further than that, my friend the Rajah told me that if ever I parted with it, or it was stolen, ill fortune would ever afterwards pursue me. Now, Mr Donovan, I am not a superstitious man, but I confess that in this instance I am weak enough to believe that the Rajah's words will come true, and that some strange calamity will befall either me or mine.'

'Without attaching any importance to that,' I answered, 'I confess that it is a serious business, and I will do what I can to recover this extraordinary goblet. But you say you leave for Egypt tomorrow?'

'Yes. I am going out on a government commission, and shall probably be absent six months.'

'Then I had better travel down to Esher with you at once, as I like to start at the fountain head in such matters.'

The Colonel was most anxious that I should do this, and, requesting him to wait for a few minutes, I retired to my inner sanctum, and when I reappeared it was in the character of a venerable parson, with flowing grey hair, spectacles, and the orthodox white choker. My visitor did not recognise me until I spoke, and then he requested to know why I had transformed myself in such a manner.

I told him I had a particular reason for it, but felt it was advisable not to reveal the reason then, and I enjoined on him the necessity of supporting me in the character I had assumed, for I considered it important that none of his household should know that I was a detective. I begged that he would introduce me as the Rev John Marshall, from the Midland Counties. He promised to do this, and we took the next train down to Esher.

The Manor was a quaint old mansion, and dated back to the commencement of Queen Elizabeth's reign. The Colonel had bought the property, and being somewhat of an antiquarian, he had allowed it to remain in its original state, so far as the actual building was concerned. But he had had it done up inside a little, and furnished in great taste in the Elizabethan style, and instead of the walls being papered they were hung with tapestry.

I found that besides the goblet some antique rings and a few pieces of gold and silver had been carried off. But these things were of comparatively small value, and the Colonel's great concern was about the lost skull, which had been kept under a glass shade in what he called his 'Treasure Chamber'. It was a small room, lighted by an oriel window. The walls were wainscoted halfway up, and the upper part was hung with tapestry. In this room there was a most extraordinary and miscellaneous collection of things, including all kinds of Indian weapons; elephant trappings; specimens of clothing as worn by the Indian nobility; jewellery, including rings, bracelets, anklets; in fact, it was a veritable museum of very great interest and value.

The Colonel assured me that the door of this room was always kept locked, and the key was never out of his possession. The lower part of the chimney of the old-fashioned fireplace I noticed was protected by iron bars let into the masonry, so that the thief, I was sure, did not come down the chimney; nor did he come in at the window, for it only opened at each side, and the apertures were so small that a child could not have squeezed through. Having noted these things, I hinted to the Colonel that the thief had probably gained access to the room by means of a duplicate key. But he hastened to assure me that the lock was of singular construction, having been specially made. There were only two keys to it. One he always carried about with him, the other he kept in a secret drawer in an old escritoire in his library, and he was convinced that nobody knew of its existence. He explained the working of the lock, and also showed me the key, which was the most remarkable key I ever saw; and, after examining the lock, I came to the conclusion that it could not be opened by any means apart from the special key. Nevertheless the thief had succeeded in getting into the room. How did he manage it? That was the problem I had to solve, and that done I felt that I should be able to get a clue to the robber. I told the Colonel that before leaving the house I should like to see every member of his household, and he said I should be able to see the major portion of them at luncheon, which he invited me to partake of.

I found that his family consisted of his wife – an Anglo-Indian lady – three charming daughters, his eldest son, Ronald Odell, a young man about four-and-twenty, and a younger son, a youth of twelve. The family were waited upon at table by two parlour-maids, the butler, and a page-boy. The butler was an elderly, sedate, gentlemanly-looking man; the boy had an open, frank face, and the same remark applied to the two girls. As I studied them I saw nothing calculated to raise my suspicions in any way. Indeed, I felt instinctively that I could safely pledge myself for their honesty.

When the luncheon was over the Colonel produced cigars, and the ladies and the youngest boy having retired, the host, his son Ronald and I ensconced ourselves in comfortable chairs, and proceeded to smoke. Ronald Odell was a most extraordinary looking young fellow. He had been born and brought up in India, and seemed to suffer from an unconquerable lassitude that gave him a lifeless, insipid appearance. He was very dark, with dreamy, languid eyes, and an expressionless face of a peculiar sallowness. He was tall and thin, with hands that were most noticeable, owing to the length, flexibility, and thinness of the fingers. He sat in the chair with his body huddled up as it were; his long legs stretched straight out before him; his pointed chin resting on his chest, while he seemed to smoke his cigar as if unconscious of what he was doing.

It was natural that the robbery should form a topic of conversation as we smoked and sipped some excellent claret, and at last I turned to the Colonel, and said:

'It seems to me that there is a certain mystery about this robbery which is very puzzling. But, now, don't you think it's probable that somebody living under your roof holds the key to the mystery?'

'God bless my life, no!' answered the Colonel, with emphatic earnestness. 'I haven't a servant in the house but that I would trust with my life!'

'What is your view of the case, Mr Ronald?' I said, turning to the son.

Without raising his head, he answered in a lisping, drawling, dreamy way:

'It's a queer business; and I don't think the governor will ever get his skull back.'

'I hope you will prove incorrect in that,' I said. 'My impression is that, if the Colonel puts the matter into the hands of some clever detective, the mystery will be solved.'

'No,' drawled the young fellow, 'there isn't a detective fellow in London capable of finding out how that skull was stolen, and where it has been taken to. Not even Dick Donovan, who is said to have no rival in his line.'

I think my face coloured a little as he unwittingly paid me this compliment. Though my character for the nonce was that of a clergyman I did not enter into any argument with him; but merely remarked that I thought he was wrong. At any rate, I hoped so, for his father's sake.

Master Ronald made no further remark, but remained silent for some time, and seemingly so absorbed in his own reflections that he took no notice of the conversation carried on by me and his father; and presently, having finished his cigar, he rose, stretched his long, flexible body, and without a word left the room.

'You mustn't take any notice of my son,' said the Colonel, apologetically. 'He is very queer in his manners, for he is constitutionally weak, and has peculiar ideas about things in general. He dislikes clergymen, for one thing, and that is the reason, no doubt, why he has been so boorish towards you. For, of course, he is deceived by your garb, as all in the house are, excepting myself and wife. I felt it advisable to tell her who you are, in order to prevent her asking you any awkward questions that you might not be prepared to answer.'

I smiled as I told him I had made a study of the various characters I was called upon to assume in pursuit of my calling, and that I was generally able to talk the character as well as dress it.

A little later he conducted me downstairs, in order that I

might see the rest of the servants, consisting of a most amiable cook, whose duties appeared to agree with her remarkably well, and three other women, including a scullery-maid; while in connection with the stables were a coachman, a groom, and a boy.

Having thus passed the household in review, as it were, I next requested that I might be allowed to spend a quarter of an hour or so alone in the room from whence the skull and other things had been stolen. Whilst in the room with the Colonel I had formed an opinion which I felt it desirable to keep to myself, and my object in asking to visit the room alone was to put this opinion to the test.

The floor was of dark old oak, polished and waxed, and there was not a single board that was movable. Having satisfied myself of that fact, I next proceeded to examine the wainscoting with the greatest care, and after going over every inch of it, I came to a part that gave back a hollow sound to my raps. I experienced a strange sense of delight as I discovered this, for it, so far, confirmed me in my opinion that the room had been entered by a secret door, and here was evidence of a door. The antiquity of the house and the oak panelling had had something to do with this opinion, for I knew that in old houses of the kind secret doors were by no means uncommon.

Although I was convinced that the panel which gave back a hollow sound when rapped was a door, I could detect no means of opening it. Save that it sounded hollow, it was exactly like the other panels, and there was no appearance of any lock or spring, and as the time I had stipulated for had expired, I rejoined the Colonel, and remarked to him incidentally:

'I suppose there is no way of entering that room except by the doorway from the landing?'

'Oh no, certainly not. The window is too small, and the chimney is barred, as you know, for I saw you examining it.'

My object in asking the question was to see if he suspected in any way the existence of a secret door; but it was now very obvious that he did nothing of the kind, and I did not deem it advisable to tell him of my own suspicions.

'You say you are obliged to depart for Egypt tomorrow, Colonel?' I asked.

'Yes. I start tomorrow night.'

'Then I must ask you to give me *carte blanche* in this matter.'

'Oh, certainly.'

'And in order to facilitate my plans it would be as well to make a confidante of Mrs Odell. The rest you must leave to me.'

'What do you think the chances are of discovering the thief?' he asked, with a dubious expression.

'I shall discover him,' I answered emphatically. Whereupon the Colonel looked more than surprised, and proceeded to rattle off a string of questions with the object of learning why I spoke so decisively. But I was compelled to tell him that I could give him no reason, for though I had worked out a theory which intuitively I believed to be right, I had not at that moment a shred of acceptable proof in support of my theory, and that therefore I could not commit myself to raising suspicions against anyone until I was prepared to do something more than justify them.

He seemed rather disappointed, although he admitted the soundness of my argument.

'By the way, Colonel,' I said, as I was about to take my departure, after having had a talk with his wife, 'does it so happen that there is anything the matter with the roof of your house?'

'Not that I am aware of,' he answered, opening his eyes wide with amazement at what no doubt seemed to him an absurd question. 'Why do you ask?'

'Because I want to go on the roof without attracting the attention of anyone.'

'Let us go at once, then,' he said eagerly.

'No, not now. But I see that the greater part of the roof is flat, and leaded. Now, in the course of two or three days I shall present myself here in the guise of a plumber, and I shall be obliged by your giving orders that I am to be allowed to ascend to the roof without let or hindrance, as the lawyers say.'

'Oh, certainly I will; but it seems to me an extraordinary proceeding,' he exclaimed.

I told him that many things necessarily seemed extraordinary when the reasons for them were not understood, and with that remark I took my departure, having promised the Colonel to do everything mortal man could do to recover the lost skull.

Three days later I went down to the Manor disguised as a working plumber, and was admitted without any difficulty, as the Colonel had left word that a man was coming down from London to examine the roof. As a servant was showing me upstairs to the top landing, where a trap door in the ceiling gave access to the leads, I passed Ronald Odell on the stairs. He was attired in a long dressing-gown, had Turkish slippers on his feet, a fez on his head, and a cigar in his mouth, from which he was puffing great volumes of smoke. His face was almost ghastly in its pallor, and his eyes had the same dreamy look which I had noticed on my first visit. His hands were thrust deep in his pockets, and his movements and manner were suggestive of a person walking in his sleep, rather than a waking conscious man. This suggestion was heightened by the fact that before I could avoid him he ran full butt against me. That, however, seemed to partially arouse him from his lethargic condition, and turning round, with a fierceness of expression that I scarcely deemed him capable of, he exclaimed:

'You stupid fool, why don't you look where you are going to?'

I muttered out an apology, and he strode down the stairs growling to himself.

'Who is that?' I asked of the servant.

'That's the master's eldest son.'

'He is a queer-looking fellow.'

'I should think he was,' answered the girl with a sniggering laugh. 'I should say he has a slate off.'

'Well, upon my word I should be inclined to agree with you,' I remarked. 'What does he do?'

'Nothing but smoke the greater part of the day.'

'Does he follow no business or profession?'

'Not that I know of; though he generally goes out between six and seven in the evening, and does not come back till late.'

'Where does he go to?'

'Oh, I don't know. He doesn't tell us servants his affairs. But there's something very queer about him. I don't like his looks at all.'

'Doesn't his father exercise any control over him?'

'Not a bit of it. Why, his father dotes on him, and would try and get the moon for him if he wanted it.'

'And what about his mother?'

'Well, her favourite is young Master Tom. He's a nice lad, now, as different again to his brother. In fact, I think the missus is afraid of Mr Ronald. He doesn't treat his mother at all well. And now that the Colonel has gone away we shall all have a pretty time of it. He's a perfect demon in the house when his father is not here.'

As we had now reached the ladder that gave access to the trap door in the roof, I requested the maid to wait while I went outside.

My object in going on to the roof was to see if there was any communication between there and the 'Treasure Chamber'. But the only thing I noticed was a trap door on a flat part of the roof between two chimney stalks. I tried to lift the door, but found it fastened. So after a time I went back to where I had left the servant, and inquired of her where the communication with the other trap door was, and she answered:

'Oh, I think that's in the lumber room; but nobody ever goes in there. They say it's haunted.' I laughed, and she added, with a toss of her head, 'Well, I tell you, I've heard some very queer noises there myself. Me and Jane, the upper housemaid, sleep in a room adjoining it, and we've sometimes been frightened out of our wits.'

I requested her to show me where the room was, as I was

anxious to see if there was any leakage from the roof. This she did, and in order to reach the room we had to mount up a back staircase, and traverse a long passage. At the end of the passage she pushed open a door, saying, 'There you are, but I ain't a-going in.'

As the room was in total darkness I requested her to procure me a candle, which she at once got, and then she left me to explore the room alone. It was filled up with a miscellaneous collection of lumber, boxes and packing cases predominating. There was a small window, but it was closely shuttered, and a flight of wooden steps led to the trapdoor I had noticed on the roof. I examined these steps very carefully, and found that they were thickly encrusted with dirt and dust, and had not been trodden upon for a very long time. The door was fastened down by means of a chain that was padlocked to a staple in the wall; and chain and padlock were very rusty. The walls of the room were wainscoted, and the wainscot in places was decayed and worm-eaten. Going down on my knees, I minutely examined the floor through a magnifying glass and detected foot-marks made with slippered feet, and I found they led to one particular corner of the room where a sort of gangway had been formed by the boxes and other lumber being moved on one side. This was very suggestive, and rapping on the wainscot I found that it was hollow. For some time, I searched for a means of opening it, but without result, until with almost startling suddenness, as I passed my hand up and down the side of the woodwork, the door swung back. I had unconsciously touched the spring, and peering into the black void thus disclosed by the opening of the door, I was enabled to discern by the flickering light of the candle, the head of a flight of stone steps, that were obviously built in the thickness of the wall.

At this discovery I almost exclaimed 'Eureka!' for I now felt that I had the key to the mystery. As I did not wish the servant to know what I was doing, I went to the passage to satisfy myself that she was not observing my movements; but a dread of the ghost-haunted lumber-room had caused her to take herself off altogether.

Closing the door of the room, I returned to the aperture in the wainscot, and minutely examined the head of the steps, where I saw unmistakable traces of the slippered feet which were so noticeable in the dust that covered the floor of the room. Descending the steps, which were very narrow, I reached the bottom, and found further progress barred by a door that was without handle or lock; but, after some time, I discovered a small wooden knob sunk in the woodwork at the side, and, pressing this, the door, with almost absolute noiselessness, slid back, and lo! the 'Treasure Chamber' was revealed. In the face of this discovery, I no longer entertained a doubt that the thief had entered the room by means of this secret passage. And there was no one in the whole household upon whom my suspicions fixed with the exception of Ronald Odell. If my assumption that he was the thief was correct, the mystery was so far explained; and my next step was to discover why he had robbed his father, and what he had done with the property. He was so strange and peculiar that somehow I could not imagine that he had stolen the things merely for the sake of vulgar gain, my impression being that in carrying off the jewelled skull he was actuated by some extraordinary motive, quite apart from the mere question of theft, and this determined me to shadow him for a time in the hope that I should succeed in soon obtaining distinct evidence that my theory was correct.

Before leaving the house, I sought an interview with Mrs Odell, who was anxious to know what the result was of my investigation; but I considered it advisable, in the then state of matters, to withhold from her the discovery I had made. But, as her curiosity to learn what I had been doing on the roof was very great, I informed her that my theory was at first that there was some connection between the roof and the 'Treasure Chamber'; but, though I had not proved that to be correct, I nevertheless was of opinion that the purloiner of the articles resided in the house. Whereupon she very naturally asked me if I suspected any particular person. I answered her candidly that I did; but that, in the absence of anything like proof, I should not be justified in naming anyone. I assured her, however, that I would use the most strenuous efforts to obtain the proof I wanted. Before leaving her, I remarked in a casual sort of way:

'I suppose Mr Ronald is at the head of affairs during his father's absence?'

'Well,' she began, with evident reluctance to say anything against her son, 'Ronald is of a very peculiar disposition. He seems to live quite within himself, as it were, and takes no interest in anything. As a matter of fact, I see very little of him, for he usually spends his evenings from home, and does not return until late. The greater part of the day he keeps to his rooms. I am sure I am quite concerned about him at times.'

The confidential way in which she told me this, and the anxious expression of her face, sufficiently indicated that Ronald was a source of great trouble to her. But I refrained, from motives of delicacy, from pursuing the subject, and was about to take my departure, when she said, with great emphasis:

'I do hope, Mr Donovan, that you will be successful in recovering the goblet; for, quite apart from its intrinsic value, my husband sets great store upon it, and his distress when he found it had been stolen was really pitiable.'

I assured her that it would not be my fault if I failed, and I said that, unless the goblet had been destroyed for the sake of the jewels and the gold, I thought it was very probable that it would be recovered. I spoke thus confidently because I was convinced that I had got the key to the puzzle, and that it would be relatively easy to fit in the rest of the pieces, particularly if I could find out where Ronald Odell spent his evenings; for to me there was something singularly suggestive in his going away from home at nights. That fact was clearly a source of grief to his mother, and she had made it evident to me that she did not know where he went to, nor why he went. But it fell to my lot to solve this mystery a week later. I shadowed him to a house situated in a *cul de sac* in the very heart of the city of London. The houses in this place were tall, imposing looking buildings, and had once been the homes of gentry and people of position. Their day of glory, however, had passed, and they were now for the most part utilised as offices, and were occupied by solicitors, agents, &c. It was a quiet, gloomy sort of region, although it led out of one of the busiest thoroughfares of the great metropolis; but at the bottom of the *cul* was a wall, and beyond that again an ancient burial-place, where the dust of many generations of men reposed. The wall was overtopped by the branches of a few stunted trees that were rooted in the graveyard; and these trees looked mournful and melancholy, with their blackened branches and soot-darkened leaves.

The house to which I traced Ronald Odell was the last one in the *cul* on the left-hand side, and consequently it abutted on the graveyard. It was the one house not utilised as offices, and I ascertained that it was in the occupation of a club consisting of Anglo-Indians. But what they did, or why they met, no one seemed able to tell. The premises were in charge of a Hindoo and his wife, and the members of the club met on an average five nights a week. All this was so much more mystery, but it was precisely in accord with the theory I had been working out in my own mind.

The next afternoon I went to the house, and the door was opened to my knock by the Hindoo woman, who was a mild-eyed, sad-looking little creature; I asked her if she could give me some particulars of the club that was held there, and she informed me that it was known as 'The Indian Dreamers' Club'. But beyond that scrap of information she did not seem disposed to go.

'You had better come when my husband is here,' she said, thereby giving me to understand that her husband was absent. But as I deemed it probable that she might prove more susceptible to my persuasive influences than her husband, I asked her if she would allow me to see over the premises. She declined to do this until I displayed before her greedy eyes certain gold coins of the realm, which proved too much for her cupidity, and she consented to let me go inside. The entrance-hall was carpeted with a thick, massive carpet, that deadened every footfall, and the walls were hung with black velvet. A broad flight of stairs led up from the end of the passage, but they were masked by heavy curtains. The gloom and sombreness of the place were most depressing, and a strange, sickening odour pervaded the air. Led by the dusky woman I passed through a curtained doorway, and found myself in a most extensive apartment that ran the whole depth of the building. From this apartment all daylight was excluded, the light being obtained from a large lamp of blood-coloured glass, and which depended from the centre of the ceiling. There was also a niche at each end of the room, where a lamp of the old Roman pattern burnt. The walls of the room were hung with purple velvet curtains, and the ceiling was also draped with the same material, while the floor was covered with a rich Indian carpet into which the feet sank. In the centre of the room was a table also covered with velvet, and all round the room were most luxurious couches, with velvet cushions and costly Indian rugs. The same sickly odour that I had already noticed pervaded this remarkable chamber, which was like a tomb in its silence; for no sound reached one from the busy world without.

Although all the lamps were lighted it took me some time to accustom my eyes to the gloom and to observe all the details of the extraordinary apartment. Then I noted that on the velvet on one side of the room was inscribed in letters of gold that were strikingly conspicuous against the sombre background, this sentence:

'TO DREAM IS TO LIVE! DREAM ON
FOR TO AWAKEN IS TO DIE!'

The dim light and the sombre upholstering of the room gave it a most weird and uncanny appearance, and I could not help associating with the Indian Dreamers' Club rites and ceremonies that were far from orthodox; while the sentence on the velvet, and which I took to be the club's motto, was like the handwriting on the wall at Belshazzar's feast. It was pregnant with a terrible meaning.

While I was still engaged in examining the room a bell rang, and instantly the Hindoo woman became greatly excited, for she said it was her husband, and that he would be so fiercely angry if he found me there that she would not be responsible for the consequences. She therefore thrust me into a recess where a statue had formerly stood, but the statue had been removed, and a velvet curtain hung before the recess. Nothing could have happened more in accord with my desire than this. For I was resolved, whatever the consequences were, to remain in my place of concealment until I had solved the mystery of the club. There was an outer and an inner door, both of them being thickly padded with felt and covered with velvet.

When the woman had retired and closed these doors the silence was absolute. Not a sound came to my ears. The atmosphere was heavy, and I experienced a sense of languor that was altogether unusual.

I ventured from my place of concealment to still further explore the apartment. I found that the lounges were all of the most delightful and seductive softness, and the tapestries, the cushions, and the curtains were of the richest possible description. It certainly was a place to lie and dream in, shut off from the noise and fret of the busy world. At one end of the room was a large chest of some sort of carved Indian wood. It was bound round with iron bands and fastened with a huge brass padlock. While I was wondering to myself what this chest contained, the door opened and the Indian woman glided in. Seizing me by the arm, she whispered:

'Come, while there is yet a chance. My husband has gone upstairs, but he will return in a few minutes.'

'When do the members of the club meet?' I asked.

'At seven o'clock.'

'Then I shall remain in that place of concealment until they meet!' I answered firmly.

She wrung her hands in distress, and turned her dark eyes on me imploringly. But I gave her to understand that nothing would turn me from my resolve; and if she chose to aid me in carrying out my purpose, she might look for ample reward. Recognising that argument would be of no avail, and evidently in great dread of her husband, she muttered:

'The peril then be on your own head!' and without another word she left the room.

The peril she hinted at did not concern me. In fact, I did not even trouble myself to think what the peril might be. I was too much interested for that, feeling as I did that I was about to witness a revelation.

The hours passed slowly by, and as seven drew on I concealed myself once more in the recess, and by slightly moving the curtain back at the edge, I was enabled to command a full view of the room. Presently the door opened, and the husband of the woman came in. He was a tall, powerful, fierce-looking man, wearing a large turban, and dressed in Indian costume. He placed three or four small lamps, already lighted, and enclosed in ruby glass, on the table; and also a number of quaint Indian drinking cups made of silver, which I recognised from the description as those that had been stolen from the Manor a year or so previously, together with twelve magnificent hookahs. These preparations completed, he retired, and a quarter of an hour later he returned and wound up a large musical box which I had not noticed, owing to its being concealed behind a curtain. The box began to play muffled and plaintive music. The sounds were so softened, the music was so dreamy and sweet, and seemed so far off, that the effect was unlike anything I had ever before heard. A few minutes later, and the Indian once more appeared. This time he wore a sort of dressing-gown of some rich material braided with gold. He walked backwards, and following him in single file were twelve men, the first being Ronald Odell. Five of them were men of colour; three of the others were half-castes, the rest were whites. But they all had the languid, dreamy appearance which characterised Odell, who, as I was to subsequently learn, was their leader and president.

They ranged themselves round the table silently as ghosts; and, without a word, Ronald Odell handed a key to the Indian, who proceeded to unlock the chest I have referred to, and he took therefrom the skull goblet which had been carried off from Colonel Odell's 'Treasure Chamber' by – could there any longer be a doubt? – his own son. The skull, which was provided with two gold handles, and rested on gold claws, was placed on the table before the president, who poured into it the contents of two small bottles which were given to him by the attendant, who took them from the chest. He then stirred the decoction up with a long-handled silver spoon of very rich design and workmanship, and which I recognised, from the description that had been given to me, as one that had been taken from the Colonel's collection. As this strange mixture was stirred, the sickening, overpowering odour that I had noticed on first entering the place became so strong as to almost overcome me, and I felt as if I should suffocate. But I struggled against the feeling as well as I could. The president next poured a small portion of the liquor into each of the twelve cups that had been provided, and as he raised his own to his lips he said:

'Brother dreamers, success to our club! May your dreams be sweet and long!'

The others bowed, but made no response, and each man drained the draught, which I guessed to be some potent herbal decoction for producing sleep. Then each man rose and went to a couch, and the attendant handed him a hookah, applied a light to the bowl, and from the smell that arose it was evident the pipes were charged with opium. As these drugged opium smokers leaned back on the luxurious couches, the concealed musical-box continued to play its plaintive melodies. A drowsy languor pervaded the room, and affected me to such extent that I felt as if I must be dreaming, and that the remarkable scene before my eyes was a dream vision that would speedily fade away.

One by one the pipes fell from the nerveless grasp of the smokers, and were removed by the attendant. And when the last man had sunk into insensibility, the Indian filled a small cup with some of the liquor from the skull goblet, and drained it off. Then he charged a pipe with opium, and, coiling himself up on an ottoman, he began to smoke, until he, like the others, yielded to the soporific influences of the drug and the opium and went to sleep.

My hour of triumph had come. I stepped from my place of concealment, feeling faint and strange, and all but overcome by an irresistible desire to sleep. The potent fumes that filled the air begot a sensation in me that was not unlike drunkenness. But I managed to stagger to the table, seize the goblet and the spoon, and make my way to the door. As I gained the passage the Hindoo woman confronted me, for she was about to enter the room.

'What is the meaning of this?' she cried, as she endeavoured to bar my passage.

'Stand back!' I said, sternly. 'I am a detective officer. These things have been stolen, and I am about to restore them to their rightful owner.'

She manifested supreme distress, but recognised her powerlessness. She dared not raise an alarm, and she might as well have tried to awaken the dead in the adjoining churchyard as those heavily drugged sleepers. And so I gained the street; and the intense sense of relief I experienced as I sucked in draughts of the cold, fresh air cannot be described. Getting to the thoroughfare I hailed a cab, and drove home with my prizes, and the following morning I telegraphed to Egypt to an address the Colonel had given me, informing him that I had recovered the goblet.

The same day I went down to the Manor at Esher, and had an interview with Mrs Odell. I felt, in the interest of her son, that it was my duty to tell her all I had learnt the previous night. She was terribly distressed, but stated that she had suspected for some time that her son was given to opium smoking, though she had no idea he carried the habit to such a remarkable extreme. She requested me to retain possession of the goblet and the spoon until her husband's return, and, in the meantime, she promised to take her weak and misguided son to task, and to have the secret passage in the wall effectually stopped up.

I should mention that I had managed to save a small quantity of the liquor that was in the goblet when I removed it from the club table; and I sent this to a celebrated analytical chemist for analysis, who pronounced it to be a very powerful and peculiar narcotic, made from a combination of Indian herbs with which he was not familiar.

The denouement has yet to be recorded. A few days later Ronald Odell, after drugging himself as usual, was found dead on one of the couches at the club. This necessitated an inquest, and the verdict was that he had died from a narcotic, but whether taken with the intention of destroying life or merely to produce sleep there was no evidence to show. Although I had no evidence to offer, I was firmly convinced in my own mind that the poor weak fellow had committed suicide, from a sense of shame at the discovery I had made.

Of course, after this tragic affair, and the exposure it entailed, the Indian Dreamers' Club was broken up, and all its luxurious appointments were sold by auction, and its members dispersed. It appeared that one of the rules was that the members of the club should never exceed twelve in number. What became of the remaining eleven I never knew; but it was hardly likely they would abandon the pernicious habits they had acquired.

In the course of six months Colonel Odell returned from Egypt, and though he was much cut up by the death of his son, he was exceedingly gratified at the recovery of the peculiar goblet, which the misguided youth had no doubt purloined under the impression that it was useless in his father's treasure room, but that it would more fittingly adorn the table of the Dreamers'

Club, of which he was the president. I could not help thinking that part of the motto of the club was singularly appropriate in his case: 'Dream on, for to awaken is to die'. He had awakened from his dream, and passed into that state where dreams perplex not.

HORACE DORRINGTON

Created by Arthur Morrison (1863-1945)

Born in Poplar in London's East End, Arthur Morrison began his working life as an office boy in the architects' department of the London School Board but turned to journalism in his early twenties. By the 1890s, he was earning his living as a full-time writer. His work in that decade was divided between fiction which depicted the East End in which he had grown up – books like Tales of Mean Streets *and* A Child of the Jago *– and detective stories. His East End stories, which cast an unsentimental eye on the life of London's poor, often aroused controversy. 'Lizerunt', from* Tales of Mean Streets, *was criticised for its account of domestic violence and prostitution, and the accuracy of his picture of slum life in* A Child of the Jago *was questioned. Meanwhile Morrison's crime fiction was appearing in the pages of the deeply respectable* Strand Magazine *alongside the Sherlock Holmes stories. His best-known detective character is Martin Hewitt – one of whose adventures is also included in this collection – but, in many ways, Horace Dorrington is a more interesting and original creation. He appeared in only a handful of stories, first published in* The Windsor Magazine *in 1897 and then gathered together in a volume entitled* The Dorrington Deed-Box *in the same year. A jovial private investigator who, beneath his cheery exterior, is completely ruthless, indeed sociopathic, Dorrington is unlike any other detective from the period.*

ARTHUR MORRISON

THE CASE OF 'THE MIRROR OF PORTUGAL'

I

Whether or not this case has an historical interest is a matter of conjecture. If it has none, then the title I have given it is a misnomer. But I think the conjecture that some historical interest attaches to it is by no means an empty one, and all that can be urged against it is the common though not always declared error that romance expired fifty years at least ago, and history with it. This makes it seem improbable that the answer to an unsolved riddle of a century since should be found today in an inquiry agent's dingy office in Bedford Street, Covent Garden. Whether or not it has so been found the reader may judge for himself, though the evidence stops far short of actual proof of the identity of the 'Mirror of Portugal' with the stone wherewith this case was concerned.

But first, as to the 'Mirror of Portugal'. This was a diamond of much and ancient fame. It was of Indian origin, and it had lain in the possession of the royal family of Portugal in the time of Portugal's ancient splendour. But three hundred years ago, after the extinction of the early line of succession, the diamond, with other jewels, fell into the possession of Don Antonio, one of the half-dozen pretenders who were then scrambling for the throne. Don Antonio, badly in want of money, deposited the stone in pledge with Queen Elizabeth of England, and never redeemed it. Thus it took its place as one of the English Crown Jewels, and so remained till the overthrow and death of Charles the First. Queen Henrietta then carried it with her to France, and there, to obtain money to satisfy her creditors, she sold it to the great Cardinal Mazarin. He bequeathed it, at his death, to the French Crown, and among the Crown Jewels of France it once more found a temporary abiding place. But once more it brought disaster with it in the shape of a revolution, and again a king lost his head at the executioner's hands. And in the riot and confusion of the great Revolution of 1792 the 'Mirror of

Portugal', with other jewels, vanished utterly. Where it went to, and who took it, nobody ever knew. The 'Mirror of Portugal' disappeared as suddenly and effectually as though fused to vapour by electric combustion.

So much for the famous 'Mirror'. Whether or not its history is germane to the narrative which follows, probably nobody will ever certainly know. But that Dorrington considered that it was, his notes on the case abundantly testify.

For some days before Dorrington's attention was in any way given to this matter, a poorly dressed and not altogether prepossessing Frenchman had been haunting the staircase and tapping at the office door, unsuccessfully attempting an interview with Dorrington, who happened to be out, or busy, whenever he called. The man never asked for Hicks, Dorrington's partner; but this was very natural. In the first place, it was always Dorrington who met all strangers and conducted all negotiations, and in the second, Dorrington had just lately, in a case regarding a secret society in Soho, made his name much known and respected, not to say feared, in the foreign colony of that quarter; wherefore it was likely that a man who bore evidence of residence in that neighbourhood should come with the name of Dorrington on his tongue.

The weather was cold, but the man's clothes were thin and threadbare, and he had no overcoat. His face was of a broad, low type, coarse in feature and small in forehead, and he wore the baggy black linen peaked cap familiar on the heads of men of his class in parts of Paris. He had called unsuccessfully, as I have said, sometimes once, sometimes more frequently, on each of three or four days before he succeeded in seeing Dorrington. At last, however, he intercepted him on the stairs, as Dorrington arrived at about eleven in the morning.

'Pardon, m'sieu,' he said, laying his finger on Dorrington's arm, 'it is M Dorrington – not?'

'Well – suppose it is, what then?' Dorrington never admitted his identity to a stranger without first seeing good cause.

'I 'ave beesness – very great beesness; beesness of a large profit for you if you please to take it. Where shall I tell it?'

'Come in here,' Dorrington replied, leading the way to his private room. The man did not look like a wealthy client, but that signified nothing. Dorrington had made profitable strokes after introductions even less promising.

The man followed Dorrington, pulled off his cap, and sat in the chair Dorrington pointed at.

'In the first place,' said Dorrington, 'what's your name?'

'Ah, yas – but before – all that I tell is for ourselves alone, is it not? It is all in confidence, eh?'

'Yes, yes, of course,' Dorrington answered, with virtuous impatience. 'Whatever is said in this room is regarded as strictly confidential. What's your name?'

'Jacques Bouvier.'

'Living at –?'

'Little Norham Street, Soho.'

'And now the business you speak of.'

'The beesness is this. My cousin, Léon Bouvier – he is *coquin* – a rrrascal!'

'Very likely.'

'He has a great jewel – it is, I have no doubt, a diamond – of a great value. It is not his! There is no right of him to it! It should be mine. If you get it for me one-quarter of it in money shall be yours! And it is of a great value.'

'Where does your cousin live? What is he?'

'Beck Street, Soho. He has a shop – a café – Café des Bons Camarades. And he give me not a crrrust – if I starve!'

It scarcely seemed likely that the keeper of a little foreign café in a back street of Soho would be possessed of a jewel a quarter of whose value would be prize enough to tempt Dorrington to take a new case up. But Dorrington bore with the man a little longer. 'What is this jewel you talk of?' he asked. 'And if you don't know enough about it to be quite sure whether it is a diamond or not, what *do* you know?'

'Listen! The stone I have never seen; but that it is a diamond makes probable. What else so much value? And it is much value that gives my cousin so great care and trouble – *cochon!* Listen! I relate to you. My father – he was charcoal-burner at Bonneuil, department of Seine. My uncle – the father of my cousin – also was charcoal-burner. The grandfather – charcoal-burner also; and his father and his grandfather before him – all burners of charcoal, at Bonneuil. Now perceive. The father of my grandfather was of the great Revolution – a young man, great among those who stormed the Bastille, the Tuileries, the Hôtel de Ville, brave, and a leader. Now, when palaces were burnt and heads were falling there was naturally much confusion. Things were lost – things of large value. What more natural? While so many were losing the head from the shoulders, it was not strange that some should lose jewels from the neck. And when these things were lost, who might have a greater right to keep them than the young men of the Revolution, the brave, and the leaders, they who did the work?'

'If you mean that your respectable great-grandfather stole something, you needn't explain it any more,' Dorrington said. 'I quite understand.'

'I do not say stole; when there is a great revolution a thing is anybody's. But it would not be convenient to tell of it at the time, for the new government might believe everything to be its own. These things I do not know, you will understand – I suggest an explanation, that is all. After the great Revolution, my great-grandfather lives alone and quiet, and burns the charcoal as before. Why? The jewel is too great to sell so soon. So he gives it to his son and dies. He also, my grandfather, still burns the charcoal. Again, why? Because, as I believe, he is too poor, too common a man to go about openly to sell so great a stone. More, he loves the stone, for with that he is always rich; and so he burns his charcoal and lives contented as his father had done, and he is rich, and nobody knows it. What then? He has two sons. When he dies, which son does he leave the stone to? Each one says it is for himself – that is natural. I say it was for my father.

But however that may make itself, my father dies suddenly. He falls in a pit – by accident, says his brother; not by accident, says my mother; and soon after, she dies too. By accident too, perhaps you ask? Oh yes, by accident too, no doubt.' The man laughed disagreeably. 'So I am left alone, a little boy, to burn charcoal. When I am a bigger boy there comes the great war, and the Prussians besiege Paris. My uncle, he, burning charcoal no more, goes at night, and takes things from the dead Prussians. Perhaps they are not always quite dead when he finds them – perhaps he makes them so. Be that as it will, the Prussians take him one dark night; and they stand him against a garden wall, and pif! paf! they shoot him. That is all of my uncle; but he dies a rich man, and nobody knows. What does his wife do? She has the jewel, and she has a little money that has been got from the dead Prussians. So when the war is over, she comes to London with my cousin, the bad Léon, and she has the café – Café des Bons Camarades. And Léon grows up, and his mother dies, and he has the café, and with the jewel is a rich man – nobody knowing; nobody but me. But, figure to yourself; shall I burn charcoal and starve at Bonneuil with a rich cousin in London – rich with a diamond that should be mine? Not so. I come over, and Léon, at first he lets me wait at the café. But I do not want that – there is the stone, and I can never see it, never find it. So one day Léon finds me looking in a box, and – chut! out I go. I tell Léon that I will share the jewel with him or I will tell the police. He laughs at me – there is no jewel, he says – I am mad. I do not tell the police, for that is to lose it altogether. But I come here and I offer you one quarter of the diamond if you shall get it.'

'Steal it for you, eh?'

Jacques Bouvier shrugged his shoulders. 'The word is as you please,' he said. 'The jewel is not his. And if there is delay it will be gone. Already he goes each day to Hatton Garden, leaving his wife to keep the Café des Bons Camarades. Perhaps he is selling the jewel today! Who can tell? So that it will be well that you begin at once.'

'Very well. My fee in advance will be twenty guineas.'

'What? *Dieu!* – I have no money, I tell you! Get the diamond, and there is one quarter– twenty-five per cent – for you!'

'But what guarantee do you give that this story of yours isn't all a hoax? Can you expect me to take everything on trust, and work for nothing?'

The man rose and waved his arms excitedly. 'It is true, I say!' he exclaimed. 'It is a fortune! There is much for you, and it will pay! I have no money, or you should have some. What can I do? You will lose the chance if you are foolish!'

'It rather seems to me, my friend, that I shall be foolish to give valuable time to gratifying your cock-and-bull fancies. See here now. I'm a man of business, and my time is fully occupied. You come here and waste half an hour or more of it with a long rigmarole about some valuable article that you say yourself you have never seen, and you don't even know whether it is a diamond or not. You wander at large over family traditions which you may believe yourself or may not. You have no money, and you offer no fee as a guarantee of your *bonâ fides*, and the sum of the thing is that you ask me to go and commit a theft – to purloin an article you can't even describe, and then to give you three-quarters of the proceeds. No, my man, you have made a mistake. You must go away from here at once, and if I find you hanging about my door again I shall have you taken away very summarily. Do you understand? Now go away.'

'*Mon Dieu!* But –'

'I've no more time to waste,' Dorrington answered, opening the door and pointing to the stairs. 'If you stay here any longer you'll get into trouble.'

Jacques Bouvier walked out, muttering and agitating his hands. At the top stair he turned and, almost too angry for words, burst out, 'Sir – you are a ver' big fool – a fool!' But Dorrington slammed the door.

He determined, however, if he could find a little time, to learn a little more of Léon Bouvier – perhaps to put a man to watch at the Café des Bons Camarades. That the keeper of this place in Soho should go regularly to Hatton Garden, the diamond market, was curious, and Dorrington had met and analysed too many extraordinary romances to put aside unexamined Jacques Bouvier's seemingly improbable story. But, having heard all the man had to say, it had clearly been his policy to get rid of him in the way he had done. Dorrington was quite ready to steal a diamond, or anything else of value, if it could be done quite safely, but he was no such fool as to give three-quarters of his plunder – or any of it – to somebody else. So that the politic plan was to send Jacques Bouvier away with the impression that his story was altogether pooh-poohed and was to be forgotten.

II

Dorrington left his office late that day, and the evening being clear, though dark, he walked toward Conduit Street by way of Soho; he thought to take a glance at the Café des Bons Camarades on his way, without being observed, should Jacques Bouvier be in the vicinity.

Beck Street, Soho, was a short and narrow street lying east and west, and joining two of the larger streets that stretch north and south across the district. It was even a trifle dirtier than these by-streets in that quarter are wont to be. The Café des Bons Camarades was a little green-painted shop the window whereof was backed by muslin curtains, while upon the window itself appeared in florid painted letters the words 'Cuisine Française'. It was the only shop in the street, with the exception of a small coal and firewood shed at one end, the other buildings consisting of the side wall of a factory, now closed for the night, and a few tenement houses. An alley entrance – apparently the gate of a stableyard – stood next the café. As Dorrington walked by the steamy window, he was startled to hear his own name and some part of his office address spoken in excited tones somewhere in this dark alley entrance; and suddenly a man rather well dressed, and cramming a damaged tall hat on his head as he went, darted from the entrance and ran in the direction from which Dorrington had come. A stoutly built Frenchwoman, carrying on her face every indication of extreme excitement, watched him from the gateway, and Dorrington made no doubt that it was in her voice that he had heard his name mentioned. He walked briskly to the end of the short street, turned at the end, and hurried round the block of houses, in hope to catch another sight of the man. Presently he saw him, running, in Old Compton Street, and making in the direction of Charing Cross Road. Dorrington mended his pace, and followed. The man emerged where Shaftesbury Avenue meets Charing Cross Road, and, as he crossed, hesitated once or twice, as though he thought of hailing a cab, but decided rather to trust his own legs. He hastened through the byways to St Martin's Lane, and Dorrington now perceived that one side and half the back of his coat was dripping with wet mud. Also it was plain, as Dorrington had suspected, that his destination was Dorrington's own office in Bedford Street. So the follower broke into a trot, and at last came upon the muddy man wrenching at the bell and pounding at the closed door of the house in Bedford Street, just as the housekeeper began to turn the lock.

'M'sieu Dorrington – M'sieu Dorrington!' the man exclaimed, excitedly, as the door was opened.

"E's gawn 'ome long ago,' the caretaker growled; 'you might 'a known that. Oh, 'ere 'e is though – good evenin', sir.'

'I am Mr Dorrington,' the inquiry agent said politely. 'Can I do anything for you?'

'Ah yes – it is important – at once! I am robbed!'

'Just step upstairs, then, and tell me about it.'

Dorrington had but begun to light the gas in his office when his visitor broke out, 'I am robbed, M'sieu Dorrington, robbed by my cousin – *coquin!* Rrrobbed of everything! Rrrobbed I tell you!' He seemed astonished to find the other so little excited by the intelligence.

'Let me take your coat,' Dorrington said, calmly. 'You've had a

ARTHUR MORRISON

downer in the mud, I see. Why, what's this?' he smelt the collar as he went toward a hat-peg. 'Chloroform!'

'Ah yes – it is that rrrascal Jacques! I will tell you. This evening I go into the gateway next my house – Café des Bons Camarades – to enter by the side door, and – paf! – a shawl is fling across my face from behind – it is pull tight – there is a knee in my back – I can catch nothing with my hand – it smell all hot in my throat – I choke and I fall over – there is no more. I wake up and I see my wife, and she take me into the house. I am all muddy and tired, but I feel – and I have lost my property – it is a diamond – and my cousin Jacques, he has done it!'

'Are you sure of that?'

'Sure? Oh yes – it is certain, I tell you – certain!'

'Then why not inform the police?'

The visitor was clearly taken aback by this question. He faltered, and looked searchingly in Dorrington's face. 'That is not always the convenient way,' he said. 'I would rather that you do it. It is the diamond that I want – not to punish my cousin – thief that he is!'

Dorrington mended a quill with ostentatious care, saying encouragingly as he did so, 'I can quite understand that you may not wish to prosecute your cousin – only to recover the diamond you speak of. Also I can quite understand that there may be reasons – family reasons perhaps, perhaps others – which may render it inadvisable to make even the existence of the jewel known more than absolutely necessary. For instance, there may be other claimants, Monsieur Léon Bouvier.'

The visitor started. 'You know my name then?' he asked. 'How is that?'

Dorrington smiled the smile of a sphinx. 'M Bouvier,' he said, 'it is my trade to know everything – everything.' He put the pen down and gazed whimsically at the other. 'My agents are everywhere. You talk of the secret agents of the Russian police – they are nothing. It is my trade to know all things. For instance' – Dorrington unlocked a drawer and produced a book (it was but an office diary), and, turning its pages, went on. 'Let me see – B. It is my trade, for instance, to know about the Café des Bons Camarades, established by the late Madame Bouvier, now unhappily deceased. It is my trade to know of Madame Bouvier at Bonneuil, where the charcoal was burnt, and where Madame Bouvier was unfortunately left a widow at the time of the siege of Paris, because of some lamentable misunderstanding of her husband's with a file of Prussian soldiers by an orchard wall. It is my trade, moreover, to know something of the sad death of that husband's brother – in a pit – and of the later death of his widow. Oh yes. More,' (turning a page attentively, as though following detailed notes) 'it is my trade to know of a little quarrel between those brothers – it might even have been about a diamond, just such a diamond as you have come about tonight – and of jewels missed from the Tuileries in the great Revolution a hundred years ago.' He shut the book with a bang and returned it to its place. 'And there are other things – too many to talk about,' he said, crossing his legs and smiling calmly at the Frenchman.

During this long pretence at reading, Bouvier had slid farther and farther forward on his chair, till he sat on the edge, his eyes staring wide, and his chin dropped. He had been pale when he arrived, but now he was of a leaden grey. He said not a word.

Dorrington laughed lightly. 'Come,' he said, 'I see you are astonished. Very likely. Very few of the people and families whose *dossiers* we have here' (he waved his hand generally about the room) 'are aware of what we know. But we don't make a song of it, I assure you, unless it is for the benefit of clients. A client's affairs are sacred, of course, and our resources are at his disposal. Do I understand that you become a client?'

Bouvier sat a little farther back on his chair and closed his mouth. 'A – a – yes,' he answered at length, with an effort, moistening his lips as he spoke. 'That is why I come.'

'Ah, now we shall understand each other,' Dorrington replied genially, opening an ink-pot and clearing his blotting-pad. 'We're not connected with the police here, or anything of that sort, and except so far as we can help them we leave our client's affairs alone. You wish to be a client, and you wish me to recover your lost diamond. Very well, that is business. The first thing is the usual fee in advance – twenty guineas. Will you write a cheque?'

Bouvier had recovered some of his self-possession, and he hesitated. 'It is a large fee,' he said.

'Large? Nonsense! It is the sort of fee that might easily be swallowed up in half a day's expenses. And besides – a rich diamond merchant like yourself!'

Bouvier looked up quickly. 'Diamond merchant?' he said. 'I do not understand. I have lost my diamond – there was but one.'

'And yet you go to Hatton Garden every day.'

'What!' cried Bouvier, letting his hand fall from the table, 'you know that too?'

'Of course,' Dorrington laughed, easily; 'it is my trade, I tell you. But write the cheque.'

Bouvier produced a crumpled and dirty cheque-book and complied, with many pauses, looking up dazedly from time to time into Dorrington's face.

'Now,' said Dorrington, 'tell me where you kept your diamond, and all about it.'

'It was in an old little wooden box – so.' Bouvier, not yet quite master of himself, sketched an oblong of something less than three inches long by two broad. 'The box was old and black – my grandfather may have made it, or his father. The lid fitted very tight, and the inside was packed with fine charcoal powder with the diamond resting in it. The diamond – oh, it was great; like that – so.' He made another sketch, roughly square, an inch and a quarter across. 'But it looked even much greater still, so bright, so wonderful! It is easy to understand that my grandfather did not sell it – beside the danger. It is so beautiful a thing, and it is such great riches – all in one little box. Why should not a poor charcoal-burner be rich in secret, and look at his diamond, and get all the few things he wants by burning his charcoal? And there was the danger. But that is long ago. I am a man of beesness, and I desired to sell it and be rich. And that Jacques – he has stolen it!'

'Let us keep to the point. The diamond was in a box. Well, where was the box?'

'On the outside of the box there were notches – so, and so. Round the box at each place there was a tight, strong, silk cord – that is two cords. The cords were round my neck, under my shirt, so. And the box was under my arm – just as a boy carries his satchel, but high up – in the armpit, where I could feel it at all times. Tonight, when I come to myself, my collar was broken at the stud – see – the cords were cut – and all was gone!'

'You say your cousin Jacques has done this. How do you know?'

'Ah! But who else? Who else could know? And he has always tried to steal it. At first, I let him wait at the Café des Bons Camarades. What does he do? He pries about my house, and opens drawers; and I catch him at last looking in a box, and I turn him out. And he calls me a thief! *Sacré!* He goes – I have no more of him; and so – he does this!'

'Very well. Write down his name and address on this piece of paper, and your own.' Bouvier did so. 'And now tell me what you have been doing at Hatton Garden.'

'Well, it was a very great diamond – I could not go to the first man and show it to sell. I must make myself known.'

'It never struck you to get the stone cut in two, did it?'

'Eh? What? – *Nom de chien!* No!' He struck his knee with his hand. 'Fool! Why did I not think of that? But still' – he grew more thoughtful – 'I should have to show it to get it cut, and I did not know where to go. And the value would have been less.'

'Just so – but it's the regular thing to do, I may tell you, in cases like this. But go on. About Hatton Garden, you know.'

'I thought that I must make myself known among the merchants of diamonds, and then, perhaps, I should learn the ways, and one day be able to sell. As it was, I knew nothing – nothing at all. I

waited, and I saved money in the café. Then, when I could do it,
I dressed well and went and bought some diamonds of a dealer –
very little diamonds, a little trayful for twenty pounds, and I try
to sell them again. But I have paid too much – I can only sell for
fifteen pounds. Then I buy more, and sell them for what I give.
Then I take an office in Hatton Garden – that is, I share a room
with a dealer, and there is a partition between our desks. My wife
attends the café, I go to Hatton Garden to buy and sell. It loses me
money, but I must lose till I can sell the great diamond. I get to
know the dealers more and more, and then tonight, as I go home
–' he finished with an expressive shrug and a wave of the hand.

'Yes, yes, I think I see,' Dorrington said. 'As to the diamond
again. It doesn't happen to be a *blue* diamond, does it?'

'No – pure white; perfect.'

Dorrington had asked because two especially famous diamonds
disappeared from among the French Crown Jewels at the time of
the great Revolution. One blue, the greatest coloured diamond
ever known, and the other the 'Mirror of Portugal'. Bouvier's
reply made it plain that it was certainly not the first which he had
just lost.

'Come,' Dorrington said, 'I will call and inspect the scene of
your disaster. I haven't dined yet, and it must be well past nine
o'clock now.'

They returned to Beck Street. There were gates at the dark
entry by the side of the Café des Bons Camarades, but they were
never shut, Bouvier explained. Dorrington had them shut now,
however, and a lantern was produced. The paving was of rough
cobble stones, deep in mud.

'Do many people come down here in the course of an evening?'
Dorrington asked.

'Never anybody but myself.'

'Very well. Stand away at your side door.'

Bouvier and his wife stood huddled and staring on the threshold
of the side door, while Dorrington, with the lantern, explored the
muddy cobble stones. The pieces of a broken bottle lay in a little

137

heap, and a cork lay a yard away from them. Dorrington smelt the cork, and then collected together the broken glass (there were but four or five pieces) from the little heap. Another piece of glass lay by itself a little way off, and this also Dorrington took up, scrutinising it narrowly. Then he traversed the whole passage carefully, stepping from bare stone to bare stone, and skimming the ground with the lantern. The mud lay confused and trackless in most places, though the place where Bouvier had been lying was indicated by an appearance of sweeping, caused, no doubt, by his wife dragging him to his feet. Only one other thing beside the glass and cork did Dorrington carry away as evidence, and that the Bouviers knew nothing of; for it was the remembrance of the mark of a sharp, small boot-heel in more than one patch of mud between the stones.

'Will you object, Madame Bouvier,' he asked, as he handed back the lantern, 'to show me the shoes you wore when you found your husband lying out here?'

Madame Bouvier had no objection at all. They were what she was then wearing, and had worn all day. She lifted her foot and exhibited one. There was no need for a second glance. It was a loose easy cashmere boot, with spring sides and heels cut down flat for indoor comfort.

'And this was at what time?'

It was between seven and eight o'clock, both agreed, though they differed a little as to the exact time. Bouvier had recovered when his wife raised him, had entered the house with her, at once discovered his loss, and immediately, on his wife's advice, set out to find Dorrington, whose name the woman had heard spoken of frequently among the visitors to the café in connection with the affair of the secret society already alluded to. He had felt certain that Dorrington would not be at his office, but trusted to be directed where to find him.

'Now,' Dorrington asked of Bouvier (the woman had been called away), 'tell me some more about your cousin. Where does he live?'

'In Little Norham Street; the third house from this end on the right and the back room at the top. That is unless he has moved just lately.'

'Has he been ill recently?'

'Ill?' Bouvier considered. 'Not that I can say – no. I have never heard of Jacques being ill.' It seemed to strike him as an incongruous and new idea. 'Nothing has made him ill all his life – he is too good in constitution, I think.'

'Does he wear spectacles?'

'Spectacles? *Mais non!* Never! Why should he wear spectacles? His eyes are good as mine.'

'Very well. Now attend. Tomorrow you must not go to Hatton Garden – I will go for you. If you see your cousin Jacques you must say nothing, take no notice; let everything proceed as though nothing had happened; leave all to me. Give me your address at Hatton Garden.'

'But what is it you must do there?'

'That is my business. I do my business in my own way. Still I will give you a hint. Where is it that diamonds are sold? In Hatton Garden, as you so well know – as I expect your cousin knows if he has been watching you. Then where will your cousin go to sell it? Hatton Garden, of course. Never mind what I shall do there to intercept it. I am to be your new partner, you understand, bringing money into the business. You must be ill and stay at home till you hear from me. Go now and write me a letter of introduction to the man who shares the office with you. Or I will write it if you like, and you shall sign it. What sort of a man is he?'

'Very quiet – a tall man, perhaps English, but perhaps not.'

'Ever buy or sell diamonds with him?'

'Once only. It was the first time. That is how I learned of the half-office to let.'

The letter was written, and Dorrington stuffed it carelessly into his pocket. 'Mr Hamer is the name, is it?' he said. 'I fancy I have met him somewhere. He is short-sighted, isn't he?'

'Oh yes, he is short-sighted. With *pince-nez.*'

'Not very well lately?'

'No – I think not. He takes medicine in the office. But you will be careful, eh? He must not know.'

'Do you think so? Perhaps I may tell him, though.'

'Tell him? *Ciel* – no! You must not tell people! No!'

'Shall I throw the whole case over, and keep your deposit fee?'

'No – no, not that. But it is foolish to tell to people!'

'I am to judge what is foolish and what wise, M Bouvier. Good evening!'

'Good evening, M Dorrington; good evening.' Bouvier followed him out to the gate. 'And will you tell me – do you think there is a way to get the diamond? Have you any plan?'

'Oh yes, M Bouvier, I have a plan. But, as I have said, that is my business. It may be a successful plan, or it may not; that we shall see.'

'And – and the *dossier.* The notes that you so marvellously have, written out in the book you read. When this business is over you will destroy them, eh? You will not leave a clue?'

'The notes that I have in my books,' answered Dorrington, without relaxing a muscle of his face, 'are my property, for my own purposes, and were mine before you came to me. Those relating to you are a mere item in thousands. So long as you behave well, M Bouvier, they will not harm you, and, as I said, the confidences of a client are sacred to Dorrington & Hicks. But as to keeping them – certainly I shall. Once more – good evening!'

Even the stony-faced Dorrington could not repress a smile and something very like a chuckle as he turned the end of the street and struck out across Golden Square towards his rooms in Conduit Street. The simple Frenchman, only half a rogue – even less than half – was now bamboozled and put aside as effectually as his cousin had been. Certainly there was a diamond, and an immense one; if only the Bouvier tradition were true, probably the famous 'Mirror of Portugal'; and nothing stood between Dorrington and absolute possession of that diamond but an ordinary sort of case such as he dealt with every day. And he had made Bouvier pay a fee for the privilege of putting him completely on the track of it! Dorrington smiled again.

His dinner was spoilt by waiting, but he troubled little of that. He spread before him, and examined again, the pieces of glass and the cork. The bottle had been a druggist's ordinary flat bottle, graduated with dose-marks, and altogether seven inches high, or thereabout. It had, without a doubt, contained the chloroform wherewith Léon Bouvier had been assaulted, as Dorrington had judged from the smell of the cork. The fact of the bottle being corked showed that the chloroform had not been bought all at once – since in that case it would have been put up in a stoppered bottle. More probably it had been procured in very small quantities (ostensibly for toothache, or something of that kind) at different druggists, and put together in this larger bottle, which had originally been used for something else. The bottle had been distinguished by a label – the usual white label affixed by the druggist, with directions as to taking the medicine – and this label had been scraped off; all except a small piece at the bottom edge by the right hand side, whereon might be just distinguished the greater part of the letters N, E. The piece of glass that had lain a little way apart from the bottle was not a part of it, as a casual observer might have supposed. It was a fragment of a concave lens, with a channel ground in the edge.

III

At ten precisely next morning, as usual, Mr Ludwig Hamer mounted the stairs of the house in Hatton Garden, wherein he rented half a room as office. He was a tall, fair man, wearing thick convex *pince-nez*. He spoke English like a native, and, indeed, he called himself an Englishman, though there were those who doubted the Briticism of his name. Scarce had he entered his office when Dorrington followed him.

The room had never been a very large one, and now a partition divided it in two, leaving a passage at one side only, by the window. On each side of this partition stood a small pedestal table, a couple of chairs, a copying-press, and the other articles usual in a meagrely furnished office. Dorrington strode past Bouvier's half of the room and came upon Hamer as he was hanging his coat on a peg. The letter of introduction had been burnt, since Dorrington had only asked for it in order to get Hamer's name and the Hatton Garden address without betraying to Bouvier the fact that he did not already know all about it.

'Good morning, Mr Hamer,' said Dorrington, loudly. 'Sorry to see you're not well' – he pointed familiarly with his stick at a range of medicine bottles on the mantelpiece – 'but it's very trying weather, of course. You've been suffering from toothache, I believe?'

Hamer seemed at first disposed to resent the loudness and familiarity of this speech, but at the reference to toothache he started suddenly and set his lips.

'Chloroform's a capital thing for toothache, Mr Hamer, and for – for other things. I'm not in your line of business myself, but I believe it has even been used in the diamond trade.'

'What do you mean?' asked Hamer, flushing angrily.

'Mean? Why, bless me – nothing more than I said. By the way, I'm afraid you dropped one of your medicine bottles last night. I've brought it back, though I'm afraid it's past repair. It's a good job you didn't quite clear the label off before you took it out with you, else I might have had a difficulty.' Dorrington placed the fragments on the table. 'You see you've just left the first letter of "EC" in the druggist's address, and the last "N" of Hatton Garden, just before it. There doesn't happen to be any other Garden in EC district that I know of, nor does the name of any other thoroughfare end in N – they are mostly streets, or lanes, or courts, you see. And there seems to be only one druggist in Hatton Garden – capital fellow, no doubt – the one whose name and address I observe on those bottles on the mantelpiece.'

Dorrington stood with his foot on a chair, and tapped his knee carelessly with his stick. Hamer dropped into the other chair and regarded him with a frown, though his face was pale. Presently he said, in a strained voice, 'Well?'

'Yes; there *is* something else, Mr Hamer, as you appear to suggest. I see you're wearing a new pair of glasses this morning; pity you broke the others last night, but I've brought the piece you left behind.' He gathered up the broken bottle, and held up the piece of concave lens. 'I think, after all, it's really best to use a cord with *pince-nez*. It's awkward, and it catches in things, I know, but it saves a breakage, and you're liable to get the glasses knocked off, you know – in certain circumstances.'

Hamer sprang to his feet with a snarl, slammed the door, locked it, and turned on Dorrington. But now Dorrington had a revolver in his hand, though his manner was as genial as ever.

'Yes, yes,' he said; 'best to shut the door, of course. People listen, don't they? But sit down again. I'm not anxious to hurt you, and, as you will perceive, you're quite unable to hurt me. What I chiefly came to say is this: last evening my client, M Léon Bouvier, of this office and the Café des Bons Camarades, was attacked in the passage adjoining his house by a man who was waiting for him, with a woman – was it really Mrs Hamer? But there, I won't ask – keeping watch. He was robbed of a small old wooden box, containing charcoal and – a diamond. My name is Dorrington – firm of Dorrington & Hicks, which you may have heard of. That's my card. I've come to take away that diamond.'

Hamer was pale and angry, but, in his way, was almost as calm as Dorrington. He put down the card without looking at it. 'I don't understand you,' he said. 'How do you know I've got it?'

'Come, come, Mr Hamer,' Dorrington replied, rubbing the barrel of his revolver on his knee, 'that's hardly worthy of you. You're a man of business, with a head on your shoulders – the sort of man I like doing business with, in fact. Men like ourselves needn't trifle. I've shown you most of the cards I hold, though not all, I assure you. I'll tell you, if you like, all about your little tour round among the druggists with the convenient toothache, all about the evenings on which you watched Bouvier home, and so on. But, really, need we, as men of the world, descend to such peddling detail?'

'Well, suppose I have got it, and suppose I refuse to give it you. What then?'

'What then? But why should we talk of unpleasant things? You won't refuse, you know.'

'Do you mean you'd get it out of me by help of that pistol?'

'Well,' said Dorrington, deliberately, 'the pistol is noisy, and it makes a mess, and all that, but it's a useful thing, and I *might* do it with that, you know, in certain circumstances. But I wasn't thinking of it – there's a much less troublesome way.'

'Which?'

'You're a slower man than I took you for, Mr Hamer – or perhaps you haven't quite appreciated *me* yet. If I were to go to that window and call the police, what with the little bits of evidence in my pocket, and the other little bits that the druggists who sold the chloroform would give, and the other bits in reserve, that I prefer not to talk about just now – there would be rather an awkwardly complete case of robbery with violence, wouldn't there? And you'd have to lose the diamond after all, to say nothing of a little rest in gaol and general ruination.'

'That sounds very well, but what about your client? Come now, you call me a man of the world, and I am one. How will your client account for the possession of a diamond worth eighty thousand pounds or so? He doesn't seem a millionaire. The police would want to know about him as well as about me, if you were such a fool as to bring them in. Where did *he* steal it, eh?'

Dorrington smiled and bowed at the question. 'That's a very good card to play, Mr Hamer,' he said, 'a capital card, really. To a superficial observer it might look like winning the trick. But I think I can trump it.' He bent farther forward and tapped the table with the pistol-barrel. 'Suppose I don't care one solitary dump what becomes of my client? Suppose I don't care whether he goes to gaol or stays out of it – in short, suppose I prefer my own interests to his?'

'Ho! ho!' Hamer cried. 'I begin to understand. You want to grab the diamond for yourself then?'

'I haven't said anything of the kind, Mr Hamer,' Dorrington replied, suavely. 'I have simply demanded the diamond which you stole last night, and I have mentioned an alternative.'

'Oh, yes, yes, but we understand one another. Come, we'll arrange this. How much do you want?'

Dorrington stared at him stonily. 'I – I beg your pardon,' he said, 'but I don't understand. I want the diamond you stole.'

'But come now, we'll divide. Bouvier had no right to it, and he's out. You and I, perhaps, haven't much right to it, legally, but it's between us, and we're both in the same position.'

'Pardon me,' Dorrington replied, silkily, 'but there you mistake. We are *not* in the same position, by a long way. You are liable to an instant criminal prosecution. I have simply come, authorised by my client, who bears all the responsibility, to demand a piece of property which you have stolen. That is the difference between our positions, Mr Hamer. Come now, a policeman is just standing opposite. Shall I open the window and call him, or do you give in?'

'Oh, I give in, I suppose,' Hamer groaned. 'But you're a deal too hard. A man of your abilities shouldn't be so mean.'

'That's right and reasonable,' Dorrington answered briskly. 'The wise man is the man who knows when he is beaten, and saves further trouble. You may not find me so mean after all, but I must have the stone first. I hold the trumps, and I'm not going to let the other player make conditions. Where's the diamond?'

'It isn't here – it's at home. You'll have to get it out of Mrs Hamer. Shall I go and wire to her?'

'No, no,' said Dorrington, 'that's not the way. We'll just go together, and take Mrs Hamer by surprise, I think. I mustn't let you out of sight, you know. Come, we'll get a hansom. Is it far?'

'Bessborough Street, Pimlico. You'll find Mrs Hamer has a temper of her own.'

'Well, well, we all have our failings. But before we start, now, observe.' For a moment Dorrington was stern and menacing. 'You wriggled a little at first, but that was quite natural. Now you've given in; and at the first sign of another wriggle I stop it once and for all. Understand? No tricks, now.'

They entered a hansom at the door. Hamer was moody and silent at first, but under the influence of Dorrington's gay talk he opened out after a while. 'Well,' he said, 'you're far the cleverest of the three, no doubt, and perhaps in that way you deserve to win. It's mighty smart for you to come in like this, and push Bouvier on one side and me on the other, and both of us helpless. But it's rough on me after having all the trouble.'

'Don't be a bad loser, man!' Dorrington answered. 'You might have had a deal more trouble and a deal more roughness too, I assure you.'

'Oh yes, so I might. I'm not grumbling. But there's one thing has puzzled me all along. Where did Bouvier get that stone from?'

'He inherited it. It's the most important of the family jewels, I assure you.'

'Oh, skittles! I might have known you wouldn't tell me, even if you knew yourself. But I should like to know. What sort of a duffer must it have been that let Bouvier do him for that big stone – Bouvier of all men in the world? Why, he was a record flat himself – couldn't tell a diamond from a glass marble, I should think. Why, he used to buy peddling little trays of rotters in the Garden at twice their value! And then he'd sell them for what he could get. I knew very well he wasn't going on systematically dropping money like that for no reason at all. He had some axe to grind, that was plain. And after a while he got asking timid questions as to the sale of big diamonds, and how it was done, and who bought them, and all that. That put me on it at once. All this buying and selling at a loss was a blind.

He wanted to get into the trade to sell stolen diamonds, that was clear; and there was some value in them too, else he couldn't afford to waste months of time and lose money every day over it. So I kept my eye on him. I noticed, when he put his overcoat on, and thought I wasn't looking, he would settle a string of some sort round his neck, under his shirt-collar, and feel to pack up something close under his armpit. Then I just watched him home, and saw the sort of shanty he lived in. I mentioned these things to Mrs H, and she was naturally indignant at the idea of a chap like Bouvier having something valuable in a dishonest way, and agreed with me that if possible it ought to be got from him, if only in the interests of virtue.' Hamer laughed jerkily. 'So at any rate we determined to get a look at whatever it was hanging round his neck, and we made the arrangements you know about. It seemed to me that Bouvier was pretty sure to lose it before long, one way or another, if it had any value at all, to judge by the way he was done in other matters. But I assure you I nearly fell down like Bouvier himself when I saw what it was. No wonder we left the bottle behind where I'd dropped it, after soaking the shawl – I wonder I didn't leave the shawl itself, and my hat, and everything. I assure you we sat up half last night looking at that wonderful stone!'

'No doubt. I shall have a good look at it myself, I assure you. Here is Bessborough Street. Which is the number?'

They alighted, and entered a house rather smaller than those about it. 'Ask Mrs Hamer to come here,' said Hamer, gloomily, to the servant.

The men sat in the drawing-room. Presently Mrs Hamer entered – a shortish, sharp, keen-eyed woman of forty-five. 'This is Mr Dorrington,' said Hamer, 'of Dorrington & Hicks, private detectives. He wants us to give him that diamond.'

The little woman gave a sort of involuntary bounce, and exclaimed. 'What? Diamond? What d'ye mean?'

'Oh, it's no good, Maria,' Hamer answered dolefully. 'I've tried it every way myself. One comfort is we're safe, as long as we give it up. Here,' he added, turning to Dorrington, 'show her some of your evidence – that'll convince her.'

Very politely Dorrington brought forth, with full explanations, the cork and the broken glass; while Mrs Hamer, biting hard at her thin lips, grew shinier and redder in the face every moment, and her hard grey eyes flashed fury.

'And you let this man,' she burst out to her husband, when Dorrington had finished, 'you let this man leave your office with these things in his possession after he had shown them to you, and you as big as he is, and bigger! Coward!'

'My dear, you don't appreciate Mr Dorrington's forethought, hang it! I made preparations for the very line of action you recommend, but he was ready. He brought out a very well kept revolver, and he has it in his pocket now!'

Mrs Hamer only glared, speechless with anger.

'You might just get Mr Dorrington a whisky and soda, Maria,' Hamer pursued, with a slight lift of the eyebrows which he did not intend Dorrington to see. The woman was on her feet in a moment.

'Thank you, no,' interposed Dorrington, rising also, 'I won't trouble you. I'd rather not drink anything just now, and, although I fear I may appear rude, I can't allow either of you to leave the room. In short,' he added, 'I must stay with you both till I get the diamond.'

'And this man Bouvier,' asked Mrs Hamer, 'what is his right to the stone?'

'Really, I don't feel competent to offer an opinion, do you know,' Dorrington answered sweetly. 'To tell the truth, M Bouvier doesn't interest me very much.'

'No go, Maria!' growled Hamer. 'I've tried it all. The fact is we've got to give Dorrington the diamond. If we don't he'll just call in the police – then we shall lose the diamond and everything else too. He doesn't care what becomes of Bouvier. He's got us, that's what it is. He won't even bargain to give us a share.'

Mrs Hamer looked quickly up. 'Oh, but that's nonsense!' she

said. 'We've got the thing. We ought at least to say halves.'

Her sharp eyes searched Dorrington's face, but there was no encouragement in it. 'I am sorry to disappoint a lady,' he said, 'but this time it is my business to impose terms, not to submit to them. Come, the diamond!'

'Well, you'll give us something, surely?' the woman cried.

'Nothing is sure, madam, except that you will give me that diamond, or face a policeman in five minutes!'

The woman realised her helplessness. 'Well,' she said, 'much good may it do you. You'll have to come and get it – I'm keeping it somewhere else. I'll go and get my hat.'

Again Dorrington interposed. 'I think we'll send your servant for the hat,' he said, reaching for the bell-rope. 'I'll come wherever you like, but I shall not leave you till this affair is settled, I promise you. And, as I reminded your husband a little time ago, you'll find tricks come expensive.'

The servant brought Mrs Hamer's hat and cloak, and that lady put them on, her eyes ablaze with anger. Dorrington made the pair walk before him to the front door, and followed them into the street. 'Now,' he said, 'where is this place? Remember, no tricks!'

Mrs Hamer turned towards Vauxhall Bridge. 'It's just over by Upper Kennington Lane,' she said. 'Not far.'

She paced out before them, Dorrington and Hamer following, the former affable and business-like, the latter apparently a little puzzled. When they came about the middle of the bridge, the woman turned suddenly. 'Come, Mr Dorrington,' she said, in a more subdued voice than she had yet used, 'I give in. It's no use trying to shake you off, I can see. I have the diamond with me. Here.'

She put a little old black wooden box in his hand. He made to open the lid, which fitted tightly, and at that moment the woman, pulling her other hand free from under her cloak, flung away over the parapet something that shone like fifty points of electric light.

'There it goes!' she screamed aloud, pointing with her finger. 'There's your diamond, you dirty thief! You bully! Go after it now, you spy!'

The great diamond made a curve of glitter and disappeared into the river.

For the moment Dorrington lost his cool temper. He seized the woman by the arm. 'Do you know what you've done, you wild cat?' he exclaimed.

'Yes, I do!' the woman screamed, almost foaming with passion, while boys began to collect, though there had been but few people on the bridge. 'Yes, I do! And now you can do what you please, you thief! You bully!'

Dorrington was calm again in a moment. He shrugged his shoulders and turned away. Hamer was frightened. He came at Dorrington's side and faltered, 'I – I told you she had a temper. What will you do?'

Dorrington forced a laugh. 'Oh, nothing,' he said. 'What can I do? Locking you up now wouldn't fetch the diamond back. And besides I'm not sure that Mrs Hamer won't attend to your punishment faithfully enough.' And he walked briskly away.

'What did she do, Bill?' asked one boy of another.

'Why, didn't ye see? She chucked that man's watch in the river.'

'Garn! That wasn't his watch!' interrupted a third, 'it was a little glass tumbler. I see it!'

* * * * *

'Have you got my diamond?' asked the agonised Léon Bouvier of Dorrington a day later.

'No, I have not,' Dorrington replied drily. 'Nor has your cousin Jacques. But I know where it is, and you can get it as easily as I.'

'*Mon Dieu!* Where?'

'At the bottom of the River Thames, exactly in the centre, rather to the right of Vauxhall Bridge, looking from this side. I expect it will be rediscovered in some future age, when the bed of the Thames is a diamond field.'

The rest of Bouvier's savings went in the purchase of a boat, and in this, with a pail on a long rope, he was very busy for some time afterward. But he only got a great deal of mud into his boat.

MARTIN HEWITT

Created by Arthur Morrison (1863–1945)

Of all the rivals of Sherlock Holmes who sprang up in the years immediately following Conan Doyle's startling success with his detective, the most consistently admired was Arthur Morrison's Martin Hewitt. Hewitt shares many characteristics with Holmes. Like Holmes, he is profoundly knowledgeable in all sorts of arcane subjects and possesses a ruthlessly logical mind. Like the stories of the sage of Baker Street, Hewitt's adventures mostly appeared in the pages of The Strand Magazine *and were illustrated by Sydney Paget. He has his own Watson in the journalist Brett who narrates the stories. He even has his own version of Moriarty in the master criminal Mayes whom he faces in a series of interlinked stories in* The Red Triangle. *In other ways, though, Hewitt is Holmes's antithesis. A lawyer's clerk turned private detective, with offices on the Strand, he is not a flamboyant eccentric but a 'stoutish, clean-shaven man, of middle height, and of a cheerful, round countenance'. Unlike Holmes, who does little to dispel the belief that he is some kind of genius, Hewitt maintains that he 'has no system beyond a judicious use of ordinary faculties'. Indeed, as Morrison is at pains to point out, presumably with a nod in the direction of Conan Doyle's creation, 'the man had always as little of the aspect of the conventional detective as may be imagined'. In total, Martin Hewitt appeared in twenty-five short stories which were later collected in four volumes –* Martin Hewitt, Investigator *(1894),* The Chronicles of Martin Hewitt *(1895),* The Adventures of Martin Hewitt *(1896) and* The Red Triangle *(1903).*

ARTHUR MORRISON

THE IVY COTTAGE MYSTERY

I had been working double tides for a month: at night on my morning paper, as usual; and in the morning on an evening paper as *locum tenens* for another man who was taking a holiday. This was an exhausting plan of work, although it only actually involved some six hours' attendance a day, or less, at the two offices. I turned up at the headquarters of my own paper at ten in the evening, and by the time I had seen the editor, selected a subject, written my leader, corrected the slips, chatted, smoked, and so on, and cleared off, it was very usually one o'clock. This meant bed at two, or even three, after supper at the club.

This was all very well at ordinary periods, when any time in the morning would do for rising, but when I had to be up again soon after seven, and round at the evening paper office by eight, I naturally felt a little worn and disgusted with things by midday, after a sharp couple of hours' leaderette scribbling and paragraphing, with attendant sundries.

But the strain was over, and on the first day of comparative comfort I indulged in a midday breakfast and the first undisgusted glance at a morning paper for a month. I felt rather interested in an inquest, begun the day before, on the body of a man whom I had known very slightly before I took to living in chambers.

His name was Gavin Kingscote, and he was an artist of a casual and desultory sort, having, I believe, some small private means of his own. As a matter of fact, he had boarded in the same house in which I had lodged myself for a while, but as I was at the time a late homer and a fairly early riser, taking no regular board in the house, we never became much acquainted. He had since, I understood, made some judicious Stock Exchange speculations, and had set up house in Finchley.

Now the news was that he had been found one morning murdered in his smoking-room, while the room itself, with others, was in a state of confusion. His pockets had been rifled, and his watch and chain were gone, with one or two other small

153

articles of value. On the night of the tragedy a friend had sat smoking with him in the room where the murder took place, and he had been the last person to see Mr Kingscote alive. A jobbing gardener, who kept the garden in order by casual work from time to time, had been arrested in consequence of footprints exactly corresponding with his boots, having been found on the garden beds near the French window of the smoking-room.

I finished my breakfast and my paper, and Mrs Clayton, the housekeeper, came to clear my table. She was sister of my late landlady of the house where Kingscote had lodged, and it was by this connection that I had found my chambers. I had not seen the housekeeper since the crime was first reported, so I now said:

'This is shocking news of Mr Kingscote, Mrs Clayton. Did you know him yourself?'

She had apparently only been waiting for some such remark to burst out with whatever information she possessed.

'Yes, sir,' she exclaimed, 'shocking indeed. Pore young feller! I see him often when I was at my sister's, and he was always a nice, quiet gentleman, so different from some. My sister, she's awful cut up, sir, I assure you. And what d'you think 'appened, sir, only last Tuesday? You remember Mr Kingscote's room where he painted the woodwork so beautiful with gold flowers, and blue, and pink? He used to tell my sister she'd always have something to remember him by. Well, two young fellers, gentlemen I can't call them, come and took that room (it being to let), and went and scratched off all the paint in mere wicked mischief, and then chopped up all the panels into sticks and bits! Nice sort o' gentlemen them! And then they bolted in the morning, being afraid, I s'pose, of being made to pay after treating a pore widder's property like that. That was only Tuesday, and the very next day the pore young gentleman himself's dead, murdered in his own 'ouse, and him going to be married an' all! Dear, dear! I remember once he said —'

Mrs Clayton was a good soul, but once she began to talk someone else had to stop her. I let her run on for a reasonable time, and then rose and prepared to go out. I remembered very well the panels that had been so mischievously destroyed. They made the room the show-room of the house, which was an old one. They were indeed less than half finished when I came away, and Mrs Lamb, the landlady, had shown them to me one day when Kingscote was out. All the walls of the room were panelled and painted white, and Kingscote had put upon them an eccentric but charming decoration, obviously suggested by some of the work of Mr Whistler. Tendrils, flowers, and butterflies in a quaint convention wandered thinly from panel to panel, giving the otherwise rather uninteresting room an unwonted atmosphere of richness and elegance. The lamentable jackasses who had destroyed this had certainly selected the best feature of the room whereon to inflict their senseless mischief.

I strolled idly downstairs, with no particular plan for the afternoon in my mind, and looked in at Hewitt's offices. Hewitt was reading a note, and after a little chat he informed me that it had been left an hour ago, in his absence, by the brother of the man I had just been speaking of.

'He isn't quite satisfied,' Hewitt said, 'with the way the police are investigating the case, and asks me to run down to Finchley and look round. Yesterday I should have refused, because I have five cases in progress already, but today I find that circumstances have given me a day or two. Didn't you say you knew the man?'

'Scarcely more than by sight. He was a boarder in the house at Chelsea where I stayed before I started chambers.'

'Ah, well; I think I shall look into the thing. Do you feel particularly interested in the case? I mean, if you've nothing better to do, would you come with me?'

'I shall be very glad,' I said. 'I was in some doubt what to do with myself. Shall you start at once?'

'I think so. Kerrett, just call a cab. By the way, Brett, which paper has the fullest report of the inquest yesterday? I'll run over it as we go down.'

As I had only seen one paper that morning, I could not answer

Hewitt's question. So we bought various papers as we went along in the cab, and I found the reports while Martin Hewitt studied them. Summarised, this was the evidence given –

Sarah Dodson, general servant, deposed that she had been in service at Ivy Cottage, the residence of the deceased, for five months, the only other regular servant being the housekeeper and cook. On the evening of the previous Tuesday both servants retired a little before eleven, leaving Mr Kingscote with a friend in the smoking or sitting-room. She never saw her master again alive. On coming downstairs the following morning and going to open the smoking-room windows, she was horrified to discover the body of Mr Kingscote lying on the floor of the room with blood about the head. She at once raised an alarm, and, on the instructions of the housekeeper, fetched a doctor, and gave information to the police. In answer to questions, witness stated she had heard no noise of any sort during the night, nor had anything suspicious occurred.

Hannah Carr, housekeeper and cook, deposed that she had been in the late Mr Kingscote's service since he had first taken Ivy Cottage – a period of rather more than a year. She had last seen the deceased alive on the evening of the previous Tuesday, at half past ten, when she knocked at the door of the smoking-room, where Mr Kingscote was sitting with a friend, to ask if he would require anything more. Nothing was required, so witness shortly after went to bed. In the morning she was called by the previous witness, who had just gone downstairs, and found the body of deceased lying as described. Deceased's watch and chain were gone, as also was a ring he usually wore, and his pockets appeared to have been turned out. All the ground floor of the house was in confusion, and a bureau, a writing table, and various drawers were open – a bunch of keys usually carried by deceased being left hanging at one keyhole. Deceased had drawn some money from the bank on the Tuesday, for current expenses; how much she did not know. She had not heard or seen anything suspicious during the night. Besides Dodson and herself, there were no regular servants; there was a charwoman, who came occasionally, and a jobbing gardener, living near, who was called in as required.

Mr James Vidler, surgeon, had been called by the first witness between seven and eight on Wednesday morning. He found the deceased lying on his face on the floor of the smoking-room, his feet being about eighteen inches from the window, and his head lying in the direction of the fireplace. He found three large contused wounds on the head, any one of which would probably have caused death. The wounds had all been inflicted, apparently, with the same blunt instrument – probably a club or life preserver, or other similar weapon. They could not have been done with the poker. Death was due to concussion of the brain, and deceased had probably been dead seven or eight hours when witness saw him. He had since examined the body more closely, but found no marks at all indicative of a struggle having taken place; indeed, from the position of the wounds and their severity, he should judge that the deceased had been attacked unawares from behind, and had died at once. The body appeared to be perfectly healthy.

Then there was police evidence, which showed that all the doors and windows were found shut and completely fastened, except the front door, which, although shut, was not bolted. There were shutters behind the French windows in the smoking-room, and these were found fastened. No money was found in the bureau, nor in any of the opened drawers, so that if any had been there, it had been stolen. The pockets were entirely empty, except for a small pair of nail scissors, and there was no watch upon the body, nor a ring. Certain footprints were found on the garden beds, which had led the police to take certain steps. No footprints were to be seen on the garden path, which was hard gravel.

Mr Alexander Campbell, stockbroker, stated that he had known deceased for some few years, and had done business for him. He and Mr Kingscote frequently called on one another, and on Tuesday evening they dined together at Ivy Cottage. They sat smoking and chatting till nearly twelve o'clock, when Mr Kingscote himself let him out, the servants having gone to bed. Here the witness proceeded rather excitedly: 'That is all I know of this horrible business, and I can say nothing else. What the police mean by following and watching me —'

The Coroner: 'Pray be calm, Mr Campbell. The police must do what seems best to them in a case of this sort. I am sure you would not have them neglect any means of getting at the truth.'

Witness: 'Certainly not. But if they suspect me, why don't they say so? It is intolerable that I should be —'

The Coroner: 'Order, order, Mr Campbell. You are here to give evidence.'

The witness then, in answer to questions, stated that the French windows of the smoking-room had been left open during the evening, the weather being very warm. He could not recollect whether or not deceased closed them before he left, but he certainly did not close the shutters. Witness saw nobody near the house when he left.

Mr Douglas Kingscote, architect, said deceased was his brother. He had not seen him for some months, living as he did in another part of the country. He believed his brother was fairly well off, and he knew that he had made a good amount by speculation in the last year or two. Knew of no person who would be likely to owe his brother a grudge, and could suggest no motive for the crime except ordinary robbery. His brother was to have been married in a few weeks. Questioned further on this point, witness said that the marriage was to have taken place a year ago, and it was with that view that Ivy Cottage, deceased's residence, was taken. The lady, however, sustained a domestic bereavement, and afterwards went abroad with her family: she was, witness believed, shortly expected back to England.

William Bates, jobbing gardener, who was brought up in custody, was cautioned, but elected to give evidence. Witness, who appeared to be much agitated, admitted having been in the garden of Ivy Cottage at four in the morning, but said that he had only gone to attend to certain plants, and knew absolutely nothing of the murder. He however admitted that he had no order for work beyond what he had done the day before. Being further pressed, witness made various contradictory statements, and finally said that he had gone to take certain plants away.

The inquest was then adjourned.

This was the case as it stood – apparently not a case presenting any very striking feature, although there seemed to me to be doubtful peculiarities in many parts of it. I asked Hewitt what he thought.

'Quite impossible to think anything, my boy, just yet; wait till we see the place. There are any number of possibilities. Kingscote's friend, Campbell, may have come in again, you know, by way of the window – or he may not. Campbell may have owed him money or something – or he may not. The anticipated wedding may have something to do with it – or, again, *that* may not. There is no limit to the possibilities, as far as we can see from this report – a mere dry husk of the affair. When we get closer we shall examine the possibilities by the light of more detailed information. One *probability* is that the wretched gardener is innocent. It seems to me that his was only a comparatively blameless manœuvre not unheard of at other times in his trade. He came at four in the morning to steal away the flowers he had planted the day before, and felt rather bashful when questioned on the point. Why should he trample on the beds, else? I wonder if the police thought to examine the beds for traces of rooting up, or questioned the housekeeper as to any plants being missing? But we shall see.'

We chatted at random as the train drew near Finchley, and I mentioned *inter alia* the wanton piece of destruction perpetrated at Kingscote's late lodgings. Hewitt was interested.

'That was curious,' he said, 'very curious. Was anything else damaged? Furniture and so forth?'

'I don't know. Mrs Clayton said nothing of it, and I didn't ask her. But it was quite bad enough as it was. The decoration was really good, and I can't conceive a meaner piece of tomfoolery than such an attack on a decent woman's property.'

Then Hewitt talked of other cases of similar stupid damage by creatures inspired by a defective sense of humour, or mere love of mischief. He had several curious and sometimes funny anecdotes of such affairs at museums and picture exhibitions, where the damage had been so great as to induce the authorities to call him in to discover the offender. The work was not always easy, chiefly from the mere absence of intelligible motive; nor, indeed, always successful. One of the anecdotes related to a case of malicious damage to a picture – the outcome of blind artistic jealousy – a case which had been hushed up by a large expenditure in compensation. It would considerably startle most people, could it be printed here, with the actual names of the parties concerned.

Ivy Cottage, Finchley, was a compact little house, standing in a compact little square of garden, little more than a third of an acre, or perhaps no more at all. The front door was but a dozen yards or so back from the road, but the intervening space was well treed and shrubbed. Mr Douglas Kingscote had not yet returned from town, but the housekeeper, an intelligent, matronly woman, who knew of his intention to call in Martin Hewitt, was ready to show us the house.

'First,' Hewitt said, when we stood in the smoking-room, 'I observe that somebody has shut the drawers and the bureau. That is unfortunate. Also, the floor has been washed and the carpet taken up, which is much worse. That, I suppose, was because the police had finished their examination, but it doesn't help me to make one at all. Has *anything* – anything *at all* – been left as it was on Tuesday morning?'

'Well, sir, you see everything was in such a muddle,' the housekeeper began, 'and when the police had done –'

'Just so. I know. You "set it to rights", eh? Oh, that setting to rights! It has lost me a fortune at one time and another. As to the other rooms, now, have they been set to rights?'

'Such as was disturbed have been put right, sir, of course.'

'Which were disturbed? Let me see them. But wait a moment.'

He opened the French windows, and closely examined the catch and bolts. He knelt and inspected the holes whereinto the bolts fell, and then glanced casually at the folding shutters. He opened a drawer or two, and tried the working of the locks with the keys the housekeeper carried. They were, the housekeeper explained, Mr Kingscote's own keys. All through the lower floors Hewitt examined some things attentively and closely, and others with scarcely a glance, on a system unaccountable to me. Presently, he asked to be shown Mr Kingscote's bedroom, which had not been disturbed, 'set to rights', or slept in since the crime. Here, the housekeeper said, all drawers were kept unlocked but two – one in the wardrobe and one in the dressing table, which Mr Kingscote had always been careful to keep locked. Hewitt immediately pulled both drawers open without difficulty. Within, in addition to a few odds and ends, were papers. All the contents of these drawers had been turned over confusedly, while those of the unlocked drawers were in perfect order.

'The police,' Hewitt remarked, 'may not have observed these matters. Any more than such an ordinary thing as *this*,' he added, picking up a bent nail lying at the edge of a rug.

The housekeeper doubtless took the remark as a reference to the entire unimportance of a bent nail, but I noticed that Hewitt dropped the article quietly into his pocket.

We came away. At the front gate we met Mr Douglas Kingscote, who had just returned from town. He introduced himself, and expressed surprise at our promptitude both of coming and going.

'You can't have got anything like a clue in this short time, Mr Hewitt?' he asked.

'Well, no,' Hewitt replied, with a certain dryness, 'perhaps not. But I doubt whether a month's visit would have helped me to get anything very striking out of a washed floor and a houseful of carefully cleaned-up and "set-to-rights" rooms. Candidly, I don't think you can reasonably expect much of me. The police have a much better chance – they had the scene of the crime to examine. I have seen just such a few rooms as anyone might see in the first well-furnished house he might enter. The trail of the housemaid has overlaid all the others.'

'I'm very sorry for that; the fact was, I expected rather more of the police; and, indeed, I wasn't here in time entirely to prevent the clearing up. But still, I thought your well-known powers –'

'My dear sir, my "well-known powers" are nothing but common sense assiduously applied and made quick by habit. That won't enable me to see the invisible.'

'But can't we have the rooms put back into something of the state they were in? The cook will remember –'

'No, no. That would be worse and worse; that would only be the housemaid's trail in turn overlaid by the cook's. You must leave things with me for a little, I think.'

'Then you don't give the case up?' Mr Kingscote asked anxiously.

'Oh, no! I don't give it up just yet. Do you know anything of your brother's private papers – as they were before his death?'

'I never knew anything till after that. I have gone over them, but they are all very ordinary letters. Do you suspect a theft of papers?'

Martin Hewitt, with his hands on his stick behind him, looked sharply at the other, and shook his head. 'No,' he said, 'I can't quite say that.'

We bade Mr Douglas Kingscote good day, and walked towards the station. 'Great nuisance, that setting to rights,' Hewitt observed, on the way. 'If the place had been left alone, the job might have been settled one way or another by this time. As it is, we shall have to run over to your old lodgings.'

'My old lodgings?' I repeated, amazed. 'Why my old lodgings?'

Hewitt turned to me with a chuckle and a wide smile. 'Because we can't see the broken panel-work anywhere else,' he said. 'Let's see – Chelsea, isn't it?'

'Yes, Chelsea. But why – you don't suppose the people who

defaced the panels also murdered the man who painted them?'

'Well,' Hewitt replied, with another smile, 'that would be carrying a practical joke rather far, wouldn't it? Even for the ordinary picture damager.'

'You mean you *don't* think they did it, then? But what *do* you mean?'

'My dear fellow, I don't mean anything but what I say. Come now, this is rather an interesting case despite appearances, and it *has* interested me: so much, in fact, that I really think I forgot to offer Mr Douglas Kingscote my condolence on his bereavement. You see a problem is a problem, whether of theft, assassination, intrigue, or anything else, and I only think of it as one. The work very often makes me forget merely human sympathies. Now, you have often been good enough to express a very flattering interest in my work, and you shall have an opportunity of exercising your own common sense in the way I am always having to exercise mine. You shall see all my evidence (if I'm lucky enough to get any) as I collect it, and you shall make your own inferences. That will be a little exercise for you; the sort of exercise I should give a pupil if I had one. But I will give you what information I have, and you shall start fairly from this moment. You know the inquest evidence, such as it was, and you saw everything I did in Ivy Cottage?'

'Yes; I think so. But I'm not much the wiser.'

'Very well. Now I will tell you. What does the whole case look like? How would you class the crime?'

'I suppose as the police do. An ordinary case of murder with the object of robbery.'

'It is *not* an ordinary case. If it were, I shouldn't know as much as I do, little as that is; the ordinary cases are always difficult. The assailant did not come to commit a burglary, although he was a skilled burglar, or one of them was, if more than one were concerned. The affair has, I think, nothing to do with the expected wedding, nor had Mr Campbell anything to do in it – at any rate, personally – nor the gardener. The criminal (or one of them) was known personally to the dead man, and was well-dressed: he (or again one of them, and I think there were two) even had a chat with Mr Kingscote before the murder took place. He came to ask for something which Mr Kingscote was unwilling to part with – perhaps hadn't got. It was not a bulky thing. Now you have all my materials before you.'

'But all this doesn't look like the result of the blind spite that would ruin a man's work first and attack him bodily afterwards.'

'Spite isn't always blind, and there are other blind things besides spite; people with good eyes in their heads are blind sometimes, even detectives.'

'But where did you get all this information? What makes you suppose that this was a burglar who didn't want to burgle, and a well-dressed man, and so on?'

Hewitt chuckled and smiled again.

'I saw it – saw it, my boy, that's all,' he said. 'But here comes the train.'

On the way back to town, after I had rather minutely described Kingscote's work on the boarding-house panels, Hewitt asked me for the names and professions of such fellow lodgers in that house as I might remember. 'When did you leave yourself?' he ended.

'Three years ago, or rather more. I can remember Kingscote himself; Turner, a medical student – James Turner, I think; Harvey Challitt, diamond merchant's articled pupil – he was a bad egg entirely, he's doing five years for forgery now; by the bye he had the room we are going to see till he was marched off, and Kingscote took it – a year before I left; there was Norton– don't know what he was; "something in the City", I think; and Carter Paget, in the Admiralty Office. I don't remember any more at this moment; there were pretty frequent changes. But you can get it all from Mrs Lamb, of course.'

'Of course; and Mrs Lamb's exact address is – what?'

I gave him the address, and the conversation became disjointed. At Farringdon station, where we alighted, Hewitt called two hansoms. Preparing to enter one, he motioned me to the other, saying, 'You get straight away to Mrs Lamb's at once. She may be going to burn that splintered wood, or to set things to rights, after the manner of her kind, and you can stop her. I must make one or two small inquiries, but I shall be there half an hour after you.'

'Shall I tell her our object?'

'Only that I may be able to catch her mischievous lodgers – nothing else yet.' He jumped into the hansom and was gone.

I found Mrs Lamb still in a state of indignant perturbation over the trick served her four days before. Fortunately, she had left everything in the panelled room exactly as she had found it, with an idea of the being better able to demand or enforce reparation should her lodgers return. 'The room's theirs, you see, sir,' she said, 'till the end of the week, since they paid in advance, and they may come back and offer to make amends, although I doubt it. As pleasant-spoken a young chap as you might wish, he seemed, him as come to take the rooms. "My cousin," says he, "is rather an invalid, havin' only just got over congestion of the lungs, and he won't be in London till this evening late. He's comin' up from Birmingham," he ses, "and I hope he won't catch a fresh cold on the way, although of course we've got him muffled up plenty." He took the rooms, sir, like a gentleman, and mentioned several gentlemen's names I knew well, as had lodged here before; and then he put down on that there very table, sir,' – Mrs Lamb indicated the exact spot with her hand, as though that made the whole thing much more wonderful – 'he put down on that very table a week's rent in advance, and ses, "That's always the best sort of reference, Mrs Lamb, I think," as kind-mannered as anything – and never 'aggled about the amount nor nothing. He only had a little black bag, but he said his cousin had all the luggage coming in the train, and as there was so much p'r'aps they wouldn't get it here till next day. Then he went out and came in with his cousin at eleven that night – Sarah let 'em in her own self – and in the morning they was gone – and this!' Poor Mrs Lamb, plaintively indignant, stretched her arm towards the wrecked panels.

'If the gentleman as you say is comin' on, sir,' she pursued, 'can do anything to find 'em, I'll prosecute 'em, that I will, if it costs me ten pound. I spoke to the constable on the beat, but he only looked like a fool, and said if I knew where they were I might charge 'em with wilful damage, or county court 'em. Of course I know I can do that if I knew where they were, but how can I find 'em? Mr Jones he said his name was; but how many Joneses is there in London, sir?'

I couldn't imagine any answer to a question like this, but I condoled with Mrs Lamb as well as I could. She afterwards went on to express herself much as her sister had done with regard to Kingscote's death, only as the destruction of her panels loomed larger in her mind, she dwelt primarily on that. 'It might almost seem,' she said, 'that somebody had a deadly spite on the pore young gentleman, and went breakin' up his paintin' one night, and murderin' him the next!'

I examined the broken panels with some care, having half a notion to attempt to deduce something from them myself, if possible. But I could deduce nothing. The beading had been taken out, and the panels, which were thick in the centre but bevelled at the edges, had been removed and split up literally into thin firewood, which lay in a tumbled heap on the hearth and about the floor. Every panel in the room had been treated in the same way, and the result was a pretty large heap of sticks, with nothing whatever about them to distinguish them from other sticks, except the paint on one face, which I observed in many cases had been scratched and scraped away. The rug was drawn half across the hearth, and had evidently been used to deaden the sound of chopping. But mischief – wanton and stupid mischief – was all I could deduce from it all.

Mr Jones's cousin, it seemed, only Sarah had seen, as she admitted him in the evening, and then he was so heavily muffled that she could not distinguish his features, and would never be able to identify him. But as for the other one, Mrs Lamb was ready to swear to him anywhere.

Hewitt was long in coming, and internal symptoms of the approach of dinnertime (we had had no lunch) had made themselves felt before a sharp ring at the door-bell foretold his arrival. 'I have had to wait for answers to a telegram,' he said in explanation, 'but at any rate I have the information I wanted. And these are the mysterious panels, are they?'

Mrs Lamb's true opinion of Martin Hewitt's behaviour as it proceeded would have been amusing to know. She watched in amazement the antics of a man who purposed finding out who had been splitting sticks by dint of picking up each separate stick and staring at it. In the end he collected a small handful of sticks by themselves and handed them to me, saying, 'Just put these together on the table, Brett, and see what you make of them.'

I turned the pieces painted side up, and fitted them together into a complete panel, joining up the painted design accurately. 'It is an entire panel,' I said.

'Good. Now look at the sticks a little more closely, and tell me if you notice anything peculiar about them – any particular in which they differ from all the others.'

I looked. 'Two adjoining sticks,' I said, 'have each a small semi-circular cavity stuffed with what seems to be putty. Put together it would mean a small circular hole, perhaps a knot-hole, half an inch or so in diameter, in the panel, filled in with putty, or whatever it is.'

'A *knot-hole*?' Hewitt asked, with particular emphasis.

'Well, no, not a knot-hole, of course, because that would go right through, and this doesn't. It is probably less than half an inch deep from the front surface.'

'Anything else? Look at the whole appearance of the wood itself. Colour, for instance.'

'It is certainly darker than the rest.'

'So it is.' He took the two pieces carrying the puttied hole, threw the rest on the heap, and addressed the landlady. 'The Mr Harvey Challitt who occupied this room before Mr Kingscote, and who got into trouble for forgery, was the Mr Harvey Challitt who was himself robbed of diamonds a few months before on a staircase, wasn't he?'

'Yes, sir,' Mrs Lamb replied in some bewilderment. 'He certainly was that, on his own office stairs, chloroformed.'

'Just so, and when they marched him away because of the forgery, Mr Kingscote changed into his rooms?'

'Yes, and very glad I was. It was bad enough to have the disgrace brought into the house, without the trouble of trying to get people to take his very rooms, and I thought –'

'Yes, yes, very awkward, very awkward!' Hewitt interrupted rather impatiently. 'The man who took the rooms on Monday, now – you'd never seen him before, had you?'

'No, sir.'

'Then is *that* anything like him?' Hewitt held a cabinet photograph before her.

'Why – why – law, yes, that's *him*!'

Hewitt dropped the photograph back into his breast pocket with a contented 'Um', and picked up his hat. 'I think we may soon be able to find that young gentleman for you, Mrs Lamb. He is not a very respectable young gentleman, and perhaps you are well rid of him, even as it is. Come, Brett,' he added, 'the day hasn't been wasted, after all.'

We made towards the nearest telegraph office. On the way I said, 'That puttied-up hole in the piece of wood seems to have influenced you. Is it an important link?'

'Well – yes,' Hewitt answered, 'it is. But all those other pieces are important, too.'

'But why?'

'Because there are no holes in them.' He looked quizzically at my wondering face, and laughed aloud. 'Come,' he said, 'I won't puzzle you much longer. Here is the post office. I'll send my wire, and then we'll go and dine at Luzatti's.'

He sent his telegram, and we cabbed it to Luzatti's. Among actors, journalists, and others who know town and like a good dinner, Luzatti's is well known. We went upstairs for the sake of quietness, and took a table standing alone in a recess just inside the door. We ordered our dinner, and then Hewitt began:

'Now tell me what *your* conclusion is in this matter of the Ivy Cottage murder.'

'Mine? I haven't one. I'm sorry I'm so very dull, but I really haven't.'

'Come, I'll give you a point. Here is the newspaper account (torn sacrilegiously from my scrapbook for your benefit) of the robbery perpetrated on Harvey Challitt a few months before his forgery. Read it.'

'Oh, but I remember the circumstances very well. He was carrying two packets of diamonds belonging to his firm downstairs to the office of another firm of diamond merchants on the ground floor. It was a quiet time in the day, and halfway down he was seized on a dark landing, made insensible by chloroform, and robbed of the diamonds – five or six thousand pounds' worth altogether, of stones of various smallish individual values up to thirty pounds or so. He lay unconscious on the landing till one of the partners, noticing that he had been rather long gone, followed and found him. That's all, I think.'

'Yes, that's all. Well, what do you make of it?'

'I'm afraid I don't quite see the connection with this case.'

'Well, then, I'll give you another point. The telegram I've just sent releases information to the police, in consequence of which they will probably apprehend Harvey Challitt and his confederate, Henry Gillard, *alias* Jones, for the murder of Gavin Kingscote. Now, then.'

'Challitt! But he's in gaol already.'

'Tut, tut, consider. Five years' penal was his dose, although for the first offence, because the forgery was of an extremely dangerous sort. You left Chelsea over three years ago yourself, and you told me that his difficulty occurred a year before. That makes four years, at least. Good conduct in prison brings a man out of a five years' sentence in that time or a little less, and, as a matter of fact, Challitt was released rather more than a week ago.'

'Still, I'm afraid I don't see what you are driving at.'

'Whose story is this about the diamond robbery from Harvey Challitt?'

'His own.'

'Exactly. His own. Does his subsequent record make him look like a person whose stories are to be accepted without doubt or question?'

'Why, no. I think I see – no, I don't. You mean he stole them himself? I've a sort of dim perception of your drift now, but still I can't fix it. The whole thing's too complicated.'

'It is a little complicated for a first effort, I admit, so I will tell you. This is the story. Harvey Challitt is an artful young man, and decides on a theft of his firm's diamonds. He first prepares a hiding-place somewhere near the stairs of his office, and when the opportunity arrives he puts the stones away, spills his chloroform, and makes a smell – possibly sniffs some, and actually goes off on the stairs, and the whole thing's done. He is carried into the office – the diamonds are gone. He tells of the attack on the stairs, as we have heard, and he is believed. At a suitable opportunity he takes his plunder from the hiding-place, and goes home to his lodgings. What is he to do with those diamonds? He can't sell them yet, because the robbery is publicly notorious, and all the regular jewel buyers know him.

'Being a criminal novice, he doesn't know any regular receiver of stolen goods, and if he did would prefer to wait and get full value by an ordinary sale. There will always be a danger of detection so long as the stones are not securely hidden, so he proceeds to hide them. He knows that if any suspicion were aroused his rooms would be searched in every likely place, so he looks for an unlikely place. Of course, he thinks of taking out a panel and hiding them behind that. But the idea is so obvious that it won't do; the police would certainly take those panels out to look behind them. Therefore he determines to hide them *in* the panels. See here' – he took the two pieces of wood with the filled hole from his tail pocket and opened his penknife – 'the putty near the surface is softer than that near the bottom of the hole; two different lots of putty, differently mixed, perhaps, have been used, therefore, presumably, at different times.

'But to return to Challitt. He makes holes with a centre-bit in different places on the panels, and in each hole he places a diamond, embedding it carefully in putty. He smooths the surface carefully flush with the wood, and then very carefully paints the place over, shading off the paint at the edges so as to leave no signs of a patch. He doesn't do the whole job at once, creating a noise and a smell of paint, but keeps on steadily, a few holes at a time, till in a little while the whole wainscoting is set with hidden diamonds, and every panel is apparently sound and whole.'

'But, then – there was only one such hole in the whole lot.'

'Just so, and that very circumstance tells us the whole truth. Let me tell the story first – I'll explain the clue after. The diamonds lie hidden for a few months – he grows impatient. He wants the money, and he can't see a way of getting it. At last he determines to make a bolt and go abroad to sell his plunder. He knows he will want money for expenses, and that he may not be able to get rid of his diamonds at once. He also expects that his suddenly going abroad while the robbery is still in people's minds will bring suspicion on him in any case, so, in for a penny in for a pound, he commits a bold forgery, which, had it been successful, would have put him in funds and enabled him to leave the country with the stones. But the forgery is detected, and he is haled to prison, leaving the diamonds in their wainscot setting.

'Now we come to Gavin Kingscote. He must have been a shrewd fellow – the sort of man that good detectives are made of. Also he must have been pretty unscrupulous. He had his suspicions about the genuineness of the diamond robbery, and kept his eyes open. What indications he had to guide him we don't know, but living in the same house a sharp fellow on the look-out would probably see enough. At any rate, they led him to the belief that the diamonds were in the thief's rooms, but not among his movables, or they would have been found after the arrest. Here was his chance. Challitt was out of the way for years, and there was plenty of time to take the house to pieces if it were necessary. So he changed into Challitt's rooms.

'How long it took him to find the stones we shall never know. He probably tried many other places first, and, I expect, found the diamonds at last by pricking over the panels with a needle. Then came the problem of getting them out without attracting attention. He decided not to trust to the needle, which might possibly leave a stone or two undiscovered, but to split up each panel carefully into splinters so as to leave no part unexamined. Therefore he took measurements, and had a number of panels made by a joiner of the exact size and pattern of those in the room, and announced to his landlady his intention of painting her panels with a pretty design. This to account for the wet paint, and even for the fact of a panel being out of the wall, should she chance to bounce into the room at an awkward moment. All very clever, eh?'

'Very.'

'Ah, he was a smart man, no doubt. Well, he went to work, taking out a panel, substituting a new one, painting it over, and chopping up the old one on the quiet, getting rid of the splinters out of doors when the booty had been extracted. The decoration progressed and the little heap of diamonds grew. Finally, he came to the last panel, but found that he had used all his new panels and hadn't one left for a substitute. It must have been at some time when it was difficult to get hold of the joiner – Bank Holiday, perhaps, or Sunday, and he was impatient. So he scraped the paint off, and went carefully over every part of the surface – experience had taught him by this time that all the holes were of the same sort – and found one diamond. He took it out, refilled the hole with putty, painted the old panel and put it back. *These* are pieces of that old panel – the only old one of the lot.

'Nine men out of ten would have got out of the house as soon as possible after the thing was done, but he was a cool hand and stayed. That made the whole thing look a deal more genuine than if he had unaccountably cleared out as soon as he had got his room nicely decorated. I expect the original capital for those Stock Exchange operations we heard of came out of those diamonds. He stayed as long as suited him, and left when he set up housekeeping with a view to his wedding. The rest of the story is pretty plain. You guess it, of course?'

'Yes,' I said, 'I think I can guess the rest, in a general sort of way – except as to one or two points.'

'It's all plain – perfectly. See here! Challitt, in gaol, determines to get those diamonds when he comes out. To do that without being suspected it will be necessary to hire the room. But he knows that he won't be able to do that himself, because the landlady, of course, knows him, and won't have an ex-convict in the house. There is no help for it; he must have a confederate, and share the spoil. So he makes the acquaintance of another convict, who seems a likely man for the job, and whose sentence expires about the same time as his own. When they come out, he arranges the matter with this confederate, who is a well-mannered (and pretty well-known) housebreaker, and the latter calls at Mrs Lamb's house to look for rooms. The very room itself happens to be to let, and of course it is taken, and Challitt (who is the invalid cousin) comes in at night muffled and unrecognisable.

'The decoration on the panel does not alarm them, because, of course, they suppose it to have been done on the old panels and over the old paint. Challitt tries the spots where diamonds were left – there are none – there is no putty even. Perhaps, think they, the panels have been shifted and interchanged in the painting, so they set to work and split them all up as we have seen, getting more desperate as they go on. Finally they realise that they are done, and clear out, leaving Mrs Lamb to mourn over their mischief.

'They know that Kingscote is the man who has forestalled them, because Gillard (or Jones), in his chat with the landlady, has heard all about him and his painting of the panels. So the next night they set off for Finchley. They get into Kingscote's garden and watch him let Campbell out. While he is gone, Challitt quietly steps through the French window into the smoking-room, and waits for him, Gillard remaining outside.

'Kingscote returns, and Challitt accuses him of taking the stones. Kingscote is contemptuous – doesn't care for Challitt, because he knows he is powerless, being the original thief himself; besides, knows there is no evidence, since the diamonds are sold and dispersed long ago. Challitt offers to divide the plunder with him – Kingscote laughs and tells him to go; probably threatens to throw him out, Challitt being the smaller man. Gillard, at the open window, hears this, steps in behind, and quietly knocks him on the head. The rest follows as a matter of course. They fasten the window and shutters, to exclude observation; turn over all the drawers, etc, in case the jewels are there; go to the best bedroom and try there, and so on. Failing (and possibly being disturbed after a few hours' search by the noise of the acquisitive gardener), Gillard, with the instinct of an old thief, determines they shan't go away with nothing, so empties Kingscote's pockets and takes his watch and chain and so on. They go out by the front door and shut it after them. *Voilà tout.*'

I was filled with wonder at the prompt ingenuity of the man who in these few hours of hurried inquiry could piece together so accurately all the materials of an intricate and mysterious affair such as this; but more, I wondered where and how he had collected those materials.

'There is no doubt, Hewitt,' I said, 'that the accurate and minute application of what you are pleased to call your common sense has become something very like an instinct with you. What did you deduce from? You told me your conclusions from the examination of Ivy Cottage, but not how you arrived at them.'

'They didn't leave me much material downstairs, did they? But in the bedroom, the two drawers which the thieves found locked were ransacked – opened probably with keys taken from the dead man. On the floor I saw a bent French nail; here it is. You see, it is twice bent at right angles, near the head and near the point, and there is the faint mark of the pliers that were used to bend it. It is a very usual burglars' tool, and handy in experienced hands to open ordinary drawer locks. Therefore, I knew that a professional burglar had been at work. He had probably fiddled at the drawers with the nail first, and then had thrown it down to try the dead man's keys.

'But I knew this professional burglar didn't come for a burglary, from several indications. There was no attempt to take plate, the first thing a burglar looks for. Valuable clocks were left on mantelpieces, and other things that usually go in an ordinary burglary were not disturbed. Notably, it was to be observed that no doors or windows were broken, or had been forcibly opened; therefore, it was plain that the thieves had come in by the French window of the smoking-room, the only entrance left open at the last thing. *Therefore*, they came in, or one did, knowing that Mr Kingscote was up, and being quite willing – presumably anxious – to see him. Ordinary burglars would have waited till he had retired, and then could have got through the closed French window as easily almost as if it were open, notwithstanding the thin wooden shutters, which would never stop a burglar for more than five minutes. Being anxious to see him, they – or again, *one* of them – presumably knew him. That they had come to *get* something was plain, from the ransacking. As, in the end, they *did* steal his money, and watch, but did *not* take larger valuables, it was plain that they had no bag with them – which proves not only that they had not come to burgle, for every burglar takes his bag, but that the thing they came to get was not bulky. Still, they could easily have removed plate or clocks by rolling them up in a table-cover or other wrapper, but such a bundle, carried by well-dressed men, would attract attention – therefore it was probable that they were well-dressed. Do I make it clear?'

'Quite – nothing seems simpler now it is explained – that's the way with difficult puzzles.'

'There was nothing more to be got at the house. I had already in my mind the curious coincidence that the panels at Chelsea had been broken the very night before that of the murder, and determined to look at them in any case. I got from you the name of the man who had lived in the panelled room before Kingscote, and at once remembered it (although I said nothing about it) as that of the young man who had been chloroformed for his employer's diamonds. I keep things of that sort in my mind, you see – and, indeed, in my scrapbook. You told me yourself about his imprisonment, and there I was with what seemed now a hopeful case getting into a promising shape.

'You went on to prevent any setting to rights at Chelsea, and I made enquiries as to Challitt. I found he had been released only a few days before all this trouble arose, and I also found the name of another man who was released from the same establishment only a few days earlier. I knew this man (Gillard) well, and knew that nobody was a more likely rascal for such a crime as that at Finchley. On my way to Chelsea I called at my office, gave my clerk certain instructions, and looked up my scrapbook. I found the newspaper account of the chloroform business, and also a photograph of Gillard – I keep as many of these things as I can collect. What I did at Chelsea you know. I saw that one panel was of old wood and the rest new. I saw the hole in the old panel, and I asked one or two questions. The case was complete.'

We proceeded with our dinner. Presently I said: 'It all rests with the police now, of course?'

'Of course. I should think it very probable that Challitt and Gillard will be caught. Gillard, at any rate, is pretty well known. It will be rather hard on the surviving Kingscote, after engaging me, to have his dead brother's diamond transactions publicly exposed as a result, won't it? But it can't be helped. *Fiat justitia*, of course.'

'How will the police feel over this?' I asked. 'You've rather cut them out, eh?'

'Oh, the police are all right. They had not the information I had, you see; they knew nothing of the panel business. If Mrs

Lamb had gone to Scotland Yard instead of to the policeman on the beat, perhaps I should never have been sent for.'

The same quality that caused Martin Hewitt to rank as mere 'common sense' his extraordinary power of almost instinctive deduction kept his respect for the abilities of the police at perhaps a higher level than some might have considered justified.

We sat some little while over our dessert, talking as we sat, when there occurred one of those curious conjunctions of circumstances that we notice again and again in ordinary life, and forget as often, unless the importance of the occasion fixes the matter in the memory. A young man had entered the dining-room, and had taken his seat at a corner table near the back window. He had been sitting there for some little time before I particularly observed him. At last he happened to turn his thin, pale face in my direction, and our eyes met. It was Challitt – the man we had been talking of!

I sprang to my feet in some excitement.

'That's the man!' I cried. 'Challitt!'

Hewitt rose at my words, and at first attempted to pull me back. Challitt, in guilty terror, saw that we were between him and the door, and turning, leaped upon the sill of the open window, and dropped out. There was a fearful crash of broken glass below, and everybody rushed to the window.

Hewitt drew me through the door, and we ran downstairs. 'Pity you let out like that,' he said, as he went. 'If you'd kept quiet we could have sent out for the police with no trouble. Never mind – can't help it.'

Below, Challitt was lying in a broken heap in the midst of a crowd of waiters. He had crashed through a thick glass skylight and fallen, back downward, across the back of a lounge. He was taken away on a stretcher unconscious, and, in fact, died in a week in hospital from injuries to the spine.

During his periods of consciousness he made a detailed statement, bearing out the conclusions of Martin Hewitt with the most surprising exactness, down to the smallest particulars.

He and Gillard had parted immediately after the crime, judging it safer not to be seen together. He had, he affirmed, endured agonies of fear and remorse in the few days since the fatal night at Finchley, and had even once or twice thought of giving himself up. When I so excitedly pointed him out, he knew at once that the game was up, and took the one desperate chance of escape that offered. But to the end he persistently denied that he had himself committed the murder, or had even thought of it till he saw it accomplished. That had been wholly the work of Gillard, who, listening at the window and perceiving the drift of the conversation, suddenly beat down Kingscote from behind with a life-preserver. And so Harvey Challitt ended his life at the age of twenty-six.

Gillard was never taken. He doubtless left the country, and has probably since that time become 'known to the police' under another name abroad. Perhaps he has even been hanged, and if he has been, there was no miscarriage of justice, no matter what the charge against him may have been.

JUDITH LEE

Created by Richard Marsh (1857-1915)

After a false start as a writer of stories for boys' magazines, Richard Heldmann reinvented himself, took the pseudonym of Richard Marsh and began to pump out reams of fiction in the crime and supernatural genres. His novel, The Beetle, *published in 1897, the same year as Bram Stoker's* Dracula, *is the tale of a shape-shifting devotee of ancient Egyptian gods stalking the fog-shrouded streets of late Victorian London. It was a great commercial success, outselling Stoker's work, and was made into a silent film in 1919, two years before Count Dracula made his debut on a cinema screen. Other horror novels followed, as well as crime fiction (*Philip Bennion's Death, The Datchet Diamonds*) and collections of short stories with titles like* The Seen and the Unseen *and* Both Sides of the Veil. *His work appeared in most of the periodicals of the day from* The Strand Magazine *to* Belgravia: A London Magazine. *When the Judith Lee stories first appeared in* The Strand Magazine *in 1911, the editor hailed the character as 'fortunate possessor of a gift which gives her a place apart in detective fiction'. Judith Lee is a young woman drawn into detective work of a kind because of this gift – her ability to read lips. She is forever seeing people discuss wicked plots and outrageous crimes, unaware that their words have been understood by the young woman across the room. The stories about her, including 'Conscience', are dependent on wild and improbable coincidences (Miss Lee always seems to be in the right spot at the right time) but they are still fun to read.*

CONSCIENCE

I had been spending a few days at Brighton, and was sitting one morning on the balcony of the West Pier pavilion, listening to the fine band of the Gordon Highlanders. The weather was beautiful – the kind one sometimes does get at Brighton – blue skies, a warm sun, and just that touch in the soft breeze which serves as a pick-me-up. There were crowds of people. I sat on one end of a bench. In a corner, within a few feet of me, a man was standing, leaning with his back against the railing – an odd-looking man, tall, slender, with something almost Mongolian in his clean-shaven, round face. I had noticed him on that particular spot each time I had been on the pier. He was well tailored, and that morning, for the first time, he wore a flower in his button-hole. As one sometimes does when one sees an unusual-looking stranger, I wondered hazily what kind of person he might be. I did not like the look of him.

Presently another man came along the balcony and paused close to him. They took no notice of each other; the newcomer looked attentively at the crowd promenading on the deck below, almost ostentatiously disregarding the other's neighbourhood. All the same, the man in the corner whispered something which probably reached his ears alone – and my perception – something which seemed to be a few disconnected words:

'Mauve dress, big black velvet hat, ostrich plume; four-thirty train.'

That was all he said. I do not suppose that anyone there, except the man who had paused and the lazy-looking girl whose eyes had chanced for a moment to wander towards his lips, had any notion that he had spoken at all. The newcomer remained for a few moments idly watching the promenaders; then, turning, without vouchsafing the other the slightest sign of recognition, strolled carelessly on.

It struck me as rather an odd little scene. I was constantly being made an unintentional confidante of what were meant to be secrets; but about that brief sentence which the one had whispered to the other there was a piquant something which struck me as amusing – the more especially as I believed I had seen the lady to whom the words referred. As I came on the pier I had been struck by her gorgeous appearance, as being a person who probably had more money than taste.

Some minutes passed. The Mongolian-looking man remained perfectly quiescent in his corner. Then another man came strolling along – big and burly, in a reddish-brown suit, a green felt hat worn slightly on one side of his head. He paused on the same spot on which the first man had brought his stroll to a close, and he paid no attention to the gentleman in the corner, who looked right away from him, even while I could see his lips framing precisely the same sentence:

'Mauve dress, big black velvet hat, ostrich plume; four-thirty train.'

The big man showed by no sign that he had heard a sound. He continued to do as his predecessor had done – stared at the promenaders, then strolled carelessly on.

This second episode struck me as being rather odder than the first. Why were such commonplace words uttered in so mysterious a manner? Would a third man come along? I waited to see – and waited in vain. The band played 'God Save the King', the people rose, but no third man had appeared. I left the Mongolian-looking gentleman still in his corner and went to the other side of the balcony to watch the people going down the pier. I saw the gorgeous lady in the mauve dress and big black picture hat with a fine ostrich plume, and I wondered what interest she might have for the round-faced man in the corner, and what she had to do with the four-thirty train. She was with two or three equally gorgeous ladies and one or two wonderfully attired men; they seemed to be quite a party.

The next day I left Brighton by an early train. In the compartment I was reading the *Sussex Daily News*, when a paragraph caught my eye. 'Tragic Occurrence on the Brighton

Line'. Late the night before the body of a woman had been found lying on the ballast, as if she might have fallen out of a passing train. It described her costume – she was attired in a pale mauve dress and a big black picture hat in which was an ostrich-feather plume. There were other details – plenty of them – but that was enough for me.

When I read that and thought of the man leaning against the railing I rather caught my breath. Two young men who were facing each other at the other end of the compartment began to talk about the paragraph in tones which were audible to all.

'Do you see that about the lady in the mauve dress who was found on the line? Do you know, I shouldn't wonder a bit if it was Mrs Farningham – that's her rig-out to a T. And I know she was going up to town yesterday afternoon.'

'She did go,' replied the other; 'and I'm told that when she started she'd had about enough cold tea.'

The other grinned – a grin of comprehension.

'If that's so I shouldn't wonder if the poor dear opened the carriage door, thinking it was some other door, and stepped out on to the line. From all I hear, it seems that she was quite capable of doing that sort of thing when she was like that.'

'Oh, quite; not a doubt of it. And she was capable of some pretty queer things when she wasn't like that.'

I wondered; these young gentlemen might be right; still, the more I thought the more I wondered.

I was very much occupied just then. It was because I had nearly broken down in my work that I had gone for those few days to Brighton. I doubt if I even glanced at a newspaper for some considerable time after that. I cannot say that the episode wholly faded from my memory, but I never heard what was the sequel of the lady who was found on the line, or, indeed, anything more about her.

I accepted an engagement with a deaf and dumb girl who was about to travel with her parents on a long voyage, pretty nearly round the world. I was to meet them in Paris, and then go on with them to Marseilles, where the real journey commenced. The night before I started some friends gave me a sort of send-off dinner at the Embankment Hotel. We were about halfway through the meal when a man came in and sat by himself at a small round table, nearly facing me. I could not think where I had seen him before. I was puzzling my brain when a second man came across the room and strolled slowly by his table. He did not pause, nor did either allow a sign to escape him to show that they were acquaintances, yet I distinctly saw the lips of the man who was seated at the table frame about a dozen words:

'White dress, star in her hair, pink roses over left breast. Tonight.'

The stroller went carelessly on, and for a moment my heart seemed to stand still. It all came back to me – the pier, the band of the Gordon Highlanders, the man with his back against the railings, the words whispered to the two men who had paused beside him. The diner in front of me was the Mongolian-looking man; I should have recognised him at once had not evening dress wrought such a change in him. That whispered sentence made assurance doubly sure. The party with whom I was dining had themselves been struck by the appearance of the lady in the white frock, with the diamond star in her hair and the pink roses arranged so daintily in the corsage of her dress. There had been a laughing discussion about who was the nicest-looking person in the room; more than one opinion had supported the claim of the lady with the diamond star.

In the middle of that dinner I found myself all at once in a quandary, owing to that very inconvenient gift of mine. I recalled the whisper about the lady in the mauve dress, and how the very next day the body of a lady so attired had been found on the Brighton line. Was the whispered allusion to the lady in the white dress to have a similar unpleasant sequel? If there was fear of anything of the kind, what was I to do?

My friends, noticing my abstraction, rallied me on my inattention.

'May I point out to you,' observed my neighbour, 'that the waiter is offering you asparagus, and has been doing so for about five minutes?'

Looking round, I found that the waiter was standing patiently at my side. I allowed him to help me. I was about to eat what he had given me when I saw someone advancing across the room whom I knew at once, in spite of the alteration which evening dress made in him – it was the big, burly man in the red-brown suit.

The comedy – if it were a comedy – was repeated. The big man, not, apparently, acknowledging the existence of the solitary diner, passed his table, seemingly by the merest chance, in the course of his passage towards another on the other side of the room. With a morsel of food on his fork poised midway between the plate and his mouth, the diner moved his lips to repeat his former words:

'White dress, star in her hair, pink roses over left breast. Tonight.'

The big man had passed, the morsel of food had entered the diner's mouth; nothing seemed to have happened, yet I was on the point of springing to my feet and electrifying the gaily-dressed crowd by crying, 'Murder!'

More than once afterwards I wished I had done so. I do not know what would have happened if I had; I have sometimes asked myself if I could say what would not have happened. As a matter of fact, I did nothing at all. I do not say it to excuse myself, nor to blame anyone, but it seemed to me, at the moment, that to do anything was impossible, because those with whom I was dining made it so. I was their guest; they took care to make me understand that I owed them something as my hosts. They were in the merriest mood themselves; they seemed to regard it as of the first importance that I should be merry too. To the best of my ability I was outwardly as gay as the rest of them. The lady in the white dress, with her party, left early. I should have liked to give her some hint, some warning – I did neither; I just let her go.

As she went across the room one or two members of our party toasted her under their breath. The solitary diner took no heed of her whatever. I had been furtively watching him the whole time, and he never once glanced in her direction. So far as I saw, he was so absorbed in his meal that he scarcely raised his eyes from the table; I knew, unfortunately, that I could not have mistaken the words which I had seen his lips forming. I tried to comfort myself with the reflection that they could not have referred to the vision of feminine loveliness which had just passed from the room.

The following morning I travelled by the early boat-train to Dover. When the train had left the station I looked at my *Telegraph*. I read a good deal of it; then, at the top of a column on one of the inside pages, I came upon a paragraph headed: 'Mysterious Affair at the Embankment Hotel'. Not very long after midnight – in time, it seemed, to reach the paper before it went to press – the body of a young woman had been found in the courtyard of the hotel. She was in her night attire. She was recognised as one of the guests who had been staying in the hotel; she had either fallen or been thrown out of her bedroom window.

Something happened to my brain so that I was unconscious of the train, in which I was a passenger, as it sped onwards.

What did that paragraph mean? Could the woman who had been found in her night attire in the courtyard of the Embankment Hotel be the woman who had worn the white dress and a diamond star in her pretty brown hair? There was nothing to show that she was. There was nothing to connect that lightly clothed body with the whispered words of the solitary diner, with a touch of the Mongol in his face; yet I wondered if it were not my duty to return at once to London and tell my story. But, after all, it was such a silly story; it amounted to nothing; it proved nothing. Those people were waiting for me in Paris; I could not desert them at the last moment, with all our passages booked, for what might turn out to be something even more fantastic than a will-o'-the-wisp.

So I went on to Paris, and, with them, nearly round the world;

and I can say, without exaggeration, that more than once that curious-looking gentleman's face seemed to have gone with me. Once, in an English paper which I picked up after we had landed at Hong Kong, I read about the body of a woman which had been found on the Great Western Railway line near Exeter station – and I wondered. When I went out into the streets and saw on the faces of the people who thronged them something which recalled the solitary diner at the Embankment Hotel – I wondered still more.

More than two years elapsed. In the summer of the third I went to Buxton, as I had gone to Brighton, for a rest. I was seated one morning in the public gardens, with my thoughts on the other side of the world – we had not long returned from the Sandwich Islands – and I was comparing that land of perpetual summer with the crisp freshness of the Buxton air. With my thoughts still far away, my eyes passed idly from face to face of those around me, until presently I became aware that under the shade of a tree on my left a man was sitting alone. When I saw his face my thoughts came back with a rush; it was the man who had been on the pier at Brighton, and at the Embankment Hotel, and who had travelled with me round the world. The consciousness of his near neighbourhood gave me a nasty jar; as at the Embankment Hotel there was an impulsive moment when I felt like jumping on to my feet and denouncing him to the assembled crowd. He was dressed in a cool grey suit; as at Brighton, he had a flower in his button-hole; he sat upright and impassive, glancing neither to the left nor right, as if nothing was of interest to him.

Then the familiar comedy, which I believe I had rehearsed in my dreams, began again. A man came down the path from behind me, passing before I had seen his face, and under the shady tree paused for an instant to light a cigarette, and I saw the lips of the man on the chair forming words:

'Grey dress, lace scarf, Panama hat; five-five train.'

His lips framed those nine words only; then the man with the cigarette passed on, and I really do believe that my heart stood still. Comedy? I had an uncomfortable conviction that this was a tragedy which was being played – in the midst of that light-hearted crowd, in that pleasant garden, under those laughing skies. I waited for the action to continue – not very long. In the distance I saw a big, burly person threading his way among the people towards that shady tree, and I knew what was coming. He did not pause even for a single instant, he just went slowly by, within a foot of the chair, and the thin lips shaped themselves into words:

'Grey dress, lace scarf, Panama hat; five-five train.'

The big man sauntered on, leaving me with the most uncomfortable feeling that I had seen sentence of death pronounced on an innocent, helpless fellow creature. I did not propose to sit still this time and allow those three uncanny beings, undisturbed, to work their evil wills. As at the hotel, the question recurred to me – what was I to do? Was I to go up and denounce this creature to his face? Suppose he chose to regard me as some ill-conducted person, what evidence had I to adduce that any statements I might make were true? I decided, in the first place, to leave him severely alone; I had thought of another plan.

Getting up from my chair I began to walk about the gardens. As had not been the case on the two previous occasions, there was no person in sight who answered to the description – 'Grey dress, lace scarf, Panama hat'. I was just about to conclude that this time the victim was not in plain view, when I saw a Panama hat in the crowd on the other side of the band. I moved quickly forward; it was certainly on a woman's head. There was a lace scarf spread out upon her shoulders, a frock of a very light shade in grey. Was this the woman whose doom had been pronounced? I went more forward still, and, with an unpleasant sense of shock, recognised the wearer.

I was staying at the Empire Hotel. On the previous afternoon, at teatime, the lounge had been very full. I saw a tall lady, who seemed to be alone, glancing about as if looking for an empty table. As she seemed to have some difficulty in finding one, and as I had a table all to myself, I suggested, as she came near, that she should have a seat at mine. The manner in which she received my suggestion took me aback. I suppose there are no ruder, more ill-bred creatures in the world than some English women. Whether she thought I wished to force my company upon her and somehow scrape an acquaintance I cannot say. She could not have treated my suggestion with more contemptuous scorn had I tried to pick her pocket. She just looked down at me, as if wondering what kind of person I could be that I had dared to speak to her at all, and then, without condescending to reply, went on. I almost felt as if she had given me a slap across my face.

After dinner I saw her again in the lounge. She wore some very fine jewellery – she was a very striking woman, beautifully gowned. A diamond brooch was pinned to her bodice. As she approached I saw it was unfastened; it fell within a foot of where I was sitting. I picked it up and offered it to her, with the usual formula.

'I think this is your brooch – you have just dropped it.'

How do you think she thanked me? She hesitated a second to take the brooch, as if she thought I might be playing her some trick. Then, when she saw that it was hers, she took it and looked it carefully over – and what do you suppose she said?

'You are very insistent.'

That was all, every word – in such ineffable tones! She was apparently under the impression that I had engineered the dropping of that diamond brooch as a further step in my nefarious scheme to force on her the dishonour of my acquaintance.

This was the lady who in the public gardens was wearing a light grey dress, a lace scarf, and a Panama hat. What would she say to me if I told her about the man under the shady tree and his two friends? Yet, if I did not tell her, should I not feel responsible for whatever might ensue? That she went in danger of her life I was as sure as that I was standing there. She might be a very unpleasant, a very foolish woman, yet I could not stand by and allow her quite possibly to be done to death, without at least warning her of the danger which she ran. The sooner the warning was given the better. As she turned into a side path I turned into another, meaning to meet her in the centre of hers and warn her there and then.

The meeting took place, and, as I had more than half expected, I entirely failed to do what I had intended. The glance she fixed on me when she saw me coming and recognised who I was conveyed sufficient information. It said, as plainly as if in so many words, that if I dared to insult her by attempting to address her it would be at my own proper peril. None the less, I did dare. I remembered the woman in the mauve dress, and the woman in the white, and the feeling I had had that by the utterance of a few words I might have saved their lives. I was going to do my best to save hers, even though she tried to freeze me while I was in the act of doing so.

We met. As if scenting my design, as we neared each other she quickened her pace to stride right past. But I was too quick for her; I barred the way. The expression with which, as she recognised my intention, she regarded me! But I was not to be frightened into dumbness.

'There is something I have to say to you which is important – of the very first importance – which it is essential that I should say and you should hear. I have not the least intention of forcing on you my acquaintance, but with your sanction –'

I got as far as that, but I got no farther. As I still continued to bar her path, she turned right round and marched in the other direction. I might have gone after her, I might have stopped her – I did move a step or two; but when I did she spoke to me over her shoulder as she was moving:

'If you dare to speak to me again I shall claim the protection of the police, so be advised.'

I was advised. Whether the woman suffered from some obscure form of mental disease or not I could not say; or with what majesty she supposed herself to be hedged around, which made it the height of presumption for a mere outsider to venture

to address her – that also was a mystery to me. As I had no wish
to have a scene in the public gardens, and as it appeared that there
would be a scene if I did any more to try to help her, I let her
go.

I saw her leave the gardens, and when I had seen that I strolled
back. There, under the shady tree, still sat the man with the touch
of the Mongol in his face.

After luncheon, which I took at the hotel, I had a surprise.
There, in the hall, was my gentleman, going through the front
door. I spoke to the hall porter.

'Is that gentleman staying in the house?' The porter intimated
that he was. 'Can you tell me what his name is?' The porter
answered promptly, perhaps because it was such an unusual
name:

'Mr John Tung.' Then he added, with a smile, 'I used to be
in the Navy. When we were on the China station I was always
meeting people with names like that – this gentleman is the first
I've met since.'

An idea occurred to me. I felt responsible for that woman, in
spite of her stupidity. If anything happened to her it would lie
at my door. For my own sake I did not propose to run the risk.
I went to the post office and I sent a telegram to John Tung,
Empire Hotel. The clerk on the other side of the counter seemed
rather surprised as he read the words which I wished him to wire.

'I suppose this is all right?' he questioned, as if in doubt.

'Perfectly all right,' I replied. 'Please send that telegram at
once.'

I quitted the office, leaving that telegraph clerk scanning my
message as if he were still in doubt if it was in order. In the course
of the afternoon I had another idea. I wrote what follows on a
sheet of paper.

'You threw the woman in the mauve dress on to the Brighton
line; you were responsible for the death of the woman in the
white dress at the Embankment Hotel; you killed the woman
who was found on the Great Western line near Exeter station; but

you are going to do no mischief to the woman in the grey dress and the lace scarf and the Panama hat, who is going up to town by the five-five.

'Be sure of that.

'Also you may be sure that the day of reckoning is at hand, when you and your two accomplices will be called to a strict account. In that hour you will be shown no more mercy than you have shown.

'That is as certain as that, at the present moment, you are still alive. But the messengers of justice are drawing near.'

There was no beginning and no ending, no date, no address – I just wrote that and left it so. It was wild language, in which I took a good deal for granted that I had no right to take; and it savoured a good deal of melodrama and highfalutin. But then, my whole scheme was a wild-cat scheme; if it succeeded it would be because of that, as it were, very wild-cat property. I put my sheet of paper into an envelope, and I wrote outside it in very large, plain letters, 'Mr John Tung'. Then I went into the lounge of the hotel for tea – and I waited.

And I kept on waiting for quite a considerable time. It was rather early for tea, but as time passed and people began to gather together, and there were still no signs of the persons whose presence I particularly desired, I began to fidget. If none of them appeared I should have to reconsider my plan of campaign. I was just on the point of concluding that the moment had come when I had better think of something else, when I saw Mr John Tung standing in the doorway and with him his two acquaintances. This was better than I had expected. Their appearance together in the public room of the hotel suggested all sorts of possibilities to my mind.

I had that missive prepared. I waited until I had some notion of the quarter of the room in which they proposed to establish themselves, then I rose from my chair and, crossing to the other side of the lounge, left on a table close to that at which they were about to sit – I hoped unnoticed – the envelope on which 'Mr

John Tung' was so plainly written. Then I watched for the march of events.

What I had hoped would occur did happen. A waiter, bustling towards the newcomers, saw the envelope lying on a vacant table, picked it up, perceived that it was addressed to Mr John Tung, and bore it to that gentleman. I could not hear, but I saw what was said. The waiter began:

'Is this your letter, sir?'

Mr Tung glanced, as if surprised, at the envelope which the man was holding, then took it from between his fingers and stared at it hard.

'Where did you get this?' he asked.

'It was on that table, sir.'

'What table?'

'The one over there, sir.'

Mr Tung looked in the direction in which the man was pointing, as if not quite certain what he meant.

'How came it to be there? Who put it there?'

'Can't say, sir. I saw an envelope lying on the table as I was coming to you, and when I saw your name on it I thought it might be yours. Tea, sir?'

'Tea for three, and bring some buttered toast.'

The waiter went. Mr Tung remained staring at the envelope as if there were something in its appearance which he found a little puzzling. One of his companions spoke to him; but as his back was towards me I could not see what he said – I could guess from the other's answer.

'Some rubbish; a circular, I suppose – the sort of thing one does get in hotels.'

Then he opened the envelope, and – I had rather a funny feeling. I was perfectly conscious that from the point of view of a court of law I had not the slightest right to pen a single one of the words which were on the sheet of paper inside that envelope. For all I could prove, Mr Tung and his friends might be the most innocent of men. I might find it pretty hard to prove that the Mongolian-looking gentleman had whispered either of the brief, jerky sentences which I had seen him whisper; and, even if I could get as far as that, there still remained the difficulty of showing that they bore anything like the construction which I had put upon them. If I had misjudged him, if my deductions had been wrong, then Mr Tung, when he found what was in that envelope, would be more than justified in making a fine to-do. It was quite possible, since I could not have eyes at the back of my head, that someone had seen me leave that envelope on the table, in which case my authorship might be traced, and I should be in a pretty awkward situation. That woman in the grey dress would be shown to have had right on her side when she declined, with such a show of scorn, to allow me even to speak to her. So, while Mr Tung was tearing open the envelope and taking out the sheet of paper, I had some distinctly uncomfortable moments. Suppose I had wronged him – what was I to do? Own up, make a clean breast of it – or run away?

I had not yet found an answer when I became perfectly certain that none was required. My chance shot had struck him like a bombshell; the change which took place in his countenance when he began to read what was written on that piece of paper was really curious. I should have said he had a visage over whose muscles he exercised great control – Mongols have as a rule. But those words of mine were so wholly unexpected that when he first saw them his expression was, on the instant, one of stunned amazement. He glanced at the opening words, then, dropping his hands to his sides, gazed round the room, as if he were wondering if there were anyone there who could have written them. Then he raised the sheet of paper again and read farther. And, as he read, his breath seemed to come quicker, his eyes dilated, the colour left his cheeks, his jaw dropped open. He presented a unique picture of the surprise which is born of terror.

His companions, looking at him, were affected as he was,

without knowing why. The big, burly man leaned towards him; I saw him mutter:

'You look as if you'd had a stroke. What's the matter? What's that you've got there? Don't look like that. Everyone is staring at you. What's up?'

Mr Tung did not reply; he looked at the speaker, then at the sheet of paper — that time I am sure he did not see what was on it. Then he crumpled the sheet of paper up in his hand, and without a word strode across the lounge into the hall beyond. His two companions looked after him in bewildered amazement; then they went also, not quite so fast as he had done, but fast enough. And all the people in the lounge looked at each other. The manner of the exit of these three gentlemen had created a small sensation.

My little experiment had succeeded altogether beyond my anticipation. It was plain that I had not misjudged this gentleman. It would be difficult to find a more striking illustration than that presented by Mr John Tung of the awful accusing conscience which strikes terror into a man's soul. I could not afford to let my acquaintance with these three interesting gentlemen cease at this moment; the woman in the grey dress must still not be left to their tender mercies.

After what seemed to me to be a sufficient interval, I left my tea and went after them into the hall. I was just in time. The three men were in the act of leaving the hotel. As they were moving towards the door a page came up, an official envelope in his hand.

'Mr John Tung? A telegram for you, sir.'

Mr Tung took it as if it were some dangerous thing, hesitated, glanced at the men beside him, tore it open, read what was on the flimsy sheet of pink paper, and walked so quickly out of the building that his gait almost approached a run. His companions went after him as if they were giving chase. My wire had finished what those few plain words on the sheet of paper had begun.

I was lingering in the hall, rather at a loss as to what was the next step that I had better take, when the woman in the grey dress came out of the lift, which had just descended. A cab was at the door, on which was luggage. Although she must have seen me very clearly, she did not recognise my presence, but passed straight out to the cab. She was going up to London by the five-five train.

I no longer hesitated what to do. I, too, quitted the hotel and got into a cab. It still wanted ten minutes to five when I reached the station. The train was standing by the platform; the grey-frocked lady was superintending the labelling of her luggage – apparently she had no maid. She was escorted by a porter, who had her luggage in charge, to a first-class carriage. On the top of her luggage was the tell-tale thing which has probably done more harm than good – the dressing-bag which is so dear to the hearts of many women, which ostentatiously proclaims the fact that it contains their jewels, probably their money, all that they are travelling with which they value most. One has only to get hold of the average travelling woman's dressing-bag to become possessed of all that she has – from the practical thief's point of view – worth taking – all contained in one portable and convenient package.

At the open door of the compartment next to the one to which the porter ushered her, the big, burly man was standing – rather to my surprise. I thought I had startled him more than that. Presently who should come strolling up but his more slightly built acquaintance. Apparently he did not know him now; he passed into the compartment at whose door he was standing, without a nod or sign of greeting. My glance travelling down the platform, I saw that standing outside a compartment only a few doors off was Mr John Tung.

This did not suit me at all. I did not propose that those three gentlemen should travel with the grey-frocked lady by the five-five train to town. Rather than that I would have called in the aid of the police, though it would have been a very queer tale that I should have had to tell them. Perhaps fortunately, I hit upon what the old-time cookery books used to call 'another way'. I had done so well with one unexpected message that I thought I would try another. There were ten minutes before the train started – still time.

I rushed to the ladies' waiting-room. I begged a sheet of paper and an envelope from the attendant in charge. It was a sheet of paper which she gave me – and on it I scribbled:

'You are watched. Your intentions are known.

'The police are travelling by the five-five train to London in attendance on the lady in the grey dress. If they do not take you on the road they will arrest you when you reach town.

'Then heigh-ho for the gallows!'

I was in doubt whether or not to add that last line, I daresay if I had had a second or two to think I should not have added it; but I had not. I just scrawled it off as fast as I could, folded the sheet of paper, slipped it into the envelope, which I addressed in large, bold letters to Mr John Tung. The attendant had a little girl with her, of, perhaps, twelve or thirteen years old, who was acting as her assistant. I took her to the waiting-room door, pointed out Mr Tung, and told her that if she would slip that envelope into the gentleman's hand and come back to me without having told him where she got it from, I would give her a shilling.

Officials were examining tickets, doors were being closed, preparations were being made to start, when that long-legged young person ran off on her errand. She gave Mr Tung the envelope as he was stepping into the carriage.

He had not time even to realise that he had got it before she was off again. I saw him glance with a startled face at the envelope, open it hurriedly, scan what was within, then make a dart into the compartment by which he was standing, emerge with a bag in his hand, and hurry from the station. Conscience had been too much for him again. The big, burly man, seeing him going, went hurrying after him, as the train was in the very act of starting. As it moved along the platform the face of the third man appeared at the window of his compartment, gazing in apparent astonishment after the other two. He might go to London by the five-five if he chose. I did not think it mattered if he went alone. I scanned the newspapers very carefully the next day; as there was no record of anything unusual having happened during the journey or afterwards I concluded that my feeling that nothing was to be feared from that solitary gentleman had been well founded, and that the lady in the grey dress had reached her destination in comfort and safety. What became of Mr Tung when he left the station I do not know; I can only say that he did not return to the hotel. That Buxton episode was in August. About a month afterwards, towards the close of September, I was going north. I started from Euston station. I had secured my seat, and, as there were still several minutes before the train went off, I strolled up and down the platform. Outside the open door of one of the compartments, just as he had done at Buxton station, Mr Tung was standing!

The sight of him inspired me with a feeling of actual rage. That such a dreadful creature as I was convinced he was should go through life like some beast of prey, seeking for helpless victims whom it would be safe to destroy – that he should be standing there, so well-dressed, so well fed, so seemingly prosperous, with all the appearance about him of one with whom the world went very well – the sight of him made me positively furious. It might be impossible, for various reasons, to bring his crimes home to him, but I could still be a thorn in his side, and might punish him in a fashion of my own. I had been the occasion to him of one moment in which conscience had mastered him and terror held him by the throat. I might render him a similar service a second time.

I was seized with a sudden desire to give him a shock which would at least destroy his pleasure for the rest of that day. Recalling what I had done at Buxton, I went to the bookstall and purchased for the sum of one penny an envelope and a sheet of paper. I took these to the waiting-room, and on the sheet of paper I wrote three lines – without even a moment's consideration:

'You are about to be arrested. Justice is going to be done.

'Your time has come.

'Prepare for the end.'

I put the sheet of paper containing these words into the envelope, and, waylaying a small boy, who appeared to have been delivering a parcel to someone in the station, I instructed him to hand my gentleman the envelope and then make off. He did his part very well. Tung was standing sideways, looking down the platform, so that he did not see my messenger approaching from behind; the envelope was slipped into his hand almost before he knew it, and the boy was off. He found himself with an envelope in his hand without, I believe, clearly realising whence it had come – my messenger was lost in the crowd before he had turned; it might have tumbled from the skies for all he could say with certainty.

For him the recurrence of the episode of the mysterious envelope was in itself a shock. I could see that from where I stood. He stared at it, as he had done before, as if it had been a bomb which at any moment might explode. When he saw his own name written on the face of the envelope, and the fashion of the writing, he looked frantically around, as if eagerly seeking for some explanation of this strange thing. I should say, for all his appearance of sleek prosperity, that his nerves were in a state of jumps. His lips twitched; he seemed to be shaking; he looked as if it would need very little to make him run. With fingers which I am sure were trembling he opened the envelope; he took out the sheet of paper – and he read.

When he had read he seemed to be striving to keep himself from playing the cur; he looked across the platform with such an expression on his face and in his eyes! A constable was advancing towards him, with another man by his side. The probability is that, scared half out of his senses, conscience having come into its own, he misinterpreted the intention of the advancing couple.

Those three lines, warning him that he was about to be arrested, that his time had come, to prepare for the end, synchronised so perfectly with the appearance of the constable and his companion, who turned out to be a 'plain clothes man' engaged in the company's business, that in his suddenly unnerved state he jumped to the conclusion that the warning and its fulfilment had come together – that those two officers of the law were coming to arrest him there and then.

Having arrived at that conclusion, he seems to have passed quickly to another – that he would not be taken alive. He put his hand into his jacket pocket, took out a revolver, which had no doubt been kept there for quite another purpose, put the muzzle to his brow, and while the two men – thinking of him not at all – were still a few yards off, he blew his brains out. He was dead before they reached him – killed by conscience.

They found his luggage in the compartment in which he had been about to travel. The contents of his various belongings supplied sufficient explanation of his tragic end. He lived in a small flat off the Marylebone Road – alone; the address was contained in his bag. When the police went there they found a miscellaneous collection of articles which had certainly, in the original instance, never belonged to him. There were feminine belongings of all sorts and kinds. Some of them were traced to their former owners, and in each case the owner was found to have died in circumstances which had never been adequately explained. This man seemed to have been carrying on for years, with perfect impunity, a hideous traffic in robbery and murder – and the victim was always a woman. His true name was never ascertained. It was clear, from certain papers which were found in his flat, that he had spent several years of his youth in the East. He seemed to have been a solitary creature – a savage beast alone in its lair. Nothing was found out about his parents or his friends; nor about two acquaintances of whom I might have supplied some particulars. Personally, I never saw nor heard anything of either of them again.

I went on from Euston station by that train to the north. Just as we were about to start, a girl came bundling into my compartment whom I knew very well.

'That was a close shave,' she said, as she took her seat. 'I thought I should have missed it; my taxi-cab burst a tyre. What's this I heard them saying about someone having committed suicide on the platform? Is it true?'

'I believe there was something of the kind; in fact, I know there was. It has quite upset me.'

'Poor dear! You do look out of sorts. A thing like that would upset anyone.' She glanced at me with sympathetic eyes. 'I was talking about you only yesterday. I was saying that a person with your power of what practically amounts to reading people's thoughts ought to be able to do a great deal of good in the world. Do you think you ever do any good?'

The question was asked half laughingly. We were in a corridor carriage. Two women at the other end of it suddenly got up and went, apparently, in search of another. I had been in no state to notice anything when I had got in; now I realised that one of the women who had risen was the one who had worn the grey dress at Buxton. She had evidently recognised me on the instant. I saw her whisper to her companion in the corridor, before they moved off:

'I couldn't possibly remain in the same compartment with that half-bred gipsy-looking creature. I've had experience of her before.'

I was the half-bred gipsy-looking creature. The experience she had had of me was when I saved her life at Buxton. That I did save her life I am pretty sure. I said to my friend, when they had gone:

'I hope that sometimes I do do a little good; but even when I do, for the most part it's done by stealth, and not known to fame; and sometimes, even, it's not recognised as good at all.'

'Is that so?' replied my friend. 'What a very curious world it is.'

When I thought of what had happened on the platform which we were leaving so rapidly behind, I agreed with her with all my heart and soul.

LADY MOLLY OF
SCOTLAND YARD

Created by Baroness Orczy (1865–1947)

Born in Budapest into the Hungarian aristocracy, Emmuska Orczy moved with her parents to England when she was in her teens. She studied at art schools in London, where she met her husband, an illustrator, and her first published works were versions of Hungarian fairy tales which she translated and he illustrated. Her first historical novel appeared at the end of the 1890s, as did her first detective story. Nearly all her later work was in those two genres. Much the most famous character she created is Sir Percy Blakeney, 'The Scarlet Pimpernel', who first appeared in a drama on the London stage and then in a series of novels and short stories. Blakeney is an apparently effete Englishman who, in reality, is none other than the Scarlet Pimpernel, the daring and mysterious saviour of French aristocrats from the revolutionary guillotine. Orczy also created two memorable detectives. The first was 'The Old Man in the Corner', who solves baffling crimes whilst barely stirring from his seat in a London teashop. He appeared in magazine stories from 1901 and his adventures were later collected in three volumes. The second was Lady Molly Robertson-Kirk, a fictional detective working for Scotland Yard some years before women in real life were able to join the police. The Lady Molly stories are narrated by her fervent, occasionally fawning, admirer and assistant, Mary Granard. First published in 1910, they reflect some of the more irritating assumptions of the period about class and gender but are written with much of the same energy and élan that Orczy demonstrated in her Pimpernel books.

THE MAN IN THE INVERNESS CAPE

I

I have heard many people say – people, too, mind you, who read their daily paper regularly –that it is quite impossible for anyone to 'disappear' within the confines of the British Isles. At the same time these wise people invariably admit one great exception to their otherwise unimpeachable theory, and that is the case of Mr Leonard Marvell, who, as you know, walked out one afternoon from the Scotia Hotel in Cromwell Road and has never been seen or heard of since.

Information had originally been given to the police by Mr Marvell's sister Olive, a Scotchwoman of the usually accepted type: tall, bony, with sandy-coloured hair, and a somewhat melancholy expression in her blue-grey eyes.

Her brother, she said, had gone out on a rather foggy afternoon. I think it was the 3rd of February, just about a year ago. His intention had been to go and consult a solicitor in the City – whose address had been given him recently by a friend – about some private business of his own.

Mr Marvell had told his sister that he would get a train at South Kensington Station to Moorgate Street, and walk thence to Finsbury Square. She was to expect him home by dinnertime.

As he was, however, very irregular in his habits, being fond of spending his evenings at restaurants and music-halls, the sister did not feel the least anxious when he did not return home at the appointed time. She had her dinner in the *table d'hôte* room, and went to bed soon after ten.

She and her brother occupied two bedrooms and a sitting-room on the second floor of the little private hotel. Miss Marvell, moreover, had a maid always with her, as she was somewhat of an invalid. This girl, Rosie Campbell, a nice-looking Scotch lassie, slept on the top floor.

It was only on the following morning, when Mr Leonard did

not put in an appearance at breakfast that Miss Marvell began to feel anxious. According to her own account, she sent Rosie in to see if anything was the matter, and the girl, wide-eyed and not a little frightened, came back with the news that Mr Marvell was not in his room, and that his bed had not been slept in that night.

With characteristic Scottish reserve, Miss Olive said nothing about the matter at the time to anyone, nor did she give information to the police until two days later, when she herself had exhausted every means in her power to discover her brother's whereabouts.

She had seen the lawyer to whose office Leonard Marvell had intended going that afternoon, but Mr Statham, the solicitor in question, had seen nothing of the missing man.

With great adroitness Rosie, the maid, had made inquiries at South Kensington and Moorgate Street stations. At the former, the booking clerk, who knew Mr Marvell by sight, distinctly remembered selling him a first-class ticket to one of the City stations in the early part of the afternoon; but at Moorgate Street, which is a very busy station, no one recollected seeing a tall, red-haired Scotchman in an Inverness cape – such was the description given of the missing man. By that time the fog had become very thick in the City; traffic was disorganised, and everyone felt fussy, ill-tempered, and self-centred.

These, in substance, were the details which Miss Marvell gave to the police on the subject of her brother's strange disappearance.

At first she did not appear very anxious; she seemed to have great faith in Mr Marvell's power to look after himself; moreover, she declared positively that her brother had neither valuables nor money about his person when he went out that afternoon.

But as day succeeded day and no trace of the missing man had yet been found, matters became more serious, and the search instituted by our fellows at the Yard waxed more keen.

A description of Mr Leonard Marvell was published in the leading London and provincial dailies. Unfortunately, there was no good photograph of him extant, and descriptions are apt to prove vague.

Very little was known about the man beyond his disappearance, which had rendered him famous. He and his sister had arrived at the Scotia Hotel about a month previously, and subsequently they were joined by the maid Campbell.

Scotch people are far too reserved ever to speak of themselves or their affairs to strangers. Brother and sister spoke very little to anyone at the hotel. They had their meals in their sitting-room, waited on by the maid, who messed with the staff. But, in face of the present terrible calamity, Miss Marvell's frigidity relaxed before the police inspector, to whom she gave what information she could about her brother.

'He was like a son to me,' she explained with scarcely restrained tears, 'for we lost our parents early in life, and as we were left very, very badly off, our relations took but little notice of us. My brother was years younger than I am – and though he was a little wild and fond of pleasure, he was as good as gold to me, and has supported us both for years by journalistic work. We came to London from Glasgow about a month ago, because Leonard got a very good appointment on the staff of the *Daily Post*.'

All this, of course, was soon proved to be true; and although, on minute inquiries being instituted in Glasgow, but little seemed to be known about Mr Leonard Marvell in that city, there seemed no doubt that he had done some reporting for the *Courier*, and that latterly, in response to an advertisement, he had applied for and obtained regular employment on the *Daily Post*.

The latter enterprising halfpenny journal, with characteristic magnanimity, made an offer of £50 reward to any of its subscribers who gave information which would lead to the discovery of the whereabouts of Mr Leonard Marvell.

But time went by, and that £50 remained unclaimed.

II

Lady Molly had not seemed as interested as she usually was in cases of this sort. With strange flippancy – wholly unlike herself – she remarked that one Scotch journalist more or less in London did not vastly matter.

I was much amused, therefore, one morning about three weeks after the mysterious disappearance of Mr Leonard Marvell, when Jane, our little parlour-maid, brought in a card accompanied by a letter.

The card bore the name 'Miss Olive Marvell'. The letter was the usual formula from the chief, asking Lady Molly to have a talk with the lady in question, and to come and see him on the subject after the interview.

With a smothered yawn my dear lady told Jane to show in Miss Marvell.

'There are two of them, my lady,' said Jane, as she prepared to obey.

'Two what?' asked Lady Molly with a laugh.

'Two ladies, I mean,' explained Jane.

'Well! Show them both into the drawing-room,' said Lady Molly, impatiently.

Then, as Jane went off on this errand, a very funny thing happened; funny, because during the entire course of my intimate association with my dear lady, I had never known her act with such marked indifference in the face of an obviously interesting case. She turned to me and said:

'Mary, you had better see these two women, whoever they may be; I feel that they would bore me to distraction. Take note of what they say, and let me know. Now, don't argue,' she added with a laugh, which peremptorily put a stop to my rising protest, 'but go and interview Miss Marvell and Co.'

Needless to say, I promptly did as I was told, and the next few seconds saw me installed in our little drawing-room, saying polite preliminaries to the two ladies who sat opposite to me.

I had no need to ask which of them was Miss Marvell. Tall, ill-dressed in deep black, with a heavy crape veil over her face, and black cotton gloves, she looked the uncompromising Scotchwoman to the life. In strange contrast to her depressing appearance, there sat beside her an over-dressed, much behatted, peroxided young woman, who bore the stamp of *the* profession all over her pretty, painted face.

Miss Marvell, I was glad to note, was not long in plunging into the subject which had brought her here.

'I saw a gentleman at Scotland Yard,' she explained, after a short preamble, 'because Miss – er – Lulu Fay came to me at the hotel this very morning with a story which, in my opinion, should have been told to the police directly my brother's disappearance became known, and not three weeks later.'

The emphasis which she laid on the last few words and the stern look with which she regarded the golden-haired young woman beside her, showed the disapproval with which the rigid Scotchwoman viewed any connection which her brother might have had with the lady, whose very name seemed unpleasant to her lips.

Miss – er – Lulu Fay blushed even through her rouge, and turned a pair of large, liquid eyes imploringly upon me.

'I – I didn't know. I was frightened,' she stammered.

'There's no occasion to be frightened now,' retorted Miss Marvell, 'and the sooner you try and be truthful about the whole matter, the better it will be for all of us.'

And the stern woman's lips closed with a snap, as she deliberately turned her back on Miss Fay and began turning over the leaves of a magazine which happened to be on a table close to her hand.

I muttered a few words of encouragement, for the little actress looked ready to cry. I spoke as kindly as I could, telling her that if indeed she could throw some light on Mr Marvell's present whereabouts it was her duty to be quite frank on the subject.

She 'hem'-ed and 'ha'-ed for a while, and her simpering ways were just beginning to tell on my nerves, when she suddenly started talking very fast.

'I am principal boy at the Grand,' she explained with great volubility; 'and I knew Mr Leonard Marvell well – in fact – er – he paid me a good deal of attention and –'

'Yes – and –?' I queried, for the girl was obviously nervous.

There was a pause. Miss Fay began to cry.

'And it seems that my brother took this young – er – lady to supper on the night of February 3rd, after which no one has ever seen or heard of him again,' here interposed Miss Marvell, quietly.

'Is that so?' I asked.

Lulu Fay nodded, whilst heavy tears fell upon her clasped hands.

'But why did you not tell this to the police three weeks ago?' I ejaculated, with all the sternness at my command.

'I – I was frightened,' she stammered.

'Frightened? Of what?'

'I am engaged to Lord Mountnewte and –'

'And you did not wish him to know that you were accepting the attentions of Mr Leonard Marvell – was that it? Well,' I added, with involuntary impatience, 'what happened after you had supper with Mr Marvell?'

'Oh! I hope – I hope that nothing happened,' she said through more tears; 'we had supper at the Trocadero, and he saw me into my brougham. Suddenly, just as I was driving away, I saw Lord Mountnewte standing quite close to us in the crowd.'

'Did the two men know one another?' I asked.

'No,' replied Miss Fay; 'at least, I didn't think so, but when I looked back through the window of my carriage I saw them standing on the kerb talking to each other for a moment, and then walk off together towards Piccadilly Circus. That is the last I have seen of either of them,' continued the little actress with a fresh flood of tears. 'Lord Mountnewte hasn't spoken to me since, and Mr Marvell has disappeared with my money and my diamonds.'

'Your money and your diamonds?' I gasped in amazement.

'Yes; he told me he was a jeweller, and that my diamonds wanted re-setting. He took them with him that evening, for he said that London jewellers were clumsy thieves, and that he would love to do the work for me himself. I also gave him two hundred pounds, which he said he would want for buying the gold and platinum required for the settings. And now he has disappeared – and my diamonds – and my money! Oh! I have been very – very foolish –and –'

Her voice broke down completely. Of course, one often hears of the idiocy of girls giving money and jewels unquestioningly to clever adventurers who know how to trade upon their inordinate vanity. There was, therefore, nothing very out of the way in the story just told me by Miss – er – Lulu Fay, until the moment when Miss Marvell's quiet voice, with its marked Scotch burr, broke in upon the short silence which had followed the actress's narrative.

'As I explained to the chief detective-inspector at Scotland Yard,' she said calmly, 'the story which this young – er – lady tells is only partly true. She may have had supper with Mr Leonard Marvell on the night of February 3rd, and he may have paid her certain attentions; but he never deceived her by telling her that he was a jeweller, nor did he obtain possession of her diamonds and her money through false statements. My brother was the soul of honour and loyalty. If for some reason which Miss – er – Lulu Fay chooses to keep secret, he had her jewels and money in his possession on the fatal February 3rd, then I think his disappearance is accounted for. He has been robbed and perhaps murdered.'

Like a true Scotchwoman she did not give way to tears, but even her harsh voice trembled slightly when she thus bore witness to her brother's honesty, and expressed the fears which assailed her as to his fate.

Imagine my plight! I could ill forgive my dear lady for leaving me in this unpleasant position – a sort of peacemaker between two women who evidently hated one another, and each of whom was trying her best to give the other 'the lie direct'.

I ventured to ring for our faithful Jane and to send her with an imploring message to Lady Molly, begging her to come and disentangle the threads of this muddled skein with her clever fingers; but Jane returned with a curt note from my dear lady, telling me not to worry about such a silly case, and to bow the two women out of the flat as soon as possible and then come for a nice walk.

I wore my official manner as well as I could, trying not to betray the 'prentice hand. Of course, the interview lasted a great deal longer, and there was considerably more talk than I can tell you of in a brief narrative. But the gist of it all was just as I have said. Miss Lulu Fay stuck to every point of the story which she had originally told Miss Marvell. It was the latter uncompromising lady who had immediately marched the younger woman off to Scotland Yard in order that she might repeat her tale to the police. I did not wonder that the chief promptly referred them both to Lady Molly.

Anyway, I made excellent shorthand notes of the conflicting stories which I heard; and I finally saw, with real relief, the two women walk out of our little front door.

III

Miss – er – Lulu Fay, mind you, never contradicted in any one particular the original story which she had told me, about going out to supper with Leonard Marvell, entrusting him with £200 and the diamonds, which he said he would have reset for her, and seeing him finally in close conversation with her recognised *fiancé*, Lord Mountnewte. Miss Marvell, on the other hand, very commendably refused to admit that her brother acted dishonestly towards the girl. If he had her jewels and money in his possession at the time of his disappearance, then he had undoubtedly been robbed, or perhaps murdered, on his way back to the hotel, and if Lord Mountnewte had been the last to speak to him on that fatal night, then Lord Mountnewte must be able to throw some light on the mysterious occurrence.

Our fellows at the Yard were abnormally active. It seemed, on the face of it, impossible that a man, healthy, vigorous, and admittedly sober, should vanish in London between Piccadilly Circus and Cromwell Road without leaving the slightest trace of himself or of the valuables said to have been in his possession.

Of course, Lord Mountnewte was closely questioned. He was a young Guardsman of the usual pattern, and, after a great deal of vapid talk which irritated Detective-Inspector Saunders not a little, he made the following statement:

'I certainly am acquainted with Miss Lulu Fay. On the night in question I was standing outside the Troc, when I saw this young lady at her own carriage window talking to a tall man in an Inverness cape. She had, earlier in the day, refused my invitation to supper, saying that she was not feeling very well, and would go home directly after the theatre; therefore I felt, naturally, a little vexed. I was just about to hail a taxi, meaning to go on to the club, when, to my intense astonishment, the man in the Inverness cape came up to me and asked me if I could tell him the best way to get back to Cromwell Road.'

'And what did you do?' asked Saunders.

'I walked a few steps with him and put him on his way,' replied Lord Mountnewte, blandly.

In Saunders's own expressive words, he thought that story 'fishy'. He could not imagine the arm of coincidence being quite so long as to cause these two men – who presumably were both in love with the same girl, and who had just met at a moment when one of them was obviously suffering pangs of jealousy – to hold merely a topographical conversation with one another. But it was equally difficult to suppose that the eldest son and heir of the Marquis of Loam should murder a successful rival and then rob him in the streets of London.

Moreover, here came the eternal and unanswerable questions: If Lord Mountnewte had murdered Leonard Marvell, where and how had he done it, and what had he done with the body?

I dare say you are wondering by this time why I have said nothing about the maid, Rosie Campbell.

Well, plenty of very clever people (I mean those who write

letters to the papers and give suggestions to every official department in the kingdom) thought that the police ought to keep a very strict eye upon that pretty Scotch lassie. For she was very pretty, and had quaint, demure ways which rendered her singularly attractive, in spite of the fact that, for most masculine tastes, she would have been considered too tall. Of course, Saunders and Danvers kept an eye on her – you may be sure of that – and got a good deal of information about her from the people at the hotel. Most of it, unfortunately, was irrelevant to the case. She was maid-attendant to Miss Marvell, who was feeble in health, and who went out but little. Rosie waited on her master and mistress upstairs, carrying their meals to their private room, and doing their bedrooms. The rest of the day she was fairly free, and was quite sociable downstairs with the hotel staff.

With regard to her movements and actions on that memorable 3rd of February, Saunders – though he worked very hard – could glean but little useful information. You see, in a hotel of that kind, with an average of thirty to forty guests at one time, it is extremely difficult to state positively what any one person did or did not do on that particular day.

Most people at the Scotia remembered that Miss Marvell dined in the *table d'hôte* room on that 3rd of February; this she did about once a fortnight, when her maid had an evening 'out'.

The hotel staff also recollected fairly distinctly that Miss Rosie Campbell was not in the steward's room at suppertime that evening, but no one could remember definitely when she came in.

One of the chambermaids who occupied the bedroom adjoining hers, said she heard her moving about soon after midnight; the hall porter declared that he saw her come in just before half past twelve when he closed the doors for the night.

But one of the ground-floor valets said that, on the morning of the 4th, he saw Miss Marvell's maid, in hat and coat, slip into the house and upstairs, very quickly and quietly, soon after the front doors were opened, namely, about 7.00 am.

Here, of course, was a direct contradiction between the chambermaid and hall porter on the one side, and the valet on the other, whilst Miss Marvell said that Campbell came into her room and made her some tea long before seven o'clock every morning, including that of the 4th.

I assure you our fellows at the Yard were ready to tear their hair out by the roots, from sheer aggravation at this maze of contradictions which met them at every turn.

The whole thing seemed so simple. There was nothing 'to it' as it were, and but very little real suggestion of foul play, and yet Mr Leonard Marvell had disappeared, and no trace of him could be found.

Everyone now talked freely of murder. London is a big town, and this would not have been the first instance of a stranger – for Mr Leonard Marvell was practically a stranger in London – being enticed to a lonely part of the city on a foggy night, and there done away with and robbed, and the body hidden in an out-of-the-way cellar, where it might not be discovered for months to come.

But the newspaper-reading public is notably fickle, and Mr Leonard Marvell was soon forgotten by everyone save the chief and the batch of our fellows who had charge of the case.

Thus I heard through Danvers one day that Rosie Campbell had left Miss Marvell's employ, and was living in rooms in Findlater Terrace, near Walham Green.

I was alone in our Maida Vale flat at the time, my dear lady having gone to spend the weekend with the Dowager Lady Loam, who was an old friend of hers; nor, when she returned, did she seem any more interested in Rosie Campbell's movements than she had been hitherto.

Yet another month went by, and I for one had absolutely ceased to think of the man in the Inverness cape, who had so mysteriously and so completely vanished in the very midst of busy London, when, one morning early in January, Lady Molly made her appearance in my room, looking more like the landlady of a disreputable gambling-house than anything else I could imagine.

'What in the world –?' I began.

'Yes! I think I look the part,' she replied, surveying with obvious complacency the extraordinary figure which confronted her in the glass.

My dear lady had on a purple cloth coat and skirt of a peculiarly vivid hue, and of a singular cut, which made her matchless figure look like a sack of potatoes. Her soft brown hair was quite hidden beneath a 'transformation', of that yellow-reddish tint only to be met with in very cheap dyes.

As for her hat! I won't attempt to describe it. It towered above and around her face, which was plentifully covered with brick-red and with that kind of powder which causes the cheeks to look a deep mauve.

My dear lady looked, indeed, a perfect picture of appalling vulgarity.

'Where are you going in this elegant attire?' I asked in amazement.

'I have taken rooms in Findlater Terrace,' she replied lightly. 'I feel that the air of Walham Green will do us both good. Our amiable, if somewhat slatternly, landlady expects us in time for luncheon. You will have to keep rigidly in the background, Mary, all the while we are there. I said that I was bringing an invalid niece with me, and, as a preliminary, you may as well tie two or three thick veils over your face. I think I may safely promise that you won't be dull.'

And we certainly were not dull during our brief stay at 34, Findlater Terrace, Walham Green. Fully equipped, and arrayed in our extraordinary garments, we duly arrived there, in a rickety four-wheeler, on the top of which were perched two seedy-looking boxes.

The landlady was a toothless old creature, who apparently thought washing a quite unnecessary proceeding. In this she was evidently at one with every one of her neighbours. Findlater Terrace looked unspeakably squalid; groups of dirty children congregated in the gutters and gave forth discordant shrieks as our cab drove up.

Through my thick veils I thought that, some distance down the road, I spied a horsy-looking man in ill-fitting riding-breeches and gaiters, who vaguely reminded me of Danvers.

Within half an hour of our installation, and whilst we were eating a tough steak over a doubtful table cloth, my dear lady told me that she had been waiting a full month, until rooms in this particular house happened to be vacant. Fortunately the population in Findlater Terrace is always a shifting one, and Lady Molly had kept a sharp eye on No 34, where, on the floor above, lived Miss Rosie Campbell. Directly the last set of lodgers walked out of the ground-floor rooms, we were ready to walk in.

My dear lady's manners and customs, whilst living at the above aristocratic address, were fully in keeping with her appearance. The shrill, rasping voice which she assumed echoed from attic to cellar.

One day I heard her giving vague hints to the landlady that her husband, Mr Marcus Stein, had had a little trouble with the police about a small hotel which he had kept somewhere near Fitzroy Square, and where 'young gentlemen used to come and play cards of a night'. The landlady was also made to understand that the worthy Mr Stein was now living temporarily at His Majesty's expense, whilst Mrs Stein had to live a somewhat secluded life, away from her fashionable friends.

The misfortunes of the pseudo Mrs Stein in no way marred the amiability of Mrs Tredwen, our landlady. The inhabitants of Findlater Terrace care very little about the antecedents of their lodgers, so long as they pay their week's rent in advance, and settle their 'extras' without much murmur.

This Lady Molly did, with a generosity characteristic of an ex-lady of means. She never grumbled at the quantity of jam and marmalade which we were supposed to have consumed every week, and which anon reached titanic proportions. She tolerated Mrs Tredwen's cat, tipped Ermyntrude – the tousled lodging-house slavey – lavishly, and lent the upstairs lodger her spirit-lamp and curling-tongs when Miss Rosie Campbell's got out of order.

A certain degree of intimacy followed the loan of those curling-tongs. Miss Campbell, reserved and demure, greatly sympathised with the lady who was not on the best of terms with the police. I kept steadily in the background. The two ladies did not visit each other's rooms, but they held long and confidential conversations on the landings, and I gathered, presently, that the pseudo Mrs Stein had succeeded in persuading Rosie Campbell that, if the police were watching No 34, Findlater Terrace, at all, it was undoubtedly on account of the unfortunate Mr Stein's faithful wife.

I found it a little difficult to fathom Lady Molly's intentions. We had been in the house over three weeks and nothing whatever had happened. Once I ventured on a discreet query as to whether we were to expect the sudden re-appearance of Mr Leonard Marvell.

'For if that's all about it,' I argued, 'then surely the men from the Yard could have kept the house in view, without all this inconvenience and masquerading on our part.'

But to this tirade my dear lady vouchsafed no reply.

She and her newly acquired friend were, about this time, deeply interested in the case known as the 'West End Shop Robberies', which no doubt you recollect, since they occurred such a very little while ago. Ladies who were shopping in the large drapers' emporiums during the crowded and busy sale time, lost reticules, purses, and valuable parcels, without any trace of the clever thief being found.

The drapers, during sale-time, invariably employ detectives in plain clothes to look after their goods, but in this case it was the customers who were robbed, and the detectives, attentive to every attempt at 'shoplifting', had had no eyes for the more subtle thief.

I had already noticed Miss Rosie Campbell's keen look of

excitement whenever the pseudo Mrs Stein discussed these cases with her. I was not a bit surprised, therefore, when, one afternoon at about teatime, my dear lady came home from her habitual walk, and, at the top of her shrill voice, called out to me from the hall:

'Mary! Mary! They've got the man of the shop robberies. He's given the silly police the slip this time, but they know who he is now, and I suppose they'll get him presently. 'Tisn't anybody I know,' she added, with that harsh, common laugh which she had adopted for her part.

I had come out of the room in response to her call, and was standing just outside our own sitting-room door. Mrs Tredwen, too, bedraggled and unkempt, as usual, had sneaked up the area steps, closely followed by Ermyntrude.

But on the half-landing just above us the trembling figure of Rosie Campbell, with scared white face and dilated eyes, looked on the verge of a sudden fall.

Still talking shrilly and volubly, Lady Molly ran up to her, but Campbell met her halfway, and the pseudo Mrs Stein, taking vigorous hold of her wrist, dragged her into our own sitting-room.

'Pull yourself together, now,' she said with rough kindness; 'that owl Tredwen is listening, and you needn't let her know too much. Shut the door, Mary. Lor' bless you, m'dear, I've gone through worse scares than these. There! You just lie down on this sofa a bit. My niece'll make you a nice cup o' tea; and I'll go and get an evening paper, and see what's going on. I suppose you are very interested in the shop robbery man, or you wouldn't have took on so.'

Without waiting for Campbell's contradiction to this statement, Lady Molly flounced out of the house.

Miss Campbell hardly spoke during the next ten minutes that she and I were left alone together. She lay on the sofa with eyes wide open, staring up at the ceiling, evidently still in a great state of fear.

I had just got tea ready when Lady Molly came back. She had an evening paper in her hand, but threw this down on the table directly she came in.

'I could only get an early edition,' she said breathlessly, 'and the silly thing hasn't got anything in it about the matter.'

She drew near to the sofa, and, subduing the shrillness of her voice, she whispered rapidly, bending down towards Campbell:

'There's a man hanging about at the corner down there. No, no; it's not the police,' she added quickly, in response to the girl's sudden start of alarm. 'Trust me, my dear, for knowing a 'tec when I see one! Why, I'd smell one half a mile off. No; my opinion is that it's your man, my dear, and that he's in a devil of a hole.'

'Oh! He oughtn't to come here,' ejaculated Campbell in great alarm. 'He'll get me into trouble and do himself no good. He's been a fool!' she added, with a fierceness wholly unlike her usual demure placidity, 'getting himself caught like that. Now I suppose we shall have to hook it – if there's time.'

'Can I do anything to help you?' asked the pseudo Mrs Stein. 'You know I've been through all this myself, when they was after Mr Stein. Or perhaps Mary could do something.'

'Well, yes,' said the girl, after a slight pause, during which she seemed to be gathering her wits together; 'I'll write a note, and you shall take it, if you will, to a friend of mine – a lady who lives in the Cromwell Road. But if you still see a man lurking about at the corner of the street, then, just as you pass him, say the word "Campbell", and if he replies "Rosie", then give *him* the note. Will you do that?'

'Of course I will, my dear. Just you leave it all to me.'

And the pseudo Mrs Stein brought ink and paper and placed them on the table. Rosie Campbell wrote a brief note, and then fastened it down with a bit of sealing-wax before she handed it over to Lady Molly. The note was addressed to Miss Marvell, Scotia Hotel, Cromwell Road.

'You understand?' she said eagerly. 'Don't give the note to the man unless he says "Rosie" in reply to the word "Campbell".'

'All right – all right!' said Lady Molly, slipping the note into her reticule. 'And you go up to your room, Miss Campbell; it's no good giving that old fool Tredwen too much to gossip about.'

Rosie Campbell went upstairs, and presently my dear lady and I were walking rapidly down the badly lighted street.

'Where is the man?' I whispered eagerly as soon as we were out of earshot of No 34.

'There is no man,' replied Lady Molly, quickly.

'But the West End shop thief?' I asked.

'He hasn't been caught yet, and won't be either, for he is far too clever a scoundrel to fall into an ordinary trap.'

She did not give me time to ask further questions, for presently, when we had reached Reporton Square, my dear lady handed me the note written by Campbell, and said:

'Go straight on to the Scotia Hotel, and ask for Miss Marvell; send up the note to her, but don't let her see you, as she knows you by sight. I must see the chief first, and will be with you as soon as possible. Having delivered the note, you must hang about outside as long as you can. Use your wits; she must not leave the hotel before I see her.'

There was no hansom to be got in this elegant quarter of the town, so, having parted from my dear lady, I made for the nearest Underground station, and took a train for South Kensington.

Thus it was nearly seven o'clock before I reached the Scotia. In answer to my inquiries for Miss Marvell, I was told that she was ill in bed and could see no one. I replied that I had only brought a note for her, and would wait for a reply.

Acting on my dear lady's instructions, I was as slow in my movements as ever I could be, and was some time in finding the note and handing it to a waiter, who then took it upstairs.

Presently he returned with the message: 'Miss Marvell says there is no answer.'

Whereupon I asked for pen and paper at the office, and wrote the following brief note on my own responsibility, using my wits as my dear lady had bidden me to do.

'Please, madam,' I wrote, 'will you send just a line to Miss Rosie Campbell? She seems very upset and frightened at some news she has had.'

Once more the waiter ran upstairs, and returned with a sealed envelope, which I slipped into my reticule.

Time was slipping by very slowly. I did not know how long I should have to wait outside in the cold, when, to my horror, I heard a hard voice, with a marked Scotch accent, saying:

'I am going out, waiter, and shan't be back to dinner. Tell them to lay a little cold supper upstairs in my room.'

The next moment Miss Marvell, with coat, hat, and veil, was descending the stairs.

My plight was awkward. I certainly did not think it safe to present myself before the lady; she would undoubtedly recollect my face. Yet I had orders to detain her until the appearance of Lady Molly.

Miss Marvell seemed in no hurry. She was putting on her gloves as she came downstairs. In the hall she gave a few more instructions to the porter, whilst I, in a dark corner in the background, was vaguely planning an assault or an alarm of fire.

Suddenly, at the hotel entrance, where the porter was obsequiously holding open the door for Miss Marvell to pass through, I saw the latter's figure stiffen; she took one step back as if involuntarily, then, equally quickly, attempted to dart across the threshold, on which a group – composed of my dear lady, of Saunders, and of two or three people scarcely distinguishable in the gloom beyond – had suddenly made its appearance.

Miss Marvell was forced to retreat into the hall; already I had heard Saunders's hurriedly whispered words:

'Try and not make a fuss in this place, now. Everything can go off quietly, you know.'

Danvers and Cotton, whom I knew well, were already standing one each side of Miss Marvell, whilst suddenly amongst this group I recognised Fanny, the wife of Danvers, who is one of our female searchers at the Yard.

'Shall we go up to your own room?' suggested Saunders.

'I think that is quite unnecessary,' interposed Lady Molly. 'I feel convinced that Mr Leonard Marvell will yield to the inevitable quietly, and follow you without giving any trouble.'

Marvell, however, did make a bold dash for liberty. As Lady Molly had said previously, he was far too clever to allow himself to be captured easily. But my dear lady had been cleverer. As she told me subsequently, she had from the first suspected that the trio who lodged at the Scotia Hotel were really only a duo – namely, Leonard Marvell and his wife. The latter impersonated a maid most of the time; but among these two clever people the three characters were interchangeable. Of course, there was no Miss Marvell at all. Leonard was alternately dressed up as man or woman, according to the requirements of his villainies.

'As soon as I heard that Miss Marvell was very tall and bony,' said Lady Molly, 'I thought that there might be a possibility of her being merely a man in disguise. Then there was the fact – but little dwelt on by either the police or the public – that no one seems ever to have seen brother and sister together, nor was the entire trio ever seen at one and the same time.

'On that 3rd of February Leonard Marvell went out. No doubt he changed his attire in a lady's waiting-room at one of the railway stations; subsequently he came home, now dressed as Miss Marvell, and had dinner in the *table d'hôte* room so as to set up a fairly plausible alibi. But ultimately it was his wife, the pseudo Rosie Campbell, who stayed indoors that night, whilst he, Leonard Marvell, when going out after dinner, impersonated the maid until he was clear of the hotel; then he reassumed his male clothes once more, no doubt in the deserted waiting-room of some railway station, and met Miss Lulu Fay at supper, subsequently returning to the hotel in the guise of the maid.

'You see the game of criss-cross, don't you? This interchanging of characters was bound to baffle everyone. Many clever scoundrels have assumed disguises, sometimes impersonating members of the opposite sex to their own, but never before have I known two people play the part of three. Thus, endless contradictions followed as to the hour when Campbell the maid went out and when she came in, for at one time it was she herself who was seen by the valet, and at another it was Leonard Marvell dressed in her clothes.'

He was also clever enough to accost Lord Mountnewte in the open street, thus bringing further complications into this strange case.

After the successful robbery of Miss Fay's diamonds, Leonard Marvell and his wife parted for a while. They were waiting for an opportunity to get across the Channel and there turn their booty into solid cash. Whilst Mrs Marvell, *alias* Rosie Campbell, led a retired life in Findlater Terrace, Leonard kept his hand in with West End shop robberies.

Then Lady Molly entered the lists. As usual, her scheme was bold and daring; she trusted her own intuition and acted accordingly.

When she brought home the false news that the author of the shop robberies had been spotted by the police, Rosie Campbell's obvious terror confirmed her suspicions. The note written by the latter to the so-called Miss Marvell, though it contained nothing in any way incriminating, was the crowning certitude that my dear lady was right, as usual, in all her surmises.

And now Mr Leonard Marvell will be living for a couple of years at the tax-payers' expense; he has 'disappeared' temporarily from the public eye.

Rosie Campbell – *i.e.* Mrs Marvell – has gone to Glasgow. I feel convinced that two years hence we shall hear of the worthy couple again.

MADELYN MACK

Created by Hugh Cosgro Weir (1884-1934)

Born in Illinois, Hugh Cosgro Weir began his career as a journalist when he was still in his teens and soon graduated to writing fiction for the many pulp magazines that flourished in America in the early years of the twentieth century. He also showed an early interest in the burgeoning new film industry, selling his stories for adaptation and writing his own screenplays. Before his early death at the age of 49, he also established his own advertising agency and set up a magazine publishing company. His best remembered fiction is the volume of short stories entitled Miss Madelyn Mack, Detective, *first published in 1914. Madelyn Mack is an interesting creation, far more unusual and original than most of the other female detectives of the period. Weir goes to great lengths to emphasise her genius as a criminologist and, like Holmes, she attracts much admiring attention for her startling deductive abilities. Also like Holmes, she has her Watson (in the journalist Nora Noraker) and her eccentricities – she carries a locket around her neck in which she keeps cola berries to keep her awake for days at a stretch when she is on a particularly demanding case. (Sadly, as the story below reveals, her classical education is lacking and she can't distinguish between Latin poets and Greek poets.) Thanks to Weir's contacts in Hollywood, several of the Madelyn Mack stories were made into short films starring Alice Joyce, a popular actress who appeared in more than 200 movies in the silent era.*

THE MISSING BRIDEGROOM

I

Two million dollars and the most beautiful girl in the county were to be Norris Endicott's in another twenty-five minutes.

He was emphatically in love with Bertha Van Sutton, but cared nothing for her millions, in spite of the remembrance of his own uncertain income as a struggling architect. The next half-hour was to bring him all that a reasonable man could ask in this uncertain world.

This was his position and outlook at the Van Sutton home at seven forty pm. Someone has said that a moment can change the course of a battle. Also it can revolutionise a man's life – perhaps end it altogether – and pitchfork him into another. At five minutes past eight – the hour that Endicott was to have made Bertha Van Sutton his wife – he had vanished from 'The Maples' as completely and mysteriously as though the balmy earth outside had opened and swallowed him. The expectant bridegroom literally had been whisked into oblivion.

At twenty minutes before eight o'clock, Willard White, glancing into his room, found Endicott pacing the floor, his tall, closely knit figure showing to excellent advantage in his evening clothes, a quiet smile, as of anticipation, on his face as he held a match to his cigarette.

'Nervous, old man?' White called banteringly, holding the door ajar.

Endicott turned with a laugh. 'Nervous? When the best girl in the world is about to be mine – all mine? Of course I'm nervous, but it's because I am so happy I can hardly keep my feet on the ground!' (Which was a somewhat hysterical, but thoroughly human remark, you would agree, had you ever worshipped at the shrine of Bertha Van Sutton!)

At five minutes past eight the orchestra shifted the music of Mendelssohn's 'Wedding March' to their racks, the leader cleared his throat in expectation of the signal to raise his baton, and the chattering throngs of guests, scattered through the lavishly decorated house from the conservatory to the veranda, swept into the long red-and-gold drawing-room, with the bower of palms and orchids at the end drawing admiring exclamations even from the most cynical dowagers. Adolph Van Sutton's millions assuredly had set a fit stage for the most talked-of wedding of the season.

Outside, Adolph himself was fumbling nervously with his cuffs as the bridal party ranged itself in whispering ranks for the entry. Bertha Van Sutton had just appeared with Ethel Allison, her chief bridesmaid and chum since boarding-school days. As she took the arm of her father, she made a picture to justify the half-audible sighs of envy from the bevy of attendants. With the folds of her long veil reaching almost to the hem of her gown and the sweep of her train, her figure looked almost regal in spite of her girlish slenderness. Her dark hair, piled in a great, loose coil, heightened the impression, which might have given her the suggestion of haughtiness had it not been for the magnetism of her smile.

The smile was bubbling in her eyes as she glanced around with the surprised question, 'Where's Norris?'

Her father looked up quickly, but it was Ethel Allison who answered, 'Willard White has just gone after him, Bert. Here he comes now!'

The best man came hurriedly through the door. As he paused, he wiped his forehead with his handkerchief.

'Where's Norris, Willard?' Miss Allison asked impatiently.

'He's gone!'

'Gone!' The bridesmaid's voice rose to a shrill falsetto.

The best man shook his head in a sort of blind bewilderment. 'He's gone,' he repeated, mechanically.

The bride whirled. Adolph Van Sutton strode forward and seized White by the arm.

'What, under Heaven, are you giving us, man?'

225

White stiffened his shoulders as though the sharp grasp had awakened him from his daze.

'Norris Endicott is not in this house, sir!' he cried, as if realising for the first time the full import of his announcement.

In the drawing-room, the orchestra-leader, with a final look at the empty door, lowered his baton with a snort of disgust and plumped sullenly back in his chair. The jewel-studded ranks of the crowding guests elevated their eyebrows in polite wonder. In the corner, the palms that were to have sheltered the bride beckoned impatiently.

On the velvet carpet, outside, lay a white, silent figure. It was Bertha Van Sutton who had fallen, an unconscious heap in the folds of her wedding finery.

Upstairs in the groom's apartment, a circle of dishevelled men were staring at one another in tongue-tied bewilderment. Norris Endicott might have vanished into thin air, evaporated. The man who was to wed the Van Sutton heiress had been blotted out, eliminated.

As the group edged uneasily toward the door, a stray breeze, fragrant with the evening odours of the flower-lined lawn below, swept through the open window. A small object, half buried in the curtain folds, fell with a soft thud to the floor. The nearest man stooped toward it almost unconsciously. It was a silver ball, perhaps three-quarters of an inch in diameter. With a shrug, he passed it to Adolph Van Sutton. The latter dropped it mechanically into his pocket.

II

The five o'clock sun was splashing its waning glow down on to the autumn-thinned trees when I pushed open the rustic gate of 'The Rosary' the next afternoon to carry the sombre problem that was beyond me to the wizard skill of Madelyn Mack.

I was frankly tired after the day's buffetings. And there was a soothing restfulness in the velvet green of the close-cropped lawn, with its fat box hedges and the scarlet splashes of its canna beds that brought me to an almost involuntary pause lest I break the spell. Madelyn Mack's rose garden beyond was a wreck of shrivelled bushes, but my pang at the memory of its faded glories was softened by the banks of asters and cosmos marshalled before it as though to hide its emptiness. The snake-like coil of a black hose was pouring a playful spray into a circle of scarlet sage at the side of the gravelled path, with the gaunt figure of Andrew Bolton crouching, hatless, near it, trimming a ragged line of grass with a pair of long shears.

With a sigh I turned toward the quaint chalet nestling ahead. I might have been miles from the rumble of the work-a-day world.

I smiled – somewhat cynically, I will confess – as I pulled the old-fashioned knocker. There were few persons yet who knew, as I did, the shadows surrounding the wedding-night vanishing of Norris Endicott. Could Madelyn solve the problem that had already taken rank as the most baffling police case of five years?

The sphinx-like face of Susan Bolton greeted me on the other side of the door. She was dressed for the street in her prim bonnet and black silk gown.

'Miss Madelyn said you would be here, Miss Noraker,' she greeted me. 'I thought I might meet you on my way to the Missionary Tea.'

Crime and a Missionary Tea! I smiled at the incongruity as I protested, 'But I never told her I was coming! How in the world –'

Susan threw up her mittened hands. 'Law, child, don't you know she has a way of finding out things?'

A sudden laugh and the friendly bark of a dog sounded from the end of the hall. A slight figure in black stepped toward me with her two hands extended. At her heels, Peter the Great trotted lazily.

'I am glad you came before six!' she said, as she seized and held both of my hands, a distinctively Madelyn Mack habit. 'I was afraid you would be delayed. The trolley service to the Van Sutton place is abominable!'

'But why did you want me before six?' I cried. 'And how did you know I was coming at all? And how –'

Madelyn released my hands with a smile. 'Really, you must give me time to catch my breath! Come into the den with Peter the Great, and toast yourself while we cross-examine each other.'

It was not until she was drawn up before the crackling log in the great open fireplace, with the dog curled contentedly on the jaguar skin at her feet, that she spoke again, and then it was in the rapid-fire fashion that showed me she was 'hot on a winding trail,' as she would express it.

'I will answer your questions first,' she began, as she rested her chin on her left hand in her favourite attitude and peered across at me, her eyes glowing with the restless energy of her mood. 'I telephoned the *Bugle* office this morning and was told that you had just left for "The Maples". Of course, I knew that Nora Noraker, the star reporter, would be put on the Van Sutton case at once, and I had a shrewd idea from past experience that you would bring the problem to me before night. As I am to meet Adolph Van Sutton here at six, I was anxious to review the field with you before his arrival. I was retained in the case this afternoon, as I rather expected to be, after I had read the early editions of the papers and saw that the police would have to abandon their obvious theory.'

I raised my eyebrows. 'What is that?'

She shrugged her shoulders. 'Murder! I had not read half a dozen paragraphs before I saw that this, of course, was absurd, and that even the police would have to admit as much before night.'

'But they haven't!' I cut in triumphantly. 'Detective Wiley gave out an interview just before I left – said there was no doubt that Endicott had been made away with!'

'Then the more fool he!' Madelyn stirred the gnarled log in the fireplace until a shower of yellow sparks went dancing up the chimney. 'I could show him his mistake in three sentences.'

For a moment she sat staring at me, with her long lashes veiling a slow smile.

'Do they use gas or electricity at "The Maples"?' she asked, abruptly.

I thought for a moment. 'Both,' I answered. 'Why?'

'Was either burning in Endicott's room at the time of his disappearance?'

I shook my head with a helpless smile.

Madelyn rubbed her hands gently through the long, shaggy hair of Peter the Great. We both sat staring into the fire for quite five minutes. 'Did Endicott dress at "The Maples" for the ceremony?' she demanded suddenly. 'Or did he dress before he appeared at the house?' I could feel her eyes studying me as I pondered the question.

I looked up finally with an expression of rueful bewilderment.

'Oh, Nora! Nora!' she cried, with a little stamp of her foot. 'Where are your eyes and your ears? And you at the house all day!'

'I rather flattered myself that I had found out all there was to find,' I answered somewhat petulantly.

Madelyn reached over to the divan by her elbow and selected a copy of the *Bugle* from the stack of crumpled papers that it contained. It was not until she had read slowly through the five-column report of the Van Sutton mystery – two columns of which I had contributed myself – that she looked up. 'I presume you have mentioned here everything of importance?'

I nodded. 'Norris Endicott was above suspicion – morally and financially. He had few friends – that is, close friends – but no enemies. There was absolutely no one who wished him ill, no one who might have a reason for doing so, unless –'

Madelyn noted my hesitation with a swift flash. 'You mean his defeated rivals for Miss Van Sutton's hand?'

'You have taken the words out of my mouth. There were two of them, and both were present at the wedding – that didn't take place. Curiously enough, one of the two was Endicott's best man,

Willard White. The other he also knew more or less intimately – Richard Bainbridge, the civil engineer.' I gazed across at her as I paused. To my disappointment, she was studying the carpet, with her thoughts obviously far away. 'That is all, I think,' I finished rather lamely.

The log in the fireplace fell downward with a shower of fresh sparks. Peter the Great growled uneasily. Madelyn took the dog's head in her lap, and was silent so long I thought she had forgotten me.

Suddenly she leaned back in her chair and her eyes half closed.

'One more question, Nora, if you please. I believe you said in your report that, when the group of searchers were leaving Endicott's vacant room, a small silver ball rolled from the sill to the floor. Do you happen to know whether the ball is solid or hollow?'

I smiled. 'It is hollow. I examined it this afternoon. But surely such a trivial incident –'

Madelyn pushed back her chair with a quick gesture of satisfaction. 'How often must I tell you that nothing is trivial – in crime? That answer atones for all of your previous failures, Nora. You may go to the head of the class! No, not another word!' she interrupted as I stared at her. 'I don't want to think or talk – now. I must have some music to clear my brain if I am to scatter these cobwebs!'

I sank back with a sigh of resignation and watched her as she stepped across to the phonograph, resting on the cabinet of records in the corner. I knew from experience that she had veered into a mood in which I would have gained an instant rebuke had I attempted to press the case farther. Patiently or impatiently, I must await her pleasure to reopen our discussion.

'What shall it be?' she asked almost gaily, with her nervous alertness completely gone as she stooped over the record case. 'How would the quartet from *Rigoletto* strike your mood? I think it would be ideal, for my part.'

From Verdi we circled to Donizetti's *Lucia*, and then, in an odd whim, her hand drew forth a haphazard selection from *William Tell*. It was the latter part of the ballet music, and the record was perhaps half completed when the door opened – we had not heard the bell – and Susan announced Adolph Van Sutton.

Madelyn rose, but she did not stop the machine. Mr Van Sutton plumped nervously into the seat that she extended to him, gazing with obvious embarrassment at her radiant face as she stood with her head bent forward and a faint smile on her lips, completely under the sway of Rossini's matchless music.

She stopped the machine sharply at the end of the record. When she whirled back toward us, *William Tell* had been forgotten. She was again the sharp-eyed, sharp-questioning ferret, with no thought beyond the problem of the moment. I think the transformation astonished our caller even more than the glimpse of her unexpected mood at his entrance. I could imagine that his matter-of-fact, commercial mind was floundering in the effort to understand the remarkable young woman before him.

Madelyn changed her seat to one almost directly opposite her nervous client. She was about to speak when she noted his eyes turned questioningly in my direction.

'This is my friend, Miss Noraker, Mr Van Sutton,' she announced formally. 'I believe you have met before.'

Mr Van Sutton polished his glasses with his handkerchief as he responded somewhat dubiously. 'Miss Noraker is a – a reporter, I believe? Don't you think, Miss Mack, that our conversation should be, er – private?'

I had already risen when Madelyn motioned to me to pause. 'Miss Noraker is not here in her newspaper capacity. She is a personal friend who has accompanied me in so many of my cases that I look upon her almost as a lieutenant. You can rest assured that nothing which you or I would wish kept silent will be published!'

Mr Van Sutton's face cleared, and he bowed to me as if in apology. 'Very well, Miss Mack. I am sure I can rely upon your discretion perfectly.'

I resumed my chair at a sign from Madelyn, and our visitor stared out into the grey dusk, with the lines of his clean-shaven face showing the uneasiness and worry of the past twenty-four hours.

Madelyn was the first to speak. 'Will you tell me candidly, Mr Van Sutton, why you objected so persistently to your daughter's marriage?'

Our caller swung around in his chair as though a shot had been fired at his elbow. 'What do you mean, young woman?'

Madelyn dropped her chin on to her hand and the fleeting twinkle I know so well flashed into her eyes. 'Six months ago, you positively refused to consider Norris Endicott as your daughter's suitor. Three months ago he approached you again and you refused him a second time. It was only four weeks ago, that you gave your consent – a somewhat grudging one, if I must be plain – and the date of the wedding was fixed almost immediately.'

Adolph Van Sutton stared across at Madelyn with widening eyes. The flush faded from his cheeks, leaving them a dull white.

'I employed you, Miss Mack, to trace Norris Endicott, not to burrow into my personal affairs!'

Madelyn stepped toward the door. 'I will send in the bill for my services within the week, Mr Van Sutton. Did you leave your hat in the hall?'

'Am I to understand that you are throwing up the case?'

'Yes, sir.'

Adolph Van Sutton thrust his hands restlessly into his pockets. 'I – I beg your pardon, Miss Mack! Please sit down, and overlook a nervous man's excitability. You can hardly understand the strain I am under. You were asking me – what was it you were asking me? Ah, you were inquiring into my relations with young Endicott!'

Mr Van Sutton rolled his handkerchief into a ball between his hands as Madelyn coldly resumed her chair. 'There is really nothing to tell you. You are a woman of the world, Miss Mack. I objected to Mr Endicott as a husband for my daughter because, frankly, he was a poor man – and Bertha has hardly been raised in a manner that would teach her economy. Have I made myself clear?' He dropped his handkerchief into his pocket and his lips tightened. 'Bertha had her own way in the end – as she generally does – and I gave in. Is there anything more?'

'I believe that personally you preferred Willard White as a son-in-law. Am I right?'

'What of it?'

Madelyn gave a little sigh. 'Nothing – nothing! You have been very patient, Mr Van Sutton. I am going to ask you just one question more – before we leave for "The Maples". Does the second storey veranda under Mr Endicott's window extend along the entire side of the house?'

I think that we both stared at her.

'The second storey veranda?' repeated Mr Van Sutton. 'I thought you told me that you had never been to my home!'

Madelyn snapped her fingers with a suggestion of impatience. 'I know there must be such a veranda! There could be no other way –' she bit her sentence through as though checking an unspoken thought. 'Unless I am mistaken, it extends from the front entirely to the rear. Am I correct?'

'You are, but –'

Madelyn pressed the bell at her elbow. 'I see you have brought your automobile. I will take the liberty of asking you to share our dinner here. Then we can start for "The Maples" immediately afterward. With luck we should reach there shortly after eight. Is that agreeable to you?'

'Really, Miss Mack –'

But Madelyn waved her hand, and the matter was settled.

III

The clock was exactly on the stroke of eight when our machine whirled through the broad gate of 'The Maples', after an invigorating dash through the New Jersey shadows. At the end of the driveway we saw the colonial mansion, whose wedding

233

night festivities had been so abruptly shattered.

If we had expected a house buried in the gloom of mystery we were disappointed. 'The Maples' was a blaze of light from cellar to attic. It was not until the automobile stopped at the front veranda, and the solemn face of the butler presented itself with its mutely questioning glance, that we found our first hint of crime or tragedy.

Mr Van Sutton conducted us at once to the library – a long, high, massively furnished room toward the end of the central hall extending entirely through the house. At the door, he turned with a short bow.

'It is needless to say, of course, that the house and its inmates are at your service. I am completely ignorant of your methods, Miss Mack. If you will let me know –'

He stopped, for Madelyn had walked over to one of the long dormer windows and stood staring out into the darkness, with her hands beating a low tattoo on the glass.

'Is Mr Endicott's room on this side?' she asked without turning.

'Almost directly overhead.'

'And the drawing-room – where the ceremony was to have been performed – I take it, is on the other side?'

There was a faraway note in her voice, which told me that she hardly heard Mr Van Sutton's formal assent.

For perhaps three minutes she remained peering out into the shadowy lawn, as oblivious to our presence as though she had been alone. Our host was pacing back and forth over the polished floor when she whirled.

'Will you take me up to Mr Endicott's room now, please?'

Mr Van Sutton strode to the door with an air of relief. 'I, myself, will escort you.'

Madelyn did not speak during the ascent to the upper floor. Once Mr Van Sutton ventured a remark, but she made no effort to reply, and he desisted with a shrug. She did not even break her silence when he threw open the door of a chamber at the end of the corridor, and we realised that we were in the room of the missing bridegroom.

For a moment we paused at the threshold, as our guide found the switch and turned on the electric lights. It was a large, airy apartment, with a small alcove at one end containing a bed, and a door at the other end opening into a marble-tiled bathroom. An effort had been made to preserve the contents exactly as they had been found on the previous evening. The dressing table was still strewn with a varied assortment of toilet articles, as though they had just been dropped. The curtain of one window was jerked to the top, while its companion hung decorously to the sill.

Madelyn darted merely a cursory glance at the room. Stepping across to the writing-table, she seized the wastepaper basket leaning against its side. It was empty. In spite of this fact, she lifted it to the table and whipped out a small magnifying glass from her handbag. For fully five minutes she bent over it, studying the woven straw with as much eagerness as a miner searching for gold dust.

When she straightened, her eyes flashed uncertainly around the walls. Directly opposite was an asbestos grate of gas logs. She sank on to her knees before it, the magnifying glass again to her eyes.

'Is there anything I can do for you, Miss Mack?' Mr Van Sutton asked impatiently.

She did not even glance in our direction. Rising to her feet, she stepped back to the writing-table where two ashtrays were resting. 'Were these Mr Endicott's?'

'I – I suppose so. Why?'

Madelyn carried the trays nearer to the light. One held a litter of ashes; the second tray both ashes and crumbling cigarette stubs. I caught a curious flicker of satisfaction in her eyes.

'Mr Endicott must have been something of a smoker, wasn't he?' she asked, as though mentioning a self-evident fact.

'On the contrary, he was not!' retorted Mr Van Sutton.

'Good!' she cried so heartily that we both stared at her. As she returned the trays, her abstraction vanished. I even caught the fragment of a tune under her breath when she threw open the door of the roomy closet at the other side of the room. It was Schumann's *Traumerei*.

A man's light grey street suit was hanging from the row of clothes hooks on the wall. On the floor, a pair of shoes had been tossed. It did not need our host's terse comment to tell us that they belonged to Norris Endicott.

'You will find nothing there, Miss Mack,' he volunteered. 'The police have had the pockets inside out half a dozen times!'

A cry from Madelyn interrupted him. She had passed the suit with a shrug and had seized the discarded shoes.

'What is it?' Mr Van Sutton demanded, pressing forward.

Madelyn tossed the shoes back to the floor. Closing the door, she stood tapping her jade bracelet. Again I thought that I heard the strains of *Traumerei*. 'I was once asked to name a detective's first rule of guidance,' she said irrelevantly. 'I answered to remember always that nothing is trivial – in crime.' She paused. 'Every day I find something new to prove the correctness of my rule!'

'But surely you have discovered nothing –'

Madelyn gazed at the owner of 'The Maples' with her peculiar twinkle. 'There are two persons in this house with whom I would like a few moments' conversation. They are the butler and Miss Van Sutton's maid. Could you have them sent to the library?'

'Certainly. Is there anything else?'

Madelyn reached absently across to the ashtrays again. There seemed a peculiar fascination for her in their prosaic litter.

'Could I also have the honour of a short interview with your daughter?'

Mr Van Sutton inclined his head and stepped into the hall. As I followed him, the door was closed sharply behind us. I whirled around and heard the key turn. Madelyn had locked herself in.

Mr Van Sutton straightened with a frown. Then, without a word, he spun about on his heels and strode toward his daughter's boudoir. I descended the stairs alone.

It was almost a quarter of an hour later that Madelyn rejoined me. She nodded briefly to the butler, who was sitting on the edge of a chair as stiffly erect as a ramrod. But she did not pause. Hardly deigning a glance at me, she stepped over to the long shelves of books, built higher than her arms could reach, and her hand zigzagged along the rich leather bindings and gilt letters. Selecting a massive morocco volume from one of the central rows, she dropped into the nearest seat. The book was an encyclopedia, extending from the letter 'H' to the letter 'N'.

As she spread it open in her lap, apparently for the first time she recalled the butler. She glanced up.

'You will excuse me?'

'Yes, madam!'

'I will be through in a moment!'

'Yes, madam!'

Jenkins' face resumed its stolidness, and Madelyn's gaze dropped to her book. She could not have read a dozen lines, however, when she closed it and sprang to her feet. She paced across the library, her hands behind her back.

'I have only one question to ask, Jenkins.'

'Yes, madam!'

'I wish to know whether Mr Endicott ordered a tray of ashes brought up to his room last night?'

Jenkins' eyes widened and his hands dropped to his sides. 'A tray of ashes?' he stammered.

'I believe that is what I said!'

With a visible effort Jenkins recovered his composure. His twenty years' training had not been in vain. 'No, madam!' he answered in a rather dubious tone.

'Are you absolutely sure? I may tell you that a great deal depends upon your answer!'

Jenkins' voice recovered its steadiness. 'I am quite sure!'

'Is it possible that you would not know?'

'I am confident that I would know!'

Madelyn sank into the leather rocker by her side, with an expression of the most genuine disappointment that I have ever seen her exhibit. In the silence that followed, the ticking of the colonial clock in the corner sounded with harsh distinctness. Outside in the hall I fancied I heard a repressed cough. Miss Van Sutton's maid evidently was awaiting her turn. Madelyn's slight, black-garbed figure had fallen back in her chair, and her right hand was pressed over her eyes.

'Would you mind leaving the room for a few moments, Nora? No, Jenkins, I wish that you would stay. I find that I have another question for you.'

Annette, the maid, was walking back and forth in the hall as I opened the door. She glanced toward me, but did not speak. I had hardly noted the details of her figure, however, when the door of the library opened again and the butler followed me. Dull wonder was written on his face as he nodded shortly to the girl to take his place.

My thoughts were broken by the swish of skirts on the stairs. The next moment I faced Adolph Van Sutton and his daughter. This was the first time during the day that I had seen the latter. She had remained locked in her room since morning, denying all interviewers, and only giving Detective Wiley a scant five minutes after his third request. I had expected to find evidences of a pronounced strain after her prostration of the previous evening, but I was startled by her pallor as her father took her arm and led her down the hall.

Of all the heart-broken women, whether of cottage or mansion, with whom my newspaper career has brought me in contact, there was no figure more pathetic than that of the heiress of the Van Sutton millions as she swayed toward me on that eventful night.

Bertha Van Sutton crossed wearily into the library as the maid emerged. 'I have one favour to request, Miss Mack, and if you have ever suffered in your lifetime, you will grant it. Please be as brief as possible!'

'Do you want me here?' her father asked.

Madelyn had walked over to the bookshelves, and was again

delving into the pages of the morocco encyclopedia. 'I would prefer not!' she answered without looking up.

It was well toward half past nine (I had glanced at my watch a dozen times) when the two women in the library emerged. The form of Bertha Van Sutton was bent even more than before, and it was evident at a glance that the strain of the interview had brought her almost to the point of a collapse.

As I started forward, the light flashed for an instant on a round gleaming object in Madelyn Mack's hand. It was the small silver ball that had been found in Norris Endicott's room.

At that moment, the front bell tinkled through the house. There was a short conversation in the vestibule, and then Jenkins ushered a tall, loosely jointed figure into the hall. It was Detective Wiley of the Newark headquarters. (Of course, the affair at 'The Maples' had come under the jurisdiction of the New Jersey police.)

The detective's ruddy face, with its stubble of beard, was flushed with an unusual excitement, and his stiff, sandy moustache stood out in two bristling lines from his mouth. He received Madelyn's bow with a short, half-contemptuous nod, as he snapped out, 'I'm right after all, Mr Van Sutton! It's murder – nothing more nor less!'

'Murder!' The gasp came from Bertha Van Sutton. For an instant I thought she was about to faint.

Wiley glanced around the group with a suggestion of conscious importance which did not leave him, even in the tension of the moment.

'We have found Mr Endicott's clothes in Thompson's Creek – and the coat is covered with blood!'

Madelyn Mack gently led Bertha Van Sutton to the chair I had vacated. One hand was stroking the girl's temples as she turned.

'You are wrong, Mr Wiley!' she said quietly. 'For the peace of mind of this household, I am willing to stake my reputation that you are wrong.'

Detective Wiley whirled with a sneer. 'Really, you astound me, my lady policeman! May I humbly inquire how your pink tea wisdom deduces so much?'

Madelyn smoothed the folds of her coat as she straightened. 'I have promised Miss Van Sutton that if she and her father will call at "The Rosary" tomorrow afternoon at four, I will give them a complete explanation of this unfortunate affair! You may call also if you are interested, Mr Wiley – and don't arrest the murderer in the meantime! Will you kindly loan us your motor for the trip back to town, Mr Van Sutton?'

IV

I confess that I approached Madelyn Mack's chalet the next day with pronounced scepticism. The morning papers of both New York and Newark had been crammed with the discovery of Norris Endicott's blood-stained garments, and were full of hysterical praise for the 'masterly work' of Detective Joseph Wiley.

Someone had found that Madelyn Mack had also been retained in the case, and the reporters had tried in vain to obtain an interview. In the face of her silence, the applause for the police had become even more emphasised.

She was alone when I entered; but, as I pointed to the clock just on the verge of four, she held up her hand. The bell sounded through the house, and the next moment Susan conducted Adolph Van Sutton and his daughter into the room.

In the confusion of the greeting, the signs of nervous strain on Madelyn's face struck me sharply. It did not need her weary admission to tell me that she had spent a racking day, nor that she had had frequent recourse to the stimulant of her cola berries. Even her hair, about whose arrangement she generally was precise to the point of nervousness, was dishevelled, and once, when Peter the Great thrust his nose into her lap, she ordered him impatiently away.

The Van Suttons had hardly seated themselves when there

was a step in the hall and the last guest of the afternoon made his appearance. There was not the slightest hint of ill humour in Madelyn's greeting as Detective Wiley somewhat awkwardly took the hand that she extended to him.

'Have you traced the murderer yet, Mr Wiley?'

'No, but I expect to have him in custody within the next twenty-four hours!' Detective Wiley dropped heavily into his chair and crossed his knees.

'May I ask if you have found the body?'

'I can't say that we have, but we have certain information which –'

Madelyn walked over to the end of the room where she could face the entire group. She was the only one of us who was standing.

'Then I am more fortunate than you are!'

The detective bounded from his seat, his sandy moustache – the barometer of his emotions – bristling. 'I am not a man to trifle with, Miss Mack. Do you mean to tell me –'

'That I have discovered the body of Norris Endicott? You have caught my meaning exactly!'

Wiley stood staring at her in a sort of tongue-tied amazement. A gasp recalled me to the other occupants of the room. Bertha Van Sutton was devouring Madelyn's face as though pleading with her to end her suspense. Her father was stroking her hand.

Madelyn stepped to the door and threw it open. On the threshold stood a young man in a brown tweed suit, with a purple lump showing just at the edge of his hair. He stared at us as though he were dazed by a sudden light.

Bertha Van Sutton darted across the room, with a cry, and threw herself into his arms.

It was Norris Endicott.

Madelyn sprang to her side, with a query intensely practical – and intensely feminine. 'Has she fainted?'

'I – I think so.' Norris Endicott stood gazing down at his burden helplessly.

'We must carry her into the next room then – take hold of her shoulders, please! No, the rest of you stand back! It needs a woman to take care of a woman!'

Detective Wiley strode over to the desk telephone and called police headquarters. He had just turned from the instrument when the door opened and Madelyn returned.

'She is all right, I assure you!' she cried hastily, as Adolph Van Sutton started from his chair. 'I have left her with Mr Endicott. On the whole, he is the best nurse we could find. Sit down, Mr Wiley. You will find that rocker more comfortable, Mr Van Sutton. It is not a long story that I have to tell, but it contains its tragedy – and we have to thank Providence that it isn't a double one!'

She paused, as though marshalling her thoughts. Detective Wiley surveyed her uneasily.

'I am sorry to inform you, Mr Van Sutton, that your daughter is a widow! Or perhaps – as I wish to be entirely frank – I should say that I am glad to convey this announcement to you!' Her slight, black figure bent forward. 'Your daughter's husband was one of the greatest scamps that ever went unpunished!'

'But my daughter never had a husband. Miss Mack! You forget –'

'I forget nothing! Has it ever occurred to you that there might be a chapter in Miss Van Sutton's life unknown to you? Pray keep your seat, my dear sir! You are a man of the world and a father. You have the knowledge of the one and the heart of the other. When I tell you that during your daughter's college days – Nora, will you kindly pour Mr Van Sutton a little of that brandy? Thank you!'

Madelyn did not change her position as the owner of 'The Maples' gulped down the liquor. She waited until he had finished, her chin still on her hand, her eyes never shifting.

'Let me give you the explanation of our mystery in a few words, Mr Van Sutton. The wedding ceremony of Wednesday night was not performed – because your daughter was already a wife!

Norris Endicott disappeared from "The Maples" – eliminated himself – to save her from one of the most agonising alternatives that ever confronted a woman!'

Behind me, I heard Detective Wiley give a cry of sudden comprehension.

'Incredible, impossible as it may seem, Miss Van Sutton did not know of the barrier to her marriage until the ceremony was less than an hour distant. What she would have done under other circumstances I don't know. It was the man, who was waiting to lead her to the altar, who came to her rescue!'

Madelyn spoke in as emotionless a tone as though she were discussing the weather. There was even a bored note in her voice as though the glamour of the problem had left her – with its solution.

'To understand the situation, we must go back quite five years. When Miss Van Sutton was a senior at Vassar she fell in love with the matinee idol of a New York stock company. Reginald Winters was a man with a character as shallow as his heart. Bluntly, he knew of your wealth, and schemed to gain a part of it. You don't find the situation unusual, do you? In the end, he persuaded Miss Bertha to elope with him. But he made a slight error. He did not investigate your disposition until after the marriage.

'He was too shrewd to risk an open avowal and a paternal storm. Rather a canny villain, as a matter of fact! He set on foot a series of inquiries which showed him, too late, that, rather than accept him in your house, you would lose your daughter.

'A disinherited heiress did not appeal to him. Less than a week after the elopement, your daughter awoke to the fact that she was deserted. Mr Van Sutton, you must calm yourself! I warn you I will not relate the sequel unless you do!

'Fate plays us queer pranks. Or is it Fate? I come now to the first suggestion of the fantastic. A year later, Miss Van Sutton read in a report of a wreck – somewhere in the West, I believe – that Reginald Winters had been killed. I don't know what her emotions were. I imagine she was like the prisoner who inhales his first breath of freedom.

'I think you can guess the next chapter? Am I verging too much on the lines of the woman novelist? It was not until the evening which was to have made her the bride of Norris Endicott that she discovered her ghastly mistake – which another hour would have made still more ghastly.

'Reginald Winters not only was living, but he had followed her to her father's door. To make our melodrama complete, in a characteristic note he reminded her of the disagreeable fact that she was his wife.'

Madelyn's eyes closed wearily. When she opened them, the lines of strain on her face seemed more intense than ever – in contrast to her light tone.

'In a novel, the bride, driven to desperation, would have killed her Nemesis. But women of real life seldom have the desperation of those of romance. Bertha Van Sutton turned to the last refuge in the world that the woman in the novel would have sought. She carried her burden and her problem to the man who was waiting to place his wedding ring on her finger.

'She dismissed her maid, bolted the door of her room, and stepped out on to the veranda below, with a dark cloak thrown over her white dress. Once at Norris Endicott's apartment, it was a matter of only an instant to bring him to the window.

'He comprehended the situation in a flash. Of course, it was obvious enough – after the first shock. The marriage could not take place. But how could it be prevented? The girl could have told the truth, of course. Was there no other way? And then Endicott made his decision. He must disappear – until he could find and reckon with the man who was threatening her. A Don Quixotic plan? Could you have made a better one? He sent Miss Van Sutton back to her room, and made his preparations for flight.

'It was not until the clock struck eight, however, that he nerved himself to the crucial step, and swung out from the veranda to the lawn below. It was a drop of perhaps twelve feet, and he made it without accident. While Willard White was calling his name through the room, he was watching him from the shadows of the yard.

'Now we come again to the unkindness of Fate. He was threading his way through the shrubbery adjoining Thompson's Creek when his foot caught in a vine and he was thrown to the ground. His head struck on a stone and for nearly an hour he lay unconscious. When he struggled to his feet, his coat and collar were matted with blood.

'Without a thought of possible consequences, he dropped them into the water. I believe that is where you found them, Mr Wiley. It was nearly daylight when he reached his rooms, almost exhausted.

'He had but one coherent thought. He must find Reginald Winters – without delay and without publicity. The note, which the actor had written to Miss Van Sutton, contained the address of his hotel – an obscure Fourth Avenue boarding-house in New York. It was easy enough to find the hotel – but the man was out.

'All of that day and night he watched the building, like a hungry dog watches a bone. It was not until this morning that Winters returned. Then he reappeared in the street so quickly that Endicott had no time to follow him up to his room.

'The actor swung off toward Broadway, with Endicott stubbornly following him. At Thirty-fourth Street and Sixth Avenue, there was a tie-up of the surface cars, and the crossing was jammed. I see you are anticipating what followed! Well – the wheel of fortune turned abruptly. Winters plunged into the swarm of vehicles, absorbed in his thoughts. Just before he reached the curb, a dray swayed before him. He dodged – too late. The rearing team crushed him to the pavement.

'When they picked him up he was quite dead.

'It was over his body that Norris Endicott and I met for the first time – with the realisation that Bertha van Sutton was free.

'As a matter of fact, I had been "shadowing" Mr Endicott, as you would express it, Mr Wiley, for several hours.' Madelyn pushed back her chair and walked across the room, drawing long, deep breaths.

'Have I made myself quite clear?'

'Are you a woman or a wizard?' gasped Adolph Van Sutton.

Detective Wiley sprang to his feet. 'I'm doing what I never thought I would have to do, Miss Mack.' He held out his hand. 'Apologising to a petticoat detective! But I don't see how on earth you did it!'

Madelyn shrugged. 'Now we are descending to the commonplace.' She leaned against the mantel with a yawn. Adolph Van Sutton thrust an unlighted cigar nervously into his mouth.

'Have you done me the honour to remember a certain maxim of mine – that nothing is trivial in crime? But – this is not a lecture on deduction!

'Miss Van Sutton's connection with the affair really was plain after that first newspaper report. By the way, Nora, did you write the description of the bride's wedding dress? I thought I recognised your style. May I congratulate you? From the viewpoint –'

'Aren't we veering from the subject, Miss Mack?' Detective Wiley broke in impatiently.

'Do you think so?' Madelyn's eyes rested on his florid face. 'I was particularly interested, Nora, in your account of the bride's coiffure. I agree with you that it was decidedly becoming. I remember that you mentioned that her *point d'esprit* veil was fastened by two long pins, each with a sterling silver ball as a head.'

A sudden light broke over me. 'And the silver ball that was found in Norris Endicott's room was one of those, of course!'

Madelyn smiled. 'Your penetration amazes me! It was your own report of the case that gave me my first and most important clue before we left this house.

'I think you will agree that my inference was plain enough.

Miss Van Sutton had visited Norris Endicott's room after she was dressed for the ceremony – and consequently just before his disappearance. She had kept the fact secret – and she was so agitated that she did not miss the loss of a valuable hair ornament. Why?

'There was another question that I put to myself. How had she reached the room? The discovery of the silver ball on the sill suggested, of course, the window. What was under the window? Here I found that a second-storey veranda extended along the entire side of the house. Miss Van Sutton then had only to step out of her own window to find a channel of communication ready made for her. You see I had a fairly good working foundation before we entered "The Maples".

'You may recall that I found much interest in Endicott's ashtrays. Have you ever studied the relation of tobacco to human emotions, Mr Wiley? You will find it a singularly suggestive field of thought, I assure you.

'The number of cigarette-ends impressed you, perhaps, as it did me. I don't know whether you noticed that, in nearly every case, the cigarette had only been half consumed – and was so torn and crushed as to suggest that it had been thrown aside in disgust. What was the natural conclusion? Obviously, that a man in an extreme state of nervous excitement had been smoking. Now, what could agitate Norris Endicott so remarkably? Not his approaching wedding, surely! Then what? How about the sudden necessity of eliminating himself from that wedding?

'In the closet, you may remember, I found a pair of the bridegroom's shoes. In their way, their presence was exceedingly remarkable. On the hooks, above, was the street suit which Endicott had taken off in preparing for the ceremony. The shoes, however, were the thin-soled, expensive footwear that a man would use only on dress occasions. What had become of the street shoes that you would expect to find in the closet? My course of reasoning was simple. After Endicott had dressed for the wedding, something had occurred which forced him to change

247

back to his heavier boots. What? The knowledge, of course, that he was about to leave the house on a rough trip. We now have the conclusion that he vanished of his own volition, that he knew where and why he was going, and that he made certain plans for leaving.

'It was the next point which I found the most baffling – and which led me into my first error.' Madelyn came to a pause by the rug of Peter the Great. The dog rose, yawning, to his feet and thrust his nose into her hand.

'Perhaps you are wondering, Mr Van Sutton, why I locked myself into the room after you and Miss Noraker had left? Frankly, I was not satisfied with my investigation – and I wanted to be alone. For instance, there was an object on Mr Endicott's dressing table that puzzled me greatly. Under ordinary circumstances I might not have noticed it. It was the second tray of ashes.

'They were not tobacco ashes. It didn't need a second glance to tell me that they had come from a wood fire. Certainly there had not been a wood fire in that room – and, if there had been, why the necessity of preserving so small a part of the ashes?

'I will admit frankly that I was about to give up the problem in disgust when I remembered my examination of the wastepaper basket and the grate. I had reasoned that Mr Endicott's flight had been made necessary after he entered the house. By what? What more likely than a message, perhaps a note, perhaps a telegram? In nine cases out of ten, a nervous man would have burned or destroyed such a message; but, in spite of my closest search, I found no traces of it. It was not until I was moving away from my saucer of ashes that my search was rewarded. In the tray was a single torn fragment of white paper.

'There were no others. Either the shreds had been carefully gathered up after the message was destroyed – which was hardly likely – or the fragment before me had been torn from a corner in a moment of agitation. But why had I found it in the ashes?'

Madelyn glanced up at Mr Van Sutton with an abrupt turning of the subject. 'Do you ever read Ovid?'

The owner of 'The Maples' gazed at her with a frown of bewilderment.

'Really, you are missing a decided treat, Mr Van Sutton. There is a quaint charm about those early Greek poets for which I have looked in vain in our modern literature. Ovid's verses on love, for instance, and his whimsical letters to maidens who have fallen early victims to the divine passion –'

'Are you joking or torturing me, Miss Mack?'

Madelyn's face grew suddenly grave.

'I am sorry. Believe me, I beg your pardon! But – it was Ovid who showed me the purpose of the tray of ashes! In one of his most famous verses there is a recipe for sympathetic ink, designed to assist in the writing of discreet love letters, I believe.

'It is astonishingly simple. No mysterious chemicals, no visits to a pharmacist. Instead of ink, you write your letters in – milk! Of course, the words are invisible. Apparently you are leaving no trace on the paper. Rub the sheet with wood ashes, however, and your message is perfectly legible! I don't know where Ovid found the recipe. It has survived, though, for seventeen hundred years. There is only one caution in its use. Make sure that the milk is not skimmed!

'A letter in invisible ink, you will admit, was thoroughly in keeping with the other details of our mystery. The encyclopedia in the library convinced me that I had made no mistake in my recipe – and then I turned to the butler, and my theory received its first jar. Mr Endicott had ordered no saucer of ashes. Moreover, no note, no telegram, not even a telephone call had come for him.

'For a moment, I was absolutely hopeless. Then I sent you from the room, Nora, so that Jenkins would not feel constrained to silence – and put the question which solved the problem.

'It was not Jenkins, however, who gave me my answer. It was Miss Van Sutton's maid. The tray of ashes had not been ordered by the groom. It had been ordered – by the bride.

'I may as well add here that Miss Van Sutton explained to me later that this had been the method of communication between her and Reginald Winters. She had suggested it herself in her college days when Ovid was almost her daily companion. It was Winters' custom to scribble his initial on the corner of the paper. This was her clue, of course, that the apparently blank sheet contained a communication.'

Madelyn stooped over the shaggy form of Peter the Great, and his tongue caressed her hand.

'It was at this juncture that Miss Van Sutton was ushered into the library. I did not ask her for the note. I was well enough acquainted with my sex to know that this would be useless. I told her what was in it – and requested her to tell me if I was wrong.'

Madelyn walked back to her chair, and, for the first time during her recital, the lines in her face relaxed.

'She gave me the note – I believe that is all. Of course, Winters' address told me where I would find Norris Endicott, and I located him this morning. Is there anything else?'

There was no answer.

'Nora,' said Madelyn, turning to me. 'Would you mind starting the phonograph? I think that Rubinstein's "Melody in F" would suit my mood perfectly. Thank you!'

Early in the following week the postponed wedding of Norris Endicott and Bertha Van Sutton was quietly performed, and the couple departed on a tour of Europe. The bride did not see the body of Reginald Winters. Months afterward, however, I learned that she had bought a secluded grave lot for the man who had so nearly brought disaster to her life.

In Madelyn Mack's relic case today, there are two objects of peculiar interest to me. One is a small silver ball, perhaps three-quarters of an inch in diameter. The other is an apparently blank sheet of paper – except for a bold, dashing 'W' in the upper right-hand corner.

ADDINGTON PEACE

Created by B Fletcher Robinson (1870-1907)

Born in Liverpool, Bertram Fletcher Robinson moved with his family to Devon as a boy and was educated in Newton Abbot and at Jesus College, Cambridge. An enthusiastic sportsman who won a rugby blue at university and rowed for his college, he qualified as a barrister in 1896 but never practised the law. Instead he turned to writing as a career and worked as a journalist and editor on a variety of newspapers and magazines before his early death at the age of only 36. Robinson is justly celebrated by Sherlockians for his role in the creation of The Hound of the Baskervilles, *the most famous of all Holmes stories. A friend of Conan Doyle, he told him of the legends of ghostly hounds and the two men originally planned to collaborate on a story set on Dartmoor.* The Hound of the Baskervilles *is dedicated to Robinson. (Wild conspiracy theorists have claimed not only that Doyle stole his ideas from Robinson but that he was involved in poisoning him. This seems – how shall I put it? – unlikely.) Robinson was also a friend of PG Wodehouse, with whom he wrote a number of comic playlets. His great contribution to crime fiction is the volume of short stories chronicling the adventures of the astute police inspector, Addington Peace, which was first published in 1905. Narrated by Peace's Watson, an aspiring artist named Phillips who lives in the flat below the detective's and learns that crime-solving is more exciting than art, these are fine examples of the Edwardian crime story.*

THE VANISHED MILLIONAIRE

I stood with my back to the fire, smoking and puzzling over it. It was worth all the headlines the newspapers had given it; there was no loophole to the mystery.

Both sides of the Atlantic knew Silas J Ford. He had established a business reputation in America that had made him a celebrity in England from the day he stepped off the liner. Once in London his syndicates and companies and consolidations had startled the slow-moving British mind. The commercial sky of the United Kingdom was overshadowed by him and his schemes. The papers were full of praise and blame, of puffs and denunciations. He was a millionaire; he was on the verge of a smash that would paralyse the markets of the world. He was an abstainer, a drunkard, a gambler, a most religious man. He was a confirmed bachelor, a woman hater; his engagement was to be announced shortly. So was the gossip kept rolling with the limelight always centred upon the spot where Silas J Ford happened to be standing.

And now he had disappeared, vanished, evaporated.

On the night of December 18th, a Thursday, he had left London for Meudon Hall, the fine old Hampshire mansion that he had rented from Lord Beverley. The two most trusted men in his office accompanied him. Friday morning he had spent with them; but at three o'clock the pair had returned to London, leaving their chief behind. From four to seven he had been shut up with his secretary. It was a hard time for everyone, a time verging upon panic, and at such times Silas J Ford was not an idle man.

At eight o'clock he had dined. His one recreation was music, and after the meal he had played the organ in the picture-gallery for an hour. At a quarter past eleven he retired to his bedroom, dismissing Jackson, his body servant, for the night. Three-quarters of an hour later, however, Harbord, his secretary, had been called to the private telephone, for Mr Ford had brought an extension wire from the neighbouring town of Camdon. It was a London message, and so urgent that he decided to wake his chief. There was no answer to his knock, and on entering the room he found that Mr Ford was not in bed. He was surprised, but in no way suspicious, and started to search the house. He was joined by a footman, and, a little later, by Jackson and the butler. Astonishment changed to alarm. Other servants were roused to aid in the quest. Finally, a party, provided with lanterns from the stables, commenced to examine the grounds.

Snow had fallen early in the day, covering the great lawns in front of the entrance porch with a soft white blanket, about an inch in thickness. It was the head-groom who struck the trail. Apparently Mr Ford had walked out of the porch, and so over the drive and across the lawn towards the wall that bounded the public road. This road, which led from Meudon village to the town of Camdon, crossed the front of Meudon Hall at a distance of some quarter of a mile.

There was no doubt as to the identity of the footprints, for Silas Ford affected a broad, square-toed boot, easily recognisable from its unusual impression.

They tracked him by their lanterns to the park wall, and there all trace of him disappeared. The wall was of rough stone, easily surmountable by an active man. The snow that covered the road outside had been churned into muddy paste by the traffic of the day; there were no further footprints observable.

The party returned to the house in great bewilderment. The telephone to London brought no explanation, and the following morning Mr Harbord caught the first train to town to make inquiries. For private reasons his friends did not desire publicity for the affair, and it was not until the late afternoon, when all their investigations had proved fruitless, that they communicated with Scotland Yard. When the papers went to press the whereabouts of the great Mr Ford still remained a mystery.

In keen curiosity I set off up the stairs to Inspector Peace's room. Perhaps the little detective had later news to give me.

I found him standing with his back to the fire puffing at his cigarette with a plump solemnity. A bag, neatly strapped, lay on the rug at his feet. He nodded a welcome, watching me over his glasses.

'I expected you, Mr Phillips,' he said. 'And how do you explain it?'

'A love affair or temporary insanity,' I suggested vaguely.

'Surely we can combine those solutions,' he smiled. 'Anything else?'

'No. I came to ask your opinion.'

'My mind is void of theories, Mr Phillips, and I shall endeavour to keep it so for the present. If you wish to amuse yourself by discussing possibilities, I would suggest your consideration of the reason why, if he wanted to disappear quietly, he should leave so obvious a track through the snow of his own lawn. For myself, as I am leaving for Camdon via Waterloo Station in twenty-three minutes, I shall hope for more definite data before night.'

'Peace,' I asked him eagerly, 'may I come with you?'

'If you can be ready in time,' he said.

It was past two o'clock when we arrived at the old town of Camdon. A carriage met us at the station. Five minutes more and we were clear of the narrow streets and climbing the first bare ridge of the downs. It was a desolate prospect enough – a bare expanse of windswept land that rose and fell with the sweeping regularity of the Pacific swell. Here and there a clump of ragged firs showed black against the snow. Under that gentle carpet the crisp turf of the crests and the broad plough lands of the lower ground alike lay hidden. I shivered, drawing my coat more closely about me.

It was half an hour later that we topped a swelling rise and saw the grey towers of the ancient mansion beneath us. In the shelter of the valley by the quiet river, that now lay frozen into silence, the trees had grown into splendid woodlands, circling the hall on the further side. From the broad front the white lawns crept down to the road on which we were driving. Dark masses of shrubberies and the tracery of scattered trees broke their silent levels. The park wall that fenced them from the road stood out like an ink line ruled upon paper.

'It must have been there that he disappeared,' I cried, with a speculative finger.

'So I imagine,' said Peace. 'And if he has spent two nights on the Hampshire downs, he will be looking for a fire today. You have rather more than your fair share of the rug, Mr Phillips, if you will excuse my mentioning it.'

A man was standing on the steps of the entrance porch when we drove up. As we unrolled ourselves he stepped forward to help us. He was a thin, pale-faced fellow, with fair hair and indeterminate eyes.

'My name is Harbord,' he said. 'You are Inspector Addington Peace, I believe.'

His hand shook as he stretched it out in a tremulous greeting. Plainly the secretary was afraid, visibly and anxiously afraid.

'Mr Ransom, the manager of Mr Ford's London office, is here,' he continued. 'He is waiting to see you in the library.'

We followed him through a great hall into a room lined with books from floor to ceiling. A stout, dark man, who was pacing it like a beast in a cage, stopped at the sight of us. His face, as he turned, looked pinched and grey in the full light.

'Inspector Peace, eh?' he said. 'Well, Inspector, if you want a reward name it. If you want to pull the house down only say the word. But find him for us, or, by Heaven, we're done.'

'Is it as bad as that? '

'You can keep a secret, I suppose. Yes – it couldn't well be worse. It was a tricky time; he hid half his schemes in his own head; he never trusted even me altogether. If he were dead I could plan something, but now...'

He thumped his hand on the table and turned away to the window.

'When you last saw Mr Ford was he in good health? Did he stand the strain?'

'Ford had no nerves. He was never better in his life.'

255

'In these great transactions he would have his enemies. If his plans succeeded there would be many hard hit, perhaps ruined. Have you any suspicion of a man who, to save himself, might make away with Mr Ford?'

'No,' said the manager, after a moment's thought. 'No, I cannot give you a single name. The players are all big men, Inspector. I don't say that their consciences would stop them from trying such a trick, but it wouldn't be worth their while. They hold off when gaol is the certain punishment.'

'Was this financial crisis in his own affairs generally known?'

'Certainly not.'

'Who would know of it?'

'There might be a dozen men on both sides of the Atlantic who would suspect the truth. But I don't suppose that more than four people were actually in possession of the facts.'

'And who would they be?'

'His two partners in America; myself, and Mr Harbord there.'

Peace turned to the young man with a smile and a polite bow.

'Can you add any names to the list?' he asked.

'No,' said Harbord, staring at the detective with a puzzled look, as if trying to catch the drift of his questions.

'Thank you,' said the inspector; 'and now, will you show me the place where this curious disappearance occurred?'

We crossed the drive, where the snow lay torn and trampled by the carriages, and so to the white, even surface of the lawn. We soon struck the trail, a confused path beaten by many footprints. Peace stooped for a moment, and then turned to the secretary with an angry glance.

'Were you with them?' he said.

'Yes.'

'Then why, in the name of common sense, didn't you keep them off his tracks? You have simply trampled them out of existence, between you.'

'We were in a hurry, Inspector,' said the secretary, meekly. 'We didn't think about it.'

We walked forward, following the broad trail until we came to a circular patch of trodden snow. Evidently the searchers had stopped and stood talking together. On the further side I saw the footprints of a man plainly defined. There were some half-dozen clear impressions and they ended at the base of the old wall, which was some six feet in height.

'I am glad to see that you and your friends have left me something, Mr Harbord,' said the inspector.

He stepped forward and, kneeling down, examined the nearest footprint.

'Mr Ford dressed for dinner?' he inquired, glancing up at the secretary.

'Certainly! Why do you ask?'

'Merely that he had on heavy shooting boots when he took this evening stroll. It will be interesting to discover what clothes he wore.'

The inspector walked up to the wall, moving parallel to the tracks in the snow. With a sudden spring he climbed to the top and seated himself while he stared about him. Then on his hands and knees he began to crawl forward along the coping. It was a quaint spectacle, but the extraordinary care and vigilance of the little man took the farce out of it.

Presently he stopped and looked down at us.

'Please stay where you are,' he said, and disappeared on the further side.

Harbord offered me a cigarette, and we waited with due obedience till the inspector's bullet head again broke the horizon as he struggled back to his position on the coping of the wall.

He seemed in a very pleasant temper when he joined us; but he said nothing of his discoveries, and I had grown too wise to inquire. When we reached the entrance-hall he asked for Jackson, the valet, and in a couple of minutes the man appeared. He was a tall, hatchet-faced fellow, very neatly dressed in black. He made a little bow, and then stood watching us in a most respectful attitude.

'A queer business this, Jackson,' said Addington Peace.

'Yes, sir.'

'And what is your opinion on it?'

'To be frank, sir, I thought at first that Mr Ford had run away; but now I don't know what to make of it.'

'And why should he run away?'

'I have no idea, sir; but he seemed to me rather strange in his manner yesterday.'

'Have you been with him long?'

'No, sir. I was valet to the Honourable John Dorn, Lord Beverley's second son. Mr Ford took me from Mr Dorn at the time he rented the Hall.'

'I see. And now, will you show me your master's room. I shall see you again later, Mr Harbord,' he continued; 'in the meanwhile I will leave my assistant with you.'

We sat and smoked in the secretary's room. He was not much of a talker, consuming cigarette after cigarette in silence. The winter dusk had already fallen when the inspector joined us, and we retired to our rooms to prepare for dinner. I tried a word with Peace upon the staircase, but he shook his head and walked on.

The meal dragged itself to an end somehow, and we left Ransom with a second decanter of port before him. Peace slipped away again, and I consoled myself with a book in the library until half past ten, when I walked off to bed. A servant was switching off the light in the hall when I mounted the great staircase.

My room was in the old wing at the farther side of the picture-gallery, and I had some difficulty in steering my way through the dark corridors. The mystery that hung over the house had shaken my nerves, and I remember that I started at every creak of a board and peered into the shadows as I passed along with Heaven knows what ghostly expectations. I was glad enough to close my door upon them and see the wood fire blazing cheerfully in the open hearth.

★ ★ ★ ★ ★

I woke with a start that left me sitting up in bed, with my heart thumping in my ribs like a piston-rod. I am not generally a light sleeper, but that night, even while I snored, my nerves were active. Someone had tapped at my door – that was my impression.

I listened with the uncertain fear that comes to the newly waked. Then I heard it again – on the wall near my head this time. A board creaked. Someone was groping his way down the dark corridor without. Presently he stopped, and a faint line of illumination sprang out under my door. It winked, and then grew still. He had lit a candle.

Assurance came with the streak of light.

What was he doing, groping in the dark, if he had a candle with him? I crept over to the door, opened it, and stared cautiously out.

About a score feet away a man was standing – a striking figure against the light he carried. His back was towards me, but I could see that his hand was shading the candle from his eyes while he stared into the shadows that clung about the further end of the corridor.

Presently he began to move forward.

The picture-gallery and the body of the house lay behind me. The corridor in which he stood terminated in a window, set deep into the stone of the old walls. The man walked slowly, throwing the light to right and left. His attitude was of nervous expectation – that of a man who looked for something that he feared to see.

At the window he stopped, staring about him and listening. He examined the fastenings, and then tried a door on his right. It was locked against him. As he did so I caught his profile against the light. It was Harbord, the secretary. From where I stood he was not more than forty feet away. There was no possibility of a mistake.

As he turned to come back I retreated into my room, closing the door. The fellow was in a state of great agitation, and I could hear him muttering to himself as he walked. When he had passed by I peeped out to see him and his light dwindle, reach the corner by the picture-gallery, and fade into a reflection – a darkness.

I took care to turn the key before I got back into bed.

I woke again at seven, and, hurrying on my clothes, set off to tell Peace all about it. I took him to the place, and together we examined the corridor. There were only two rooms beyond mine. The one on the left was an unoccupied bedroom; that on the right was a large store-room, the door of which was locked. The housekeeper kept the key, we learnt upon inquiry. Whom had Harbord followed? The problem was beyond me. As for Inspector Peace, he did not indulge in verbal speculations.

It was in the central hall that we encountered the secretary on his way to the breakfast-room. The man looked nervous and depressed; he nodded to us, and was passing on, when Peace stopped him.

'Good morning, Mr Harbord,' he said. 'Can I have a word with you?'

'Certainly, Inspector. What is it?'

'I have a favour to ask. My assistant and myself have our hands full here. If necessary could you help us by running up to London, and...'

'For the day?' he interrupted.

'No. It may be an affair of three or four days.'

'Then I must refuse. I am sorry, but...'

'Don't apologise, Mr Harbord,' said the little man, cheerfully. 'I shall have to find someone else – that is all.'

We walked into the breakfast-room, and a few minutes later Ransom appeared with a great bundle of letters and telegrams in his hand. He said not a word to any of us, but dropped into a chair, tearing open the envelopes and glancing at their contents. His face grew darker as he read, and once he thumped his hand upon the table with a crash that set the china jingling.

'Well, Inspector?' he said at last.

The little detective's head shook out a negative.

'Perhaps you require an incentive,' he sneered. 'Is it a matter of a reward?'

'No, Mr Ransom; but it is becoming one of my personal reputation.'

'Then, by thunder! you are in danger of losing it. Why don't you and your friend hustle, instead of loitering around as if you were paid by the day? I tell you, man, there are thousands – hundreds of thousands – melting, slipping through our fingers, every hour, every hour.'

He sprang from his seat and started his walk again – up and down, up and down, as we had first seen him.

'Shall you be returning to London?'

At the question the manager halted in his stride, staring sharply down into the inspector's bland countenance.

'No,' he said, 'I shall stay here, Mr Addington Peace, until such time as you have something definite to tell me.'

'I have an inquiry to make which I would rather place in the hands of someone who has personal knowledge of Mr Ford. Neither Mr Harbord nor yourself desire to leave Meudon. Is there anyone else you can suggest?'

'There is Jackson – Ford's valet,' said the manager, after a moment's thought. 'He can go, if you think him bright enough. I'll send for him.'

While the footman who answered the bell was gone upon his errand, we waited in an uneasy silence. There was the shadow of an ugly mystery upon us all. Jackson, as he entered, was the only one who seemed at his ease. He stood there – a tall figure of all the respectabilities.

'The inspector here wishes you to go to London, Jackson,' said the manager. 'He will explain the details. There is a fast train from Camdon at eleven.'

'Certainly, sir. Do I return tonight?'

'No, Jackson,' said Peace. 'It will take a day or two.'

The man took a couple of steps towards the door, hesitated, and then returned to his former place.

'I beg your pardon, sir,' he began, addressing Ransom. 'But I would rather remain at Meudon under present circumstances.'

'What on earth do you mean?' thundered the manager.

'Well, sir, I was the last to see Mr Ford. There is, as it were, a suspicion upon me. I should like to be present while the search continues, both for his sake – and my own.'

'Very kind of you, I'm sure,' growled Ransom. 'But you either do what I tell you, Jackson, or you pack your boxes and clear out. So be quick and make up your mind.'

'I think you are treating me most unfairly, sir. But I cannot be persuaded out of what I know to be my duty.'

'You impertinent rascal!' began the furious manager. But Peace was already on his feet with a hand outstretched.

'Perhaps, after all, I can make other arrangements, Mr Ransom,' he said. 'It is natural that Jackson should consider his own reputation in this affair. That is all, Jackson; you may go now.'

It was half an hour afterwards, when the end of breakfast had dispersed the party, that I spoke to Peace about it, offering to go to London myself and do my best to carry out his instructions.

'I had bad luck in my call for volunteers,' he said.

'I should have thought they would have been glad enough to get the chance of work. They can find no particular amusement in loafing about the place all day.'

'Doubtless they all had excellent reasons,' he said with a smile. 'But, anyway, you cannot be spared, Mr Phillips.'

'You flatter me.'

'I want you to stay in your bedroom. Write, read, do what you like, but keep your door ajar. If anyone passes down the corridor, see where he goes, only don't let him know that you are watching him if you can help it. I will take my turn at half past one. I don't mean to starve you.'

I obeyed. After all, it was, in a manner, promotion that the inspector had given me; yet it was a tedious, anxious time. No one came my way, barring a sour-looking housemaid. I tried to argue out the case, but the deeper I got the more conflicting grew my theories. I was never more glad to see a friendly face than when the little man came in upon me.

The short winter's afternoon crept on, the inspector and I taking turn and turn about in our sentry duty. Dinner-time came and went. I had been off duty from nine, but at ten thirty I poured out a whisky and soda and went back to join him. He was sitting in the middle of the room smoking a pipe in great apparent satisfaction.

'Bedtime, isn't it?' I grumbled, sniffing at his strong tobacco.

'Oh no,' he said. 'The fact is, we are going to sit up all night.'

I threw myself on a couch by the window without reply. Perhaps I was not in the best of tempers; certainly I did not feel so.

'You insisted on coming down with me,' he suggested.

'I know all about that,' I told him. 'I haven't complained, have I? If you want me to shut myself up for a week I'll do it; but I should prefer to have some idea of the reason why.'

'I don't wish to create mysteries, Mr Phillips,' he said kindly; 'but, believe me, there is nothing to be gained in vague discussions.'

I know that settled it as far as he was concerned, so I nodded my head and filled a pipe. At eleven he walked across the room and switched off the light.

'If nothing happens, you can take your turn in four hours from now,' he said. 'In the meanwhile get to sleep. I will keep the first watch.'

I shut my eyes; but there was no rest in me that night. I lay listening to the silence of the old house with a dull speculation. Somewhere far down in the lower floor a great gong-like clock chimed the hours and quarters. I heard them every one, from twelve to one, from one to two. Peace had stopped smoking. He sat as silent as a cat at a mouse hole.

It must have been some fifteen minutes after two that I heard the faint, faint creak of a board in the corridor outside. I sat up, every nerve strung to a tense alertness. And then there came a sound I knew well, the soft drawing touch of a hand groping in the darkness as someone felt his way along the panelled walls. It passed us and was gone. Yet Peace never moved. Could he have fallen asleep? I whispered his name.

'Hush!'

The answer came to me like a gentle sigh.

One minute, two minutes more and the room sprang into sight under the glow of an electric hand-lamp. The inspector rose from his seat and slid through the door, with me upon his heels. The light he carried searched the clustered shadows but the corridor was empty, nor was there any place where a man might hide.

'You waited too long,' I whispered impatiently.

'The man is no fool, Mr Phillips. Do you imagine that he was not listening and staring like a hunted beast? A noisy board, a stumble, or a flash of light, and we should have wasted a tiring day.'

'Nevertheless he has got clear away.'

'I think not.'

As we crept forward I saw that a strip of the oak flooring along the walls was grey with dust. If it had been in such a neglected state in the afternoon I should surely have noticed it. In some curiosity I stooped to examine the phenomenon.

'Flour,' whispered the little man, touching my shoulder.

'Flour?'

'Yes. I sprinkled it myself. Look – there is the first result.'

He steadied his light as he spoke, pointing with his other hand. On the powdery surface was the half footprint of a man.

The flour did not extend more than a couple of feet from the walls, so that it was only here and there that we caught up the trail. We had passed the bedroom on the left – yet the footprints still went on; we were at the store-room door, yet they still were visible before us. There was no other egress from the corridor. The tall window at the end was, as I knew, a good twenty feet from the ground. Had this man also vanished off the earth like Silas Ford?

Suddenly the inspector stopped, grasping my arm. The light

he held fell upon two footprints set close together. They were at right angles to the passage. Apparently the man had passed into the solid wall!

'Peace, what does this mean?'

You, sir, sitting peaceably at home, with a good light and an easy conscience, may think I was a timid fool; yet I was afraid – honestly and openly afraid. The little detective heard the news of it in my voice, for he gave me a reassuring pat upon the back.

'Have you never heard of a "priest's hole"?' he whispered. 'In the days when Meudon Hall was built, no country-house was without its hiding-place. Protestants and priests, Royalists and Republicans, they all used the secret burrow at one time or another.'

'How did he get in?'

'That is what we are here to discover; and as I have no wish to destroy Mr Ford's old oak panels I think our simplest plan will be to wait until he comes back again.'

The shadows leapt upon us as Peace extinguished the light he carried. The great window alone was luminous with the faint starlight that showed the tracery of its ancient stonework; for the rest, the darkness hedged us about in impenetrable barriers. Side by side, we stood by the wall in which we knew the secret entrance must exist.

It may have been ten minutes or more when from the distance – somewhere below our feet, or so it seemed to me – there came the faint echo of a closing door. It was only in such cold silence that we could have heard it. The time ticked on. Suddenly, upon the black of the floor, there shone a thin reflection like the slash of a sword – a reflection that grew into a broad gush of light as the sliding panel in the wall, six feet from where we stood, rose to the full opening. There followed another pause, during which I could see Peace draw himself together as if for some unusual exertion.

A shadow darkened the reflection on the floor, and a head came peering out. The light but half displayed the face, but I could see that the teeth were bare and glistening, like those of a man in some deadly expectation. The next moment he stepped across the threshold.

With a spring like the rush of a terrier, Addington Peace was upon him, driving him off his balance with the impact of the blow. One loud scream he gave that went echoing away into the distant corridors. But, before I could reach them, the little detective had him down, though he still kicked viciously until I lent a hand. The click of the handcuffs on his wrists ended the matter.

It was Ford's valet, the man Jackson.

We were not long by ourselves. I heard a quick patter of naked feet from behind us, and Harbord, the secretary, came running up, swinging a heavy stick in his hand. Ransom followed close at his heels. They both stopped at the edge of the patch of light in which we were, staring from us to the gaping hole in the wall.

'What in thunder are you about?' cried the manager.

'Finding a solution to your problem,' said the little detective, getting to his feet. 'Perhaps, gentlemen, you will be good enough to follow me.'

He stepped through the opening in the wall, and lifted the candle which the valet had placed on the floor whilst he was raising the panel from within. By its light I could see the first steps of a flight which led down into darkness.

'We will take Jackson with us,' he continued. 'Keep an eye on him, Mr Phillips, if you please.'

It was a strange procession that we made. First Peace, with the candle, then Ransom, with the valet following, while I and Harbord brought up the rear. We descended some thirty steps, formed in the thickness of the wall, opened a heavy door, and so found ourselves in a narrow chamber, some twelve feet long by seven broad. Upon a mattress at the further end lay a man, gagged and bound. As the light fell upon his features, Ransom sprang forward, shouting his name.

'Silas Ford, by thunder!'

With eager fingers we loosened the gag and cut the ropes that bound his wrists. He sat up, turning his long, thin face from one to the other of us as he stretched the cramp from his limbs.

'Thank you, gentlemen,' said he. 'Well, Ransom, how are things?'

'Bad, sir; but it's not too late.'

He nodded his head, passing his hands through his hair with a quick, nervous movement.

'You've caught my clever friend, I see. Kindly go through his pockets, will you? He has something I must ask him to return to me.'

We found it in Jackson's pocket-book – a cheque, antedated a week, for five thousand pounds, with a covering letter to the manager of the bank. Ford took the bit of stamped paper, twisting it to and fro in his supple fingers.

'It was smart of you, Jackson,' he said, addressing the bowed figure before him. 'I give you credit for the idea. To kidnap a man just as he was bringing off a big deal – well, you would have earned the money.'

'But how did you get down here?' struck in the manager.

'He told me that he had discovered an old hiding-place – a "priest's hole" he called it, and I walked into the trap as the best man may do sometimes. As we got to the bottom of that stairway he slipped a sack over my head, and had me fixed in thirty seconds. He fed me himself twice a day, standing by to see I didn't holloa. When I paid up he was to have twenty-four hours' start; then he would let you know where I was. I held out awhile, but I gave in tonight. The delay was getting too dangerous. Have you a cigarette, Harbord? Thank you. And who may you be?'

It was to the detective he spoke.

'My name is Peace, Inspector Addington Peace, from Scotland Yard.'

'And I owe my rescue to you?'

The little man bowed.

'You will have no reason to regret it. And what did they think had become of me, Inspector?'

'It was the general opinion that you had taken to yourself wings, Mr Ford.'

* * * * *

It was as we travelled up to town next day that Peace told me his story. I will set it down as briefly as may be.

'I soon came to the conclusion that Ford, whether dead or alive, was inside the grounds of Meudon Hall. If he had bolted, for some reason, by-the-way, which was perfectly incomprehensible, a man of his ability would not have left a broad trail across the centre of his lawn for all to see. There was, moreover, no trace of him that our men could ferret out at any station within reasonable distance. A motor was possible, but there were no marks of its presence next morning in the slush of the roads. That fact I learnt from a curious groom who had aided in the search, and who, with a similar idea upon him, had carefully examined the highway at daybreak.

'When I clambered to the top of the wall I found that the snow upon the coping had been dislodged. I traced the marks, as you saw, for about a dozen yards. Where they ended I, too, dropped to the ground outside. There I made a remarkable discovery.

'Upon a little drift of snow that lay in the shallow ditch beneath were more footprints. But they were not those of Ford. They were the marks of long and narrow boots, and led into the road, where they were lost in the track of a flock of sheep that had been driven over it the day before.

'I took a careful measurement of those footprints. They might, of course, belong to some private investigator; but they gave me an idea. Could some man have walked across the lawn in Ford's boots, changed them to his own on the top of the wall, and so departed? Was it the desire of someone to let it be supposed that Ford had run away?

'When I examined Ford's private rooms I was even more fortunate. From the boot-boy I discovered that the master had three pairs of shooting-boots. There were three pairs in the stand. Someone had made a very serious mistake. Instead of hiding the pair he had used on the lawn, he had returned them to their place. The trick was becoming evident. But where was Ford? In the house or grounds, dead or alive, but where?

'I was able, through my friend the boot-boy, to examine the boots on the night of our arrival. My measurements corresponded with those that Jackson, the valet, wore. Was he acting for himself, or was Harbord, or even Ransom, in the secret? That, too, it was necessary to discover before I showed my hand.

'Your story of Harbord's midnight excursion supplied a clue. The secretary had evidently followed some man who had disappeared mysteriously. Could there be the entrance to a secret chamber in that corridor? That would explain the mystification of Harbord as well as the disappearance of Silas Ford. If so Harbord was not involved.

'If Ford were held a prisoner he must be fed. His gaoler must of necessity remain in the house. But the trap I set in the suggested journey to town was an experiment singularly unsuccessful, for all the three men I desired to test refused. However, if I were right about the secret chamber I could checkmate the blackmailer by keeping a watch on him from your room, which commanded the line of communications. But Jackson was clever enough to leave his victualling to the night-time. I scattered the flour to try the result of that ancient trick. It was successful. That is all. Do you follow me?'

'Yes,' said I; 'but how did Jackson come to know the secret hiding-place?'

'He has long been a servant of the house. You had better ask his old master.'

MARK POIGNAND
& KALA PERSAD

Created by Headon Hill (1857–1927)

Born in the Suffolk coastal town of Lowestoft, Francis Edward Grainger began his career as a journalist but turned to writing fiction in his thirties. Under the pseudonym 'Headon Hill', taken from the name of a beauty spot on the Isle of Wight, Grainger produced a large number of crime stories for the monthly magazines throughout the late Victorian and Edwardian eras. His hardback fiction, with titles such as The Hour-Glass Mystery, Caged, *and* Guilty Gold, *proved popular for more than thirty years without ever turning him into a bestselling author. He created several crime-solving characters, the most Sherlockian of which was the private detective Sebastian Zambra. However, his most original creations were Kala Persad, a wizened Hindu sage, and Mark Poignand, the young man who brings him to London. In England, Poignand opens a 'Confidential Advice' agency and makes use of Kala Persad's wisdom and insights into human nature to solve a series of mysteries. Poignand, a not particularly likeable individual, tends to keep the old fakir in seclusion from English society and to take sole credit for the pair's achievements but it is always Kala Persad who puts him on the right track. The stories are suffused with the kind of patronising assumptions about Indian life and Indian individuals that were commonplace at the time but these are sometimes undercut by their actual plots and by the ingenuity with which Kala Persad works out how and by whom crimes were committed. A collection of the stories,* The Divinations of Kala Persad, *was published in 1895.*

THE DIVINATION OF THE KODAK FILMS

High up in the topmost turret of Okeover Castle sat Kala Persad, his leathery face glued to the window, and his eyes blazing like coals of fire at a group upon the terrace a hundred feet below.

There were five persons in all who were focussed by those piercing orbs from the point of vantage in the tower. Three of the group had been upon the terrace some time; the other two had come up in succession within the last few minutes. The original trio consisted of an elderly lady, fur-clad and stately, having by her side a sweet-faced girl, so like in feature that they could only be mother and daughter, and of Mark Poignand, who had been slowly pacing up and down with them since breakfast. To them had come up the stone steps from the park a young lady of dashing carriage and stylish, tailor-made costume, carelessly swinging a Kodak by its leather strap; and she in turn had been followed at the interval of a couple of minutes by a dapper, well-groomed man of five-and-thirty, who, despite his short stature, was of distinctly military bearing.

Presently the group separated, and after a brief interval Mark Poignand appeared in the doorway of the turret-chamber. Kala Persad was still squatting cross-legged on the chair which he had drawn to the window, but at the sound of his master's footsteps he looked up and thrust forward his silver-stubbled chin in peering curiosity.

'The Sahib has read the riddle?' he asked eagerly.

'No, indeed,' replied Poignand; 'and clever as you are, Kala, I should be very much surprised to hear that you had. Surely you don't mean...?' he continued, as he noted the glitter of the snake-charmer's eye.

'Bah!' interrupted Kala Persad, in the half-contemptuous tone that always irritated Poignand, though it never failed to reassure him. 'Bah! The vultures which perch on the summits of the Ghats sight more prey in an hour than the tigers of the jungle in a whole moon. The hiding-place of the Mem Sahib's jewels is known to thy servant, and it remains but to put forth thy hand to restore them to their owners.'

'Where are they, then?' asked Poignand breathlessly.

'The Sahib must first tell me this – so that by no chance do I go astray,' proceeded Kala Persad leisurely. 'The short Sahib who came on the terrace but now is he who saw and chased the robbers, is he not?'

'Yes, that is Sir Frederick Cranstoun; but for Heaven's sake don't keep me waiting; where are the jewels?'

'The Sahib saw a young Missee Baba come from the great maidan (park) with a black box in her hand, swinging it thus? Well, in that box lies hid the secret of our desires. Let the Sahib procure and open that box without delay, and he will discover the secret of the jewels which the old Mem Sahib deplores.'

Mark Poignand regarded the old man with half-dubious wonder. 'It is too late in the day for me to go back on your counsels now, Kala,' he said; 'otherwise I should say that you were at fault at last. Miss Hicks is an American lady, well known in society, and of great wealth.

'What possible connection can she have with the professional burglars who were caught almost in the very act of stealing Lady Hertslet's diamonds? The box she had in her hand is simply an instrument for taking sun pictures – a pastime to which, I have ascertained, she is much given; and, besides, I very much doubt if it would hold all the jewellery that was abstracted from the safe.'

'I have spoken; it is for the Sahib to act,' replied the snake-charmer curtly; and adjusting the folds of his scarlet turban, he turned to contemplate the landscape in dignified silence. Poignand, knowing his moods, smiled softly, and quietly left the room. Making his way down the winding staircase to the chamber that had been allotted to him in the main wing of the castle, he lighted a cigarette and sat down to think out his follower's strange assertion.

The more he gave his mind to it, the more astounding did the old snake-charmer's ultimatum seem. The burglary, which was the cause of his presence at Okeover Castle, had been a very commonplace affair, only interesting to the world at large because of the enormous value of the family jewels stolen. Two nights previously the usual little comedy had been played while Lady Hertslet and her guests were at dinner, the servants, as usual on such occasions, being busy in the lower part of the house. The ladder, which in country mansions seems to be kept ready for the special benefit of cracksmen, had been brought from an out-building, and by this means an entry had been effected through the window of her ladyship's dressing-room, where was the safe containing the celebrated Hertslet diamonds. After prudently locking the doors leading on to the landing and into the adjoining bedroom, the burglars lost no time in getting to work.

Meanwhile the party in the dining-room was making merry in happy ignorance of what was going on upstairs. Besides the hostess and her daughter, Mildred, there were present that night only the two guests staying at the castle – Sir Frederick Cranstoun, a captain in the 23rd Hussars; and Miss Stella Hicks, an American heiress, better known in Paris and London than her native New York. Towards the close of dinner an argument was started between Mildred Hertslet and Miss Hicks as to the height of a certain Swiss waterfall, and on it becoming known that Sir Frederick had a photograph of the falls in question which would decide the point there and then, he was requested to fetch it from his bedroom.

The baronet of course complied, and went at once for the picture, his way taking him past the room in which the thieves were at work. As he came opposite the door, his attention was attracted by a gleam of light underneath, which was suddenly extinguished, as though on account of his approach, and, thinking it strange, he went close up and listened. At first there was dead silence within, but after a minute some faint whispering reached him, and he was confirmed in the conviction that something was wrong. Believing himself justified by the circumstances, he turned the handle of the door, only to find the latter locked, and to hear the scuffling sounds of hasty flight.

His first course was to shout lustily for help, and his second to hurry round through Lady Hertslet's bedchamber, rightly guessing that there would be another door thence into the dressing-room. On finding that also locked, he attacked it with such success that it gave way just as the head of the last burglar was disappearing below the window-sill, and just as the alarmed servants came trooping up the staircase to his aid. Without a moment's hesitation, Sir Frederick plunged down the ladder, and reached ground in time to catch a glimpse of the thieves as they sped across the terrace towards the park.

Despite the fact that he was in evening dress, hatless, and lightly shod, the baronet gave chase at once, and pursued the three flying forms right across the moonlit expanse, through a fringe of wood on the opposite side, and into the high road, which, after a half-mile stretch, led to the railway station in the village of Okeover. Here the burglars ran into the arms of a couple of policemen and a posse of railway officials, who, owing to the wise foresight of the butler at the castle in despatching a groom on a fast horse, were ready ambushed in the booking-office.

Sir Frederick Cranstoun, who had stuck to the chase with dogged persistency, came up just as the capture had been effected, and a couple of men servants, who had followed in his wake, arrived at brief intervals a few seconds later.

The three men were secured and taken to the county town, where they were subsequently identified as notorious metropolitan house-breakers; and the evidence against them was as complete as could be wished for, since Sir Frederick was close on their heels all the way, and sundry implements of their profession were found upon them. The only thing necessary to general satisfaction that was not found, either on the burglars or anywhere else, was the case containing the Hertslet diamonds. It was not in the broken-open safe; it had not been left in the dressing-room, and the most careful search along the route taken by the flying thieves failed to reveal the slightest trace of it. The box and the diamonds had vanished apparently into the infinities of space.

A policeman, and especially a provincial policeman, when he has once got the handcuffs on the undoubted perpetrator of a crime, is apt to look on the case as finished and done with, so far as he himself is concerned. Lady Hertslet saw at once that if she trusted to the superintendent of the county police to find her jewels she would be in a fair way never to see them again. Without saying so in so many words, the officer allowed it to be seen pretty plainly that he thought it unreasonable of her to expect more from him than the procuring of vengeance on the criminals in the shape of a good rousing sentence. There was small comfort in this, seeing that in the superintendent's opinion the men would be sure to get seven years, and that the best chance of finding the jewels would be in watching them on coming out, when they would probably make for the spot where they had hidden their plunder during their flight.

Lady Hertslet was not the sort of woman to stand official nonsense. Having received the report, evidently intended to be final, of the futile police search along the ground traversed, she said nothing, but quietly despatched her steward to town for Mark Poignand, whose successes in elucidating mysteries had reached her ears. He had presented himself without delay, but on hearing the circumstances had at once pronounced the case to be outside the limits of his ordinary practice.

'You see, Lady Hertslet,' he said, 'such small reputation as my bureau possesses has been gained in tracking out guilty persons. Here the thieves are already in custody. There is no mystery to be cleared up. What you wish me to engage in seems to be nothing more nor less than a game of hide-and-seek, and I can lay claim to no particular ability in that line.'

'I only know that my jewels are worth eighty thousand pounds, and that it is a game well worth your playing if you care to undertake it,' was the reply.

Poignand thought for a moment. He had stated his honest conviction that a simple search was not more in his way of business than in anyone else's; but over and above this was the objection that it was not a case in which Kala Persad, from his lair in the Strand, could profitably employ his instinctive faculties. The old man could hardly be expected to point out the whereabouts of a missing jewel-case that must be hidden somewhere in a stretch of country he had never seen, even if his talents extended to hitting off-hand on secret hiding-places.

'If I am to make the attempt, it will be necessary for me to confide in you a private detail of my method,' Poignand said at last. 'I have a very shrewd assistant upon whom I greatly rely in these investigations, and I should require his presence here unknown to the members of your household, for his very existence is one of my trade secrets. The difficulty is that he is a foreigner – a Hindoo – and I do not quite see how to introduce him into the castle without exciting general curiosity.'

'That can easily be arranged,' replied Lady Hertslet eagerly. 'My steward is thoroughly to be trusted, and not a soul else need know of your man's presence. He can have the turret room at the top of the west tower, into which no one ever goes, and whence there is a clear view over nearly the whole of the route taken by the burglars on their way to the station. There is a separate door at the foot of the tower, by which he can get in and out after dark should he want to, and he would be able to see pretty well everything that is going on nearer home – if that would be an advantage.'

'We never know in these cases,' replied Poignand oracularly; and then, having concluded his final arrangements, he returned to town to bring Kala Persad upon the scene. Late the same evening, which was the one following the burglary, the old snake-charmer was smuggled – a mass of shawls and wraps – into the western tower, where he was safely installed in the turret chamber, Poignand himself being accommodated in the main wing of the castle with the avowed object of finding the jewels.

Kala Persad's dogmatic assertion with reference to Miss Hicks' Kodak was made the morning after their arrival. As a well-known figure in society, Poignand was received on an equal footing, and he had already taken advantage of this to learn what he could of his hostess and her daughter, as well as of his fellow guests. Nothing had transpired to suggest any mystery of the kind indicated. Lady Hertslet was a widow of enormous wealth, which would one day be inherited by her only daughter, and Poignand had not to exercise much of his ingenuity to discover that between Mildred Hertslet and Sir Frederick Cranstoun there existed an attachment which had not yet found favour with her mother. From a worldly point of view this was not, perhaps, surprising when certain stray bits of club gossip came to Poignand's recollection that, for a baronet, Sir Frederick was a poor man.

Miss Hicks gave the impression of being a fair specimen of the American heiress who is at home everywhere but in her own land. Very sprightly and agreeable, with perhaps a tinge of what in an English girl would be termed fastness, but which in ladies from over the Atlantic is allowed to pass as piquancy, she was considerably older than Mildred, and a year or two back had been the heroine of a rumour assigning her in matrimony to an Italian duke, a rumour since falsified by the duke marrying someone else. Her visit to Okeover Castle was the result of a long-standing invitation, the Hertslets having known her in London during several seasons.

Pondering Kala Persad's imputation in the privacy of his chamber, Poignand reflected that the worst he had heard of Miss Hicks was an inordinate desire to marry a 'title', but that was a weakness common to most of her fellow countrywomen, and one which in no way justified a suspicion of having appropriated her hostess's diamonds. The odds, too, were heavy against her having stumbled by chance on the hiding-place, which a careful police search had failed to reveal.

Poignand had not yet commenced the preliminaries of the investigation, and he decided to complete these before definitely following the line laid down for him by the snake-charmer. The first item in his programme was naturally to interview and closely question the man who had been hot on the trail of the flying burglars, and who might have seen something during that wild career which should throw a new light on the situation. He had intended to get hold of Sir Frederick immediately after breakfast, but the baronet had set out for the stroll from which he had only just returned, and the interval had been spent in examining the broken safe and in hearing Lady Hertslet once again recapitulate the facts so far as they were known to her.

Quitting his room, Poignand set out to find Sir Frederick, and came upon him in the entrance hall at the foot of the grand staircase, where he was engaged in reading the barometer. He looked up at the sound of footsteps, and nodded coldly. Something in the baronet's manner in the drawing-room on the previous evening had given Poignand an impression of want of sympathy, which he attributed rather to a general dislike of the profession of 'gentleman detective' than to antipathy to his present errand. It was a feeling that he had had to encounter before, and he quite understood it.

'The glass is falling steadily; we are to have rain, I suppose,' said Sir Frederick in a tone of annoyance.

'I hope not – at any rate till I have gone over the ground,' replied Poignand. 'It might obliterate possible traces, you see. By the way, I was going to ask you to be good enough to accompany me, so that there may be no chance of my missing the exact course of the chase.'

'Oh, very well,' was the reply; 'I have personally conducted four parties – of police and servants from the house – over the ground already. One more won't make any difference.'

The antagonistic ring in his voice was so unmistakable that Poignand's thoughts unconsciously reverted to Kala Persad sitting alone in his watch tower. If, instead of to the American heiress, the old man's finger had pointed to this ill-tempered captain of Hussars, who was so chary of his help, while of all others able to be most helpful, he would have felt more sure of his clue. As it was, he began to think that, after all, there might be lower depths in this apparently simple case.

'In the course of the morning I may avail myself of your assistance,' said Poignand. 'In the meanwhile just a question or two, please. Did you lose sight of the thieves at any point in the pursuit – long enough, I mean, to give them a chance to conceal the jewel-case?'

'That's a funny thing to ask,' said Sir Frederick, regarding him with a queer look of suspicion. 'It almost implies that I may have seen them hide the case, and know where it is.'

'Come, come,' said Poignand; 'that is your suggestion – not mine, remember.'

'Well, then,' proceeded the other, 'I had them well in view across the open stretch of park, and in the road leading up to the village and station. In the belt of wood that lies between the park and the road it was different. Without ever really losing them I saw them of course less distinctly, and once or twice may have been guided rather by the sound of their scrunching through the bushes than by sight. They never stopped, though. Of that I am quite certain.'

'In that open stretch across the park did you notice the jewel-case?'

'The third man was carrying a square box, which from Lady Hertslet's description must have been the case.'

'And when you emerged from the wood into the road, had he it still?' asked Poignand.

'I can only say that I did not see it,' returned Sir Frederick; 'and what is more, I haven't seen it since, if, as I believe, that is what you are trying to get at,' he added with a sudden rush of petulance, as he turned into the adjacent billiard-room and slammed the door behind him.

Poignand stood where he was left, whistling softly to himself, and staring round with a vacant gaze that took in nothing of the antlers and the armour and the old oak panelling upon which it rested. The strange behaviour of the baronet filled him with a suspicion which it was hard to reconcile with the probabilities of the case. Had it not been for the obvious desire of Sir Frederick

Cranstoun to become connected by marriage with the Hertslets, Poignand would have concluded at once that he knew the whereabouts of the jewels, and meant to preserve them for his own use; but, on the other hand, it was extremely unlikely that a man would want to rob the lady to whose daughter's hand he aspired. Putting it on no higher grounds, he would be taking goods which, if his hopes were realised, would fall into his hand in the ordinary course of events, for was not Mildred Hertslet her mother's only child?

Poignand was suddenly delivered from the deadlock in his ruminations by a lively voice at his elbow, and turning, he saw the elegant figure of Miss Stella Hicks posed on the bottom stair. She had changed her dress since her stroll in the park, and wore a morning toilette that was one of Worth's happiest efforts. Her gracious smile was in striking contrast to the sulkiness with which he had just been met, and she greeted him with a frank familiarity that was quite refreshing.

'Well, reader of the inscrutable,' she said, 'I suppose it isn't fair to pump you on your all-important quest, but I should dearly like to know – have you got an inkling yet?'

'Not the very faintest,' was the reply. 'I have no more idea of where the jewels are than you have, Miss Hicks. I don't despair, though, for I have not begun my search yet, and it is even possible that it may not take the form of a search in the ordinary sense of the word.'

He watched her narrowly as he said this, and got his reward. She had been leaning idly against the wall at the foot of the staircase, but she started forward now and eyed him keenly.

'Why, how else could you find them?' she asked eagerly. 'I am so interested in anything like detective work,' she added apologetically, as though anxious to furnish a reason for her curiosity.

'Ah! But this is a very uninteresting case, you see,' said Poignand, with intentional levity. 'What you ladies enjoy is the excitement of mystery, and of hunting down and fixing the guilt on some unhappy wretch. That has all been done for me by Sir Frederick Cranstoun, though he might have finished the job while he was about it by not losing sight of the jewel-case.'

'H'm – yes!' ejaculated the fair American, in a tone which made Poignand wonder whether it was only her native drawl or intended to be significant. 'But you haven't answered my question yet: if you ain't going to look for these diamonds, how do you reckon to find them?'

Again he studied her closely as he made answer: 'I am thinking of having a shot at the burglars themselves. It might be possible to induce one of them to split, on the promise of being let down lightly, and, at any rate, it seems worthwhile getting an order to see them in gaol for the purpose of trying.'

'Oh! That's your plan, is it?' she murmured softly. 'Do you know, I don't think much of it; for if I was a burglar, I am quite sure I should keep my knowledge to myself;' and she passed on, rather abruptly, to the morning-room, whence the sound of Mildred's piano floated through the hall.

Poignand stood looking after her with half-closed eyes. 'So you don't think much of my plan, do you, my lady?' he soliloquised. 'In that case I wonder why that shade of anxiety shot across your fascinating features when I mentioned it. Well, you needn't alarm yourself in that direction, for my plan, as you call it, doesn't happen to be the first item in the programme. There's something in the air that puzzles me, and I'm inclined to believe that, after all, there's more here than a mere hunt among hedgerows and fern coppices. Yes, I'll play old Kala's card first and have a look at that Kodak.'

He turned and retraced his steps up the broad staircase to the main landing, whence to the right and left branched the corridors, flanked by the principal bedrooms. Lady Hertslet, in showing him over the scene of the robbery, had informed him as to the occupation of the different rooms, and he knew that Miss Hicks was accommodated in the first room in the left passage. Lady Hertslet's apartments and those of her daughter opened on to the landing itself, while his own and Sir Frederick's rooms were in the passage running to the right.

Poignand went straight to his own room and stood for a few minutes listening intently inside the open doorway. There was no sound audible nearer than the strains of the piano far away on the ground floor. The music had changed to a duet, and he knew that for the present Miss Hicks was safely accounted for. He went out into the passage, and the silence near at hand still prevailed.

Looking up and down the length of both the passages, he could see no sign of a living creature, and it became evident that the housemaids having finished their morning work in that part of the house had retired to the regions below. There was no cause for hesitation. Gliding across the thickly carpeted landing into the further passage, he boldly opened the door of the American's room and entered.

Poignand's eyes roved over the dainty luxury of the room, passing by the glittering gold and silver toilet accessories and costly paraphernalia, which stamped Lady Hertslet's guest as a wealthy woman, without fastening on anything in particular till he caught sight of the Kodak. It stood on a small table at the head of the bed amid a number of requisites for developing and fixing, of which, as the possessor of a Kodak himself and an amateur photographer of no mean order, he thoroughly understood the uses. In an instant the camera was in his hands, and the briefest of inspections proved that, taken literally, Kala Persad's imputation was unfounded. There was nothing in the Kodak beyond its own mechanism, and the spool of film on which the pictures were taken.

'No jewels here,' murmured Poignand to himself. 'Strange, too, that there should be absolutely nothing, for the old man is never wholly at fault. By the way, he did not say definitely that I should find the jewels in the Kodak, but only "the secret of our desires". I wonder whether there is anything on this film of a compromising nature. It might be as well to develop it, and see what artistic effects the fair Stella has been after.'

He glanced quickly at the photographic requisites on the table, and found what he wanted in a box of spare film spools. One of these he substituted for the spool in the camera, placing the latter in his pocket. The automatic register on the instrument told him that only one film on this spool had been used, and having readjusted the register at that number, he left the Kodak as he had found it, and quietly regained his own room.

He had brought his own Kodak with him, and was well supplied with the necessary chemicals for developing negatives. All that remained was to shut the shutters, light his portable red lamp, and set to work in the extemporised dark-room to bring into being the as yet latent image secured by the American heiress.

Gradually, under his skilful treatment, the pale cream colour of the film began to change into fantastic shapes, assuming momentarily fresh forms and shades which in that dim light gave no idea of the subject beyond an indistinct blur of waving foliage and rustic scenery. But a plunge in the fixing bath soon cleared the cloudiness away, and it was safe to admit the daylight again. Hastily unfastening the shutters, Poignand held the developed film up to the sunny sky, devoured every detail of the negative, and burst into a low chuckle of triumph.

The picture represented a woodland glade. In the centre was an aged oak, and some ten feet up where the boughs began to branch, clung Sir Frederick Cranstoun! He had thrust one arm into a hollow that ran downwards from the fork of the trunk, and there was an agonised expression on his face which said, 'I can't reach it,' as plain as words could speak.

Poignand hastily washed the dishes, hustled the chemicals into a drawer, and taking the negative with him, went downstairs again. The click of balls in the billiard-room and the notes of the piano told him that he might safely leave the castle without meeting those he wished to avoid, and a couple of minutes later he was speeding across the park towards the belt of wood on the far side.

When he reached the shelter of the trees he went more leisurely, noting the different landmarks, and comparing them from time to time with the picture. The wood was about a quarter of a mile broad, and it was not till he came to about the centre that he reached the object of his search in the form of a large oak tree standing a little apart in the middle of a clearing. There was no doubt about it; the tree was the original of the one portrayed in the negative.

He went forward and examined the trunk. To his surprise there were indications that it had been scaled as far as the first fork, not once, but several times – or, at any rate, by several people. The chipping of the bark told that tale unerringly. Looking again, he saw that the height of the hollow from the ground was not so great that anyone passing could not have tossed the jewel-case in with a vigorous heave, and the idea came to him that Sir Frederick must have seen the action. But why had he concealed his knowledge, and, above all, were the jewels hidden in the hollow of the oak still?

Five minutes spent in arduous clambering, and five more in straining to the extremity of his reach, solved the latter question in a triumphant affirmative. Poignand's arms were longer than Sir Frederick's by the necessary couple of inches, and when he touched ground Lady Hertslet's jewel-case, intact and heavy laden, was safe in his clutch. His first and obvious duty was to restore it to its owner, but the most difficult part of his task lay in explaining the means by which the result had been obtained. Though he had solved the main issue, the heart of the mystery was untouched. Sir Frederick's knowledge or suspicion of the burglars' hiding-place, his unwillingness to help, his secret attempt to secure the jewels, and, above all, the strange action of Miss Hicks in following him to indelibly record that attempt, and her concealment of her discovery, all seemed inexplicable.

He recrossed the park, and mounted the steps to the terrace. The castle was basking in the hot rays of the autumn noonday sun, for the rain which Sir Frederick had feared – doubtless, lest the soft ground should betray his next visit to the oak – still held off. Poignand was passing along the front of the mansion towards the morning-room, where he expected to find Lady Hertslet, when, on nearing one of the French windows of the billiard-room, the sound of voices brought him to a halt. The speakers, Sir Frederick and Miss Hicks, though they conversed in guarded tones, were plainly quarrelling, and the first words he heard thrilled the listener with the prescience of coming revelation.

'You have no proof of my knowledge' said the baronet passionately.

'The fact that I have taxed you with it, and that you do not deny it, is proof enough for me,' replied the American, with an emphasis on the last word.

'And, assuming that it is so, you have no proof that it is a guilty knowledge – that I wanted the things for myself,' said Sir Frederick.

'Don't you fall into any such error,' retorted Miss Hicks, lapsing into Yankeeism in her excitement. 'I spotted you in the wood this morning, and snapped you with my Kodak. I've got a counterfeit presentment of you groping for those diamonds quite good enough for my purpose, I reckon, when it's developed.'

'Good Heavens, woman! and what is your object in all this suspicion and espionage?' exclaimed the baronet, evidently restraining himself with difficulty. 'What is the price of your silence? For anyone who would act as you have acted is to be bought; of that I am very sure.'

'And you are right,' was the reply, 'though the price is not such a very terrible one. What you have to do to secure me as an ally is to give up all idea of marrying Mildred Hertslet, and make me Lady Cranstoun. Apart from this awkward fix you've got yourself into, I've got dollars enough to make it quite worth your while.'

Poignand waited breathlessly for the reply. There was a short pause, the sound of a choking sob of rage, and then Sir Frederick said:

'Infamous creature! So the motive of all this is a paltry title. You may ruin my happiness, but you shall never reap the fruits of your scheming. I shall go at once to Lady Hertslet, and tell her the whole truth – how, without being positive, I thought I saw one of the thieves hurl the case into the hollow of the tree as he rushed by; and how, foolishly enough, I conceived the idea of gaining her favour, and furthering my suit, by restoring the jewel-case myself into her hands. When, in the evil of your own nature, you suspected me of evil design, and followed me into the wood, I was endeavouring to forestall this man Poignand, having been prevented by the police search from making the attempt yesterday. If Lady Hertslet believes me – well and good; if not, I have lost Mildred; but in any case you shall not profit by my folly.'

Every word, every inflexion of voice, proved the sincerity of his statement, and Poignand read the situation like a book. The American had thought it possible that Sir Frederick suspected the hiding-place, and either placing her own base construction on his conduct, or, more probably divining his real motive, had seized the opportunity for getting him into her power and securing the coveted title. How would she take her defeat? Fiendishly, maliciously, it seemed.

'Don't make any mistake!' she cried. 'When I have circulated my print of "the baronet after the jewel-case, or Sir Frederick Cranstoun up a tree" you won't have much reputation left, I guess. Your story may avail with your friends, but the mud will stick in public.'

Poignand walked in through the window and ostentatiously laid the jewel-case on the billiard table. Sir Frederick, who was fuming out of the room, paused in perplexity, and Miss Hicks gave a scream of surprise.

'Yes, I've found the missing jewels,' said Poignand cheerily. 'And I have also heard the interesting conversation that has just taken place. Miss Hicks, I should advise you to drop it. You have given yourself away in the presence of a witness, you see. You are likely to come off, socially, a good deal worse than Sir Frederick, if I tell of the pretty bargain you tried to make. And I shouldn't advise you to place any reliance on the proof you thought you had got, for I am open to prophesy, without making any admissions, that when you develop the film in your Kodak, you will find it a failure.'

The beaten woman understood what had happened, and knew that she was helpless. With a stifled snarl of rage she fled from the room, while Sir Frederick came forward and wrung Poignand's hand.

'And now we will take the jewel-case to its owner,' said Poignand, when he had briefly explained the origin of his discovery. 'I shall tell her that but for you I might never have been successful, and, after all, that is but the simple truth. It is all that need ever be known of the matter – now that our American heiress has got her claws clipped.'

It came out at the trial that the burglars had lain hid in the oak tree to reconnoitre before the robbery, and had then discovered the hollow which in their subsequent flight they used as a cache. As for the process of reasoning by which Kala Persad arrived at his unerring intuition, it never received fuller elucidation than in his own words to Poignand:

'You see, Sahib, Sir Frederick only free man who could be knowing where jewels were. What for Missee American follow him into wood with box if not to do with the secret? When two curious things happen close together, they bound to have to do with each other.'

Profound philosophy which at least had the merit of being right.

JOHN PYM

Created by David Christie Murray (1847-1907)

Born in West Bromwich, Murray was the son of a printer and began his career working in his father's business. After a brief, unhappy period in the army, he settled into the life of a journalist and worked as a foreign correspondent covering the Russo-Turkish War of 1877-8. He began to write fiction in the late 1870s and, by the time of his death, he had published several dozen novels and volumes of short stories. Well-travelled, Murray lived abroad for much of the 1880s and 1890s and visited Australia, Canada and the USA on lecture tours. The Investigations of John Pym, a collection of stories previously published in magazines, appeared in 1895. 'The Case of Muelvos Y Sagra' is not a very good story but it is an interesting one and it reveals all too clearly Conan Doyle's powerful impact on his fellow writers of short fiction for the magazines. John Pym is not so much a rival of Sherlock Holmes, more a copy. He has been given so many of the attributes of Baker Street's most famous inhabitant – his mastery of arcane subjects, his experiments in chemistry, his pipe-smoking while pondering a problem, his own faithful Watson his friend Ned Venables – that Murray has difficulty establishing any individuality for him at all. And the plot of this particular story is so blatantly lifted from one of Holmes's most famous adventures, published a couple of years earlier, that it is a wonder Doyle did not sue Murray for plagiarism.

THE CASE OF MUELVOS Y SAGRA

At the time of which I, Ned Venables, write, my friend John Pym gave little promise of becoming known to the world at large. I used to think him the most irritating man of my acquaintance, though he was for years my dearest friend. There was hardly a walk of life in which he might not have achieved success, and he did practically nothing. He has the largest and most varied intellectual armoury of any man I know, but he spent all his time in furbishing his weapons and adding new ones with no apparent object. He studied by turns anatomy, medicine, chemistry, natural history, geology, botany, language and literatures; amassing learning at a frightful rate, and doing nothing with it all. I am a man of action, and it has been the business of my life to lay before the public, piping hot, every new thing that I have learned and seen. To a man of my habits and my way of thinking, there was something scarcely tolerable in the spectacle of this astonishing savant grubbing and grinding among his books for ever, and leaving all the wide fields of his learning sterile and unused. When in the course of some one of our talks he would pour out on me some stream of hard-won fact and brilliant theory, I used to ask him impatiently what was the good of all his erudition whilst it lay unused. He used to laugh and confess to an insatiable curiosity. Then he would announce a new study – had a six months' craze for hydraulics, or astronomy, or microscopy. It was enough for him that he had discovered himself to be ignorant anywhere. He would not rest until he had patched that hole in his armour.

He came out of his books at last in a sufficiently astonishing manner.

Pym and I were one night seated in his rooms, when our old friend Dr Macquarrie came in and joined in our talk.

'Well,' said the doctor, 'what's the latest addition to that palatial lumber-room of useless knowledge?'

Macquarrie was quite of my way of thinking about Pym's capacities, and the pity of his brilliant, useless life. Old Pym, who is an ugly man, with a nose like a crag and a brow like a cliff, has the sweetest smile I ever knew. It fairly transforms his face. He turned laughingly at the question.

'I'm invading your own special ground, Mac,' he answered. 'I've turned toxicologist.'

'Have you, indeed?' said the doctor. 'Well since that's your momentary line, Pym, I wish you'd do a little thing for me.'

'Indeed!' said Pym, idly, 'and what may that be?'

'I've a case just now,' returned Macquarrie, 'that worries the life out of me, or thereabouts. To tell ye the plain truth, I'm nine-tenths convinced of foul play in it. I'll not tell ye the names, but here are the circumstances. There's a lady patient o' mine, by birth a Spaniard. She's a charming woman, verging on the sixties. She has charge of a fine little fellow of about three years of age, a nephew of hers, son of a dead sister five and twenty years younger than herself. Now this child has suffered from symptoms that clean bother me. That he's suffering from some kind of irritant poison I haven't any manner o' doubt in the world, but what it is and how it was administered I'm completely at a loss to guess. The symptoms are extraordinarily contradictory. There are signs of poisoning by strychnia, which have looked at moments unmistakable. Then the child has suffered from a maddening irritation of the skin, from hot sweats and cold sweats, tremblings, and a remarkable imitation of St Vitus's dance. The latest symptom is the breaking out of a festering wound on the little wretch's foot. Three days ago there was no sign of that to my certain knowledge.'

I asked Macquarrie what made him suspicious of foul play.

'A year ago,' he answered, 'the child's infant brother died with a partial manifestation of the same symptoms. At that time a certain person was staying in the house. He is staying there now, or was until yesterday. He's a Spanish Brazilian, this fellow, and he's the uncle of my little sufferer. The child's an orphan, and is now sole heir to a very considerable estate. Should he die, this saffron-coloured scoundrel inherits in his stead.'

'Does the child's aunt and guardian suspect this man?' asked Pym.

'That I know she does right well,' the doctor answered. 'And there's a part of the mystery! The fellow's so dreaded since his latest visit, and what we take for its result, that he has not been allowed a second's intercourse with the child. He has had no opportunity, so far as we can make out, of administering anything of a deleterious nature. There's nothing but suspicion in the former case, and nothing but suspicion in this. The fact is that this child is sick, and sick almost unto death of the very symptoms which killed his infant brother a year back when this man was in the house, and the mystery is, that the man has never been allowed near the victim. He has full motive for crime, for he is a gambler and hard-up, and if the child died he would immediately be wealthy.'

'It's a queer business,' said Pym. He rose up to knock the ashes from his pipe, and stood thoughtfully whilst he refilled and relit it. 'The motive's clear enough,' he said after a pause, 'but the suspicion seems to rest on what may be a pure coincidence.'

'The motive and coincidence together,' cried Macquarrie.

'Just so,' said Pym, in a dull inward way, 'just so.' He sat, nursing his foot after a way he had, and staring into the fire, and pulling mechanically at his pipe. He roused himself to ask a single question.

'Is the child out of danger?'

'I'm half disposed to hope so,' Macquarrie answered. 'I shall know better tomorrow.'

'This fellow's away, is he?' Pym asked; and then in answer to the doctor's puzzled look, 'This Spanish Brazilian fellow. He's away?'

'Yes,' the doctor answered. 'He's away. He has some mercantile business in Southampton which he says will keep him a day or two; when the rascal left the child was supposed to be in extremis. Whether he's guilty or no, he'll be sorry to come back and find him well again, I know, though he was mightily moved with concern for the puir thing's welfare when he went away.'

'You speak of the child's guardian as being a charming woman,' said Pym. 'Why does a charming woman admit into her house a man whom she conceives to be capable of murder?'

'That's the pity of it,' cried Macquarrie. 'The house is not hers, but his. He is joint guardian with her, and she lives on his sufferance. He's away in the Brazils when he's at home, and this is his third visit to London for years past.'

No more was said on this topic at the time, but when at a late hour Macquarrie rose to leave us, Pym asked him, with some little urgency, I fancied, to call on the following evening. I took my leave shortly afterwards and went upstairs to bed. Pym and I were old chamber chums, but when he had taken to making all manner of horrible stenches with chemicals some four or five years before, I had left him to his devices, and had rented the suite of rooms over him.

I saw nothing of him next day, except for the chance glimpse of his face I caught as he passed me in a hansom in the neighbourhood of the Zoological Gardens. But at night, as I was sitting at work at my desk, I heard a dull battering just under my feet, and recognising a signal long in use between us, I descended to Pym's chambers.

'Here he is,' said Pym, as I entered. 'Now, Mac, if I wanted to go tiger-shooting, or if I ever got into a tight and desperate corner, this same old Ned Venables is the man I should like to have with me. He's as tough as wire, he's as cool as a cucumber, he's as keen as a terrier, and there's nothing on the earth, or in the water under it, that knows how to frighten him.'

I feel a certain sense of immodesty in setting down this rhodomontade, and I feel that all the more keenly because I know how far it is from being true. I have been frightened pretty often in my time, and the only merit I claim in that regard is that I have never let anybody see it. I never knew but one man who really loved danger. I loathe it, but I have a reputation to consider.

'Now, Mac,' Pym continued, 'if I can persuade you to introduce me to this lady, you know enough of me by this time to be sure that your confidence in me will be utterly respected. I don't say I'm right, but I do say I may be. The theory's so wild that I won't expose myself to any man's laughter by proclaiming it, until I've tried it.'

'Well,' said Macquarrie, 'it's a serious matter, but with you and Venables here I can trust it. I do suspect the Brazilian rascal, and I do believe that if he comes back again he may make another trial. If you think you can guess what fiend's tricks he works by, I'll give you all the authority I've got – and it isn't much – to try. The lady's name is Murios, and she's in the Albert Road, Regent's Park. The Brazilian rascal's name is Muelvos y Sagra. Prefix Josef, and ye have'm in full. The child's greatly better, but I promised to take another luik at him tonight, and if ye're agreeable I'll introduce you to the lady at once.'

'What is this all about?' I asked. 'And why am I wanted?'

'Ned, old fellow,' said Pym, laying both hands upon my shoulders, 'do this one thing for me.'

'My dear Jack,' I answered, 'if you put it in that way I'll do anything.'

So I went off in contented ignorance. Whatever Pym's game was, it was blind man's buff to me. We boarded a four-wheeler, and were driven to the street Macquarrie had named. Pym and I were left in the vehicle whilst the doctor entered a decent-looking, retired little house, cosy, and with a feel of home about it, even when looked at from outside. I spoke once to Pym, but he returned no answer. Presently a servant came out and requested us to enter. We obeyed, and Macquarrie introduced us to a stately, sad-mannered lady, who had once been beautiful and was still venerably sweet, with her snow-white bands of hair, and her delicate brunette complexion, her fine arched eyebrows and large, short-sighted brown eyes. This was the Senora Murios. She received us in musical Spanish speech, expressing a hope that she was understood, and regretting that she had no English. Pym easily reassured her on that point, and for my own part I had had twelve months of that wretched, inactive Carlist war, and could get on well enough. I have scraped acquaintance with two or three languages in that way.

I need not detail the conversation, but it came to this: Pym saw a possible solution to the mystery of the child's illness. He

earnestly begged the lady's confidence, and he asked to be allowed
to see the rooms respectively occupied by Senor Muelvos y Sagra
and the child. The lady for her part assented, and at that moment
there came a noisy summons at the street door.

'That is Josef,' said Senora Murios, rising to her feet, and
clasping her hands with a look of abject terror. 'What shall I do?
What shall I say?'

'These gentlemen are friends of yours.' said Macquarrie, 'and
known to you through me. There is no cause for alarm, believe
me.'

The Senora was right in her recognition of Senor Josef's knock.
I don't think I should have liked the swarthy man, even if I had
not come prepared to dislike and suspect him, and yet he was not
altogether an ill-looking fellow. He was scrupulously dressed,
though he had just come off a journey, and he wore a gold-rimmed
pince-nez, perched delicately on the bridge of his thin nose. His
fine arched eyebrows were black as jet, but his close-cropped hair
and his dandy little moustache and imperial were almost white.
There was a spurious look of good breeding about the man, to
which his tall and slender figure added some affect. His eyes were a
good deal too close together for my liking, and if ever I saw pitiless
and greedy 'Self' written on a human face I saw it on his, as he
stood bowing from right to left in the act of drawing off his gloves
from his lean, long-fingered hands. It was easy to see that whatever
else he was, the fellow was no fool. He had a fine though narrow
dome of head, and his whole face was expressive of intelligence – a
malignant intelligence – a snake's deified.

Macquarrie accepted the situation created by this gentleman's
arrival with a suave coolness which excited my admiration.

'You will be delighted, sir, to learn that your little charge is
out of danger.'

'Delighted,' said Senor Josef, smiling and bowing, but I saw
him bite his underlip. 'That is indeed good news.'

'These gentlemen,' pursued Macquarrie, 'are Englishmen of
eminence, whom I have taken the liberty to introduce to the

Senora Murios. They have the advantage of speaking Spanish, which is not a common pleasure among my countrymen.'

The Senor bowed and shook hands with both of us. He was enchanted to make our acquaintance. He regretted infinitely that it was absolutely necessary that he should tear himself away. He had brought home his baggage, but he had to keep an appointment at a little distance only. He bade us goodnight with sorrow, and trusted that he would have the pleasure of seeing us again. And so he bowed himself out, smiling and protesting, and all the while, as was to be seen plainly enough, wondering who we two strangers were, and casting suspicious guesses here and there as to the meaning of our presence.

We stood in silence when he had left us, and heard the sharp click of his heels upon the pavement as he walked away.

'Oh!' whispered Senora Murios, in a frightened voice to Pym, 'if he knew why you were here, sir, he would kill me. He is not a man to be watched or spied upon.'

Pym begged to see the rooms at once, and for a second time she assented. But she led the way tremulously, and at Pym's request I followed. Our frightened guide led us, to begin with, to a bedroom on the first floor. It was a chamber of the most ordinary type, plainly and even rather meagrely furnished. The only thing in any degree unusual about it was that in place of the common plaster and wallpaper it was lined with plain stained deal. The ceiling was of the same construction, a fact I might not have noticed if I had not observed that Pym scrutinised it with the closest attention.

'The child's bed stood here?' he asked after a time.

'Yes,' the lady answered. 'The child's bed stood there. Since his seizure it has been taken to my own room.'

'Thank you,' said Pym, gravely. 'There is nothing further to look for here.'

Our guide moved towards the door, but stopped with a face of terror at the noise of cab wheels in the street outside. The sound went by, and she led the way again.

'This,' she said, opening a door on the next landing, 'is the bedroom of the child's uncle.'

We entered after her, and I looked about me again, discerning nothing uncommon in the aspect or arrangement of the room. The bed was old-fashioned and heavy, and between its foot and the projecting bulk of a heavy mahogany wardrobe there was but just sufficient space to allow of the wardrobe door being opened. Pym went straight to this antique piece of furniture and looked into its shadowed recess. It seemed at first sight to be quite empty.

'The candle, madame, if you please,' said Pym. He took the light and knelt upon the floor, with his head and shoulders projected in the wardrobe. By-and-by an odd little gasp escaped him, and he withdrew his head. His face at that instant was fully illumined, and I saw that he was ghastly pale, and that his eyes were blazing with some inward fire. He rose from his knees, and reaching his left hand towards me, held out a small clay flowerpot somewhat larger than a common tumbler. I did not understand his agitation or guess at the meaning of his discovery, but there was no mistaking the fact that he was at once shaken and triumphant. At a gesture from him I took the candle in my unoccupied hand, and he drew from the flowerpot a tangle of thin whip-cord, at the end of which was fastened a little arrangement in rusted wire. Pym examined this with a prolonged intentness, which gave me time to scrutinise it also. It was made of two pieces of wire, each perhaps six inches in length. Each piece was doubled in the centre. The centre ends then ran together for an inch, when they diverged, and each of the further ends formed a hook. The two pieces were fastened together firmly at the bend by a smaller piece of wire, which had been bound about them by the aid of a pair of pliers. Below this was a little wire circle, which could be used to bring the four curves closer to each other.

'That will do,' said Pym at last, replacing the worthless-looking tangle pretty much as he had found it. A little rough sand fell from the flowerpot as he did this, and falling on his knees, he scrupulously removed it from the carpet grain by grain. Then he replaced the flowerpot in the wardrobe, and rising to his feet, closed the door, and handed the candlestick to Senora Murios in silence.

'What is it?' she asked, whisperingly, with an added terror in her eyes. 'You have found something?'

'Everything, I think,' said Pym. 'I shall have more to say downstairs.'

She looked at him wonderingly, but he stood without regarding her, his face still pale, his clean-shaven lips compressed in a hard, straight line, and his eyes veritably blazing. I, who had known him so closely for so many years, had no hint of a doubt about him in my mind, wholly in the dark as I was. He was always a daring theorist, but he treated theory as theory, and was, like all fine thinkers, slow to proclaim certainty.

When we reached the lower room, Macquarrie started and stared at him, his face was so transfigured. Senora Murios stood, with the unextinguished candle in her hand, waiting with a piteous look of bewilderment and fear. Pym planted himself squarely on the hearthrug, facing us all.

'I have little doubt, madame,' he said, in the slow and precise way in which a man speaks a language which is not often on his tongue, 'that Josef Muelvos y Sagra is once a murderer in fact and twice a murderer in intent. I say this with a complete sense of the gravity of the statement. I believe myself to understand the diabolical means by which he has worked, and I trust to take him red-handed in a last attempt. But to succeed, I must have nothing less than your full trust and confidence.'

She looked from Pym to Macquarrie, from Macquarrie to me, and back again to Pym.

'You are an English gentleman,' she said, after a painfully undecided pause. 'Dr Macquarrie is almost my only English friend. He tells me you are all-accomplished, and good and upright. I will take his word.'

'Thank you,' said Pym. 'Tell me,' he continued, still speaking in Spanish, but addressing himself to Macquarrie, 'when do you think the child might be safely trusted to sleep in his own room again alone?'

'Impossible to say,' the doctor answered.

'We must wait then,' said Pym. 'But when that time comes, Senora Murios, I shall ask you to trust me. In the meantime, I should advise the child's removal from this house at the earliest safe hour. Other means than those I suspect may be employed against him.'

'What means do you suspect?' she asked, panting in her speech.

'Pardon me if I even seem to add to your suspense,' said Pym, gravely. 'I have reason for it. I have only to ask you for one promise. When the time arrives, will you permit this gentleman and myself to watch over your charge for that one night? We shall ask to have the door locked and to be in darkness.' She gazed at us all three in turn with her pathetic, troubled, and short-sighted look, but she finally assented by a mere inclination of the head. 'The next matter is entirely at your discretion, but I should be happier to know that for that one night you would be willing to absent yourself from the house.'

Old Pym's ugly face was handsome with sincerity and earnestness. His sturdy figure and his manly, quiet voice spoke honesty. The Senora held out her hand to him with a sudden impulse.

'I trust you,' she said. 'I trust you altogether.'

We left upon this understanding, and Pym kept his secret to himself. The days went by, and I had from him or from the doctor occasional news of the child. He was recovering fast, but was suffering from a form of eczema, hearing which Pym merely nodded with 'Just so, just so'. The Spanish Brazilian was still in London, unexpectedly detained, he said, by the prolongation of certain business negotiations. A full month went by before I found myself called upon. Pym came into my rooms at about the end of that time. He was very grave and stern, and I guessed the hour was near.

'That business with our exotic friend comes off tonight,' he said. 'Shall you be ready?' I was keen-set with curiosity and answered 'Yes' at once. 'All right,' said Pym. 'Come down to me at eight o'clock.'

He went away without another word, and left me on the tenterhooks, feeling as if a big battle were announced for next morning. I ought to know that sensation.

Eight o'clock came, and down I went to Pym's rooms. He was already dressed for out of doors, and when I entered he was toying with a small, short-handled butterfly net. He had fixed a string arrangement by which he could close the mouth of the net at a jerk, and he was testing this with an intentness which seemed absurdly trivial under the circumstances. But when he had fairly satisfied himself as to its smooth working, he folded it up and stowed it away under the light dust coat he wore. I concluded that he had a use for it, and forbore to question him. He armed himself further with a dark lantern, and then announced his readiness to start.

We found a hansom waiting, and the driver, evidently instructed beforehand, set off at a brisk pace. It was a clouded night, and cold, with a touch of wet mist in the air. The hansom set us down at a public-house, and Pym led the way in. He walked through the bar and into a snuggery behind it.

'We may have to wait here for a little while,' he said. We sat silent and alone for perhaps half an hour, and then the potman came in with a note. Pym read it and put it in his pocket. 'The coast is clear,' he said calmly. 'We can go now.'

The mist had thickened to a drizzle, and the night had grown bleak and windy, but we were within five minutes' distance of the house we sought. When we reached it, we found the street door already open and the Senora awaiting us. She was so terribly agitated that she could scarcely speak, but she made us understand that she was supposed to be absent from the house, and had made arrangements to spend the night away from it. Senor Muelvos y Sagra had made a pretence of being out of town, but he had returned that evening, bringing with him a large black despatch box, which he had himself carried to his own room.

'That will do,' said Pym. 'You will act most wisely by showing us to the child's room at once, and leaving the house immediately. Your servants know that you are here?'

'I have but one,' the unhappy lady answered, 'but I could trust her with my soul.'

A minute later we were in the lower bedroom, in the dark. Two chairs had been placed for us near the window. Pym turned the key in the lock, and then withdrew it. We heard the opening and closing of the street door, and a retreating step in the passage below. The solitary domestic had retired.

Pym had fired the wick of his dark lantern before leaving the hall, and he now set it on the floor at his feet. I could see just a dim glow-worm sort of light shining in the ventilator at the top, but that was all. We sat as still as a pair of ghosts, and could hear each other's breathing and the ticking of our own and each other's watches. The time went on with incredible slowness, but my eyes had grown accustomed to the darkness, which was faintly illuminated by the street lamps outside, and I could make out everything in the chamber in a dim and shadowy way. Cabs went by with roar and clatter, footsteps passed the house, and voices, and the time dragged along. A clock at some distance struck the quarters with an interminable stretch betwixt each and each.

It was near midnight when a rapid but light footstep came along the street, and paused below. The rattle of a latch-key sounded in the lock, faintly, and the door was stealthily opened and as stealthily closed. Then a step came creaking up the stair, and paused outside our room. A cautious hand tried the door. We heard the sputter of a match, and a light gleamed through the keyhole.

Then the footsteps went murderously stealing upstairs and by-and-by we heard them creaking overhead. I put my heart into my ears and listened. There was a faint noise of hollow iron; then a snap as of a key in a lock, then a pause, then footsteps again, then the creak of a floor, and then a faint rasp upon the floor above, as if one dry substance slid upon another. Pym's hand touched mine, and it was like fire. I turned silently to look at him, and in the dimness saw him beckon upwards. I looked, and there, right above the child's cot, was a square of faint light, and whilst I was wondering what this might mean, something dropped through it and came slowly down. The thing was living. It had a body shaped like two eggs, a lesser and a larger, and a number of limbs that writhed at the air as if they sought to grasp something. Then I knew the meaning of Pym's butterfly net. He rose without a sound, and waited for the hideous thing to descend with the net open below it. It came down writhing into the waiting net, there was a faint clicking noise and Pym with a loud voice cried:

'The lantern! Quick! I have it.'

Before I could snatch the lantern from the floor, the ceiling was shaken as if by a heavy fall.

'Now,' said Pym, 'let us have a look at you.' I flashed the lantern, and there on the floor, struggling in the butterfly net, was a gigantic spider, covered with coarse, reddish grey hair. 'Take this,' said Pym thrusting something into my hand. I felt at once that it was a revolver. 'If that scoundrel tries to get downstairs, stop him.'

I rushed for the door, forgetting in my excitement that it was locked, and tugged at it until Pym followed with the key. The child was awake, and screamed in an agony of terror. Pym threw open the window, and blew a policeman's whistle again and again. I stood guarding the stair. Feet came running, and a voice called out to know what was the matter.

'Attempted murder!' Pym's voice answered. 'Wait there till I let you in.'

Four of us went upstairs, two policemen lantern in hand, and we two spectators of that awful crime. I tried the door, and found it locked. I called, but no answer came. I made a rush and burst it open with one flatfooted thrust, and at that instant a shot sounded.

When we entered, we found that Josef Muelvos y Sagra had gone to his account.

On the bed stood a large despatch box, which opened both at the lid and at the front. It had a false bottom, on which was distributed, to the depth of five or six inches, a coarse grey sand, which had not long ago been sprinkled with water. Below the false bottom burned a spirit lamp. In one corner of the sanded space lay a flowerpot of the size and shape I knew already. Within it was the dead and shrunken body of a mouse.

By this time the quaking domestic was doing her best to soothe the frightened child.

Pym brought up his captive, and delivered a brief lecture to the bewildered officers.

'This, gentlemen, is the largest and most formidable of the Mygalidae. It is commonly known as the great South American Hairy Spider. It is exceedingly fierce and venomous, though its powers of offence have been greatly exaggerated by the ignorant. Its bite has often been reported as fatal to adults, but I have met with no authentic record. It has been frequently known to be fatal to young children. When irritated, as you observe it is at present by the pressure of this contrivance of wire, it becomes additionally dangerous. It demands a high temperature, and an air not too devoid of moisture. I shall ask you to observe, gentlemen, that this wardrobe has no bottom, and that a hole has been cut through the floor of this apartment. Remark further, that the bed of the child whose life was attempted lies directly below the orifice.'

He detached the handle of the net and dropped the dreadful thing, net and all, into the despatch box, blew out the spirit lamp, and locked up the struggling insect.

We left one officer to guard the body of the suicide-murderer, and we accompanied the other to the local police office, where Pym told his story. When at the close of this wild night we found ourselves at home again, I gave a loose rein to my astonishment.

'Well,' said Pym simply, 'I know no other poison which could produce all the effects that Mac detailed. Then came in that symptom of maddening irritation of the skin. Those short reddish grey hairs come off at a touch and produce precisely that effect. It is that fact which has led to the superstitious belief that mere contact with this insect is fatal. Then the villain himself came from Brazil, which is the home of this particular beast. I was less puzzled to diagnose the case than to work out the means by which the crime might be committed.'

And there is the unvarnished history of John Pym's first criminal investigation.

CHRISTOPHER QUARLES

Created by Percy James Brebner (1864–1922)

Born in London, the son of a bank manager, Brebner began his own working life in the Stock Exchange but soon decided that writing was more to his taste. His fiction, written under both his own name and the pseudonym Christian Lys, includes examples of many of the most popular genres of the era. The Fortress of Yadasara, *first published in 1899, is a 'lost world' adventure about a man who stumbles upon a land in the Caucasus where medieval knights still roam;* Princess Maritza *from 1907 is a Ruritanian tale of an English soldier's adventures in a fictional European country;* The Brown Mask *of 1911 is a historical romance about a highwayman in the late seventeenth century. Brebner's only significant contribution to crime fiction consists of the short stories featuring Christopher Quarles, a brilliant but eccentric professor and amateur detective whose services are regularly sought by the tales' narrator, the police officer Murray Wigan. As Wigan diligently searches for clues, Quarles, often assisted by his granddaughter Zena, constructs elaborate, seemingly fanciful theories on the basis of slender facts to explain the mysteries they are investigating. Quarles's theories always turn out to be correct. He appeared in two volumes of stories,* Christopher Quarles: College Professor and Master Detective, *published in 1914, and* The Master Detective *which appeared two years later.*

THE SEARCH FOR THE MISSING FORTUNE

Whenever he had solved a case, if not to the world's satisfaction, to his own, Quarles seldom mentioned it again. He professed to think little of his achievement, a pose which I have no doubt concealed a considerable amount of satisfaction and self-complacency. Of the curious case connected with the Bryants, he was, however, rather proud; and, since it resulted in making things easier for Zena and me, I have every reason to be satisfied.

It began in a strange way. A simple looking old man, his clothes a size too large for him, walked into a large pawnbroker's one day, and, handing him a scarf-pin, asked how much could be given for it. The pin was no use to him. He didn't want to pawn it, but to sell it. The customer was requested to put a price upon his property, and, after some hesitation, he asked whether twenty pounds would be too much. The man in the shop went into a back room ostensibly to consult his superior, in reality to send for the police. It happened that a quantity of jewellery had been stolen from a well-known society lady a few weeks before, and pawnbrokers had had special notice of the fact; hence the firm's precaution. The simple old man had offered for twenty pounds a diamond that was worth at least twenty times that amount.

Being interested in the jewel robbery, I was naturally keen to know all that could be discovered about this simple old man, and I will give the story as I told it to Christopher Quarles after I had made the most minute inquiries.

The old man's name was Sims – James Sims – and for the last year he had resided with a niece, who was married and living at Fulham. Until twelve months ago he had been manservant to an old gentleman named Ottershaw, living at Norbiton, who he said had given him the pin. Mr Ottershaw was a retired Indian servant, who chose to live a lonely life, and was evidently an erratic individual.

Although there was no direct evidence on the point, nothing to show that he had any income beyond his pension, nor any property beyond the old house at Norbiton which he had bought, the idea got abroad that he was an exceedingly wealthy man. Sims declared that he had never seen any evidence of great wealth. His master was aware of what was said, and used to chuckle about it, but he never in any way endorsed the story. At the same time he didn't deny it, and, indeed, fostered the idea to some extent by saying that he hoped to keep his anxious relatives waiting until he was a hundred.

These relatives consisted of two nephews and a niece, the children of Mr Ottershaw's sister, who had been some years his senior. Both the nephews – George and Charles Bryant – were married; the niece was a spinster whose sole interest in life was foreign missions. The Bryants had money, just sufficient to obviate the necessity to work, and, so far as the two brothers were concerned, they were undoubtedly chiefly concerned in waiting for a dead man's shoes. Miss Bryant hoped to become rich for the sake of her missionary work. All of them were convinced of their uncle's wealth.

The old gentleman did not attain his century. He caught a chill, pneumonia set in, and in three days he was dead. Sims declared that about a month before his death his master had given him the pin with the remark: 'You've been a good servant, Sims. This is a little gift in recognition of the fact. It's worth a few pounds, and should you outlive me and find yourself hard up, you can turn it into money.' Sims had not found himself hard up, he had saved enough to live quietly upon, but his great-niece, of whom he was very fond, was going to be married, and he thought he would turn the pin into money as a nest egg for her.

Mr Ottershaw's will was a curiosity. It began with a very straightforward statement that the testator was aware that his relatives had for long past been hoping for his death. No doubt they would have come to live with him had he allowed it, to see that his money did not go to strangers. 'They have their reward,' the will went on. 'I leave all I am possessed of to George, Charles, and Mary Bryant in equal shares, without any restrictions whatever. But, since during my lifetime my nephews and niece have undoubtedly speculated concerning my wealth, I feel it would be a pity if my death were to rob them suddenly of so pleasant an occupation. Frankly, I would take what wealth I have with me if I could. This being impossible, I suppose, I have placed it in a safe place, so that, in order to find it, my relatives will still be able to speculate and exercise their ingenuity. For their guidance I may say that I deposited it in this place while alone in one of the rooms of my house at Norbiton, that I did not send it out of the house, yet if the house is burnt down, or pulled down brick by brick, it will not be found.'

The will then went on to provide that the house should not be sold for five years, nor anything taken out of it. During this period his nephews and niece were to have free access to it whenever they wished, or any person they might appoint could visit it. If they chose they could let it furnished for five years. They could burn it or pull it down if they liked, but if it were intact at the end of five years, it was to be sold, and the proceeds equally divided.

'These are the only conditions,' the will concluded; 'but, as I am doing so much for my relatives, I may just mention two things which I should like done, but they are in no way commands. On the finding of my wealth, if it is found, I should like ten per cent of it given to a society or societies for the feeble-minded. And, as I have explained to my relatives more than once, I should like to be cremated, but I leave the decision to them. If cremation is considered too expensive, I must be buried in the usual way.'

Although the house at Norbiton was still intact, I was told by George Bryant that during the last twelve months every nook and cranny had been searched without avail. He still believed that the wealth was hidden somewhere, but he had begun to doubt whether it would ever be found. Naturally, when he heard of Sims's attempt to sell a diamond pin, his hopes revived. His brother Charles had always thought that Sims knew something, but he himself had not thought so. Now the affair was on an entirely different footing.

When I had told my story in the empty room at Chelsea I think we were all three convinced that this was the toughest problem we had ever tackled.

'Did the relatives respect the old man's wish and have the body cremated?' Zena asked.

'No; he was buried in a cemetery at Kingston.'

'Then they don't deserve to find the money, and I hope they won't.'

'I do not like the relatives,' I returned; 'but in this matter there is something to be said for them. They have always been opposed to cremation, a fact which Mr Ottershaw knew quite well, and, recognizing the contemptuous tone of the will, not unreasonably, I think, they decided that the wish was expressed only to annoy them, and that their uncle had no real desire to be cremated.'

'One of your absurd questions,' said Quarles.

'It seems to me I have never asked a more natural or a more sensible one,' said Zena.

'I won't argue, my dear,' Quarles returned. 'I presume that paper you have there, Wigan, is a copy of the wording of the will?'

'Yes,' and I handed it to him.

'Of course, you do not think Sims has any connection with this jewel robbery you have been engaged upon?'

'No; he would not be selling so valuable a stone for twenty pounds.'

'And you have come to the conclusion that his story is a plain statement of facts?'

'I think so.'

'You are not sure?'

'Well, one cannot close one's eyes to the possibility that he may dislike the Bryants as much as his master did, and may be keeping his master's secret,' I answered.

'Or he may have learned the secret by chance,' said Zena.

'He may,' said the professor. 'You questioned him upon that point, Wigan?'

'He says he knows nothing.'

'What has become of the pin?'

'It is in the hands of the police at present, but will be handed back to him. There is no evidence whatever that he is not the rightful owner. The Bryants wanted to have him arrested.'

Quarles spread out the paper, and began reading parts of the will in a slow, thoughtful manner.

'"Frankly I would take what wealth I have with me if I could".' And Quarles repeated the sentence twice. 'That might imply that there was no wealth to speak of; and, following this idea for a moment, the permission to burn the house or pull it down might suggest a hope in the old man's mind that the frantic search for what did not exist would result in the destruction of even that which did – the house and furniture. The fact that he desires ten per cent of the wealth, if it is found, to go to imbeciles rather favours this notion; and his wish to be cremated may be an attempt to make his relatives spend money upon him from whom they were destined to receive nothing.'

'It would be a grim joke,' I said.

'A madman's humour, perhaps,' said Zena.

'He goes on: "This being impossible, I suppose", and then says he has hidden his wealth. He did not seem quite certain that he could not take it with him, did he?'

'You think –'

'No, no,' said Quarles, 'I haven't got as far as thinking anything definite yet. The will then explains in a riddle where the treasure is hidden. He was alone in a room. He didn't send the treasure out of the house. The statements are so deliberate that I am inclined to believe in a treasure of some sort.'

'So am I,' I answered, 'because of the valuable pin he gave to his man.'

'When was this will made?' asked Quarles.

'Nine years ago.'

'Living as he did, he would hardly spend his pension,' the professor went on. 'Money would accumulate in nine years, and, since there is no evidence that he did anything else with it, we may assume that the hoard was periodically added to, and, therefore, he must have placed it where he could get at it without much difficulty.'

For a moment Quarles studied the paper.

'I think we may take his statements literally,' he went on; 'so unless the treasure was very small, small enough to be concealed inside a brick, it seems obvious that it was not hidden in the walls of the house, or it would have been found in the process of pulling down.'

'If we are to be quite literal, we must remember that he says brick by brick,' I pointed out. 'It might therefore be hidden in a brick.'

'I have thought of that,' Quarles returned; 'but in pulling down bricks would get broken, especially a hollow brick, as this would be. I think we may take the words to mean only total demolition, and that there is no special significance in the expression "brick by brick". Burning does away with the idea that the treasure may be hidden in woodwork.'

'If he put it under a ground–floor room or under a cellar neither pulling down nor a fire would disclose it,' said Zena.

'Every flag in the cellars has been taken up,' I answered; 'and all the ground underneath the house has been dug up.'

'Is there a well?' she asked.

'No; that was the first thing I looked for when I came there.'

'He says in a room,' Quarles went on. 'I don't think that means a cellar.'

'Do you think the treasure was small in bulk and placed in his coffin?' said Zena eagerly, leaning forward in her chair as she asked the question.

'Certainly in that case he would be perfectly justified in saying that he didn't send it out of the house,' said Quarles.

'It is most improbable,' I said. 'To begin with, Mr Ottershaw wished to be cremated, so would hardly leave any such instructions. And, further, Sims saw him placed in his coffin, and says nothing was buried with the body.'

'It is an interesting problem,' said the professor; 'but one does not feel very much inclined to help the Bryants.'

'Then you have a theory?' I asked.

'I haven't got so far as theory; I am only rather keen to try my wits. There is a shadowy idea at the back of my brain which may be gone by morning. If it hasn't, we'll go and see Sims.'

Next morning when I went to Chelsea, as I had arranged to do, I found Quarles waiting for me, and we went to Fulham together. Sims had two rooms in his niece's house, but took his meals with the family. We went into his sitting room and he was quite ready to talk about Mr Ottershaw. I told him that Quarles was a gentleman who thought he could find the hidden money.

'I shall be very glad if he does,' said Sims. 'The Bryants will know then that I had nothing to do with it. Mr Charles has been the worst; but since I tried to sell that pin Mr George has been as bad.'

'I take it you don't like the Bryants,' said Quarles.

'I don't dislike them, only when they bother me.'

'Your master didn't like them?'

'Didn't he? I never heard him say. He wasn't in the habit of saying much to anybody, not even to me.'

'You were fond of him?'

'Loved him. He wasn't what you would call a lovable character, but I loved him, and he liked me. You see, him and me were born in the same neighbourhood, five miles out of Worcester; and when he came back from India he came down there to see an old friend, since dead, and I happened to be there at the time out of a job. That's how we came together fifteen years ago.'

'You didn't go at once to Norbiton?'

'Not until three years afterward.'

'Where were you during those three years?'

'In several places, part of the time in Switzerland, and in Germany.'

'Now about this treasure, Mr Sims?'

'Bless you, sir, I don't believe in it.'

'The will very distinctly mentions it.'

'I know. I've heard such a lot about that will from the Bryants that I know it almost by heart. It was a joke, that's what I think.

311

Why, Mr Charles has asked me more than once whether I didn't slip it into his coffin.'

'Mr Ottershaw gave you no such instructions, I suppose,' said Quarles.

'The only instructions he gave was that I was to lay him out, and to see him put into his coffin if he was buried, and, whatever happened, to see him decently carried out of the house. There was some talk of his being cremated, and I suppose the master didn't know how they would take him away then. No doubt he thought the Bryants would have a woman to lay him out, so he left a letter for me to show them. The master always did hate women.'

'And you did this for him?'

'Gladly, and I helped the undertaker lift him into the coffin. I was there when he was screwed down, so were Mr George and Mr Charles. There was nothing but the body buried; nothing.'

'The Bryants wouldn't have him cremated, I understand,' said Quarles.

'And quite right, too,' said Sims. 'It's a heathenish custom, that's what I think.'

'And you don't believe there was any large sum of money?'

'No, I don't. I should have seen some sign of it.'

'Your master gave you a very valuable pin,' said Quarles; 'I don't suppose you had seen that before.'

'It's true, I hadn't.'

'There may have been other valuables where that came from.'

'I don't think it,' said Sims. 'I don't believe the master himself knew it was so valuable.'

As we walked up the Fulham Road I asked the professor what he thought of Sims.

'Simple – and honest, I fancy.'

'You're not quite sure?'

'Not quite, but then I am not sure of anything in this affair yet. I suggest we go and see Mr George Bryant. I want his permission to go over the house at Norbiton.'

George Bryant lived at Wimbledon, and we found him at home. Much of our conversation went over old ground, and need not be repeated here; but the professor was evidently not very favourably impressed with Bryant. Nor did Bryant appear to think much of Quarles. He smiled contemptuously at some of his questions, and, when asked for permission to visit the house at Norbiton, he said he must consult his brother and sister.

'Except that I am keenly interested in the affair as a puzzle, I don't care one way or the other,' said Quarles. 'Whether you handle the money or not is immaterial to me, but I have a strong impression that I can find it.'

'In that case, of course –'

'There are conditions,' said Quarles, 'and one or two more questions.'

'I am willing to answer any questions.'

'Did you often visit your uncle?'

'Only twice in ten years, and on each occasion he was not very well – a touch of gout, which was what made him so ill-tempered, I imagine. My brother Charles was with me on one occasion; my sister, I believe, never went there.'

'Yet you all expected to profit by his death?'

'His letters certainly gave us to understand that we should, and so far the will was no surprise to us.'

'Has the clause in the will which forbids the removal of anything from the house been observed?' Quarles asked.

'Most certainly.'

'I mean with regard to trifling things.'

'Nothing has been taken. Of course, the will has been complied with.'

'It wasn't with regard to Mr Ottershaw's cremation.'

'We did what we considered to be right, and I refuse to discuss that question. For my own part, I believe if James Sims could be forced to speak the mystery would be at an end. I cannot help feeling that the police have failed in their duty by not having him arrested.'

'I daresay that is a question my friend Detective Wigan will refuse to discuss,' said the professor. 'Do you care to hear my conditions? You can talk them over with your brother and sister when you consider whether I shall be allowed to go over the house or not.'

'I shall be glad to know your fee,' said Bryant.

For a moment I thought that Quarles was going to lose his temper.

'I charge no fee,' he said quietly, after a momentary pause; 'but if the money is found through me, you must give ten per cent for the benefit of imbeciles according to the wish of the deceased, and you must pay me ten per cent. That will leave eighty per cent for you to divide.'

'Preposterous!' Bryant exclaimed.

'As you like. Those are my conditions, and I must receive with the permission to visit the house a properly witnessed document, showing that the three of you agree to my terms.'

'I am afraid you will wait in vain.'

'It is your affair,' said Quarles, with a shrug of his shoulders. 'Remember I can find the money, and I believe I am the only man who can.'

On our way back to town I asked Quarles whether he expected to get the permission.

'Certainly I do. George Bryant is too greedy for money to miss such a chance.'

'And do you really mean that you can find the money?'

'At any rate, I mean the Bryants to pay heavily for it if I do.'

Quarles was right. Three days later the permit and the required document arrived, and we went to Norbiton.

As I had visited the house already, I was prepared to act as guide to the professor, but he showed only a feeble interest in the house itself. The only room he examined with any minuteness was the bedroom Mr Ottershaw had used, and he seemed mainly to be proving to his own satisfaction that certain possibilities which had occurred to him were not probabilities.

PERCY JAMES BREBNER

'There's a ten per cent reward hanging to this, Wigan,' he chuckled. 'We're out to make money on this occasion. Bryant seems to have spoken the truth. The place appears to be much as Mr Ottershaw left it.'

He had opened a cupboard in the bedroom, and took up two or three pairs of boots to look at.

'Large feet, hadn't he? Went in for comfort rather than elegance. I never saw uglier boots. But they are well made, nothing cheap about them.'

'You don't expect to find the money in his boots, do you?'

'Never heard of hollow heels, Wigan?' he asked.

'You couldn't hide much money if every boot in the house had a hollow heel.'

'No, true. I wasn't thinking of hollow heels particularly.'

Then he took up a stout walking-stick which was standing in the corner of the cupboard, felt its weight, and walked across the room with it to try it.

'Nothing hollow about this, at any rate,' he said, after examining the ferrule closely.

When we returned to the hall he was interested in the sticks in the stand.

'He was fond of stout ones, Wigan,' laughed Quarles. 'Well, I don't think there is much to interest us here.'

Our inspection of the house had been of the most casual kind. We hadn't even looked into some of the rooms, and the odd corners and fireplaces to which I had given considerable attention on my former visit hardly received a passing glance from Quarles.

'Have you looked at everything you want to see?' I asked in astonishment.

'I think so. You said the cellars had been dug up, so they are of no interest, and I warrant the Bryants have already searched in every likely and unlikely place. What is the use of going over the same ground, or in examining cabinets and drawers for false backs and false bottoms, when others have done it for us?'

'What is your next move, then?'

315

'I think we may as well go back to Chelsea and talk about it.'

I must admit that, in spite of my knowledge of Quarles, I thought he was beaten this time, and that he was using bluff to hide his disappointment. I thought he had gone to Norbiton with a fixed idea in his mind, only to discover that he had made a mistake. He would not discuss the affair on our way back to Chelsea; but when we reached the house, he called for Zena, and the three of us retired to the empty room.

'Well, dear, is the ten per cent reward to make us rich beyond the dreams of avarice?' asked Zena.

'It is impossible to say.'

'Then you haven't found the money?'

'We haven't counted it yet,' was the answer. 'Let us consider the points. The first is this: Nine years before his death, Mr Ottershaw made his will, frankly expressing a wish that he could take his money with him. Therefore, I think we may assume that he was not in love with his relatives, and was not delighted that his death should profit them. The next sentence in the will seems to express a doubt as to whether the treasure could be taken or not, and I suggest that something occurred about that time to make it appear feasible. So we get a riddle, and if it is to be read literally, as I believe it is meant to be, there can apparently be only one possible hiding-place – somewhere in the ground underneath the house. This is so obvious that one would hardly expect it to be the solution, and so there is particular significance in his statement that he didn't send it out of the house. He hid it, he says, when he was alone in one of the rooms. Let us suppose it was his bedroom. From there he certainly could not bury his treasure in the ground. We have decided that the hiding-place could not be in any part of the brickwork or in the woodwork, therefore we are driven to the conclusion that it was placed in some piece of furniture or some receptacle made for the purpose. Since I believe he thought it possible to take his wealth with him, the latter supposition seems to me the more probable.'

'In banknotes a large sum would only occupy a small space,' I said.

'I don't think the treasure was in money,' said Quarles. 'The fact that a diamond was given to Sims and not money suggests that the treasure was in precious stones. If he spent everything he could in this way, giving hard cash for a gem, and thus doing away with the necessity for inquiry and references, the lack of evidence regarding his wealth is partly explained. Great wealth can be sunk in a very small parcel of gems, and if he hoped to take his wealth with him it must be small in bulk.'

'So that it could be placed in his coffin, you mean,' said Zena.

'Sims declares nothing was placed in his coffin,' said Quarles; 'he is most definite upon the point.'

'And I have already pointed out that, since he wished to be cremated, Mr Ottershaw would hardly make any such arrangement,' I said.

'He may have wished to be cremated, but he may not have expected to be,' said Quarles. 'As a matter of fact, he left certain instructions which point to a doubt. Sims was to lay him out and see that he was decently cared for. So anxious was Mr Ottershaw about this that he left a letter for Sims to show to the Bryants. This is a most significant fact.'

'Then you suspect the man Sims,' said Zena.

'We will go a step further before I answer that question. Today, Wigan, we have made a curious discovery. All Mr Ottershaw's walking-sticks were very stout ones, and that he really used them, not merely carried them, the condition of the ferrules proves. Moreover, there was a curious fact about his boots. They were large, the right one being a little larger than the other, and the right boot in every pair was the least trodden down – indeed, showed little wear either inside or out. I wonder if Sims could explain this?'

Zena was leaning forward, her eyes fixed upon the professor, and I was thinking of a boot with a hollow heel.

'Let's go back to the will for a moment,' said Quarles. 'Although

Mr Ottershaw desired to be cremated, he did not put it in the form of a condition, as he might reasonably have done. He even mentions the expense, and, in fact, gives his relatives quite a good excuse for not doing as he desires. It seems to me he didn't care much one way or the other, and that his object was to make the relatives suffer for their greed, and suffer all the more because he didn't actually leave the money away from them. It was Zena's absurd question, Wigan, and her anger that the Bryants had not carried out the old man's wish, which gave me the germ of a theory. I believe if they had had him cremated they would have found the treasure. He gave them a chance which they lost by burying him.'

'Then you believe Sims carried out his master's wishes?' I said. 'I do.'

'And managed to have the treasure buried with him?'

'I do not believe Sims knows anything about a treasure,' said Quarles; 'and I think he speaks the truth when he says that nothing but the body was buried. But Sims knew more about his master than anyone else. He could tell us something about their doings in Switzerland and Germany, for instance. He was very fond of his master, and was trusted by him.'

'We want to know what happened just after Mr Ottershaw's death,' I said. 'To know what occurred abroad will not help us much.'

'I think it will,' Quarles returned. 'Supposing Mr Ottershaw had an accident abroad which necessitated the amputation of his right leg, and supposing, in Germany perhaps, he got the very best artificial limb money could purchase?'

'A wooden leg!' I exclaimed.

'Yes, not of the old sort, but the very best the instrument makers could devise. Mr Ottershaw became proud of that leg and told no one about it. Only his man knew. His right boot showed less sign of wear, because he helped that leg with a stout stick. The wooden foot would not stain the inside of a boot with moisture as a real foot does. When the Bryants went to see him he complained of gout, an excuse for not walking, and so giving them a chance of discovering the leg. Then came the idea of secreting the treasure, and I suggest that it consists of gems concealed in that wooden leg. He didn't want the leg removed after his death, so Sims laid him out. Probably the leg is fitted with a steel, fire-resisting receptacle which would have been found among the débris had the body been cremated.'

'Then the treasure is buried with him,' said Zena. 'Will they open the grave?'

'I am not sure whether the old man succeeded in carrying his wealth with him after all,' said Quarles. 'Sims was fond of and sentimental about his master, and as we talked to him, Wigan, it seemed to me there was something he had no intention of telling us. He was particularly insistent that nothing but the body had been buried, and appeared almost morbidly anxious to tell nothing but the exact truth. Tomorrow we will go to Fulham and ask him whether he removed the wooden leg before the coffin was screwed down.'

Quarles's conjecture proved to be right. Sims had been sentimental about the leg because his master was so proud of it, and the night before the coffin was fastened down had crept silently into the room and taken it off, placing a thick shawl rolled up under the shroud, so that the corpse would appear as it was before. It had not occurred to him at the time that his master was so anxious that the leg should be buried with him, but since that night he had wondered whether he had done wrong. The wooden leg was hidden in his bedroom. When he was told that it probably contained the treasure, his fear and amazement were almost painful to witness. He was evidently quite innocent of any idea of robbery.

Ingeniously concealed in the top part of the leg we found a steel cylinder, full of gems. Mr Ottershaw must have made a lot of money while he was in India, for Quarles's ten per cent of the value obtained for the jewels came to over twelve thousand pounds.

'Half of it goes to Zena as a wedding present,' he said on the day he banked the money. 'I shouldn't wait long if I were you, Wigan.'

'But, grandfather, I –'

'My dear, I'm not always thinking only of myself. You have your life before you and I want you to be happy. My only condition is that there shall always be a place at your fireside for me.'

The tears were in Zena's eyes as she kissed him, but she looked at me and I knew my waiting time was nearly over.

'Now I shall rest on my laurels, Wigan, and trouble no more about mysteries,' said Quarles.

He meant it, but I very much doubt whether a ruling passion is so easily controlled. We shall see.

JOHN THORNDYKE

Created by R Austin Freeman (1862–1943)

Dr John Thorndyke was a medical practitioner turned detective who was one of the earliest forensic scientists in crime fiction. He appeared in a series of novels and collections of short stories, beginning with The Red Thumb Mark *in 1907, a tale that highlights the then fledgling science of fingerprints, and ending with* The Jacob Street Mystery *in 1942. He was the creation of Richard Austin Freeman who, like his character, had trained as a doctor and then turned, not to detective work, but to writing. Invalided home from Africa's Gold Coast, where he had been working for the Colonial Service, he supplemented his income with short stories for the late Victorian magazine press. His first real success came with stories written in collaboration with another medic and published in 1902 under the pseudonym of 'Clifford Ashdown' about a gentlemanly conman named Romney Pringle. Thorndyke arrived on the scene five years later and Freeman continued to write about him until shortly before his death. Freeman's fiction is not to everyone's taste – Julian Symons once described reading him as 'very much like chewing dry straw' – but he was admired by many fellow writers from Raymond Chandler to George Orwell. He is often described as the inventor of the 'inverted detective story' in which the crime and its perpetrator are shown at the beginning and the author then unfolds the detective's method of discovering them. His earlier stories, such as 'The Mandarin's Pearl' below, are very much in the Holmes tradition and show Thorndyke meticulously using his wide-ranging knowledge of all kinds of sciences to reveal the truth.*

THE MANDARIN'S PEARL

Mr Brodribb stretched out his toes on the kerb before the blazing fire with the air of a man who is by no means insensible to physical comfort.

'You are really an extraordinarily polite fellow, Thorndyke,' said he.

He was an elderly man, rosy-gilled, portly, and convivial, to whom a mass of bushy, white hair, an expansive double chin, and a certain prim sumptuousness of dress imparted an air of old-world distinction. Indeed, as he dipped an amethystine nose into his wine glass, and gazed thoughtfully at the glowing end of his cigar, he looked the very type of the well-to-do lawyer of an older generation.

'You are really an extraordinarily polite fellow, Thorndyke,' said Mr Brodribb.

'I know,' replied Thorndyke. 'But why this reference to an admitted fact?'

'The truth has just dawned on me,' said the solicitor. 'Here am I, dropping in on you, uninvited and unannounced, sitting in your own armchair before your fire, smoking your cigars, drinking your Burgundy – and deuced good Burgundy, too, let me add – and you have not dropped a single hint of curiosity as to what has brought me here.'

'I take the gifts of the gods, you see, and ask no questions,' said Thorndyke.

'Devilish handsome of you, Thorndyke – unsociable beggar like you, too,' rejoined Mr Brodribb, a fan of wrinkles spreading out genially from the corners of his eyes; 'but the fact is I have come, in a sense, on business – always glad of a pretext to look you up, as you know – but I want to take your opinion on a rather queer case. It is about young Calverley. You remember Horace Calverley? Well, this is his son. Horace and I were schoolmates, you know, and after his death the boy, Fred, hung on to me rather. We're near neighbours down at Weybridge, and very good friends. I like Fred. He's a good fellow, though cranky, like all his people.'

'What has happened to Fred Calverley?' Thorndyke asked, as the solicitor paused.

'Why, the fact is,' said Mr Brodribb, 'just lately he seems to be going a bit queer – not mad, mind you – at least, I think not – but undoubtedly queer. Now, there is a good deal of property, and a good many highly interested relatives, and, as a natural consequence, there is some talk of getting him certified. They're afraid he may do something involving the estate or develop homicidal tendencies, and they talk of possible suicide – you remember his father's death – but I say that's all bunkum. The fellow is just a bit cranky, and nothing more.'

'What are his symptoms?' asked Thorndyke.

'Oh, he thinks he is being followed about and watched, and he has delusions; sees himself in the glass with the wrong face, and that sort of thing, you know.'

'You are not highly circumstantial,' Thorndyke remarked.

Mr Brodribb looked at me with a genial smile.

'What a glutton for facts this fellow is, Jervis. But you're right, Thorndyke; I'm vague. However, Fred will be here presently. We travel down together, and I took the liberty of asking him to call for me. We'll get him to tell you about his delusions, if you don't mind. He's not shy about them. And meanwhile I'll give you a few preliminary facts. The trouble began about a year ago. He was in a railway accident, and that knocked him all to pieces. Then he went for a voyage to recruit, and the ship broke her propeller-shaft in a storm and became helpless. That didn't improve the state of his nerves. Then he went down the Mediterranean, and after a month or two, back he came, no better than when he started. But here he is, I expect.'

He went over to the door and admitted a tall, frail young man whom Thorndyke welcomed with quiet geniality, and settled in a chair by the fire. I looked curiously at our visitor. He was a typical neurotic – slender, fragile, eager. Wide-open blue eyes with broad pupils, in which I could plainly see the characteristic 'hippus' – that incessant change of size that marks the unstable nervous equilibrium – parted lips, and wandering taper fingers, were as the stigmata of his disorder. He was of the stuff out of which prophets and devotees, martyrs, reformers, and third-rate poets are made.

'I have been telling Dr Thorndyke about these nervous troubles of yours,' said Mr Brodribb presently. 'I hope you don't mind. He is an old friend, you know, and he is very much interested.'

'It is very good of him,' said Calverley. Then he flushed deeply, and added: 'But they are not really nervous, you know. They can't be merely subjective.'

'You think they can't be?' said Thorndyke.

'No, I am sure they are not.' He flushed again like a girl, and looked earnestly at Thorndyke with his big, dreamy eyes. 'But you doctors,' he said, 'are so dreadfully sceptical of all spiritual phenomena. You are such materialists.'

'Yes,' said Mr Brodribb; 'the doctors are not hot on the supernatural, and that's the fact.'

'Supposing you tell us about your experiences,' said Thorndyke persuasively. 'Give us a chance to believe, if we can't explain away.'

Calverley reflected for a few moments; then, looking earnestly at Thorndyke, he said:

'Very well; if it won't bore you, I will. It is a curious story.'

'I have told Dr Thorndyke about your voyage and your trip down the Mediterranean,' said Mr Brodribb.

'Then,' said Calverley, 'I will begin with the events that are actually connected with these strange visitations. The first of these occurred in Marseilles. I was in a curio-shop there, looking over some Algerian and Moorish tilings, when my attention was attracted by a sort of charm or pendant that hung in a glass case. It was not particularly beautiful, but its appearance was quaint and curious, and took my fancy. It consisted of an oblong block of ebony in which was set a single pear-shaped pearl more than three-quarters of an inch long. The sides of the ebony block were lacquered – probably to conceal a joint – and bore a number of Chinese characters, and at the top was a little gold image with a hole through it, presumably for a string to suspend it by. Excepting for the pearl, the whole thing was uncommonly like one of those ornamental tablets of Chinese ink.

'Now, I had taken a fancy to the thing, and I can afford to indulge my fancies in moderation. The man wanted five pounds for it; he assured me that the pearl was a genuine one of fine quality, and obviously did not believe it himself. To me, however, it looked like a real pearl, and I determined to take the risk; so I paid the money, and he bowed me out with a smile – I may almost say a grin – of satisfaction. He would not have been so well pleased if he had followed me to a jeweller's to whom I took it for an expert opinion; for the jeweller pronounced the pearl to be undoubtedly genuine, and worth anything up to a thousand pounds.

'A day or two later, I happened to show my new purchase to some men whom I knew, who had dropped in at Marseilles in their yacht. They were highly amused at my having bought the thing, and when I told them what I had paid for it, they positively howled with derision.

'"Why, you silly guffin," said one of them, a man named Halliwell, "I could have had it ten days ago for half a sovereign, or probably five shillings. I wish now I had bought it; then I could have sold it to you."

'It seemed that a sailor had been hawking the pendant round the harbour, and had been on board the yacht with it.

'"Deuced anxious the beggar was to get rid of it, too," said Halliwell, grinning at the recollection. "Swore it was a genuine pearl of priceless value, and was willing to deprive himself of it for the trifling sum of half a jimmy. But we'd heard that sort of thing before. However, the curio man seems to have speculated on the chance of meeting with a greenhorn, and he seems to have pulled it off. Lucky curio man!"

'I listened patiently to their gibes, and when they had talked themselves out I told them about the jeweller. They were most frightfully sick; and when we had taken the pendant to a dealer in gems who happened to be staying in the town, and he had offered me five hundred pounds for it, their language wasn't fit for a divinity students' debating club. Naturally the story got noised abroad, and when I left, it was the talk of the place. The general opinion was that the sailor, who was traced to a tea-ship that had put into the harbour, had stolen it from some Chinese passenger; and no less than seventeen different Chinamen came forward to claim it as their stolen property.

'Soon after this I returned to England, and, as my nerves were still in a very shaky state, I came to live with my cousin Alfred, who has a large house at Weybridge. At this time he had a friend staying with him, a certain Captain Raggerton, and the two men appeared to be on very intimate terms. I did not take to Raggerton at all. He was a good-looking man, pleasant in his manners, and remarkably plausible. But the fact is – I am speaking in strict confidence, of course – he was a bad egg. He had been in the Guards, and I don't quite know why he left; but I do know that he played bridge and baccarat pretty heavily at several clubs, and that he had a reputation for being a rather uncomfortably lucky player. He did a good deal at the race-meetings, too, and was in general such an obvious undesirable that I could never understand my cousin's intimacy with him, though I must say that Alfred's habits had changed somewhat for the worse since I had left England.

'The fame of my purchase seems to have preceded me, for when, one day, I produced the pendant to show them, I found that they knew all about it. Raggerton had heard the story from a naval man, and I gathered vaguely that he had heard something that I had not, and that he did not care to tell me; for when my cousin and he talked about the pearl, which they did pretty often, certain significant looks passed between them, and certain veiled references were made which I could not fail to notice.

'One day I happened to be telling them of a curious incident that occurred on my way home. I had travelled to England on one of Holt's big China boats, not liking the crowd and bustle of the regular passenger-lines. Now, one afternoon, when we had been at sea a couple of days, I took a book down to my berth, intending to have a quiet read till teatime. Soon, however, I dropped off into a doze, and must have remained asleep for over an hour. I awoke suddenly, and as I opened my eyes, I perceived that the door of the state-room was half open, and a well-dressed Chinaman, in native costume, was looking in at me. He closed the door immediately, and I remained for a few moments paralysed by the start that he had given me. Then I leaped from my bunk, opened the door, and looked out. But the alleyway was empty. The Chinaman had vanished as if by magic.

'This little occurrence made me quite nervous for a day or two, which was very foolish of me; but my nerves were all on edge – and I am afraid they are still.'

'Yes,' said Thorndyke. 'There was nothing mysterious about the affair. These boats carry a Chinese crew, and the man you saw was probably a Serang, or whatever they call the gang-captains on these vessels. Or he may have been a native passenger who had strayed into the wrong part of the ship.'

'Exactly,' agreed our client. 'But to return to Raggerton. He listened with quite extraordinary interest as I was telling this story, and when I had finished he looked very queerly at my cousin.

"'A deuced odd thing, this, Calverley," said he. "Of course, it may be only a coincidence, but it really does look as if there was something, after all, in that –"

"'Shut up, Raggerton," said my cousin. "We don't want any of that rot."

"'What is he talking about?" I asked.

"'Oh, it's only a rotten, silly yarn that he has picked up somewhere. You're not to tell him, Raggerton."

"'I don't see why I am not to be told," I said, rather sulkily. "I'm not a baby."

'"No," said Alfred, "but you're an invalid. You don't want any horrors."

'In effect, he refused to go into the matter any further, and I was left on tenterhooks of curiosity.

'However, the very next day I got Raggerton alone in the smoking-room, and had a little talk with him. He had just dropped a hundred pounds on a double event that hadn't come off, and I expected to find him pliable. Nor was I disappointed, for, when we had negotiated a little loan, he was entirely at my service, and willing to tell me everything, on my promising not to give him away to Alfred.

'"Now, you understand," he said, "that this yarn about your pearl is nothing but a damn silly fable that's been going the round in Marseilles. I don't know where it came from, or what sort of demented rotter invented it; I had it from a Johnnie in the Mediterranean Squadron, and you can have a copy of his letter if you want it."

'I said that I did want it. Accordingly, that same evening he handed me a copy of the narrative extracted from his friend's letter, the substance of which was this:

'About four months ago there was lying in Canton Harbour a large English barque. Her name is not mentioned, but that is not material to the story. She had got her cargo stowed and her crew signed on, and was only waiting for certain official formalities to be completed before putting to sea on her homeward voyage. Just ahead of her, at the same quay, was a Danish ship that had been in collision outside, and was now laid up pending the decision of the Admiralty Court. She had been unloaded, and her crew paid off, with the exception of one elderly man, who remained on board as ship-keeper. Now, a considerable part of the cargo of the English barque was the property of a certain wealthy mandarin, and this person had been about the vessel a good deal while she was taking in her lading.

'One day, when the mandarin was on board the barque, it happened that three of the seamen were sitting in the galley smoking and chatting with the cook – an elderly Chinaman named Wo-li – and the latter, pointing out the mandarin to the sailors, expatiated on his enormous wealth, assuring them that he was commonly believed to carry on his person articles of sufficient value to buy up the entire lading of a ship.

'Now, unfortunately for the mandarin, it chanced that these three sailors were about the greatest rascals on board; which is saying a good deal when one considers the ordinary moral standard that prevails in the forecastle of a sailing-ship. Nor was Wo-li himself an angel; in fact, he was a consummate villain, and seems to have been the actual originator of the plot which was presently devised to rob the mandarin.

'This plot was as remarkable for its simplicity as for its cold-blooded barbarity. On the evening before the barque sailed, the three seamen, Nilsson, Foucault, and Parratt, proceeded to the Danish ship with a supply of whisky, made the ship-keeper royally drunk, and locked him up in an empty berth. Meanwhile Wo-li made a secret communication to the mandarin to the effect that certain stolen property, believed to be his, had been secreted in the hold of the empty ship. Thereupon the mandarin came down hot-foot to the quayside, and was received on board by the three seamen, who had got the covers off the after-hatch in readiness. Parratt now ran down the iron ladder to show the way, and the mandarin followed; but when they reached the lower deck, and looked down the hatch into the black darkness of the lower hold, he seems to have taken fright, and begun to climb up again. Meanwhile Nilsson had made a running bowline in the end of a loose halyard that was rove through a block aloft, and had been used for hoisting out the cargo. As the mandarin came up, he leaned over the coaming of the hatch, dropped the noose over the Chinaman's head, jerked it tight, and then he and Foucault hove on the fall of the rope. The unfortunate Chinaman was dragged from the ladder, and, as he swung clear, the two rascals let go the rope, allowing him to drop through the hatches into the lower hold. Then they belayed the rope, and went down below. Parratt had already lighted a slush-lamp, by the glimmer of which they could see the mandarin swinging to and fro like a pendulum within a few feet of the ballast, and still quivering and twitching in his death-throes. They were now joined by Wo-li, who had watched the proceedings from the quay, and the four villains proceeded, without loss of time, to rifle the body as it hung. To their surprise and disgust, they found nothing of value excepting an ebony pendant set with a single large pearl; but Wo-li, though evidently disappointed at the nature of the booty, assured his comrades that this alone was well worth the hazard, pointing out the great size and exceptional beauty of the pearl. As to this, the seamen knew nothing about pearls, but the thing was done, and had to be made the best of; so they made the rope fast to the lower deck-beams, cut off the remainder and unrove it from the block, and went back to their ship.

'It was twenty-four hours before the ship-keeper was sufficiently sober to break out of the berth in which he had been locked, by which time the barque was well out to sea; and it was another three days before the body of the mandarin was found. An active search was then made for the murderers, but as they were strangers to the ship-keeper, no clues to their whereabouts could be discovered.

'Meanwhile, the four murderers were a good deal exercised as to the disposal of the booty. Since it could not be divided, it was evident that it must be entrusted to the keeping of one of them. The choice in the first place fell upon Wo-li, in whose chest the pendant was deposited as soon as the party came on board, it being arranged that the Chinaman should produce the jewel for inspection by his confederates whenever called upon.

'For six weeks nothing out of the common occurred; but then a very singular event befell. The four conspirators were sitting outside the galley one evening, when suddenly the cook uttered a cry of amazement and horror. The other three turned to see what it was that had so disturbed their comrade, and then they, too, were struck dumb with consternation; for, standing at the door of the companion-hatch – the barque was a flush-decked vessel – was the mandarin whom they had left for dead. He stood quietly regarding them for fully a minute, while they stared at him transfixed with terror. Then he beckoned to them, and went below.

'So petrified were they with astonishment and mortal fear that they remained for a long time motionless and dumb. At last they plucked up courage, and began to make furtive inquiries among the crew; but no one – not even the steward – knew anything of any passengers, or, indeed, of any Chinaman, on board the ship, excepting Wo-li.

'At daybreak the next morning, when the cook's mate went to the galley to fill the coppers, he found Wo-li hanging from a hook in the ceiling. The cook's body was stiff and cold, and had evidently been hanging several hours. The report of the tragedy quickly spread through the ship, and the three conspirators hurried off to remove the pearl from the dead man's chest before the officers should come to examine it. The cheap lock was easily picked with a bent wire, and the jewel abstracted; but now the question arose as to who should take charge of it. The eagerness to be the actual custodian of the precious bauble, which had been at first displayed, now gave place to equally strong reluctance. But someone had to take charge of it, and after a long and angry discussion Nilsson was prevailed upon to stow it in his chest.

'A fortnight passed. The three conspirators went about their duties soberly, like men burdened with some secret anxiety, and in their leisure moments they would sit and talk with bated breath of the apparition at the companion-hatch, and the mysterious death of their late comrade.

'At last the blow fell.

'It was at the end of the second dog-watch that the hands were gathered on the forecastle, preparing to make sail after a spell of bad weather. Suddenly Nilsson gave a husky shout, and rushed at Parratt, holding out the key of his chest.

'"Here you, Parratt," he exclaimed, "go below and take that accursed thing out of my chest."

"'What for?" demanded Parratt; and then he and Foucault, who was standing close by, looked aft to see what Nilsson was staring at.

'Instantly they both turned white as ghosts, and fell trembling so that they could hardly stand; for there was the mandarin, standing calmly by the companion, returning with a steady, impassive gaze their looks of horror. And even as they looked he beckoned and went below.

"'D'ye hear, Parratt?" gasped Nilsson; "take my key and do what I say, or else –"

'But at this moment the order was given to go aloft and set all plain sail; the three men went off to their respective posts, Nilsson going up the fore-topmast rigging, and the other two to the main-top. Having finished their work aloft, Foucault and Parratt, who were both in the port watch, came down on deck, and then, it being their watch below, they went and turned in.

'When they turned out with their watch at midnight, they looked about for Nilsson, who was in the starboard watch, but he was nowhere to be seen. Thinking he might have slipped below unobserved, they made no remark, though they were very uneasy about him; but when the starboard watch came on deck at four o'clock, and Nilsson did not appear with his mates, the two men became alarmed, and made inquiries about him. It was now discovered that no one had seen him since eight o'clock on the previous evening, and, this being reported to the officer of the watch, the latter ordered all hands to be called. But still Nilsson did not appear. A thorough search was now instituted, both below and aloft, and as there was still no sign of the missing man, it was concluded that he had fallen overboard.

'But at eight o'clock two men were sent aloft to shake out the fore-royal. They reached the yard almost simultaneously, and were just stepping on to the foot-ropes when one of them gave a shout; then the pair came sliding down a backstay, with faces as white as tallow. As soon as they reached the deck, they took the officer of the watch forward, and, standing on the heel of the bowsprit, pointed aloft. Several of the hands, including Foucault and Parratt, had followed, and all looked up; and there they saw the body of Nilsson, hanging on the front of the fore-topgallant sail. He was dangling at the end of a gasket, and bouncing up and down on the taut belly of the sail as the ship rose and fell to the send of the sea.

'The two survivors were now in some doubt about having anything further to do with the pearl. But the great value of the jewel, and the consideration that it was now to be divided between two instead of four, tempted them. They abstracted it from Nilsson's chest, and then, as they could not come to an agreement in any other way, they decided to settle who should take charge of it by tossing a coin. The coin was accordingly spun, and the pearl went to Foucault's chest.

'From this moment Foucault lived in a state of continual apprehension. When on deck, his eyes were for ever wandering towards the companion hatch, and during his watch below, when not asleep, he would sit moodily on his chest, lost in gloomy reflection. But a fortnight passed, then three weeks, and still nothing happened. Land was sighted, the Straits of Gibraltar passed, and the end of the voyage was but a matter of days. And still the dreaded mandarin made no sign.

'At length the ship was within twenty-four hours of Marseilles, to which port a large part of the cargo was consigned. Active preparations were being made for entering the port, and among other things the shore tackle was being overhauled. A share in this latter work fell to Foucault and Parratt, and about the middle of the second dog-watch – seven o'clock in the evening – they were sitting on the deck working an eye-splice in the end of a large rope. Suddenly Foucault, who was facing forward, saw his companion turn pale and stare aft with an expression of terror. He immediately turned and looked over his shoulder to see what Parratt was staring at. It was the mandarin, standing by the companion, gravely watching them; and as Foucault turned and met his gaze, the Chinaman beckoned and went below.

'For the rest of that day Parratt kept close to his terrified comrade, and during their watch below he endeavoured to remain awake, that he might keep his friend in view. Nothing happened through the night, and the following morning, when they came on deck for the forenoon watch, their port was well in sight. The two men now separated for the first time, Parratt going aft to take his trick at the wheel, and Foucault being set to help in getting ready the ground tackle.

'Half an hour later Parratt saw the mate stand on the rail and lean outboard, holding on to the mizzen-shrouds while he stared along the ship's side. Then he jumped on to the deck and shouted angrily: "Forward, there! What the deuce is that man up to under the starboard cat-head?"

'The men on the forecastle rushed to the side and looked over; two of them leaned over the rail with the bight of a rope between them, and a third came running aft to the mate. "It's Foucault, sir," Parratt heard him say. "He's hanged hisself from the cat-head."

'As soon as he was off duty, Parratt made his way to his dead comrade's chest, and, opening it with his pick-lock, took out the pearl. It was now his sole property, and, as the ship was within an hour or two of her destination, he thought he had little to fear from its murdered owner. As soon as the vessel was alongside the wharf, he would slip ashore and get rid of the jewel, even if he sold it at a comparatively low price. The thing looked perfectly simple.

'In actual practice, however, it turned out quite otherwise. He began by accosting a well-dressed stranger and offering the pendant for fifty pounds; but the only reply that he got was a knowing smile and a shake of the head. When this experience had been repeated a dozen times or more, and he had been followed up and down the streets for nearly an hour by a suspicious gendarme, he began to grow anxious. He visited quite a number of ships and yachts in the harbour, and at each refusal the price of his treasure came down, until he was eager to sell it for a few francs. But still no one would have it. Everyone took it for granted that the pearl was a sham, and most of the persons whom he accosted assumed that it had been stolen. The position was getting desperate. Evening was approaching – the time of the dreaded dog-watches – and still the pearl was in his possession. Gladly would he now have given it away for nothing, but he dared not try, for this would lay him open to the strongest suspicion.

'At last, in a by-street, he came upon the shop of a curio-dealer. Putting on a careless and cheerful manner, he entered and offered the pendant for ten francs. The dealer looked at it, shook his head, and handed it back.

'"What will you give me for it?" demanded Parratt, breaking out into a cold sweat at the prospect of a final refusal.

'The dealer felt in his pocket, drew out a couple of francs, and held them out.

'"Very well," said Parratt. He took the money as calmly as he could, and marched out of the shop, with a gasp of relief, leaving the pendant in the dealer's hand.

'The jewel was hung up in a glass case, and nothing more was thought about it until some ten days later, when an English tourist, who came into the shop, noticed it and took a liking to it. Thereupon the dealer offered it to him for five pounds, assuring him that it was a genuine pearl, a statement that, to his amazement, the stranger evidently believed. He was then deeply afflicted at not having asked a higher price, but the bargain had been struck, and the Englishman went off with his purchase.

'This was the story told by Captain Raggerton's friend, and I have given it to you in full detail, having read the manuscript over many times since it was given to me. No doubt you will regard it as a mere traveller's tale, and consider me a superstitious idiot for giving any credence to it.'

'It certainly seems more remarkable for picturesqueness than for credibility,' Thorndyke agreed. 'May I ask,' he continued, 'whether Captain Raggerton's friend gave any explanation as to how this singular story came to his knowledge, or to that of anybody else?'

'Oh yes,' replied Calverley; 'I forgot to mention that the seaman, Parratt, very shortly after he had sold the pearl, fell down the hatch into the hold as the ship was unloading, and was very badly injured. He was taken to the hospital, where he died on the following day; and it was while he was lying there in a dying condition that he confessed to the murder, and gave this circumstantial account of it.'

'I see,' said Thorndyke; 'and I understand that you accept the story as literally true?'

'Undoubtedly.'

Calverley flushed defiantly as he returned Thorndyke's look, and continued:

'You see, I am not a man of science: therefore my beliefs are not limited to things that can be weighed and measured. There are things, Dr Thorndyke, which are outside the range of our puny intellects; things that science, with its arrogant materialism, puts aside and ignores with close-shut eyes. I prefer to believe in things which obviously exist, even though I cannot explain them. It is the humbler and, I think, the wiser attitude.'

'But, my dear Fred,' protested Mr Brodribb, 'this is a rank fairy-tale.'

Calverley turned upon the solicitor. 'If you had seen what I have seen, you would not only believe: you would *know*.'

'Tell us what you have seen, then,' said Mr Brodribb.

'I will, if you wish to hear it,' said Calverley. 'I will continue the strange history of the Mandarin's Pearl.'

He lit a fresh cigarette and continued:

'The night I came to Beechhurst – that is my cousin's house, you know – a rather absurd thing happened, which I mention on account of its connection with what has followed. I had gone to my room early, and sat for some time writing letters before getting ready for bed. When I had finished my letters, I started on a tour of inspection of my room. I was then, you must remember, in a very nervous state, and it had become my habit to examine the room in which I was to sleep before undressing, looking under the bed, and in any cupboards and closets that there happened to be. Now, on looking round my new room, I perceived that there was a second door, and I at once proceeded to open it to see where it led to. As soon as I opened the door, I got a terrible start. I found myself looking into a narrow closet or passage, lined with pegs, on which the servant had hung some of my clothes; at the farther end was another door, and, as I stood looking into the closet, I observed, with startled amazement, a man standing holding the door half open, and silently regarding me. I stood for a moment staring at him, with my heart thumping and my limbs all of a tremble; then I slammed the door and ran off to look for my cousin.

'He was in the billiard-room with Raggerton, and the pair looked up sharply as I entered.

'"Alfred," I said, "where does that passage lead to out of my room?"

'"Lead to?" said he. "Why, it doesn't lead anywhere. It used to open into a cross corridor, but when the house was altered, the corridor was done away with, and this passage closed up. It is only a cupboard now."

'"Well, there's a man in it – or there was just now."

'"Nonsense!" he exclaimed; "impossible! Let us go and look at the place."

'He and Raggerton rose, and we went together to my room. As we flung open the door of the closet and looked in, we all three burst into a laugh. There were three men now looking at us from the open door at the other end, and the mystery was solved. A large mirror had been placed at the end of the closet to cover the partition which cut it off from the cross corridor.

'This incident naturally exposed me to a good deal of chaff from my cousin and Captain Raggerton; but I often wished that the mirror had not been placed there, for it happened over and over again that, going to the cupboard hurriedly, and not thinking of the mirror, I got quite a bad shock on being confronted by a figure apparently coming straight at me through an open door.

In fact, it annoyed me so much, in my nervous state, that I even thought of asking my cousin to give me a different room; but, happening to refer to the matter when talking to Raggerton, I found the Captain so scornful of my cowardice that my pride was touched, and I let the affair drop.

'And now I come to a very strange occurrence, which I shall relate quite frankly, although I know beforehand that you will set me down as a liar or a lunatic. I had been away from home for a fortnight, and as I returned rather late at night, I went straight to my room. Having partly undressed, I took my clothes in one hand and a candle in the other, and opened the cupboard door. I stood for a moment looking nervously at my double, standing, candle in hand, looking at me through the open door at the other end of the passage; then I entered, and, setting the candle on a shelf, proceeded to hang up my clothes. I had hung them up, and had just reached up for the candle, when my eye was caught by something strange in the mirror. It no longer reflected the candle in my hand, but instead of it, a large coloured paper lantern. I stood petrified with astonishment, and gazed into the mirror; and then I saw that my own reflection was changed, too; that, in place of my own figure, was that of an elderly Chinaman, who stood regarding me with stony calm.

'I must have stood for near upon a minute, unable to move and scarce able to breathe, face to face with that awful figure. At length I turned to escape, and, as I turned, he turned also, and I could see him, over my shoulder, hurrying away. As I reached the door, I halted for a moment, looking back with the door in my hand, holding the candle above my head; and even so *he* halted, looking back at me, with his hand upon the door and his lantern held above his head.

'I was so much upset that I could not go to bed for some hours, but continued to pace the room, in spite of my fatigue. Now and again I was impelled, irresistibly, to peer into the cupboard, but nothing was to be seen in the mirror save my own figure, candle in hand, peeping in at me through the half-open door.

And each time that I looked into my own white, horror-stricken face, I shut the door hastily and turned away with a shudder; for the pegs, with the clothes hanging on them, seemed to call to me. I went to bed at last, and before I fell asleep I formed the resolution that, if I was spared until the next day, I would write to the British Consul at Canton, and offer to restore the pearl to the relatives of the murdered mandarin.

'On the following day I wrote and despatched the letter, after which I felt more composed, though I was haunted continually by the recollection of that stony, impassive figure; and from time to time I felt an irresistible impulse to go and look in at the door of the closet, at the mirror and the pegs with the clothes hanging from them. I told my cousin of the visitation that I had received, but he merely laughed, and was frankly incredulous; while the Captain bluntly advised me not to be a superstitious donkey.

'For some days after this I was left in peace, and began to hope that my letter had appeased the spirit of the murdered man; but on the fifth day, about six o'clock in the evening, happening to want some papers that I had left in the pocket of a coat which was hanging in the closet, I went in to get them. I took in no candle as it was not yet dark, but left the door wide open to light me. The coat that I wanted was near the end of the closet, not more than four paces from the mirror, and as I went towards it I watched my reflection rather nervously as it advanced to meet me. I found my coat, and as I felt for the papers, I still kept a suspicious eye on my double. And, even as I looked, a most strange phenomenon appeared: the mirror seemed for an instant to darken or cloud over, and then, as it cleared again, I saw, standing dark against the light of the open door behind him, the figure of the mandarin. After a single glance, I ran out of the closet, shaking with agitation; but as I turned to shut the door, I noticed that it was my own figure that was reflected in the glass. The Chinaman had vanished in an instant.

'It now became evident that my letter had not served its purpose, and I was plunged in despair; the more so since, on this day, I felt again the dreadful impulse to go and look at the pegs on the walls of the closet. There was no mistaking the meaning of that impulse, and each time that I went, I dragged myself away reluctantly, though shivering with horror. One circumstance, indeed, encouraged me a little; the mandarin had not, on either occasion, beckoned to me as he had done to the sailors, so that perhaps some way of escape yet lay open to me.

'During the next few days I considered very earnestly what measures I could take to avert the doom that seemed to be hanging over me. The simplest plan, that of passing the pearl on to some other person, was out of the question; it would be nothing short of murder. On the other hand, I could not wait for an answer to my letter; for even if I remained alive, I felt that my reason would have given way long before the reply reached me. But while I was debating what I should do, the mandarin appeared to me again; and then, after an interval of only two days, he came to me once more. That was last night. I remained gazing at him, fascinated, with my flesh creeping, as he stood, lantern in hand, looking steadily in my face. At last he held out his hand to me, as if asking me to give him the pearl; then the mirror darkened, and he vanished in a flash; and in the place where he had stood there was my own reflection looking at me out of the glass.

'That last visitation decided me. When I left home this morning the pearl was in my pocket, and as I came over Waterloo Bridge, I leaned over the parapet and flung the thing into the water. After that I felt quite relieved for a time; I had shaken the accursed thing off without involving anyone in the curse that it carried. But presently I began to feel fresh misgivings, and the conviction has been growing upon me all day that I have done the wrong thing. I have only placed it for ever beyond the reach of its owner, whereas I ought to have burnt it, after the Chinese fashion, so that its non-material essence could have joined the spiritual body of him to whom it had belonged when both were clothed with material substance.

'But it can't be altered now. For good or for evil, the thing is done, and God alone knows what the end of it will be.'

As he concluded, Calverley uttered a deep sigh, and covered his face with his slender, delicate hands. For a space we were all silent and, I think, deeply moved; for, grotesquely unreal as the whole thing was, there was a pathos, and even a tragedy, in it that we all felt to be very real indeed.

Suddenly Mr Brodribb started and looked at his watch.

'Good gracious, Calverley, we shall lose our train.'

The young man pulled himself together and stood up. 'We shall just do it if we go at once,' said he. 'Goodbye,' he added, shaking Thorndyke's hand and mine. 'You have been very patient, and I have been rather prosy, I am afraid. Come along, Mr Brodribb.'

Thorndyke and I followed them out on to the landing, and I heard my colleague say to the solicitor in a low tone, but very earnestly: 'Get him away from that house, Brodribb, and don't let him out of your sight for a moment.'

I did not catch the solicitor's reply, if he made any, but when we were back in our room I noticed that Thorndyke was more agitated than I had ever seen him.

'I ought not to have let them go,' he exclaimed. 'Confound me! If I had had a grain of wit, I should have made them lose their train.'

He lit his pipe and fell to pacing the room with long strides, his eyes bent on the floor with an expression sternly reflective. At last, finding him hopelessly taciturn, I knocked out my pipe and went to bed.

* * * * *

As I was dressing on the following morning, Thorndyke entered my room. His face was grave even to sternness, and he held a telegram in his hand.

'I am going to Weybridge this morning,' he said shortly, holding the 'flimsy' out to me. 'Shall you come?'

I took the paper from him, and read:

'Come, for God's sake! FC is dead. You will understand.–
BRODRIBB.'

I handed him back the telegram, too much shocked for a
moment to speak. The whole dreadful tragedy summed up in
that curt message rose before me in an instant, and a wave of deep
pity swept over me at this miserable end to the sad, empty life.

'What an awful thing, Thorndyke!' I exclaimed at length. 'To
be killed by a mere grotesque delusion.'

'Do you think so?' he asked dryly. 'Well, we shall see; but you
will come?'

'Yes,' I replied; and as he retired, I proceeded hurriedly to
finish dressing.

Half an hour later, as we rose from a rapid breakfast, Polton
came into the room, carrying a small roll-up case of tools and a
bunch of skeleton keys.

'Will you have them in a bag, sir?' he asked.

'No,' replied Thorndyke; 'in my overcoat pocket. Oh, and here
is a note, Polton, which I want you to take round to Scotland
Yard. It is to the Assistant Commissioner, and you are to make
sure that it is in the right hands before you leave. And here is a
telegram to Mr Brodribb.'

He dropped the keys and the tool-case into his pocket, and we
went down together to the waiting hansom.

At Weybridge Station we found Mr Brodribb pacing the
platform in a state of extreme dejection. He brightened up
somewhat when he saw us, and wrung our hands with emotional
heartiness.

'It was very good of you both to come at a moment's notice,'
he said warmly, 'and I feel your kindness very much. You
understood, of course, Thorndyke?'

'Yes,' Thorndyke replied. 'I suppose the mandarin beckoned
to him.'

Mr Brodribb turned with a look of surprise. 'How did you
guess that?' he asked; and then, without waiting for a reply, he
took from his pocket a note, which he handed to my colleague.

'The poor old fellow left this for me,' he said. 'The servant found it on his dressing-table.'

Thorndyke glanced through the note and passed it to me. It consisted of but a few words, hurriedly written in a tremulous hand.

'He has beckoned to me, and I must go. Goodbye, dear old friend.'

'How does his cousin take the matter?' asked Thorndyke.

'He doesn't know of it yet,' replied the lawyer. 'Alfred and Raggerton went out after an early breakfast, to cycle over to Guildford on some business or other, and they have not returned yet. The catastrophe was discovered soon after they left. The maid went to his room with a cup of tea, and was astonished to find that his bed had not been slept in. She ran down in alarm and reported to the butler, who went up at once and searched the room; but he could find no trace of the missing one, except my note, until it occurred to him to look in the cupboard. As he opened the door he got rather a start from his own reflection in the mirror; and then he saw poor Fred hanging from one of the pegs near the end of the closet, close to the glass. It's a melancholy affair – but here is the house, and here is the butler waiting for us. Mr Alfred is not back yet, then, Stevens?'

'No, sir.' The white-faced, frightened-looking man had evidently been waiting at the gate from distaste of the house, and he now walked back with manifest relief at our arrival. When we entered the house, he ushered us without remark up on to the first floor, and, preceding us along a corridor, halted near the end. 'That's the room, sir,' said he; and without another word he turned and went down the stairs.

We entered the room, and Mr Brodribb followed on tiptoe, looking about him fearfully, and casting awestruck glances at the shrouded form on the bed. To the latter Thorndyke advanced, and gently drew back the sheet.

'You'd better not look, Brodribb,' said he, as he bent over the corpse. He felt the limbs and examined the cord, which still remained round the neck, its raggedly-severed end testifying to the terror of the servants who had cut down the body. Then he replaced the sheet and looked at his watch. 'It happened at about three o'clock in the morning,' said he. 'He must have struggled with the impulse for some time, poor fellow! Now let us look at the cupboard.'

We went together to a door in the corner of the room, and, as we opened it, we were confronted by three figures, apparently looking in at us through an open door at the other end.

'It is really rather startling,' said the lawyer, in a subdued voice, looking almost apprehensively at the three figures that advanced to meet us. 'The poor lad ought never to have been here.'

It was certainly an eerie place, and I could not but feel, as we walked down the dark, narrow passage, with those other three dimly-seen figures silently coming towards us, and mimicking our every gesture, that it was no place for a nervous, superstitious man like poor Fred Calverley. Close to the end of the long row of pegs was one from which hung an end of stout box-cord, and to this Mr Brodribb pointed with an awestruck gesture. But Thorndyke gave it only a brief glance, and then walked up to the mirror, which he proceeded to examine minutely. It was a very large glass, nearly seven feet high, extending the full width of the closet, and reaching to within a foot of the floor; and it seemed to have been let into the partition from behind, for, both above and below, the woodwork was in front of it. While I was making these observations, I watched Thorndyke with no little curiosity. First he rapped his knuckles on the glass; then he lighted a wax match, and, holding it close to the mirror, carefully watched the reflection of the flame. Finally, laying his cheek on the glass, he held the match at arm's length, still close to the mirror, and looked at the reflection along the surface. Then he blew out the match and walked back into the room, shutting the cupboard door as we emerged.

'I think,' said he, 'that as we shall all undoubtedly be subpoenaed by the coroner, it would be well to put together a few notes of the facts. I see there is a writing table by the window, and I would propose that you, Brodribb, just jot down a *précis* of the statement that you heard last night, while Jervis notes down the exact condition of the body. While you are doing this, I will take a look round.'

'We might find a more cheerful place to write in,' grumbled Mr Brodribb; 'however –'

Without finishing the sentence, he sat down at the table, and, having found some sermon paper, dipped a pen in the ink by way of encouraging his thoughts. At this moment Thorndyke quietly slipped out of the room, and I proceeded to make a detailed examination of the body: in which occupation I was interrupted at intervals by requests from the lawyer that I should refresh his memory.

We had been occupied thus for about a quarter of an hour, when a quick step was heard outside, the door was opened abruptly, and a man burst into the room. Brodribb rose and held out his hand.

'This is a sad home-coming for you, Alfred,' said he.

'Yes, my God!' the newcomer exclaimed. 'It's awful.'

He looked askance at the corpse on the bed, and wiped his forehead with his handkerchief. Alfred Calverley was not extremely prepossessing. Like his cousin, he was obviously neurotic, but there were signs of dissipation in his face, which, just now, was pale and ghastly, and wore an expression of abject fear. Moreover, his entrance was accompanied by that of a perceptible odour of brandy.

He had walked over, without noticing me, to the writing-table, and as he stood there, talking in subdued tones with the lawyer, I suddenly found Thorndyke at my side. He had stolen in noiselessly through the door that Calverley had left open.

'Show him Brodribb's note,' he whispered, 'and then make him go in and look at the peg.'

With this mysterious request, he slipped out of the room as silently as he had come, unperceived either by Calverley or the lawyer.

'Has Captain Raggerton returned with you?' Brodribb was inquiring.

'No, he has gone into the town,' was the reply; 'but he won't be long. This will be a frightful shock to him.'

At this point I stepped forward. 'Have you shown Mr Calverley the extraordinary letter that the deceased left for you?' I asked.

'What letter was that?' demanded Calverley, with a start.

Mr Brodribb drew forth the note and handed it to him. As he read it through, Calverley turned white to the lips, and the paper trembled in his hand.

'"He has beckoned to me, and I must go",' he read. Then, with a furtive glance at the lawyer: 'Who had beckoned? What did he mean?'

Mr Brodribb briefly explained the meaning of the allusion, adding: 'I thought you knew all about it.'

'Yes, yes,' said Calverley, with some confusion; 'I remember the matter now you mention it. But it's all so dreadful and bewildering.'

At this point I again interposed. 'There is a question,' I said, 'that may be of some importance. It refers to the cord with which the poor fellow hanged himself. Can you identify that cord, Mr Calverley?'

'I!' he exclaimed, staring at me, and wiping the sweat from his white face; 'how should I? Where is the cord?'

'Part of it is still hanging from the peg in the closet. Would you mind looking at it?'

'If you would very kindly fetch it – you know I – er – naturally – have a –'

'It must not be disturbed before the inquest,' said I; 'but surely you are not afraid –'

'I didn't say I was afraid,' he retorted angrily. 'Why should I be?'

With a strange, tremulous swagger, he strode across to the closet, flung open the door, and plunged in.

A moment later we heard a shout of horror, and he rushed out, livid and gasping.

'What is it, Calverley?' exclaimed Mr Brodribb, starting up in alarm.

But Calverley was incapable of speech. Dropping limply into a chair, he gazed at us for a while in silent terror; then he fell back uttering a wild shriek of laughter.

Mr Brodribb looked at him in amazement. 'What is it, Calverley?' he asked again.

As no answer was forthcoming, he stepped across to the open door of the closet and entered, peering curiously before him. Then he, too, uttered a startled exclamation, and backed out hurriedly, looking pale and flurried.

'Bless my soul!' he ejaculated. 'Is the place bewitched?'

He sat down heavily and stared at Calverley, who was still shaking with hysteric laughter; while I, now consumed with curiosity, walked over to the closet to discover the cause of their singular behaviour. As I flung open the door, which the lawyer had closed, I must confess to being very considerably startled; for though the reflection of the open door was plain enough in the mirror, my own reflection was replaced by that of a Chinaman. After a momentary pause of astonishment, I entered the closet and walked towards the mirror; and simultaneously the figure of the Chinaman entered and walked towards me. I had advanced more than halfway down the closet when suddenly the mirror darkened; there was a whirling flash, the Chinaman vanished in an instant, and, as I reached the glass, my own reflection faced me.

I turned back into the room pretty completely enlightened, and looked at Calverley with a newborn distaste. He still sat facing the bewildered lawyer, one moment sobbing convulsively, the next yelping with hysteric laughter. He was not an agreeable spectacle, and when, a few moments later, Thorndyke entered the room, and halted by the door with a stare of disgust, I was moved to join him. But at this juncture a man pushed past Thorndyke, and, striding up to Calverley, shook him roughly by the arm.

'Stop that row!' he exclaimed furiously. 'Do you hear? Stop it!'

'I can't help it, Raggerton,' gasped Calverley. 'He gave me such a turn – the mandarin, you know.'

'What!' ejaculated Raggerton.

He dashed across to the closet, looked in, and turned upon Calverley with a snarl. Then he walked out of the room.

'Brodribb,' said Thorndyke, 'I should like to have a word with you and Jervis outside.' Then, as we followed him out on to the landing, he continued: 'I have something rather interesting to show you. It is in here.'

He softly opened an adjoining door, and we looked into a small unfurnished room. A projecting closet occupied one side of it, and at the door of the closet stood Captain Raggerton, with his hand upon the key. He turned upon us fiercely, though with a look of alarm, and demanded:

'What is the meaning of this intrusion? And who the deuce are you? Do you know that this is my private room?'

'I suspected that it was,' Thorndyke replied quietly. 'Those will be your properties in the closet, then?'

Raggerton turned pale, but continued to bluster. 'Do I understand that you have dared to break into my private closet?' he demanded.

'I have inspected it,' replied Thorndyke, 'and I may remark that it is useless to wrench at that key, because I have hampered the lock.'

'The devil you have!' shouted Raggerton.

'Yes; you see, I am expecting a police officer with a search warrant, so I wished to keep everything intact.'

Raggerton turned livid with mingled fear and rage. He stalked up to Thorndyke with a threatening air, but, suddenly altering his mind, exclaimed, 'I must see to this!' and flung out of the room.

Thorndyke took a key from his pocket, and, having locked the door, turned to the closet. Having taken out the key to unhamper the lock with a stout wire, he reinserted it and unlocked the door. As we entered, we found ourselves in a narrow closet, similar to the one in the other room, but darker, owing to the absence of a mirror. A few clothes hung from the pegs, and when Thorndyke had lit a candle that stood on a shelf, we could see more of the details.

'Here are some of the properties,' said Thorndyke. He pointed to a peg from which hung a long, blue silk gown of Chinese make, a mandarin's cap, with a pigtail attached to it, and a beautifully made papier-mâché mask. 'Observe,' said Thorndyke, taking the latter down and exhibiting a label on the inside, marked 'Renouard à Paris', 'no trouble has been spared.'

He took off his coat, slipped on the gown, the mask, and the cap, and was, in a moment, in that dim light, transformed into the perfect semblance of a Chinaman.

'By taking a little more time,' he remarked, pointing to a pair of Chinese shoes and a large paper lantern, 'the make-up could be rendered more complete; but this seems to have answered for our friend Alfred.'

'But,' said Mr Brodribb, as Thorndyke shed the disguise, 'still, I don't understand –'

'I will make it clear to you in a moment,' said Thorndyke. He walked to the end of the closet, and, tapping the right-hand wall, said: 'This is the back of the mirror. You see that it is hung on massive well-oiled hinges, and is supported on this large, rubber-tyred castor, which evidently has ball bearings. You observe three black cords running along the wall, and passing through those pulleys above. Now, when I pull this cord, notice what happens.'

He pulled one cord firmly, and immediately the mirror swung noiselessly inwards on its great castor, until it stood diagonally across the closet, where it was stopped by a rubber buffer.

'Bless my soul!' exclaimed Mr Brodribb. 'What an extra-ordinary thing!'

The effect was certainly very strange, for, the mirror being now exactly diagonal to the two closets they appeared to be a single, continuous passage, with a door at either end. On going up to the mirror, we found that the opening which it had occupied was filled by a sheet of plain glass, evidently placed there as a precaution to prevent any person from walking through from one closet into the other, and so discovering the trick.

'It's all very puzzling,' said Mr Brodribb; 'I don't clearly understand it now.'

'Let us finish here,' replied Thorndyke, 'and then I will explain. Notice this black curtain. When I pull the second cord, it slides across the closet and cuts off the light. The mirror now reflects nothing into the other closet; it simply appears dark. And now I pull the third cord.'

He did so, and the mirror swung noiselessly back into its place.

'There is only one other thing to observe before we go out,' said Thorndyke, 'and that is this other mirror standing with its face to the wall. This, of course, is the one that Fred Calverley originally saw at the end of the closet; it has since been removed, and the larger swinging glass put in its place. And now,' he continued, when we came out into the room, 'let me explain the mechanism in detail. It was obvious to me, when I heard poor Fred Calverley's story, that the mirror was "faked", and I drew a diagram of the probable arrangement, which turns out to be correct. Here it is.' He took a sheet of paper from his pocket and handed it to the lawyer. 'There are two sketches. Sketch 1 shows the mirror in its ordinary position, closing the end of the closet. A person standing at A, of course, sees his reflection facing him at, apparently, A 1. Sketch 2 shows the mirror swung across. Now a person standing at A does not see his own reflection at all; but if some other person is standing in the other closet at B, A sees the reflection of B apparently at B 1 – that is, in the identical position that his own reflection occupied when the mirror was straight across.'

'I see now,' said Brodribb; 'but who set up this apparatus, and why was it done?'

'Let me ask you a question,' said Thorndyke. 'Is Alfred Calverley the next of kin?'

'No; there is Fred's younger brother. But I may say that Fred has made a will quite recently very much in Alfred's favour.'

'There is the explanation, then,' said Thorndyke. 'These two scoundrels have conspired to drive the poor fellow to suicide, and Raggerton was clearly the leading spirit. He was evidently concocting some story with which to work on poor Fred's superstitions when the mention of the Chinaman on the steamer gave him his cue. He then invented the very picturesque story of the murdered mandarin and the stolen pearl. You remember that these "visitations" did not begin until after that story had been told, and Fred had been absent from the house on a visit. Evidently, during his absence, Raggerton took down the original mirror, and substituted this swinging arrangement; and at the same time procured the Chinaman's dress and mask from the theatrical property dealers. No doubt he reckoned on being able quietly to remove the swinging glass and other properties and replace the original mirror before the inquest.'

'By God!' exclaimed Mr Brodribb, 'it's the most infamous, cowardly plot I have ever heard of. They shall go to gaol for it, the villains, as sure as I am alive.'

But in this Mr Brodribb was mistaken; for immediately on finding themselves detected, the two conspirators had left the house, and by nightfall were safely across the Channel; and the only satisfaction that the lawyer obtained was the setting aside of the will on facts disclosed at the inquest.

As to Thorndyke, he has never to this day forgiven himself for having allowed Fred Calverley to go home to his death.

NO EXIT PRESS
UNCOVERING THE BEST CRIME

'A very smart, independent publisher delivering
the finest literary crime fiction' – *Big Issue*

MEET NO EXIT PRESS, the independent publisher bringing you the best in crime and noir fiction. From classic detective novels, to page-turning spy thrillers and singular writing that just grabs the attention. Our books are carefully crafted by some of the world's finest writers and delivered to you by a small, but mighty, team.

In our 30 years of business, we have published award-winning fiction and non-fiction including the work of a Pulitzer Prize winner, the British Crime Book of the Year, numerous CWA Dagger Awards, a British million copy bestselling author, the winner of the Canadian Governor General's Award for Fiction and the Scotiabank Giller Prize, to name but a few. We are the home of many crime and noir legends from the USA whose work includes iconic film adaptations and TV sensations. We pride ourselves in uncovering the most exciting new or undiscovered talents. New and not so new – you know who you are!!

We are a proactive team committed to delivering the very best, both for our authors and our readers.

Want to join the conversation and find out more about what we do?

Catch us on social media or sign up to our newsletter for all the latest news from No Exit Press HQ.

f fb.me/noexitpress **𝕏** @noexitpress
noexit.co.uk/newsletter